Heather Kaufman gives us a biblical story with a heart for today's world, pulling out an array of joy and hope, sorrow and loss. Ultimately, this book consumed me with absolute delight. . . . *Up from Dust* is a ray of hope for every Martha who seeks and follows Jesus.

—Mesu Andrews, Christy Award–winning author

Up from Dust invites us into Jesus' inner circle with fresh insight on the life of Martha of Bethany. Taking us on an intriguing journey through heartbreak and healing, this strong debut from Heather Kaufman leads readers directly to the joy of the empty tomb.

—Connilyn Cossette, Christy Award winner
and ECPA bestselling author

UP
from
DUST

MARTHA'S STORY

HEATHER KAUFMAN

BETHANYHOUSE
a division of Baker Publishing Group
Minneapolis, Minnesota

Published by Bethany House Publishers
Minneapolis, Minnesota
www.bethanyhouse.com

Bethany House Publishers is a division of
Baker Publishing Group, Grand Rapids, Michigan

Printed in the United States of America

Library of Congress Cataloging-in-Publication Data
Names: Kaufman, Heather (Heather M.), author.
Title: Up from dust / Heather Kaufman.
Description: Minneapolis, Minnesota : Bethany House, a division of Baker Publishing Group, 2024. | Series: Women of the way
Identifiers: LCCN 2023033569 | ISBN 9781540903563 (paperback) | ISBN 9780764242823 (casebound) | ISBN 9781493445233 (ebook)
Subjects: LCGFT: Bible fiction. | Novels.
Classification: LCC PS3611.A8277 U6 2024 | DDC 813/.6--dc23/eng/20230818
LC record available at https://lccn.loc.gov/2023033569

Author is represented by Books & Such Literary Agency.

Baker Publishing Group publications use paper produced from sustainable forestry practices and post-consumer waste whenever possible.

24 25 26 27 28 29 30 7 6 5 4 3 2 1

For Tristan, Seth, and Caira.

May your sibling bond remain strong
all throughout your years.

We are brought down to the dust; our bodies cling to the ground. Rise up and help us; rescue us because of your unfailing love.

Psalm 44:25–26 NIV

prologue

65 AD
Jerusalem, Israel

Firelight illuminates their faces—these beautiful, inquisitive children with wide-open hearts. Several lean heavy against my knee and beg for stories of Yeshua. They aren't the only ones who come to me for the stories. Many come with longing. Some come with doubt. All come with questions.

The children's questions are different, for they ask with refreshing honesty, devoid of agenda. With worn arms, I scoop a wriggling little body into my lap. Most of them have heard the stories before, but gladly I will tell them again, of the man with fire for eyes and kindness for hands, the man who upset and exceeded our expectations—the Christ, Son of the living God, who came into the world.

Tonight, however, my voice trembles in the telling, and my eyes unexpectedly drip with tears. For a moment, I cannot continue. How can I convey to these dear ones the depth and breadth of all I have seen and come to cherish? I am old now and gray, and my heart is full of found things. I have found the nettling burn of sorrow. I have found the relief of joy and the gift of love. I have found the goodness of God, and it is sweet on the lips like honeycomb.

How can I begin to tell of the many things I have found? Or of the One who found me? I see His hand in my story like a weaver's shuttle through the warp, steady and sure, pulling here, loosening there, doing the work necessary for beauty. How do I tell of His capable hands, the ones that rescued me?

Before I can share the many ways I was found, I would have to begin with the day I was lost.

PART ONE

One

20 Tishri
11 AD
Bethany, Israel

Beginnings and endings often collide, one with the other. The day my sister entered the world was no different. She came reluctantly, screaming and clawing her way into our home. The midwife shook her head in confusion, for my sister was born under an auspicious moon.

Abba had taken my brother and me next door, to Abdul's home. We had been in his home before, but never in the dead of night.

"Such things are not for young girls, *Talitha*." Abba used his tender name for me—little lamb. He hadn't called me by that name in a long time.

"God be with you." Abdul clasped Abba's shoulder and drew him close.

My brother gripped my hand tightly. "I'm scared." He wasn't much younger than I was but could already look me in the eye. "Where's Machla?" he asked, speaking of Abdul's wife.

"Remember, she came earlier. To help with Ima." I swallowed hard and tried not to think of what was happening back home.

There were three dead babies after my brother. Boy, girl, then boy—all arriving before their time, all impossibly small, gone before they could take their first breath. How would this be any different? It couldn't be.

I had watched as my mother grew large, her belly swollen, her prayers expectant that now, this time, it would turn out right and she would birth a live babe. I had watched the distrust and fear leave my parents' faces as the time drew closer. And then the day came when my mother had exhaled three words: "*The final month!*" She and my father had held each other and wept with happiness.

But I knew. I always knew. This one would arrive dead too, and I would have to watch as the joy and hope died on their faces.

"I need to go," my brother whispered, releasing my hand to clutch himself. He bounced from one foot to the other.

"What? *Now?*" I hissed, glancing up at the adults, who were deep in conversation.

"Yes, now." My brother groaned, his face pained.

I sighed deeply. Six years old and yet he still waited until the last possible moment, until he was wiggling with desperation.

"Follow me." I wasn't about to interrupt the adults, so I dragged him to the side of the courtyard. Small oil lamps in hewn holes along the plastered walls offered enough light to find the animal stalls. The full moon, bulbous and loud, mocked our need for privacy.

"Here. Go here." I motioned to the nearest stall, which housed an ox.

"Here?"

"Yes. Just go. It stinks already. What's a bit more stench?" I turned as my brother lifted his tunic. Inadvertently I locked gazes with the ox, who blinked at me slowly, once, twice.

My brother tugged my hand when he was done, his young face a clear picture of relief.

"Come, children."

We both jumped, my brother ducking his head as if he'd been caught urinating in the synagogue.

Gilah, Abdul's daughter, stood at the entrance to the sleeping chamber, her face highlighted in moonlight, looking eerily beautiful. "Come this way."

I turned toward Abba, reluctant to go inside. He hadn't made us leave our home when the others had been born. Why now? I blinked back tears, thinking of the wrenching screams that had filled our courtyard as we'd been ushered out. I didn't usually turn toward Abba for comfort, seeking it instead from Ima. But now my bravado fled, and I longed to climb into his lap. He responded to the plea in my eyes by taking my free hand, then my brother's.

"I'm returning to your mother." We stood solemnly in a small circle. "You'll stay here for tonight, and in the morning, I'll send Samu for you."

"Will we need to stay that long?" I hated how small my voice sounded. I didn't want to wait for our steward to come fetch us.

"Look at the skies, child. It's nearly day already." Abba released my hand to pinch a cheek, and I ducked, not wanting Gilah to see. "It's best this way. You can rest and be out of the midwife's way."

"Will Ima be all right?" my brother piped up, but Abba had already turned from us, signaling the end of the conversation.

As he strode away, Gilah put her arm around my brother and me, shepherding us inside. We stepped timidly around the sleeping forms of family members. I counted two others—Gilah's younger brothers. "You must be so scared, so tired." Her eyes were as black and small as ripe olives, her hair falling in a thick, luxurious wave down her back. "Here, lie down and rest yourselves."

I sat next to my brother on a mat and continued to hold his hand. I was half Gilah's age and a bit cowed by her presence.

"Your mother will be all right, children." She offered us the comfort Abba had failed to give. Gilah knelt by the bedroll with a small bowl of water. My brother took a long drink before handing the bowl to me.

"Slow down, or we'll be taking another trip to the ox," I teased. My banter elicited a nervous laugh from my brother. I sipped at the water, keeping a wary eye above the rim.

"Rest yourselves. I am certain good news will arrive shortly." Gilah placed a warm hand on my knee and then lay down on her own mat across the room.

As I observed her dark form grow still, my face flushed with the knowledge I'd gleaned at the village well. Gossip was common while the girls drew water each day, and Gilah had often been the topic of such chatter. I had recently listened with fascination as three girls discussed how Abdul's daughter had yet to bloom into womanhood and how the carpenter's son had finally been betrothed to the scribe's daughter instead.

"I can't sleep." My brother was on his back, eyes wide open. I lay down next to him. "Will Ima be all right?" he asked again, voice thinned out with weariness.

I tilted my head so it touched his. "I don't know," I answered truthfully.

We were partners, he and I. Some of the boys teased my brother for how close we were, saying he'd rather be at home doing women's work with me than out playing with them. Secretly, I was pleased by our closeness. Even though he would one day outpace me in height and stature, he would never outgrow his love for me. I didn't know what was happening back home, but I would be strong for my brother no matter what.

"Do you think it's a boy or a girl?" His black curls brushed my cheek. I turned my face into their soft folds. He had the mane of a lion, just like our mother. I, on the other hand, had our father's serious dark brown locks, long and straight.

"I don't know," I murmured again. And then, sensing he wanted more, I added, "A boy, most likely, don't you think? Another little brother would be nice."

"Nice, yes." He was already drifting toward sleep.

"Or a sister to share in the household chores." The words continued to pour out as I speculated about the new child, speaking aloud the names that had already been chosen.

As sleep claimed my brother, his hand finally loosened from mine. Quiet then, I stared at the wooden beams above me, listening to the strange breathing all around me and trying to still my mind.

Truth be told, I had not let myself think on this child much. What was the point when he or she would arrive dead and disappoint us? Best to accept him or her that way from the start rather than face it surprised and broken, the way we had the other three. I rolled to my side and willed my heart to slow. Closing my eyes, I focused again on my breathing.

Loud keening startled me upright. I must have fallen asleep, for the jolt was great, and the chamber was lighter than I remembered. Heart beating quickly, my wide-eyed gaze landed on the door as another high, distant wail threaded the air.

Shivering, I lay back down and squeezed my eyes shut to ignore the creeping sense of dread. Another wail sounded, then another. I pried an eye open to stare at the other four forms in the room, all silent and slumbering. My nervous shifting jostled my brother, who moaned and mouthed something in his sleep. Now more voices joined the first. Male and female, they rose in a high pitch.

Gooseflesh spread across my arms as I sat up slowly. I touched my brother's hair, let my fingers slide into the curls briefly, and then stood. When I reached the door, I opened it as quietly as I could, but it let out a groan. Leaving it open a crack, I slipped through, silent as a spirit.

The full moon was visible, but so was the sun, peeking over the horizon, casting orange over the packed earthen floor. I crossed the empty courtyard to the double wooden doors that led to the street, expecting at any moment a hand on my shoulder and a stern reprimand. But the only one who noticed me was the ox, his large brown eyes regarding me with no judgment as I let myself out.

Several women rushed past, and I pressed myself against the wall, hoping to remain unseen. The keening sounded again, louder and more persistent. My feet moved of their own accord, taking me down the dusty road to our own front entrance. It was unbarred, one of the doors standing ajar. Several more women arrived, ducking inside. I could not force myself to enter. Motionless, I stared at the beams Abba had built with his two strong hands.

Curiosity won out. I opened the door wider and stepped inside.

The courtyard was busier than ever at this time of the morning. Women rushed back and forth, chickens clucked loudly in the coop, and animals in the side stall were restless and worried. Feet rooted to the earth like a sapling, I watched my home dissolve into uproar.

Samu raced down the stairs that led to the roof. I stretched a feeble hand to him, but he didn't see me as he rushed across the courtyard and flung open the door that led to the sleeping chamber.

That's when I heard it.

A babe crying, its voice shredding the air, searching for life. It was crying so loudly and for so long, I wondered how it could manage to draw breath. Just when I thought it could cry no longer, it stopped, emitting shuddering, deep gasps—hiccups of air entering before another series of prolonged wails. And with the wails of the babe, the cries of my father.

I'd only heard him cry once before, when we had buried the third baby. I associated that distinctive cry with death. The fresh sounds of newborn life mixed with the throbbing presence of death and my father's agony.

The door opened again, and Samu's wife, Abigail, exited, carrying a blanket so full of blood that it dripped from her hands to the ground, staining the earth red. Breath lodging in my throat, I blinked rapidly at the sight. Samu left the room as well and shut the door behind him as Abigail leaned into him for support. "A baby girl, and now with no mother," Abigail moaned. "God be praised, we did not lose them both."

"What's happening?" I turned at the sound of my brother's voice to find him standing behind me, staring at the bloody blanket.

My eyes pinched closed against the sharp pain of his presence. My sweet brother had followed me. I stood and faced him. He was nearly my height but not quite, so I could still block his view. I stood between him and the blood, the screaming, the tears. I stood between him and death with a hand on each of his shoulders. "Let's go back."

"No. What happened?" My brother, usually so docile and obedient, shrugged my hands from his shoulders and tried to duck past me.

I lunged in front of him again and gripped his shoulders more firmly this time. "Let's leave. We don't need to see any more."

"No, I want to stay!" My brother crumpled into tears. "I want Ima! I want to stay and see Ima and the baby!"

I shook my head, and then recoiled as he screamed at me. "Let me go! Let me go!"

He twisted against my grip. With all my strength, I backed him out of our home and into the dusty street. He screamed and pushed against me all the way, his young face red from exertion. I pushed him out and then down, onto the ground in the middle of the street. I knelt over him like a hen with her chick until he stopped resisting. Bowing his head in defeat and acceptance, he let me shelter him with my arms.

"Shush now. All will be well." It wouldn't, but I had to say such things for his sake. "Shush, shush, Lazarus. Shush, my brother, shush."

He cried in my arms. His shoulders pressed against me with every sob. I stared hard at the horizon, jaw tense, eyes alert. That was when I came to understand that full moons and all such things are lies.

There was nothing auspicious about this night.

Two

21 Tishri
11 AD

We hid in the vegetable garden, along the border between the herbs and the barley field. As the sun made its ascent, we nestled among the mint and listened to the village mourn. Lazarus sat with knees gathered tightly to his chest, wiping tears from wide eyes, leaving streaks of dirt behind. "What do we do?" he whispered in an empty voice.

"We sit here," I whispered back. The decision to hide had been fueled by fear and a desire to protect my brother from the harsh realities facing us back home. He couldn't see how unsettled I was. I swiped perspiration from my eyes and scooted farther away so he wouldn't notice how violently I had begun to shake.

Our home was on the outskirts of Bethany, the last dwelling before the open fields and terraced gardens that gently sloped down the mountain and ended in the fertile valley that housed our fig grove. This side of our home contained the most windows, each one small and hewn close to the top of the ten-foot wall. The second one from the right was my parents' sleeping chamber. Beyond the second one from the right lay my dead mother.

Even now, Savta, my father's mother, was most likely with the body, washing away the blood, paring the nails, and scrubbing my mother's hair. I closed my eyes and envisioned Ima's fierce black curls catching in my grandmother's gnarled fingers.

"I'm going to be sick," Lazarus moaned. He hung his head between his knees and gulped in quick, painful-sounding breaths. As I rubbed his back, I searched my mind for a way to distract him.

"Here." I plucked a handful of mint, crushing the leaves between my fingers to release their sharp scent. "This will quiet your stomach." He laid his head in my lap, my hand resting on his temple as he chewed methodically.

We sat there long enough for him to nod off, trails of saliva and flecks of mint spotting his cheeks. Long enough for me to question my decision to hide. Sooner or later, someone would come find us. Better to make oneself found than to be ferreted out and scolded.

With gentle hands, I eased Lazarus' sleeping head from my lap and stood. Without Lazarus to fret over, I would be free to find Savta.

The walk back to our home seemed longer than our desperate flight from it. When I arrived, the courtyard had calmed, although I knew it was only a matter of time before the mourners arrived.

A sudden desire to see Ima one more time flared in my chest. Why had I fled to the fields when this was the last time I could touch her hair and gaze into her kind face? She was a beautiful woman—everyone said so. I used to watch as she combed her hair in the evenings, wishing I possessed more of her good looks.

Was I too late? Had Savta and the other women already bound the body? Why had I run away scared when I should have been here with her? With a cry, I ran to the door and swung it wide, panting. The room echoed with its quiet.

I was too late.

With a sob, I stumbled to the tightly wrapped body. She was completely covered in a shroud, her hands and feet bound with strips of cloth, her face hidden by the *sudarium*, the special burial cloth.

I had run away like a little child and missed this last opportunity to see her, to give her the love and care she deserved. And now I would never see her again. With trembling fingers, I plucked at her graveclothes, weeping bitter tears and calling her name with so much longing that I nearly broke apart.

"Oh, Martha." Savta laid a warm hand on my back and regarded me with gentle eyes. "Her struggle is over, and she rests in peace."

I turned into her arms and released my sorrow into the folds of her rough mantle. Another hand rested on my shoulder and then another. Machla and Gilah stood by my side, their family in the doorway. The time for visiting the dead had arrived.

More family and friends began pressing into the room, coming to offer comfort. But the wound was too fresh for me to find peace in their words.

Savta drew me aside. "Where is your brother?"

"Asleep in the field."

"Fetch him. He must not miss the procession."

My heart banged in my chest, heavy with anger, fear, and sadness. I did not want to miss one more moment with Ima. "Can you send Abigail?"

Savta gave me a sharp look, and I quickly ducked my head in submission. "Yes, Savta, I'll fetch him."

I squeezed past the visitors, out the door, and through the courtyard, retracing my steps through the garden, sobbing as I ran. "Lazarus!" I released the name in a harsh shout. "Wake up, brother!" I tripped in my haste and sprawled in the dirt. Now anger rose to the forefront, and I ground my teeth in frustration.

"Brother!" I spat the word as I struggled to my feet. If it hadn't been for him, I would have stayed. I had only left to protect him, hadn't I? And look what it had cost me.

My right knee throbbed. I stumbled a few paces before finding my stride once again. "Lazarus!" It was a scream this time. Tears came fast, blurring my vision. I stumbled again, this time falling willingly to my knees. I bowed my head to the ground and released a shrill wail. Rocking back and forth, I keened toward the heavens. What would I do without a mother?

As quickly as the tears came, they ceased. I knelt, hunched in a quivering mound, and hiccupped quietly. Eventually I stood, wiping my nose, my eyes, and discovering that I'd overshot the place where I'd left Lazarus. I stood in the barley field, not ten paces from the first terrace leading to our fig grove.

"Brother?" I turned on my heel, a prick of worry snatching at my chest. Surely he must have heard my wailing. The lack of response terrified me. I could not lose him too.

"Lazarus?" This time his name left my lips like a hurried prayer. I ran back to the border of the field, back to the vegetable garden and the patch of mint, to the trampled nest where we had rested.

He was gone.

"Brother, where are you?" Anger fled, replaced by worry. I ran the length of the garden, calling his name, but received no response.

Mourners clogged the path home. More stood in our courtyard, dressed in sackcloth. Some played small hand drums, and others the flute. Still others raised their voices in a series of wails, tearing at their hair. Even with all the noise, the cries of my baby sister were distinct. She screeched from her perch in the wet nurse's arms as the mourners flowed into the street and the litter bearing my mother emerged not far behind. Six people shouldered her, my father at the front, near Ima's head. I ran to him, tugging at his mantle.

"Abba, it's Lazarus. I cannot find him!"

"Not now, child." He looked at me with tenderness I did not expect. Only one night had passed, and yet he appeared so much older. "Go and stand with your grandmother. I'm sure your brother is there."

But he was not.

Desperate but obedient, I fell in line with the procession as it wound its way through the village. The family tomb sat among many outside Bethany, on the other side of the mountain. Narrow pathways snaked through rocky outcroppings, joining each cave in a network of graves. To reach it, we would need to make our way through the entire village. Past the synagogue and the well, past the marketplace and its many shops.

As we traveled, we collected more people until the crowd swelled like a bloated deer and the people jostled hard against one another in tight alleyways.

I tried to shut my ears to the harried voices surrounding me. Ima's final moments had been loud, with people rushing and grasping at the last threads of life. But death was much louder. I could hardly attend to my own grief and concern for my brother through all the noise.

The crowd fell into order at the graveyard. Talk silenced as people grouped into small clusters to pick their way to the tomb. I had lost sight of the litter but now ran ahead, pushing past others and shouting my brother's name. Gilah snagged me by the shoulders.

"Lazarus," I gasped. "Have you seen him? Where is he?"

Face tight, she pointed ahead. Lazarus! He was right behind the litter, standing precariously at the top of the steps that led down to the tomb. He stood solemn and still, as if he might topple headlong down the steps. He looked like a lost lamb, powerless to aid himself, and at the sight, all resentment fled.

The pathway to the tomb was steep, and I skittered down

it—half sliding, half running, scraping my leg badly on the rocks. The litter was descending the steps into the tomb as I reached my brother's side and snatched him from the edge.

"You scared me! Where were you? Are you all right?" I wrapped him in my arms and held him tightly. At the hollow look on his face, I fell silent.

Three men rolled aside the whitewashed stone covering the entrance of the tomb. As the grating of stone against stone filled the air, a chasm in my chest opened. "Brother." I whispered the word against his ear, trying again to shake him from his stupor, but he merely shuddered in my arms and lowered his gaze. I turned again, keeping one arm around him as we faced the open tomb—together.

We'd buried our grandfather, Savta's husband, over a year ago, and last month, we'd come to move Saba's bones into an ossuary box. Lazarus had stayed outside, but I'd entered with my parents and had seen the inside of our family tomb—the place where Ima would now rest. Two rooms, front and back. We'd moved his bones from a shelf in the front into a box, then placed it in the back room, which already held the boxes of Saba's parents.

I couldn't bear to think of Ima keeping company with bones.

Worse still, of her becoming nothing but bones—eventually resting in her own little box. My chin trembled as I struggled to be strong for Lazarus.

"I don't want to go."

"What?" I turned to him in surprise.

"I don't want to go in there."

"You don't need to." I patted his arm. "The priest will say a prayer, and they will lay Ima inside, but we don't need to go in."

"No, I mean, I don't *ever* want to go inside." Lazarus looked dazed. "But I have to. This is where everyone in the family goes. We're all going to go inside. I'm going to go in there too!" His voice rose with each word until he was nearly yelling. His breath was ragged now, his eerie calm from before shattered. I shushed him, burying him deeper in my arms.

It was true. We would all enter a tomb at some point, never to come out again . . . except on the last day. But when this last day would come or what it would mean for us, I had no idea. So instead of false promises, I sang him a song. The words of the *Shema*, as old as time, words that Ima used to sing to us before bed.

"Hear, O Israel. Adonai is our God. Adonai is One." I backed us away from the tomb. "Blessed be the name of the glory of His kingdom forever and ever." They were exiting the tomb now. "You shall love Adonai with all your heart." The tomb was closed, the whitewashed stone staring at us blindly. I closed my eyes and whispered, "With all your soul, and with all your might."

Ima's burial had been quick. She died as the dawn was breaking, and before the sun set, she was in the family tomb.

And my grief was only beginning to blossom.

Death is intimate. It's as close as our skin. At least this is what the women mumble to one another at the well. They console themselves by passing around sayings—well-worn truths that speak of inevitability and Abraham's bosom, of peace, rest, and Yahweh's will. But there is no peace or rest for me, no comfort, for my mother is dead and my father as good as dead with grief.

It is just me and my brother and this infant who will not stop crying.

Lazarus loved her immediately. He continued to mourn for Ima, yes, but he found a place to put his love in this squalling girl. I waited for love to come to me too, but it refused. She was so large. She looked months and not days old. Her face grew red as a pomegranate when she screamed—which was all the time. The wet nurse struggled to make her eat. For a while, fear said she might waste away. Her weight dropped; her cries grew feeble. As others wailed and mourned and prayed over her, I waited, feeling nothing.

Then, one day, she decided to live. She roused herself and ate and ate. We had to bring in another wet nurse to meet her hungry demands. Joy cut through the village's grief but kept its distance from my heart. When I peered into her hungry face, I was filled with thoughts of how much she had already taken from me.

I avoided my sister, this wished-for one with the insatiable thirst who seemed to take and take. My brother poured out his love on her, my father cried his tears over her, but I stayed as far away as I could from the girl who had ended my mother's life. This girl who was my own flesh but who felt like an unwelcome stranger.

Mary.

Three

14 Sivan
17 AD
Six Years Later

The women of Bethany were aflutter, chattering and happy like birds in the spring. I was often on the outside of village gossip, but this time I was part of the inner circle, for the cause of the commotion was my closest of friends.

Standing in the tight cluster of women, I gazed at her, this soon-to-be bride who wore her joy like a veil. She was surrounded by excited visitors, all come to see the groom's *mattan*, his extravagant gifts to the bride, all eager to touch, see, and hear. I longed to wrap my arms around her waist and whisper my congratulations into her ear. As I caught her gaze over the heads of the others, she scrunched her nose in the expression she reserved for me. Ah, Gilah, there would be time later for us to talk.

"He wasted no time in approaching your father," Puah, the carpenter's wife, stated as she handled the gift reverently, running the beads of the necklace through calloused hands and rubbing the golden pendant between weather-cracked fingers. Gold was costly, but nothing less was expected from Simon the Pharisee.

When Abdul had announced his daughter's betrothal to such a high-standing man, the entire village had reeled from shock. None was more surprised, however, than Gilah herself.

"Of course he is eager," Yaffah, the midwife, joined in. "He's been left with a young son to care for."

Poor Rachel with her petite frame and weak countenance. She'd been ill for years, and Simon had consulted every doctor and tried innumerable remedies before she'd passed away. The thirty days of mourning had recently ended. Simon had indeed wasted little time in finding a new wife. Unlike my melancholy father, who still grieved for my mother and refused any mention of another bride.

"You will be a mother right away," Yaffah continued. "Lemuel is a sweet boy. I delivered him myself."

After my own mother's death, it'd been Gilah who had provided the most comfort. I had been surprised and wary, but the more I trusted her, the more I found her worthy of that trust. And now I knew her as the most merciful person in Bethany.

At Yaffah's mention of Lemuel, a frown passed over my friend's face, as if her joy was masking nervousness.

"Have you wondered why he chose you?" Tikvah, Gilah's cousin, questioned with a sour expression.

"I realize I'm not the choicest of women." Gilah bowed her head.

At twenty-two, she was well past the usual age of marriage. I shivered to think that I, at fourteen, was a far more obvious choice. I had yet to become a woman, however, and Abba had yet to bring forward any suitors.

My time would come soon enough. When it did, would it find me like Gilah, with expectancy shining in my eyes and red blooming in my cheeks? My belly warmed at the thought.

My cousin Zissa had recently signed a *ketubah*, a marriage contract, and she was a whole year younger than I was. She would wait the typical year until the marriage ceremony and had already begun preparing her dowry. The other girls were afire with excitement and envy.

"Simon is not bad to look at." Puah raised an eyebrow. "That aided your decision, eh? And not so old, either."

At thirty-five, Simon was indeed young. I had never considered his looks before, his expression and demeanor always appearing stern beneath his headdress. He was a common sight in Bethany and often taught in the synagogue.

"He is not . . . unpleasant in appearance." Gilah hid a smile. Her admission let loose a series of low laughs among the women, who exchanged knowing looks.

"Ah, you will bring him much comfort in his grief." Puah took hold of Gilah's arm and leaned in closely. "When I first married my Micah, he couldn't get enough of me." She reared back with a barking laugh. "Now, though, he could use a little less!" She slapped her stomach, and the women joined in her laughter.

"Be prepared for his hunger," Bina instructed. She was young and recently married to the village blacksmith, whose temper was nearly as hot as his forge. "He will be hungry for you all the time, and you won't hold much say in the matter."

"Now, Bina, don't frighten the bride." Yaffah clucked her tongue.

Bina placed one hand on her hip and wagged a finger with the other. "Frighten, no. Prepare, yes."

My cheeks warmed at her pointed words. Before I could think better of it, I opened my mouth in protest. "Shouldn't Gilah enter this marriage with hope and not dread?" My heart thrummed hard in my chest as all the women turned to me.

"You don't know what you speak of, young Martha." Bina smirked and waved her hand dismissively.

"It's true, I don't speak from experience." I scrambled to collect my thoughts. "I just . . . think Gilah should anticipate enjoying her new husband."

"Well said, Martha." Yaffah nodded.

Bina sniffed. "Hope too often disappoints. A wise woman keeps her eyes open and fixed ahead rather than gazing at the stars and dancing with dreams."

Her voice wavered at the end, and I instantly regretted my words. Who was I to talk about such things? Perhaps Bina was right. Before I could say anything further, Bina was turning away. "Don't worry yourself, child." Her words dismissed me entirely.

I stood on the fringe with my mouth hanging open, aware of my inexperience. Heat rose in me, this time not in defense of a friend but from shame.

Small and overlooked. Assessed and discarded. Alone in the middle—this was how it often was for me. The woman of my home but hardly a woman. Unmarried and young, yet full of responsibilities. Older than my years yet perceived as a wide-eyed youth. Bina's quick remark cut right to the tender core of me. So I shut both my mouth and a piece of my heart as I bowed my head in deference.

My brother's hushed voice disrupted my tumultuous thoughts. "We cannot find Mary."

I startled and turned to find Lazarus hovering over me. With a quick look to the women, I let him draw me outside their circle. At twelve, he had finally outpaced me, and I, his big sister, had to look up to speak to him.

"Aren't you supposed to be in the grove?" I hissed. "It's the beginning of the harvest." My mind skipped over his message to the irrationality of his being here at this hour. Even I should be busy at the harvest. Ripe figs spoiled quickly if left on the branch, so it was a household affair when Samu declared the harvest ready.

"Savta sent Abigail to fetch me. Mary is missing, since early morning, and she thought I'd know where to find her." Our sister often followed Lazarus around, so it made sense that Savta would seek his help.

My brother had turned into a lanky young man with curls that fell softly around his shoulders. He was kind and good and universally adored, although he was somewhat absentminded and, some would even say, peculiar. *"But not in a bad way,"* Abigail once said. *"He reminds me of a foal—all legs and potential."*

"Or a young hart," Savta had chimed in. *"He senses things the rest of us do not—more in harmony with whatever transpires in his head than in his hands."*

I couldn't disagree with this last description. My brother had certainly inherited our mother's introspective nature, although Ima had been better about grounding herself in her duties—often inviting her children into her rich inner landscape through story and song. Lazarus, however, had a vibrant mind that few fully understood, often fumbling what was right in front of him while his mind carried him far away. A trait our father decidedly disliked.

Not long after Ima's death, our father's attitude toward Lazarus had shifted. Nothing my brother did was quite right, his inclinations were all wrong, and no matter how hard Lazarus tried to please Abba, he always fell short. Our father's approval had no pattern we could trace, no firm ground we could find, which meant Lazarus often turned to me for help and affirmation.

I sighed. "Where have you looked for her?"

"Everywhere! I pray she isn't hurt or stuck somewhere."

"I'm sure she's fine." I was unconcerned, for Mary was constantly running off and ending up in odd places. At nearly six years old, she should be contributing to the household, learning the skills she would need to run her own home one day. However, instead of helping and learning from me, Savta, and Abigail, it was not uncommon for her to run away for hours on end, returning home looking half-wild.

"You're like a feral cat," I once shouted in frustration as I washed her filthy body and tried to untangle her hair.

She'd smirked and said, *"Thank you."*

Mary saved her most fiery self for me, choosing to show others different sides as best fitted her needs. Savta and Abigail were both too old to exert much control over her, for she easily outpaced and outwitted them with her antics. She displayed her sweetest self to Lazarus, who coddled her like a pet. And Abba? Well, Mary and Abba gave each other a wide berth, each unsure what to do with the other and therefore handling the relationship by avoiding it.

Now, confronted with my brother's concern, I couldn't muster up any of my own to match it and so instead turned back to the women, who had quickly filled my spot in the circle.

"Please, Martha." Lazarus' voice was urgent. "Please help me find her."

I groaned. The thought of leaving the women after being humiliated by Bina put a sour taste in my mouth. But I couldn't deny my brother and leave him to fret over our sister alone.

The women passed around another gift, a length of fine linen. I wanted to touch it too and exclaim over the softness and beautiful hue, but instead I let Lazarus lead me from the courtyard.

"Thank you, sister." Lazarus sounded relieved. I lifted a hand to quiet him. Think—I needed to think so I could find Mary quickly and return to the women.

Mary's favored hiding place was in the grove, perched high in the air, hidden in leaves. The grove, however, was currently filled with workers, so I turned my mind closer to home. "The roof." A neighbor was adding onto his home and had requested to store his lumber on our roof, which meant there were more hiding places than usual for a small, irksome girl to get lost.

"I've already looked there," Lazarus objected.

"We'll look again." I led the way to the family courtyard and up the flight of stairs leading to the roof. The space was cluttered with excess items and piles of wood. Lazarus immediately called out to Mary, as he'd surely done earlier. I shushed him with an impatient gesture.

Lazarus had a blind spot in his heart toward our sister, unable to see her defiance clearly. If she didn't want to be found, then she would make sure she wasn't. To call out our presence was to give her the opportunity to further hide herself.

Walking quietly across the earthen roof, I paused at some jars of grain, peeking behind them, and then moved on to a stack of wood. No Mary. Anger rose in my chest, despite my attempts to tame it.

It was always up to me to take care of our sister. Our father had been less than attentive with his children even while Ima was alive, but now, with her death heavy on our household, he'd withdrawn even more. Always a quiet man, he'd become nearly stoic, impossible to understand, painful to love. It was no wonder, then, that Mary clung so closely to Lazarus. Instead of compassion, however, I could only harbor irritation at being drawn away from the women to come play hide-and-seek with my stubborn sister.

My eyes snagged on a corner of the roof sectioned off by two stacks of wood. Suspicion flaring, I strained to see over the pile and into the dark depths behind. For a moment all was still, but then I heard a body shift. Triumphantly, I gestured to Lazarus with a finger to my lips. In one smooth motion, he hopped the wood and dropped into the corner, a small yelp of surprise greeting us both.

"Ah-ha!" Lazarus scooped Mary into his arms, clasping her to his chest. "There you are. We were so worried!"

Mary stared at me over Lazarus' shoulder with sullen, unrepentant eyes. Her round face was framed by matted hair, cheeks streaked with dirt.

"Didn't you hear Lazarus call for you earlier?" I raised an eyebrow, hands on my hips. "Why did you stay hidden? You've interrupted the harvest and worried Savta."

No answer. Mary simply raised one of her shoulders in a small shrug as if to say, *"And what is that to me?"*

I clenched my teeth in exasperation. "You need to think of someone other than yourself, Mary."

"Hush!" Lazarus twisted around to send me a harsh look as he cradled Mary against his chest, one hand stroking her hair. "She's found now. That's all that matters." He shifted Mary to his side, where she quickly scrambled onto his back, twining her thin arms around his neck and hugging his waist with scrawny legs. As he climbed back over the wood, she looked for all the world like a crafty jackal making off with someone's noonday meal.

Lazarus dropped to the ground, and Mary, face nestled against his neck, smirked at me.

They both had Ima's bountiful black curls, and with their faces so close together, I could scarcely tell where one head of hair began and the other ended. Not for the first time did the similarity bring me pain. As if mocking my distress, my own plain locks fell across my eyes as I turned to look over the edge of the roof. Lazarus chatted to Mary, bouncing her on his back. Her shrill laughter sounded across the roof as he tickled her exposed thighs. I shot them a peevish look before turning my attention to the courtyard next door.

From my perch, I could see the women leaving Abdul's home, their words and laughter coming to me in pieces. Now there was no chance to return and reenter the conversation. My chin dropped to my chest as I tried to deny the stab of pain flooding me. I was not a "child" the way Bina had labeled me. My body was already forming new curves and my thoughts new directions as I awaited a groom of my own. I'd left the women, however, as a reprimanded little girl, speaking about things I didn't understand, and I feared that's how I would remain. No matter how hard I tried to step into Ima's role, I would forever and only be a foolish girl.

The evening sun shone warmly through Bethany as I shifted the clay jar from one hip to the other. My expectation was heightened as I anticipated seeing Gilah at the village well. I passed neighbors' homes until I reached the marketplace with the large stone well in the middle. The usual crowd was gathered—young women filling their containers with water and their ears with gossip, ending their day with the brief respite of friendship shared over a mutual task. I scanned the crowd for Gilah and found her seated on the edge of the well, pouring a bucket of water into her jar.

"Good evening, friend!" Gilah waved as I approached. She lifted the full jar to her shoulder and motioned for me to follow her to the side of the road, where she eased her load to the ground.

"I didn't show the others the most precious of Simon's gifts to me." Gilah's face had never looked more beautiful, highlighted by joy and the setting sun. "I wanted to share it with you first." She held out her hand, and I quickly set my jar down so I could grab it in my own.

"Oh, Gilah!" I turned her hand slowly, letting the golden ring on her finger catch the last few rays of the sun. "It's magnificent," I breathed. "And is this . . . ?"

"Yes," Gilah confirmed, her voice light, almost girlish. "An amethyst."

I exhaled in wonder at the brilliance of the purple jewel embedded in the top of the ring. "You didn't show the others?"

"Of course not! Not before I had shown you." Gilah laughed

and squeezed my hand, causing me to duck my head with joy. I might be a child in Bina's eyes, but Gilah saw me truly.

"I hope Bina's words didn't frighten you." I twisted the ring on her finger so the sun played off the jewel.

"Bina struggles with bitterness." A shadow passed over Gilah's face. "It's wise to measure her words before accepting them."

Releasing Gilah's hand, I lifted my jar once more. "I'm looking forward to helping you prepare for the wedding. You've done so much for me and now I can help *you*."

It was true—Gilah had added the benefit of a wife and a mother to our household without receiving the title. In fact, I had overheard Abdul speaking with my father only months after Ima died.

"It makes good sense, Yothum. She is your second cousin and able to bear you many more children."

I was a frightened, grieving girl, sequestered behind a door, hardly daring to breathe as I listened to Abdul's words.

"No. She is but a child," my father replied.

"You married your Devorah when she was fourteen."

"No, Abdul. I do not want another wife. I have one healthy son and two daughters besides. What need is there for a young bride?"

That was the first I'd heard of Gilah being considered as a replacement for Ima. The thought had terrified and consumed me. Gilah? Why, she was not much older than I! Gilah? The girl who was trying to befriend me? Was she showing interest in me to ingratiate herself with Abba?

I'd struggled with what I'd heard, pushing Gilah away, seeing my dead mother's face in her kind, hopeful eyes. I pushed and I pushed until I could resist no longer, and it became clear that Gilah had no hopes or plans beyond drawing me beneath her wing. She never mentioned my father. Indeed, they rarely crossed paths as she diligently taught me how to manage a household, how to tend to the children and take on the mantle of womanhood, all while doing so herself in her own father's household. I loved her. It was that simple and that profound. In being denied the position of mother, she became that to me and more.

Now, as we stood in the middle of the street, jars in hand, I couldn't stop smiling. "I'll come over soon," I promised.

"Until then." Gilah gave me her crinkled-nose expression.

I was still smiling to myself as I drew near to the well. So lost in wonder was I at the special gift Gilah had shared with me that I didn't notice him at first. He was satiating his thirst from a small pouch, letting the water trickle over the stubble on his chin, wiping his face with the back of his hand. I drew near, then stopped abruptly at the sight of him.

He was scrappy and scarred. The flute, rod, and other tools strapped to his belt indicated he was a shepherd, and I was close enough now that the smell also indicated as much. Immediately, I moved to the other side of the well.

Shepherds were widely seen as vulgar, spending more time with animals than humans. I glanced around sharply and saw that it was now the two of us alone at the well. My heart beat fast and hard as uneasiness churned within me.

"Let me help you with that."

I whipped my head up at the sound of his voice. He was young! Much younger than I'd first thought. Most likely no more than eighteen. He held out a hand for my jar.

"No, it's fine. I can handle it myself."

"Please, let me. It'd be an honor to draw water for someone so beautiful."

My jaw dropped open, and I mindlessly handed him the jar. Not since Ima had died had anyone called me beautiful—not even my father or brother. The young man must be teasing.

But as he pulled on the rope and drew water for me, I could see he was embarrassed by his declaration. He lowered his gaze, avoiding my eyes. Was that a blush creeping up his neck? Could he be in earnest?

My face was sticky with sweat, my straight brown hair plastered to my brow. I brushed at the limp locks uselessly, knowing that nothing could make my hair bounce the way my siblings' curls did. My eyes were a typical dark brown, and yes, they were fringed with long lashes, but that could hardly compensate for the ordinariness of the rest of my face. My lips were too thin, my nose too sharp, and my ears too large. *Beautiful?*

"Thank you," I managed to whisper.

A grin played around his lips at my response.

I had never lingered over a man's appearance before, but now, for the first time, I studied a young man with interest. If he was indeed eighteen, then he was only a handful of years older than I was. His head was uncovered, displaying a shock of deep copper-toned hair that curled around his ears and neck.

He glanced at me, and my insides leapt at the look in his light-brown eyes, for his expression was filled with self-conscious sincerity. He'd meant it when he'd called me beautiful. My body stiffened with the knowledge, eyes locked on his face, captivated by his admiration. His arms were strong and scarred, which wasn't unusual for a shepherd. What stood out the most was one long scar that extended from the corner of his right eye to his collarbone. It made him look fierce, determined . . . handsome.

Now it was my turn to blush. I averted my gaze and focused on the water he was pouring into my jar. His accent. Northern. What had brought him all the way down to Bethany?

"Here you are. . . ." He was by my side, voice trailing off, indicating he wanted my name.

"Martha." Why had I given it to him?

"Martha." He said my name slowly, as if savoring a date cake. I didn't dare look him in the eye again, but even though I kept my gaze low, I could tell he was pleased.

Taking the proffered jar, I hoisted it onto my shoulder with a whispered "Thank you."

"You're welcome, Martha."

I turned away and realized I had forgotten how to walk. One foot in front of the other. It wasn't difficult, but my gait was stilted. What I wouldn't give for Gilah's natural grace. Her hips swayed, even with a jar on her shoulder or head. My hips rocked like a boat in a storm.

"Uri." His voice sounded rushed and urgent behind me. I turned awkwardly to find him still standing by the well, watching me. "I'm Uri." He thumped a fist to his chest, giving me a crooked and endearing smile.

I nodded in acknowledgment, spilling some of the water. He'd filled it to the brim. I usually left a little room. The water splashed at my feet, and he let out a deep laugh, which he quickly checked. "Oh, I'm sorry. I didn't intend to laugh at you. I mean . . . I wasn't laughing at *you*. . . ." He extended his arms in a plea.

It was my turn to smile. It nearly split my face in two. And then laughter I didn't recognize bubbled up inside me. It escaped like a breath, short and happy. I turned back around with my too-full jar, leaving him with my laughter and taking with me his admiration and his name.

Uri, "my light."

Four

The sun was beginning its descent as I gave the lentil stew one last stir and ladled it into a bowl. "Bring this to Abba," I instructed Mary, who sat in the kitchen corner with her cat, Chana, in her lap. "And then come right back."

She scurried to the courtyard, where Abba sat with our brother and Samu around a small fire. Turning back to the pot, I scooped two more bowls of food and followed in my sister's steps. This was often how the men ended their day—food, fire, talk. I usually listened in to their conversations, gathering snippets and piecing them into a whole. This evening, however, my mind was preoccupied with thoughts of a certain shepherd, and so I served the men distractedly. Mary and I set the stew before them, and I returned to the kitchen for the bread.

Had it been only a handful of days since I'd met him at the well? Since that time, I'd tried to see myself the way Uri had. Sheepishly, I'd peeked at my reflection in the curve of a metal basin and in every pool of water, trying earnestly to see what he saw and what the curves of my body had begun to declare. *I am beautiful.* My hand strayed to my face often, my teeth caught my lips in hidden smiles, my cheeks were rosy with this newfound knowledge that I—yes, I, Martha—was beautiful.

Uri. His name had been on my mind for days, but still, it was a shock when I heard it slip from Abba's mouth.

"I hired a man—Uri. He'll be leaving in a few days to retrieve the flock."

My hands fumbled the dish I was carrying, causing rounds of bread to scatter across the earthen floor. Abba glanced up at me with a look of surprise, but then turned back to his food. Mary helped me gather the loaves, dusting them off and returning them to the dish.

The flock. Abba had recently sold our olive grove and bought a small flock, something he'd been talking about for years. The man at the well was employed by my father? I wanted to laugh and cry at the same time. The emotions surging inside me were new, unexpected, unnamed. I had no point of reference to help orient my thoughts as I numbly placed the dish before the men and retreated to the edge of the courtyard.

"When we take Lazarus to the Temple in four days' time, I'll offer a thanksgiving sacrifice for the new flock." Abba clapped a hand on Lazarus' knee—a surprising display of affection.

"How do you feel, boy? Your time to be blessed by the elders." Samu chortled and elbowed Lazarus. "You've been waiting a long time for this moment, eh? You're more prepared than some, I'd say. You can quote the Law better than most men twice your age."

Lazarus accepted Samu's words with a small smile, but Abba grunted. "My son's sharp mind is better suited for the learning halls than the field." The statement didn't sound like a compliment as it left his lips. "If you would turn that mind of yours to practical matters, I'd be more at ease with the future of this estate."

As he typically did when confronted with Abba's brusqueness, Lazarus grew quiet, both in word and disposition. His pleased expression vanished as he silently resumed eating.

"Leave the boy alone, Yothum. He'll grow into his inheritance. You'll see." Samu waved an unconcerned hand in the air, as if Abba's words were nothing more than flies to swat away.

It was a common theme in the household of late. As Lazarus grew older, Abba grew more irritable and concerned about what he termed a "lack of aptitude" when it came to Lazarus handling the estate.

"Where is our new flock coming from?" I dared to speak up as I hovered nearby.

"Jericho," Abba answered. "I'm sending Uri the day after next to gather and pasture them along the Jordan Valley for the summer. By then the accommodations will be ready to keep them here through the winter."

Jericho, a day's journey away, but one fraught with difficulty and known for bandits. Uri was leaving on a perilous journey in two days. How would I see him again before he left?

One well-placed comment in Tikvah's hearing the next morning was all it took to figure out where Uri was staying, for if anyone delighted in the details of everyone's business, it was Tikvah. Now, to devise a way to see him.

As morning stretched to afternoon, I bundled food into a basket and crafted a small deception. If anyone asked, I was dropping off food to a cousin, not shamelessly seeking out a shepherd boy.

The slant of the afternoon sun caressed my back as I journeyed through the village streets with a heavy-laden basket. Who was this brazen girl on her way to see a man? I hardly recognized myself. Bina's words resounded in my head, creating a deafening cacophony. "*You don't know what you speak of, young Martha.*"

And then there was the matter of what Uri would think—a

young woman showing up unannounced on his doorstep. Or what others would say if they saw us. Or what my father would do if he found out.

I stopped in the marketplace, eyes full of tears, despising the conflict tearing me apart. Like a storm-tossed boat, I had no control over my own thoughts. My plan, now full of holes, lay at my feet. Who was to say that Uri would even be glad to see me? Most likely he had simply been toying with me after all, and I had been too simple to see it. This final argument shattered the plan, and I turned toward home, swiping angrily at my eyes.

"It's you! I was hoping I would see you again."

His voice—just as I'd remembered it, warm and smooth like honey. I couldn't help the small gasp that escaped my lips as I turned to face him. He stood, relaxed and smiling, with a thick piece of wood braced on one shoulder. My lips moved but no sound emerged.

It looked like he'd come from the carpenter's shop. I imagined his large frame in the small building, Puah hiding in the back, ogling him from a safe distance. The image made me smirk, which caused Uri's face to light up with delight.

"Are you on your way somewhere?" He swung the thick shepherd's rod to his other shoulder. "May I accompany you?" He glanced at my basket and sniffed appreciatively.

His manner was easy and unaffected, his voice genuine and thoughtful, and my body responded in kind. My shoulders, stoically clenched before, eased downward.

I picked my plan back up, disregarding the holes I had so easily torn in it earlier. I *would* see this through. I *would* chance his mockery and others' gossip. "In truth, I was on my way to find *you*. My father hired you to fetch his new flock."

His eyes widened, and he ran a calloused hand against the back of his neck. "I didn't realize who you were. I apologize. I have been too free in my speech—wait, did you say you were on your way to find *me*?"

This was a new attitude I hadn't seen before. Humbled and nervous, yet hopeful, he shifted from foot to foot. I hastened to put him at ease. "Please don't worry. I enjoy your conversation. I overheard my father talking of your journey tomorrow, and I wanted to bring you food." I held out the basket quickly. It dangled between us, a hurried offering.

His eyes widened even more. He avoided looking at my face and instead stared at the basket as if he didn't know what to do with it. "Oh! It was kind of your father to send this."

"N-no, you misunderstand." My words tripped over themselves. "This is from *me*." I was blushing badly and thankful he wasn't looking at my face. Having decided to go through with my plan, I was wholly committed. There was to be no doubt that the gift was from me and me alone.

He stared silently at the basket, and my arm began to ache, my feelings not far behind. I kept talking to ease the tension. "The road to Jericho, it's not long, but it's tiring, hot, dangerous. I hate to think of you traveling it alone." Why had I added that last part? I bit my lip and let my hand with the basket drop, along with my gaze.

He caught my wrist with a strong, warm touch, lifting my arm back up and moving closer so the basket was crushed between us. "No one has worried over me for quite some time." His voice had turned husky, and my gaze darted to his face to find him studying me intently.

Long lashes fringed light-brown eyes ringed with gold, as if light emanated from within. The exquisiteness of his eyes contrasted sharply with the ruggedness of the rest of his face. His nose looked like it'd been broken and reset multiple times, and the scar stretching across the right side of his face appeared raw and angry. Overarching everything—the scars, the world-weariness—was a visage of youth that made my heart squeeze painfully.

My eyes fluttered briefly over the trailing scar. "How did this happen?"

"It was years ago." He let out a quick breath. "Perhaps I'll tell you the story someday."

Heat rose in my stomach at the look in his eyes, and I shivered at the implication that there would be a "someday." The basket was still caught between us, his hand encircling my wrist. Belatedly, I realized how intimate we looked. Clearing my throat, I took a step back. "I included an assortment of foods, enough for the journey tomorrow and more besides."

He took the basket, lifting it to his face and inhaling the aromas with a pleased expression. I watched him with hungry eyes, missing the warmth of his hand immediately. How would I ever manage the nearly six months he would be away with the new flock?

"You are so kind, so thoughtful." There was no mockery in his voice as there had been in Bina's. He wasn't toying with me. I knew it, deep in my bones and down to my toes. Every word from his lips was genuine. I expected him to peek into the basket now that it was in his possession, but he didn't. Instead, he lowered it to his side, his eyes never straying from my face. I sensed that while I was in his presence, that's where his gaze would remain.

"And you needn't worry," he said. "I won't be traveling the road alone. Your father is sending a man named Tzvi to accompany me."

Tzvi had been born into our household. Indeed, my father had grown up with him. He was like an uncle to me. I would be able to breathe easier with Uri in his company, although Tzvi may wonder where Uri had received such bountiful provisions and indeed might even recognize my cooking. I ducked my head at the thought.

"It's growing dark. . . ." Uri let the words taper off, regret fringing his voice.

"Yes, I need to return home."

"You should be getting back."

We spoke at the same time, both stumbling to a stop and then grinning.

"Thank you for the food." His voice was tight with emotion. I could tell he wanted to walk me home, but now that he knew my identity, discretion restrained him. We both knew that it wouldn't do for Abba to see him with me.

"Martha," he said my name softly. "I'll think of you all along the road tomorrow." He chuckled. "Truthfully, I'll be thinking of you much longer than that."

Pride swelled in me. To catch the admiration of such a young man—shepherd or not—was traveling straight to my head. "And I, you. I won't rest easy until you're back. Please be safe." My eyes strayed to the scar again.

"Oh, you can be sure that I will." His answer was quick, decided, and—dare I think it?—possessive. "Now that I have your smile to look forward to." He backed up a few paces, keeping his eyes trained on me. His smile had been wide and easy before, but now it was different—slower, calmer, and a bit lopsided. His grin had transitioned from all-encompassing to intimate. He was giving me something he didn't give everyone, a certain look he kept in reserve. I tingled with the gift of it.

He backed up another few paces, presumably waiting for me to turn away first. I tried to comply but couldn't, my feet rooted to the spot. At last, the distance between us reached the point of absurdity—him still backing away, me still standing, foolishly smiling after him.

I shook my head, biting my lip to keep from laughing. "Good-bye, Uri. God bless you and bring you back in one piece." I checked my tongue before adding *to me*, and then I turned and dashed toward home, heart full and yet somehow light.

Not even the suspicious scampering in a dark alley—as if someone had been watching us—could penetrate my mind with worry. What did it matter if someone had seen us? What did anything matter but Uri's safe return home?

To me.

Five

22 Sivan
17 AD

A waft of breeze lifted wisps of hair and splayed them across my face, a few strands sticking to my smiling lips as I observed Lazarus.

At twelve, he was in his final year of preparation and considered a man in many ways. It was every boy's wish to go to the Holy City to receive the elders' blessing in the Temple. Lazarus had been looking forward to this day for years, and I rejoiced to see him so pleased. Abba had given the thanksgiving offering, and now we celebrated in the home of Abba's cousin Benjamin.

Benjamin worked as a potter and had eight children, who were our dearest friends. I was closest to Aviva, who was my elder by a year. She had a bright mind and playful eyes that now danced with mischief in the firelight as she told a story to the children gathered at her feet.

Mary sat with Lieba and Malka, the twins, and listened with rapt attention. I let my eyes flutter shut as I reclined on one of three benches surrounding a beautiful fountain. The food grew heavy in my stomach as I listened to Aviva.

Our cousins had become affluent in recent years, and the tiled courtyard we were enjoying was filled with lush vegetation, a fountain in the center, and a well—a far cry from our humble hearth at home. The family's rise in station, we'd learned, was in no small part due to the handiwork of Cleopas, Benjamin's third child and eldest son.

"His future is bright," Benjamin had boasted soon after our arrival. "With skill nearly surpassing my own." He'd clapped a hand on his son's broad shoulder.

I observed Benjamin's pride as he interacted with his son and ached for my brother. When would Abba learn to appreciate Lazarus for who he was instead of harboring bitterness over his perceived failings?

"Is there room for me on that bench?" Aviva smiled down at me, having finished her story.

"Certainly." I shifted and patted the seat. "Those bowls you served with tonight—they are stunning. Are they your father's handiwork?"

"Cleopas made those. He has a natural talent with paint."

"They are remarkable."

"He would be glad to hear it. He thinks of little else. Cleopas!" Aviva raised a hand to her brother. "Martha is a great admirer of your work."

My quiet cousin nodded his thanks, then joined us near the fountain, Lazarus trailing behind.

Growing up, I'd enjoyed goading Cleopas into levity, for he was often too serious for his own good. I delighted in cracking through his solemn exterior and making him laugh. But now, as he approached, my body buzzed with a new awkwardness.

Since the last time I'd seen him, Cleopas had changed dramatically. The scraggly hairs on his chin had blossomed into a full black beard, and he'd filled out his tall frame. Gone was the gangly boy I remembered. In his place stood a broad-shouldered young man with gentle eyes that carefully studied me as if memorizing a text. The transformation left me unsettled, and I could hardly meet his gaze.

"So you have begun painting your pottery." My voice squeaked as I stated the obvious. What was wrong with me? This was still Cleopas, the boy I'd grown up with, the older brother I'd never had. I forced myself to meet his eyes. "Tell me, how did you come by the art?"

Cleopas beamed, his teeth flashing white through the blackness of his beard. "The idea of taking something ordinary"—he gestured to a plain jar at the base of the fountain—"and giving it honor intrigues me." He sat abruptly by my side, causing me to startle and bump into Aviva. "I enjoy the process of taking what is lowly and transforming it into something beautiful."

He punctuated his talk with dancing hands, and even though I was entranced by his enthusiasm, my mind was too distracted by his proximity.

"It's thrilling to imbue something so fragile with intricate handiwork," he continued, eyes alight.

"A blessing indeed to harbor passion for your work," I conceded, scooting away so that our legs no longer touched. "But—and I hope you don't find this impertinent, I'm simply curious—why paint the pottery in the first place if it's simply going to break?" I raised an eyebrow with a grin, pushing past my discomfort to revisit our usual comradery. "Like you said, it's fragile. One careless move and the whole piece is shattered. Painted shards—such a pity and a waste." I clucked my tongue, hoping that I hadn't taken my teasing too far. But the old fire leapt into Cleopas' eyes as he rose to my baiting.

"Ah, Martha," he chuckled, and the sound was deep and warm. "You always did like to poke." He raised his chin. "Why are you so kind to everyone but me?"

Feeling a bit like impetuous Mary, I raised a shoulder and smirked. "Perhaps because I know you can handle it."

Cleopas leaned back with a loud laugh. My body relaxed at the sound, our legs touching once more and me no longer caring. There, I'd made him laugh—a small triumph.

"Painted shards, eh?" Cleopas turned toward me. "I know you think me overly serious, but now it's *you* who are the serious, practical one." He grinned, and I blushed. "Isn't it better to behold beauty for a moment than not at all?"

"I suppose so."

"Simply because something is fragile, does that mean it shouldn't be enjoyed to the utmost? Valued even more for its fragility?"

"You are being too philosophical now," I laughed. "Which is why you enjoy my brother's company." I looked to Lazarus, who rolled his eyes.

Cleopas shrugged. "I'm not sure about philosophical. I simply like to dwell upon ideas, tease out the deeper meaning of things."

"Interesting." I relaxed, easing against Aviva so I could better face her brother. "Wouldn't you say, though, that life is more about doing than dwelling? If all we did was dwell upon ideas, no one's ideas would ever come to fruition."

"Can life not consist of both?" His answer was immediate, expression eager. I furrowed my brow as I examined his face. He narrowed his eyes, examining me right back. "And look who is the philosophical one now. *Doing* versus *dwelling*, indeed."

My mouth fell open in surprise until I realized it was his turn to poke at me. Biting my lip to keep from laughing out loud, I shook my head and crossed my arms in a fake pout. "Hmm, even Lazarus cannot pull out the philosopher in me." I raised an eyebrow. "You must possess a natural talent for provoking me."

"A high compliment indeed." Cleopas gave a satisfied nod, another grin creeping across his face.

"Now you see what I deal with day in and day out," Aviva

spoke from her small corner of the bench, where I'd unintentionally crushed her.

At that moment, the twins skipped into view. They were small for their four years, having been born early and never quite catching up. However, what they lacked in height, they made up for in gustiness. They bounded to our bench, and each clung to one of Cleopas' legs, a squirming little bottom on each of his feet.

"Ride!" Lieba commanded.

"Ride now!" Malka clarified.

Cleopas acted startled, lifting one foot and then the other. "W-what? What is this?" An outburst of girlish giggles greeted him. "What creatures are crawling all over me?" He stood and stomped off elaborately, stopping every so often to shake a leg as if to cast off an irritant. The girls shrieked with mirth as they hung on for dear life. Aviva and I watched in amusement as Lazarus joined in the fun, tickling one girl and then the other, causing them to fall off and then have to scramble back on.

The rest of the evening passed happily, Aviva and I staying close. I caught Cleopas glancing at me on and off. At first, I returned his looks, hoping he would come over and talk. But his mood seemed altered. He quickly averted his eyes every time they met mine. I contented myself with stolen glances, checking on him and Lazarus, wondering what they were discussing.

Perhaps, I mused, Lazarus was sharing something of import with Cleopas, something to cause those searing looks he was sending my way.

Six

4 Tishri
17 AD

Months passed as I alternated between "doing" and "dwelling," my thoughts often returning to Cleopas' conversation that night in the courtyard. My natural tendency was to feverishly *do* all the tasks my hands could find to keep my mind from *dwelling* on Uri. Thankfully, there was much to occupy my hands as our family was consumed with preparations to receive its new flock. My wandering mind needed the focus, and my aching heart needed the distraction.

We planned to enclose the sheep on the sunny hillside overlooking our fig grove. It was ideal grazing land and one of my favorite spots. Sporadically dotting the hillside were three lanky sycamore fig trees. With their widespread root system and towering canopy, these trees stood out from the rest in our grove. Whereas our common fig trees lay clustered in a carpet across the valley, these stately trees stood watch on the hillside, their heart-shaped leaves fluttering in the wind.

I liked to think of them as Hananiah, Mishael, and Azariah, standing valiantly before King Nebuchadnezzar. I'd secretly named each tree after one of these heroes and especially enjoyed resting under the shade of Azariah.

Each year, when it was time to pierce their unripe fruit for fertilization, I was the first one climbing their branches with awl in hand. The view from their arms was breathtaking. If I closed my eyes, I could almost feel a hot rush of wind straight from the desert, and on the tail of the wind, the tang of salt from the Dead Sea.

Abba decided to build the permanent sheepfold near Azariah. Each morning, the men of the household set out for the hillside to construct the low building and walled enclosure that would eventually house the new flock. I often brought them a noonday meal and afterward paused beneath my tree to pray for Uri's safe return.

The last I'd heard, he and Tzvi had successfully picked up the flock and were now pasturing them near the Jordan. My thoughts kept returning to the last time I'd seen him, my heart thudding like it was too big for my chest and needed more room to expand.

It was tempting to tell Gilah about Uri, and on more than one occasion, I nearly cried aloud with the burden of my secret—needing someone, anyone, to know. But always a small check in my spirit restrained me. Would she laugh at the way I was swooning over a shepherd boy? Or worse yet, would she tell my father? I kept my affections quiet and learned to live with their weight.

Recently married, Gilah was too busy these days to spend much time with me anyway. I still noticed, however, a subtle change in my dear friend. Her brow was often furrowed, and she'd begun worrying her lip until it was red and raw.

One morning, she arrived in our courtyard with Lemuel in tow. Mary and I were grinding grain for the day's bread but stopped our work as Gilah approached, gently prying the boy from her legs.

Lemuel had thick brown hair that curled around large ears. His eyes were big with lashes longer than most girls'. He looked shyly at us from around Gilah's tunic and stuck two fingers in his mouth.

Mary instantly flew from my side to poke at the younger boy mischievously. I was about to chide and call her back, but Gilah spoke imploringly. "Would you mind letting Mary entertain him? Here, I'll take her place." She sank to her knees at the grinding stone.

My brows shot up in surprise, but I nodded permission to Mary, who quickly snatched the boy's hand in her own and dragged him away. For a while, the only sound was the scrape of grain against basalt.

"Sometimes I think Simon wishes he had no son." Gilah's voice was matter-of-fact.

I stifled a gasp. No son? But every Hebrew man wanted a son. And one as sweet as Lemuel? What could be better?

My eyes instinctively sought out the boy. He was in a corner with Mary, where she was joyously shoving a kitten into his hands while his small face brightened, teasing out a pronounced dimple in each cheek. Their two heads clustered over the kitten as their childish voices echoed in the courtyard.

"What makes you say such a thing?" I turned back to my friend. "Surely Simon is thankful for a healthy, well-tempered son."

Gilah bit her lip. "I should not have spoken. Forgive me."

"You're worried. Did something happen to upset you?"

"It's simply . . ." Her voice broke off, and she worked the grinder with even more intensity. "The way he speaks to him sometimes. It's not with kindness and love. He releases pent-up anger upon the poor boy."

I frowned, trying to imagine Simon angry. It wasn't hard to do. While I'd never seen him lose his temper, he did display an air of pride that might lend itself to anger in the right context.

"Is Lemuel a defiant child?" I asked, thinking of Mary, who most certainly fit the description.

"No, not at all! He's the sweetest of boys. He's nothing like my brothers, who were always troublemaking. Lemuel is like a pet lamb." There was obvious love in her voice as she glanced at the boy with affection. "But I wonder if that's part of the problem. Simon dislikes Lemuel's temperament, goading him sometimes in a way I find . . ." She bit her lip again and ducked her head. "Nothing, it's nothing. I cannot judge the man. He's my husband. I have already been too free with my speech."

Certainly, it wasn't unusual for a father to be stern with a son. Indeed, our father could be described as such. If anyone understood this, however, it was Gilah, who had grown up with rambunctious brothers who were constantly being chastened. To see her so distraught over Simon's treatment of Lemuel, then, left an uneasy pit in my stomach. Alarm rose in my chest as I observed her eyes darting back and forth in panic.

"Yahweh help me, I didn't want . . . I thought to avoid . . . if I had known . . ."

Her words trailed off, and I leaned close, trying to catch the threads of her worried speech.

"If you had known what? What did you want to avoid?" When she didn't answer, I laid a soft hand on her arm. "Friend, are you . . . unhappy?" Was Bina right after all? Had I been foolish to think my friend would find joy in her match with Simon?

"No," Gilah answered decisively, eyes flashing quickly to meet mine as if she'd forgotten my presence. "Don't mind my foolish words." With effort, she fixed a bright expression on her face. "Sleep eludes me lately. I am merely rambling. Besides, Lemuel needs me." Her voice caught. "He needs a mother."

Didn't she realize that I could see through the false front and brave words? By the set of her jaw, I saw her determination.

There would be no more discussion on the matter, so I left it alone and turned back to my task.

But I wondered at the glimpse Gilah had given me. Perhaps people were not always what they seemed. Underneath his mantle of righteousness, was Simon a hard man?

Seven

17 Chislev
17 AD

I began to bleed as the winter winds blew in. It was bound to happen, but I was still taken aback by the throbbing pain in my belly.

"Ah, you are a woman now," Savta murmured as she stroked my hair and prepared ginger tea to ease my discomfort. Left unspoken was the lament that I had become a woman and Ima was not here to see it. Would she be pleased, I often wondered, at the person I was becoming?

During this time, Uri and Tzvi returned to winter the flock in the newly constructed sheepfold. Being ritually impure for the prescribed seven days, I stayed at home and bemoaned my ill fortune while Abba and Lazarus eagerly spent hours inspecting the flock. Even Mary was able to partake in the joyous return and brought back reports of the names she'd given the lambs. Her enthusiasm grated on my ears, but I held my tongue, even though I had no interest in the lambs. It was the shepherd who consumed my thoughts day and night.

When my time had run its course and I could finally visit the flock, I twisted the truth and claimed curiosity, submitting to my siblings' company as an unwelcome necessity as we tramped down the hill to the sheepfold. Mary leapt ahead of us, as exuberant as a young hart, apparently not minding the wind that tore its way through the valley, whipping and lashing at our garments. I shivered from the cold but even more so from the anticipation coursing throughout my body.

"Abba is pleased with his new hire." Lazarus' voice was beginning to deepen. It cracked at the edges, sounding like a rusty door hinge—an image I would never share with him since his changing voice caused him embarrassment. Still, I hid an amused smile as he continued to talk in his rusty-hinged tone.

"Tzvi speaks highly of him, praising his great instincts, keen eye, and superior strength." There was a note of wistfulness that caused me to look at him sharply.

"And what do you think, brother?"

"I tend to agree. I wish . . ." His voice trailed off, this time cracking with hesitancy.

"What do you wish?"

"I wish Abba trusted me more. I asked him about the possibility of me shepherding the flock, and he laughed in my face."

I winced, all too easily imagining the interchange. "But why would you even wish to do so? You're not well suited for the shepherd's life."

"But still . . . perhaps I could have proved my competence."

The thought of Lazarus leading sheep over the rough Judean terrain was so improbable, it made me want to echo Abba's laughter. Lazarus simply did not possess the physical strength necessary to perform shepherding duties. He had Ima's slender build—more of a willow than an oak—and had also inherited her inquisitive mind, thriving under the scribes' tutelage. The way he spoke longingly of shepherding, a profession that was isolated from the learning halls, surprised me. I wondered if hearing praise of Uri's strength was making my brother self-conscious of his own lack. And perhaps even jealous of Abba's admiration.

"You would not do well with only sheep for company. You are far too chatty." I bumped my shoulder against his arm.

He shook his head at me and snorted.

"Besides, what would you do without your scrolls, your debates, your daily increase in knowledge? That quick mind of yours would soon grow restless." We passed Azariah, and I reached out a hand to run my fingers through the leaves.

We were now in view of the sheepfold. Mary had beat us to it and was already banging possessively on the gate. My heart picked up its pace as Uri stepped out and nudged my sister playfully with his staff. He had darkened considerably from the last time I'd seen him, and his hair now curled around his neck and brushed his shoulders. It was all I could do to keep from running to him. Instead, I kept pace with my brother and tried to keep my face open and friendly but not too familiar, which was hard to do as his eyes met mine and widened with pleasure.

"Welcome home, Uri." My voice trembled with emotion.

"Martha, thank you." To me, his voice sounded deeply intimate, and I glanced at my siblings to gauge their reactions. Nothing.

Mary was pulling on his mantle, jumping up and down and chanting, "Mazal! Mazal! Mazal!"

"Who's Mazal?" I tore my eyes from Uri and feigned interest in my sister.

"One of the lambs." Mary looked at me as if I were dense. "I told you about her." Her tone managed to be both condescending and wounded.

"I'll fetch her for you." Uri opened the gate, and Mary slithered inside. I called out for her, but Uri stopped me with a soft word. "It's all right. Come in." He shot me an amused look. "If you can stand the smell, that is."

I stood against the tall stone wall and gazed with genuine admiration at the fine flock within. Plump ewes and rams munched contentedly on grain, while spritely lambs darted in play. Uri scooped one of the gangly creatures into his arms and brought it to where we stood by the gate. Mary jumped up and down, emitting giggles of anticipation.

"If you sit and are still, you can hold her on your lap."

Mary immediately complied, and I watched with a lump in my throat as Uri knelt before her and gently eased the lamb into her waiting arms. "Mazal was born early, and I had to carry her much of the way home since she couldn't keep up with the others." His obvious tenderness with both Mary and the lamb nearly undid me, and I had to look away to keep my emotions in check.

"It's why she's so quiet," Mary murmured, obviously having heard the story of Mazal's birth before. "She's quiet and small, and I love her."

Uri stood and chuckled, the sound reverberating throughout my body. "I was intending to call her Talitha—my little lamb—but Mary had other ideas."

"My father used to call me by that name." My breath caught in my throat. It'd been years since I'd heard that name from Abba's lips. Indeed, it'd been years since I'd experienced my grieving father's love at all.

"Ah." Uri's eyes latched on to mine. "A fitting name for you."

I couldn't help it. I let my heart show in my face. It had been six months, after all, and I could wait no longer.

Two heartbeats with our eyes locked and then . . . I'm not sure what I expected to happen. Certainly not this—not the abrupt turning of his face from mine, as if my emotions were distasteful. There was no doubt he saw my expression, discerned its meaning, and yet he acted abhorred. His face was turned and now his back as he moved across the sheepfold, farther away from me. The denial was like a strike across the cheek.

Surrounded by the bleating of sheep, my heart constricted as I stared at the back of his broad shoulders. Silly and foolish. I had been silly and foolish. Oh, I wanted to keel over from humiliation! He had left enamored but had returned changed. He'd had time to reflect and had come to his senses. Tears pricked my eyes, and I stooped to hide them by petting Mazal's head.

"Tzvi says you're from Sepphoris." Lazarus followed on Uri's heels like a dog, his young, thin build even more noticeable next to Uri's robust frame.

"Yes, that's right."

"How did you end up down here?"

Sepphoris, the greatest city in all of Galilee, was situated many miles north of us—a bustling metropolis strategically located between the Sea of Galilee and the Mediterranean. My heart was aching so badly that I nearly missed Uri's reply. He rested a hand on the head of an expectant ewe, keeping his gaze trained on my brother and away from me. "That's a long story. One, perhaps, to be told fully at another time. I needed to separate myself from a dangerous group of people. It's important, Lazarus, to choose your friends wisely."

"Indeed, as Solomon instructs us, 'Whoever walks with the wise becomes wise, but the companion of fools will suffer harm.'" Lazarus stood on the other side of the ewe and nodded his head sagely.

"You speak true words, friend." Uri glanced admiringly at my brother. I waited for his gaze to flit in my direction, but it didn't come. Sinking back on my heels, I looked forlornly at my lap, where Mazal's head had come to rest.

"Betzalel often tells us that wisdom starts with the fear of the Lord and is destroyed by the fear of man," Lazarus continued.

"His tutor," I offered from my crouched position.

Even with my spoken explanation, Uri didn't look my way,

choosing instead to continue facing my brother. "What does he mean by that saying?"

Lazarus' face was alight. He was in his element when he was speaking of the Law. "The first part is self-explanatory. I think the second part means that when we are more concerned with what our fellow man thinks than what the Lord says, we display a lack of wisdom."

Uri nodded. "I agree, for if we correctly posture ourselves in reverence before the Lord, we will not be swayed back and forth by man, who is changeable. The Lord is the only one worth fearing."

"Yes, for He alone is immutable," Lazarus said brightly, surprise in his voice. "You know Torah. Where did you receive training?"

Uri shook his head with a smile. Ah! How I had missed that look! To not be the recipient was excruciating.

"I claim no formal training, but I spent time in the fields north of Jerusalem under a shepherd named Meir, and he had much to teach in the way of the Law."

"A shepherd tutor," Lazarus exclaimed. "And here Martha thought one could not be a scholar and a shepherd at the same time. How Uri proves you wrong." My brother gave me a joking wink. He couldn't know how his words drove anguish into my bones.

At my brother's jesting words, Uri finally looked in my direction, but briefly. How he must despise me! Unwittingly, Lazarus had betrayed me as a judgmental woman, quick to look down her nose at the lower class.

I opened and closed my mouth, trying to find words to remedy the situation, but also trying to keep in step with the light tone of the conversation. "I-I said no such thing. Was not David a shepherd before he was a king? Is not God Himself referenced as our shepherd? You mistook my words."

Uri's gaze settled upon me then, but I was too afraid to meet his eyes. Like a coward, I turned away. My heart was sore, like my arms after a full day at the loom or after hours at the hand mill. My heart's strength was used up, and I longed to return home, to be alone. "Come, Mary, we mustn't outstay our welcome."

"You can stay however long—"

"Savta needs us at home." I cut off Uri's words and rose to my feet, jostling Mazal's head from my lap. The lamb gave a soft bleat of protest.

"Can we take her home?" Mary whined, wrapping her thin arms around the lamb's neck.

"No, she's still suckling." My words were harsher than I intended. I bent and pried one of Mary's arms loose, softening my tone as I did so. "She needs her mother."

Mary's lower lip quivered, but she complied.

"I'll stay a little longer . . . if Uri isn't tired of my presence," Lazarus spoke eagerly.

To be a man and enjoy the ability to come and go as I wished! Lazarus could stay behind and no one would mind. I had no such freedom. Although, after Uri's rejection, I no longer had a desire to be in his company, especially alone. The sting of humiliation was strong. My cheeks burned with it, my heart leapt with it, my breath caught with it. Now my body compelled me from Uri's presence like a stone from a sling.

"Do as you wish." I unlatched the gate and slipped out, Mary's hand in mine. From my peripheral, I could see Uri was close behind us, his hand on the gate, his gaze still trained in our direction.

I did not look back. Gripping Mary's hand tighter, I walked briskly toward home, ignoring Mary's protests that I was moving too fast. Azariah's leaves brushed at my head and irritably I swatted at them as we passed quickly beneath. I bore to the right so the tree's gnarled trunk would further obscure our retreating forms, should someone still be watching.

Uri was folded into the household as easily and thoroughly as leaven into dough. With Tzvi vouching for his deft handling of the flock, Abba's mind was visibly put at ease, and he increasingly entrusted more of the flock's care to Uri, releasing Tzvi to return to other duties.

With the flock bedded for the winter, we didn't see much of Uri, which suited my wounded heart well. My mind, which had strayed to him repeatedly over the last six months, was having a hard time being redirected. Each time my thoughts reached out to him, I remembered the same scene: Uri's back turned to me, denying the look on my face. Slowly and steadily, I attempted to put to death the feelings I had once nurtured.

We endured a wet and lonely winter. Strong winds lashed through the valley and beat against our walls. Thunder rolled across the sky at night like the voice of God at Sinai. We were thankful for the rain and expectant that new growth would arise from the fields because of it.

I turned my energy inward, toward home and those within its walls. We waited out the long dark months, praying for spring, warmth, and life to return, while privately I waited for the coldness in my heart to thaw.

EIGHT

3 IYYAR
18 AD

Joy, like birdsong, filled the air. The winter had been rougher than usual, but we were now enjoying the bountiful results.

"It's the way this world is ordered," Savta said. "Pain before blessing. Dark before light. Sadness before joy. All good things come in time."

Her form had become more hunched lately, and her eyesight was rapidly failing. She spent most days in the corner of the courtyard at the loom, a task that her gnarled hands knew well. Even this, however, would soon be taken from her, as her fingers curled in on themselves more each day. I watched helplessly as she was robbed of her daily activities, small degrees at a time. Each evening, I rubbed her hands with a bit of oil, trying to release her fingers from the tightness that gripped them.

I was nearly fifteen. For a whole year my body had been straining toward womanhood, changes coming slowly. One day, however, I awoke to find my small chest had blossomed overnight. Rather than joy, a sharp pang flooded me. I clasped myself tightly and cried confused tears.

How I wished Ima was here to help make sense of all the emotions tearing through me. I'd tell her of Uri, of his words at the well that had soared through my mind like a song. I'd tell her of his denial and the deepening loneliness that threatened to overtake me.

We saw Uri more often now, as the warmer weather arrived and the sheep were let out to pasture. I avoided him as much as possible, and when thrown into his company, kept my gaze and conversation directed elsewhere.

Spring had come to Bethany, and before the hot summer months arrived, our family would turn its attention to the new flock. The sheep's coats had grown thick over the long winter months, and it was finally time to relieve them of their heavy burden.

"This is cause for great celebration." Abba clapped his hands, happier than I'd seen him in a long time.

Shearing day had finally arrived, and I, along with many women in the village, gathered by the creek that wound its way north of Bethany. After the generous winter rains, the banks were full, and it was to these banks that the men drove our flock. One by one, the sheep entered the creek and were cleansed of their filth. *It's like a mikvah,* I thought, pleased at the imagery.

"Your family's first sheepshearing." Gilah stood close to my side, her hand resting lightly on her stomach. "This truly is a day to celebrate."

Gilah was expecting her and Simon's first child. With her new responsibilities keeping her busy, I missed the closeness we used to share. After her initial outpouring of concern, something in Gilah had shifted. She was less open, more reserved, and she never talked about Simon. I'd carefully broached the subject on several occasions, trying to be discreet with my questions. Each time she'd quickly quieted me, claiming all was well. But there was no crinkled-nose expression, no familiar tipping of her head when she was in earnest. Finally, I'd stopped asking and hoped that her silence wasn't an indicator of unhappiness.

Talk of Lemuel, however, was never far from Gilah's lips. She extolled his virtues to any who would listen, and the boy clearly adored her. We watched together as he scampered in and out of the creek with Mary.

"Stay on the bank, Lemuel," Gilah cautioned. "The water is deep in some places, and you may slip."

"I'm fine, Ima," the boy called, his dark eyes dancing with mischief as he darted after Mary, back into the water.

Gilah groaned. "Lately, I don't contain the energy to discipline him the way I should."

"I'm afraid Mary is a bad influence." I grimaced. Truthfully, Lemuel's behavior had worsened in direct proportion to the amount of time he spent with my sister. No coincidence, in my mind.

The women stood upstream from the men, at enough distance that we weren't soaked by the violent thrashing of the sheep in the water. The men had an efficient system in place. Abba stood, thigh-deep in the creek, with a ewe in his arms. He held her still while Samu scrubbed at her coat. Lazarus and two other young men from the village were herding the sheep back and forth from the creek to Uri and Tzvi, whose job it was to conduct the shearing.

I wandered in their direction, mesmerized. I'd seen sheep shorn before, but it was different when the flock was your own, when the wool would land directly into your own hands and eventually onto your own back.

Uri had his mantle off and his tunic rolled up, revealing strong forearms with muscles that flexed as he worked swiftly and expertly. He took hold of the first ewe, flipped her onto her back, and pressed her tightly between his legs. Withdrawing a long knife, he cut off the wool around her tail, flinging the small pieces to the side. Once the ewe's bottom was shorn, he worked his way up her abdomen. And then with firm, long strokes of the blade all along the ewe's flanks, Uri peeled off her coat as if removing a bandage. I laughed aloud at the look on the ewe's face as she stumbled away, dazed. She shook herself and darted off, prancing like a newborn lamb.

"Martha!" Tzvi raised his voice to be heard over all the bleating, splashing, and shouts of the men. "Grab the women and bind the wool, will you?"

My gaze snapped upward. At the mention of my name, Uri looked up too and stood, panting slightly from his work as he stared at me. I couldn't read the expression in his eyes.

"Y-yes, of course." Heat rushed to my face. I'd been idly gawking instead of helping—unusual for me. I motioned for Gilah to fetch Mary and then turned to take the fleece from Uri's arms. Our hands brushed, and tingles from the touch shot through my body. Why could I not control my emotions? He was still panting from exertion, and I was close enough to feel his breath on my face. I turned away quickly before he could say anything and walked to the field where the sheep were gathered. I could bear Uri's nearness if I kept my hands busy.

Unfurling the fleece, I knelt in the grass, running my hands through the white folds. Mary knelt by my side and together we bound the fleece, working side by side. Others joined us, and soon the field was dotted with shorn lambs and bundles of fleece as women joyfully called to one another, extolling the virtues of Yothum's fine flock.

Admirably, Mary stayed by my side, choosing to assist me rather than run off with Lemuel. It was at times like these, when my sister and I joined over a mutual task, that I softened toward her. As she matured, I anticipated more of these moments.

Benjamin had come from Jerusalem to partake in the festivities, bringing Cleopas with him. They were with Abba now, inspecting the wool, but Cleopas seemed distracted, his eyes flitting to the creek with a furrow in his brow.

I followed his gaze to where Lazarus stood with Azriel and Baruch. The two were twins, sons of Betzalel. My brother looked up to them because they were his tutor's sons, but also because they were older and more experienced. I had never seen them pay Lazarus any attention before today, but now they jostled and joked with him as they ran the sheep to and from the creek. My eyes traveled back to Cleopas with compassion. He must be jealous over my brother's attention.

As the day stretched on, I transitioned from working in the fields to preparing the meal back home. It wouldn't be nearly as elaborate as Gilah's wedding banquet had been so many months ago, but it would be more celebration than our household had seen in a long time.

Gilah, along with other women in the village, assisted me in bringing out platters of bread and boiled meat, jars of wine, and bowls of date cakes. Simple and festive. The presence of meat especially increased the excitement—almost more than the wine.

Abba and Samu had built several fires around which the laborers congregated to enjoy the food. Someone pulled out a flute, and soon a melody rose in the air, accompanied by shouts and calls. Abba relaxed, his face appearing young and handsome once again in the firelight.

Uri was in another cluster of men, his deep laughter distinct from the others'. I'd observed him all day, but he'd given me no sign of special attention or notice, confirming what I already knew. Now, seeing him at ease with the others and oblivious to me, a stone rolled in front of a tomb, deciding the fate of my attraction. I had no use for unrequited love. I would not waste my thoughts any further on this man who called me beautiful one moment and ignored me the next. I was fifteen—well, nearly. I needed to release my heart to look elsewhere.

Azriel and Baruch, for instance, were both fine young men—more traditionally handsome than Uri. My eyes sought them out and found them once again with Lazarus. The three were standing apart from the rest, drinks raised in celebration. Each twin had an arm across my brother's shoulders and was laughing boisterously. Lazarus, although tall, appeared dwarfed between the twins' stocky builds.

A brief wave of unease passed through me as Lazarus puffed out his narrow chest, trying to keep up with their jabs and laughter. The twins were handsome and polished, like smooth stones in a sling. Could they be just as dangerous? Admittedly, I knew little of their characters. I hoped Lazarus was not yet again comparing himself to others and finding himself lacking.

"He needs to be careful with those two."

I startled at Cleopas' voice by my side. He stood with a drink in hand, gazing at Lazarus with worry etched on his face.

"Would you like another?" I gestured to his near-empty cup.

"No, thank you." Cleopas turned to me, eyes soft and glowing in the moonlight. "Moderation even in celebration is wise." He tipped his drink as if toasting me. "Besides, my father and I leave shortly for home."

"The twins' father is wise and good. What makes you so cautious?" I turned back to watch Lazarus, guilty and embarrassed for having contemplated the twins' good looks, as if somehow Cleopas could see inside my head and ferret out my wayward thoughts.

"One's parentage isn't always a true indicator of a child's outcome." Cleopas drained the last of his drink. "Some men are so sure of their appearance that they stop tending to the man inside—the soul."

I turned to him with a frown. "That's hardly a fair assessment. You judge them because they are handsome."

Cleopas looked distressed. "That was not my intent. I've been watching them all evening, and I sense that . . ."

"And your senses could never be wrong!" I spat, hating the biting edge of my voice. I was overreacting because I was flustered, and the conversation had leapt out of my control like a newly shorn ewe from the shearer's hold.

"I've angered you. I'm sorry." Cleopas' soft reply made my harshness seem more ridiculous. "You have . . . feelings for one of the twins?" he asked hesitantly, head downcast, demeanor abruptly subdued.

I snorted out a laugh, trying to cover my embarrassment. "No!"

A burst of laughter drew my attention to where Uri reclined next to Tzvi. Tikvah was bending low to serve him more food. Blood rushed to my face at the sight. What was she doing here? I hadn't seen her out in the field earlier. Had she come only to partake in the merriment? She was lingering much longer than necessary by Uri. His eyes shone in the firelight as he looked up at her.

With a lump in my throat, I whirled back around and stared hard at the dark tree line in the distance. My hands clenched at my sides, and without realizing it, I took a few steps out of the firelight and closer to that tree line, two steps closer to the dark.

"Martha." Cleopas' voice once again startled me. I'd nearly forgotten his presence and turned to look over my shoulder at him, belatedly realizing that tears pooled in my eyes.

"Ah, I can see I've upset you." Cleopas groaned, looking close to tears himself. "Won't you come and sit a moment before I leave?" He reached out a hand and cupped my elbow.

"There you are!" Zissa's face bounded into view. "Come and dance, cousin!" She snagged my arm from Cleopas' warm grasp with a laugh. I shot him an apologetic look as Zissa dragged me toward the fire and away from the solitude my soul suddenly craved.

We'd celebrated Zissa's wedding last month, and in that short time she'd grown even more beautiful. Marriage suited her. Would it ever suit me? I'd been so joyful earlier. What was this strange lethargy that had crept so cleverly into my heart?

Zissa and I joined hands with a long line of women snaking around the fire. I tried to catch sight of Cleopas through the flames as feminine voices rose in praise to *Jehovah-Jireh*, the God Who Provides, but I could not find him. Cleopas had left thinking I was angry with him. More tears gathered in my eyes even as my mouth opened in praise.

Later that evening, my hair cascaded long and unhindered down my back. I bent to kiss Mary, and my locks fell forward around my face, creating a peaceful tent over my sister's slumbering form. She'd fallen asleep as soon as I'd laid out her mat on the roof. We often slept up here in the summers, positioning our mats beneath the stars. The cool night air was a welcome relief from the heat of the day. I sat gently stroking Mary's back and humming softly.

I would never admit it, but I enjoyed watching her sleep. Her features, animated by mischief during the day, relaxed into a sweet countenance at night, keenly reminding me of Ima. Some nights, the resemblance brought me pain, but tonight it carried joy. I traced her delicate features, and she twitched beneath my fingers. What would happen to her once I had a family of my own? I would need to stay close, to guide her until she was wed herself one day.

The celebration had lingered long into the night. I could still see the faint glow of the fires in the distance. Abba had come home not long ago, and I was sure Lazarus would soon follow. I finished preparing for bed with one eye on the horizon. With my outer garment off, I shivered in the night wind. Softly, I padded barefoot down the stairs to the courtyard below, my long hair catching in the wind.

The courtyard was still and silent, except for the few slumbering forms of relatives too tired to return home. I stole across the earthen floor to my parents'—no, my father's—chamber. Perhaps he'd know where Lazarus was.

Aggressive snores greeted me, and I backed away with a sigh. There was no use waking him. He'd need to sleep off the drink before he was of any use. Moving to our front entrance, I noticed with alarm that the doors were barred. Did Abba not expect Lazarus back tonight? I opened the doors and stood silently staring out into the night, my arms wrapped around my middle.

"Brother, where are you?" Was he still in the company of the twins? They'd been drinking a lot, but I hadn't noticed how much Lazarus had drunk. Surely, if he was in the company of friends, he would be safe. Cleopas' worried voice, however, resounded in my mind. *"He needs to be careful with those two."*

I'd been so embarrassed by my admiration of the twins that I hadn't truly weighed Cleopas' words. Was he right to worry? I couldn't retire unless Lazarus was home, so I stood in the open doorway until the distant fires dimmed and the night creatures ceased their stirring. And still no brother. I paced back and forth, biting my nails until they bled and praying for Yahweh to stretch out His protective hand over my brother. Finally, exhausted, I closed the doors and leaned my back against them, hesitant to fasten the bar for what remained of the night.

A distant shout jerked me upright. My heart thundered in my chest as I threw open the doors once more. Eyes blurry from weariness, I blinked rapidly. Was that a man hurrying across the field? The shout rose again as the dark form stumbled, managing to right itself at the last moment. Yes! It was a man stumbling toward home. Lazarus!

Disregarding propriety, I ran out the door, into the street, and toward the figure in the field. I had nothing on but my tunic, which streamed behind me.

"Help! We need help!" The voice was masculine, but it wasn't Lazarus. Not until I was nearly within arm's reach did I recognize the man who now dropped to his knees in exhaustion.

"I discovered him facedown in the creek." Uri nearly collapsed as he laid my silent brother at my feet.

Nine

He was alive. My mind held on to this one hopeful fact as Lazarus shuddered violently in my arms, vomiting all over my chest. "Bring him inside. We need to get him inside," I gasped.

Uri and I carried Lazarus into the house and stretched him out in the courtyard. His skin shone luminous and nearly blue in the lamplight. My screams upon first seeing him had awoken the entire household, and we were soon surrounded, everyone talking at once, everyone trying to help.

The uproar was so intense that it woke Abba, who lurched from his room, stumbling and falling multiple times. Catching sight of Lazarus, he scrambled to his side, falling over him with a cry of anguish.

"Someone remove him!" I pushed at my father, attempting to clear access to Lazarus' face.

"He was unconscious when I found him," Uri panted next to me. "I pounded on his chest until he began coughing, but there's more water. He's having trouble coughing it up."

"My son. My only son." Abba lay across Lazarus' chest.

"Remove him!" I screamed into the night air. He was suffocating my brother, who was still emitting gurgling sounds with intermittent, wet coughs.

Samu grabbed my father's arm and dragged backward, but he lashed out, wrenched his arm free, and fell across Lazarus once more.

I turned to Uri and found his face close to mine. "Please."

He read the desperate look in my eyes, nodded, and moved to my father, grasping his right arm as Samu took the left. As they heaved my sobbing father backward, I flew forward to take his place.

Blood streamed from Lazarus' brow, and I recoiled with a gasp.

"It's a superficial wound." Abigail placed a steady hand on my shoulder, knelt beside me, and swiftly began cleaning the cut.

"His stomach . . . it's swollen." I rested a hand on the alarming rise in my brother's middle. "Uri said he'd already coughed up water. How much more could there be?"

"Move aside, Martha, Abigail." Samu had returned. "His cut can wait. The water in his belly cannot." Before I could protest, he pounded the heel of his palm into my brother's chest, causing him to cry out.

I cried out as well, biting my tongue to keep from bidding Samu to stop. The painful thumping, fist against flesh, tore at my ears and made me cringe, but it was necessary.

On the second blow, Lazarus coughed up water. I darted forward, but Abigail restrained me. A third blow produced more water, a fourth even more. Samu paused as my brother continued to cough. The sound was less wet than before, and my heart flickered with hope.

"Stop!"

It was Lazarus. Praise be to God! It was my brother calling out for Samu to cease. I placed a trembling hand to my mouth, tears spilling over.

"Stop!" His voice sounded strangled, both painful and beautiful to hear. I ran to Samu's side as my brother fainted.

"Run and fetch Yaffah," Samu instructed his wife as he lifted Lazarus in his arms.

Bethany had no physician, but Yaffah had years of training as a midwife and had a storehouse of herbal remedies.

Samu carried Lazarus into an interior room, and I was about to follow when I heard a soft sob.

Mary sat in the shadows on a step halfway between roof and courtyard. Her knees were drawn to her chest, and she gripped them furiously as her whole body convulsed with another sob.

"Oh, sister." I ran to her with open arms. Even though I was a mess from tending Lazarus, Mary clung to me, ignoring the vomit and burying her face in my neck.

"Is he dead?" Her voice was young, frightened.

"No. Only resting."

Mary burrowed deeper into my arms. "What happened to him? Why was Samu hitting him?"

"Samu wasn't hurting him. He was trying to make the water come out. Uri said Lazarus was in the creek and swallowed a lot of water. But Samu got it all out." Had he? Had all the water left my poor brother's body? And would he wake again from his faint?

"But why? Why was he in the creek?"

Mary's thundering sobs had turned to tired sniffles, and I stroked the back of her head while pondering the question. Why indeed? I gave the single answer I had. "I don't know."

I rose with Mary in my arms, grunting under her weight. She nuzzled my neck with her face as I carried her back to bed. The rooftop echoed with eerie quiet after so much excitement.

"Will he be all right?" Mary struggled to keep her eyes open. She looked at me through small slits. "Will Lazarus be all right?"

My breath caught in my throat. It was the same question Lazarus had asked me so many years ago on a different fateful night. Things hadn't turned out all right then. I prayed they would this night.

I covered Mary with my mantle and gave her the truthful answer I had given my brother then. "I don't know." And then, because I had come to realize this answer was only one side of the coin, I added, "But Yahweh does, and we will rest in that."

There was no sleep for me that night. Mary cried out with nightmares, and I stayed by her side until sleep fully claimed her.

Yaffah was able to revive Lazarus. Although his breathing was ragged and his body still ravaged by coughs, the water was gone. The cut on his head was long and deep. Yaffah stitched it up, declaring that he'd display a handsome scar when it was finally healed. She applied a poultice and wrapped his head with linen before leaving with a word of warning to watch him throughout the night. I stood and gazed at his sleeping form. The rise and fall of his chest hitched often with bursts of coughs.

"Go, Martha, and rest yourself." Samu sat in a corner, his head leaning against the wall.

I was about to protest, but then realized I was still covered in my brother's vomit. The least I could do was change before coming back to keep watch.

Weariness clutched at my chest as I trudged back to the roof and pulled my soiled tunic over my head, gagging as I found pieces of matted hair. Pouring water into a basin, I dipped my head in and scrubbed, splashing water over my bare skin in a makeshift bath. I pulled on a fresh tunic and, as its soft folds traveled over my head and down my body, the tears came as well, falling slow and steady down my cheeks.

I had held my brother in his time of need. I had held my sister as well. Who was there to hold me? Once I could have gone to Gilah, but that time had passed. Savta wouldn't know what to do with my tears. Her practical nature would take over and she'd simply tell me to go to bed. I was alone with my fright, which felt wild and big.

Slumping onto my knees, I hunched over until my forehead touched the floor. I cried hard and silently, rocking back and forth, seeking relief.

And then there was Abba, who was useless to comfort himself, let alone his daughter. At the thought of Abba came the image of Uri escorting him away. Even in the throes of confusion and terror, Uri's presence had steadied me. Surely, he was a gift from God. If he had not seen my brother . . . had not dragged him from the creek . . . Lazarus would be dead right now and I would still be pacing anxiously by the front door, waiting for his body to be found.

I stumbled to my feet and raced down the stairs to the room where Lazarus lay. Samu was where I'd left him. I paused in the doorway. "Where is Abba? And Uri?"

"I left them in your father's room."

Abba was passed out on the bed, and there was no sign of Uri. He must have returned to the sheepfold—alone and without acknowledgment for the role he'd played in Lazarus' rescue.

My emotions were running high, otherwise I would have thought better of my actions as I sprinted out our front door and into the street. My hair was loose and wet, my feet still bare as I hitched up my tunic around my knees and ran through the garden, the barley field, and down the hillside.

As Azariah rose in the distance, a sob tore at my throat. My feet ached, and I was shivering from the night air on my wet hair. This was ridiculous. *I* was ridiculous. I was a half-clad, barefoot girl with dripping hair and streaming eyes, running through the dead of night like her life depended on it. And yet I did not care.

Dawn wasn't far off. Already the horizon glowed with anticipation. As I neared the tree, a shadow stepped out from under its branches. This time, I recognized the form immediately. Uri opened his arms wide, and I crashed into them with a sob.

He held me tightly against his chest and rested his chin on the top of my head. His mantle was still wet from dragging my brother from the creek. I buried my face in its folds and added to its dampness with my tears.

When my emotion was spent and I'd finally quieted, I listened to the thumping of Uri's heart and let contentment wash over me. He must have been waiting for word of Lazarus and had instead been confronted with me tearing through the fields like a wild person. What must he think of me?

The new day was dawning, and with it the realization of what I'd done. I'd sought out comfort, but at what cost to my pride? Uri's arms hadn't moved since I'd entered them. If anything, he was holding me even closer. But now my body was tense with awareness. I dreaded pulling back and seeing the expression on his face, but I couldn't stay in his arms. The village would rouse itself soon and we would be seen.

"I'm sorry." I fumbled with my words, mumbling them against his chest. "I shouldn't be here." And yet I wasn't leaving. "I simply wanted to thank you." Had I? Or had it been self-interest that drove me? "My brother would be dead if not for you." That much was true.

"He is alive, then?" Uri's voice rumbled softly against my cheek.

I pulled back to give him the joyful news. "Yes, praise be to God. Samu was able to relieve him of the rest of the water, and Yaffah roused him when he fainted. He cut his head badly, but there won't be lasting wounds on that account."

"He seemed to be trying to cross the stream. I'm sure he slipped and hit his head."

"Thank God you were nearby."

"I couldn't sleep. Tzvi had returned the sheep to the fold, and I began wandering. I often do so when I cannot sleep."

"And is that often?"

"Of late, yes."

Even though we were a handbreadth apart, with his arms still around me, I was avoiding his eyes. I investigated them now and was surprised to see pain there. For a moment, I forgot my disheveled state as a new worry entered my mind. "What's wrong that you cannot sleep?"

He dropped his arms abruptly and turned away. "Nothing to concern you. I am thankful God gave me sleeplessness this night so that I might be there for your brother."

I had given up the idea that he might be attracted to me, but I still cared for his pain. "You can share with me what troubles you, Uri."

"No, I cannot!" He turned back toward me and ran a hand through his hair vigorously, as if trying to shear the hair from his own head.

"We haven't talked lately, not since you returned, but I have a good listening ear. At least that's what Gilah tells me."

He was pacing back and forth now with agitated strides.

"You don't need to worry." I scrambled at a reason for his mood. "I won't mistake your confidence for affection." My voice cracked as my cheeks flooded with embarrassment. "I know there is none between us."

He groaned and sat on a raised tree root that gnarled its way upward into a seat.

"Won't you share with me as friends? Can't we be that to each other?"

"Friends? No." The words seemed forcibly wrenched from his body. He stared up at me with hopeless eyes. "No," he repeated softly. "Not as friends. You are more than that to me—you have been from the moment I saw you."

"What can you mean?"

"Just what I've said." He rose quickly, then sat back down just as fast, his body seeming to teem with energy he couldn't contain. "God help me, I am being too free with my speech." He stared at me, taking me in head to toe, his eyes widening as they snagged on my unbound hair.

At his wide-eyed look, I was reminded of how scandalous this was—me being here, alone, with a man, with hair undone. Self-consciously, I shoved a hand through my long brown locks. My heart begged for him to continue, to explain his flustered words, but my mind balked at my blatant impropriety. Aghast, I looked down at my worn tunic. I had nothing to bind up my hair. Nervously, I spun it into a long twist, snaking it over my shoulder, curling it into a tight ball at the curve of my throat, longing for covering, shaking under his gaze.

His eyes followed my methodical movement, chest rising and falling with rapid breath.

"I-I shouldn't be here," I gasped. God help me, my feet were still bare. What had I been thinking? I shuffled backward, one hand covering the ball of hair at my neck, the other splayed across my chest. My chest! Oh, Yahweh, could he see too much? This last thought humiliated me so much, I dropped my hair and turned to run.

I'd made it two strides when he caught me. "Martha." His voice was rushed, breathless, his hand warm as he grasped my shoulder. I quivered under his touch, half turning, not wanting him to see me in such a state.

"Please let me go, Uri. I shouldn't have come." Tears clogged my voice. "I only wanted to thank you. Please don't look at me. I'm a frantic mess, and I'm fairly certain I still reek of my brother's vomit."

He chuckled at that, breaking some of the tension between us. "You don't see what I see." His hand brushed the back of my neck. "You are beautiful." His words, warm and soft, fell upon me like a benediction.

"W-what?" I turned to face him, still trying to cover as much of me as I could but filled with an aching hope that compelled me to stay. He was gazing at me with a mixture of tenderness and shyness that drew me to him like a moth to a flame.

"You think too little of yourself, I can tell. But you are strong." He lifted a hand and tangled a finger in my hair. "From the moment I saw you at the well, laughing with such joy over your friend's good fortune, my heart was yours."

His passionate words crept through my body like a flame, leaving me gaping and dumbfounded. "How can this be? You've been so distant, like I no longer existed."

At my confused outburst, he stepped backward, arms spread wide. "Because you can't. You can't exist in that way for me." He shook his head. "Don't you see? There is absolutely nothing I can offer you. You can marry well one day—very well. You deserve that. You deserve so much more than I can give you."

He took several long steps away and hung his head. "I've had plenty of time to think about it. Night after endless night in the Jordan wilderness with nothing to do but think of you." He groaned and scrubbed a hand over his face. "And in thinking of you, I saw how selfish I would be to act upon the desires of my heart."

Joy filled me slowly, like a smooth, well-aged wine, and I laughed aloud at the sensation that traveled from head to toe. Uri drew his head up abruptly at my laugh and stared at me with wondering eyes.

Nervousness fled as a strange giddiness leapt to life in my chest. I hugged myself and grinned like a fool. More laughter escaped me, and I turned quickly away, hands to my flaming cheeks.

"I shouldn't have . . . I'm sorry. I never planned to say a thing." Uri rubbed the back of his neck with a large hand, face apologetic and uncertain in the light of my reaction.

"No . . . it's just that . . . I've been trying hard to forget you, Uri."

He looked at me with such a quizzical expression that I burst into giggles. Heavens, but I needed to control myself. Who was this giddy girl? I did not recognize her.

"I've been trying hard to forget you, but my heart would not let me." My smile was so wide, my cheeks ached.

Uri stared at me for a single long moment, then tilted his head back and let out a deep, exultant shout that sent shivers down to my toes. "Surely not, Martha of Bethany." He cocked his head at me with narrowed eyes. "Surely your heart didn't need help forgetting such a brute." He gestured to himself.

"You think too little of yourself." I echoed his words, my smile slipping as he closed the distance between us.

He'd taken me swiftly into his arms before, when I was overcome with sorrow and fear, but now with our mutual declaration hanging between us, he stopped short. His breath grew ragged as he stared down at me, eyes racing across my face, arms trembling by his sides as if he fought an inner battle to keep them from grabbing hold of me.

I wasn't laughing any longer as I gulped and stared back at him. "I . . . should probably leave."

"Yes, probably," he murmured.

"But I'll return."

"Yes, please do."

I took a step back and then another, loath to leave him but also too shy to stay. He made no move to stop me, his face filled with a mixture of longing and disbelief. I stumbled my way back up the hillside, hands snatching at my wild hair, body abuzz with the knowledge that he was watching me, my heart not daring to look back.

Ten

Everything changed after the accident. Lazarus became withdrawn and moody. Even as his body healed, the health of his soul and mind worsened. I pleaded with him to talk to me, but he steadfastly refused to explain what had happened that night. Not even Abba's threats could sway him. This, perhaps, was the greatest and most upsetting change—our father's ignited wrath.

One afternoon, he stormed into the room while I changed the dressing on Lazarus' wound. Abba ordered me out in a tone that jolted me into action. I hovered outside the door in a state of dread.

"What were you thinking, son? You are the heir of this household. You cannot be careless with your life. Your absentmindedness extends too far."

I couldn't make out Lazarus' mumbled response, but whatever it was, it infuriated Abba even more.

"You are a man and past such ignorant behavior. You will never gain the respect of a household if you continue to conduct yourself in this way. Those boys—they lack judgment."

Those boys? He must mean Azriel and Baruch. I closed my eyes in pain. So Cleopas' intuition about them had been right. And I had implied he was judgmental.

"What folly did they lead you into?"

Again, my brother's mumbled reply.

"You are a disgrace and a disappointment. You are of no use to anyone, not even yourself."

I gasped and lurched back. Abba had hinted at his disappointment over Lazarus through the years but had never spoken it outright. Certainly, he was not an affectionate father, but I'd never thought him cruel. I feared his words would wound my brother more than his tumble in the creek.

After Abba stormed out, I reentered to assess the damage that had been done. Lazarus' stony expression told me all I needed to know.

It was a strange time. As our household suffered in strained silence after Lazarus' accident, I privately nurtured a deep and great joy. Uri's admiration was like a salve for my aching heart, the memory of our encounter a refuge I turned to when worries over my family overwhelmed me.

I hardly knew how to conduct myself around him. Most of the time we were apart. During the day, I was busy with household tasks, while he spent his time in the surrounding fields with the flock. It was the beginning of summer, and he'd be leaving soon to higher, cooler pastures—a reality I was steadfastly trying to ignore. Anytime we met in public, in the field, at the well, or elsewhere in the village, I could barely look at him for the joy surging through my body. He would clear his throat and try to goad me into paying him attention—a lure I never took.

I'd promised him I'd be back and yet I tarried, nervous and half-terrified of this new and wonderful thing. When I finally ventured out one evening, I was filled with doubt. Even though this time I wore my hair discreetly covered and was fully garbed in mantle and sandals, I was still defying convention by seeking out a man's company—alone. What would Ima think if she could see me now?

But the pull to be near Uri was too strong to deny. Instead of sprinting down the hill into his arms, I came to him slowly, dazed and unsure. He was waiting, most likely had been waiting each night, and he met me with an outstretched hand. I took it shyly, sliding my fingers between his. We talked in hushed tones with hands tangled and hearts thrumming beneath the moon until finally I tore myself away to return to bed.

The second time I met him, my steps were more purposeful, and it was I who reached for him first, clasping his hand in both of my own. I was eager and bashful, careful and hopeful. His eyes never strayed from me, as if he could scarcely believe I was there. We walked beneath the stars, then sat under Azariah's canopy, where he played a haunting and lilting tune on his flute that captured my breath. Like one of the lambs, I settled beneath the music, my face tilted toward him, my heart not far behind.

The third time, I barreled down the hill, taking him off guard, nearly knocking him off his feet. He caught me with a happy laugh and strong arm, and we rocked in an off-kilter embrace, our breaths mingling in the nippy night air. When we settled, I was close against his pounding heart, head resting on his shoulder. His gaze turned serious as he held me, and for a moment I couldn't breathe. But then he cleared his throat, snagged my hand, and tugged me leaping and laughing behind him as he darted farther down the hill.

With each encounter, I dared to believe a bit more that I was seen and admired by this young man, and that with him I was safe. As the time for his departure grew closer, I longed to know him deeper but wasn't sure how to ask or what his reaction might be.

One night, as we walked near the sheepfold, he dropped my hand to check the lock on the gate. I stood several paces behind him and stared at his broad shoulders with an aching heart. "Uri?"

"Yes?" He turned quickly, was back by my side in an instant, where he joined our hands again.

Mouth dry as the desert, I gazed up at him, memorizing his face, daring to reach for it with a trembling hand.

His eyes closed briefly at my touch, and when they opened again, they were filled with a warmth that traveled straight to my bones and gave me the courage to speak.

"You'll be leaving soon." My voice cracked with emotion, and I stared stubbornly at his collarbone, not trusting myself to meet his eyes. "I will pray for you every day. I . . . I want to know more about the man I'll be praying over." Swallowing hard, I risked a look at his face, and seeing how intently he watched me, quickly dropped my gaze again.

"And besides, you promised." I lightened my tone, trying to infuse a bit of teasing between us. "That day with the food basket. You said one day you'd tell me more of your story." I followed his trailing scar with curious eyes. "I'm ready to listen if you are ready to tell it. I want to know as much as you're willing to share with me."

He was quiet for a long moment, staring at our clasped hands with such a conflicted expression that I began to grow frightened.

"Uri?"

He heard the tremor in my voice and responded by drawing me close, resting an arm across my shoulders, anchoring me to his chest.

"Of course you want to know more, and you will." He pulled back. "I want you to know me, but I'm afraid when you do, you'll look at me differently."

"Never," I breathed.

He smiled, but there was sadness behind it. "What I am about to tell you is all in my past. Can you remember this?" He paused, only continuing with some difficulty. "When I share something hard or surprising with you, please remember these things are not who I am now. Ah, Martha . . . I can see already that I am frightening you." He groaned and turned away.

"No!" I clutched at his arm, angry with myself. "I want to hear. I want to know."

He faced away from me for a moment as I grasped his strong forearm with both hands and willed him to continue.

"Very well." He sighed deeply and led me to the shelter of Azariah's canopy, where he eased himself onto the gnarled root he'd first used as a seat. I settled on the ground at his feet, posturing myself to listen.

"You wouldn't think it looking at me now, but my father, Gavriel, was born into a prestigious Levitical family. He came from a line of priests, but I never met any of them because, by the time I was born, they had disowned my father."

I let out a small gasp. "But why?"

"He . . . collected taxes for the Romans."

I groaned, imagining the shame that shrouded his family. Tax collectors were often seen as little better than thieves—lining their pockets at the expense of their neighbors, all under the banner of our foreign occupiers. Little wonder the extended family had disowned Uri's father.

"My parents would argue late into the night. I don't remember over what—only that the tax commissioner was frequently at our home, and I was always banned from the house when he arrived. During one such encounter, I hid in a chest to avoid being sent away. They were arguing violently—the commissioner and my parents. I was barely seven and didn't fully understand their words."

Seven. Not much younger than I was when I'd lost Ima. The hurt behind his words was evident, and suddenly I realized how much Uri must care for me to share these hard things. A new longing rose in my chest, and I reached a hand to him, which he quickly grasped.

"Now I understand that my father had been stealing for the commissioner and was refusing to continue the practice. By keeping silent and cracking the chest lid open, I was able to observe the argument as it grew more heated, violent. The commissioner slapped my mother across the face when she tried to intervene, which ignited my father's rage. And then . . ."

"Yes?" My breath left in a rush.

"The commissioner had brought soldiers with him. They didn't need much encouragement to brutalize a Jewish couple. I often wonder why—why the senseless bloodshed. And then I recall my parents' late-night conversations. I think my father had stumbled upon sensitive information. My family had become wrapped up in something much larger and bigger than they'd bargained for."

"So, the soldiers . . . killed them?" I squeaked, horrified. When Uri nodded, I yanked my hand away to cover my face, mortified that I'd asked him to share such a painful past. "Oh, Uri . . ." I sobbed and hunched over my knees.

In an instant, he slid from the root to the ground by my side and was gently prying my hands from my face.

"Shush, love. What is this?"

"I shouldn't have asked you. . . . I'm sorry. I'm making you relive such horrible things." My mind was filled with grief on Uri's behalf, but not so addled that I hadn't recognized his term of endearment, which only made me weep more.

"Ah, Martha." He nestled me against his side until we were sitting hip to hip, backs against Azariah's roots. "You have nothing to apologize for."

Turning into him, I let Uri shelter me with a strong arm, daring to ask, "Did you see it happen?"

"Some of it, yes. And then afterward, when they'd left and I'd waited for hours to make sure the soldiers were gone, I saw the damage that had been done."

I closed my eyes, seeing my mother's bed linens filled with red, recalling the deep void that'd opened inside me as her lifeblood dripped to the ground. I'd had Lazarus to care for, which had given me a purpose. What must it have been like to go through such loss alone? My tears fell silent and fast. I ducked my head to hide them from Uri as he continued.

"I had no one to care for me—no family to claim me. I also sensed that if the people who'd killed my parents found me, they'd slaughter me on sight. The streets of Sepphoris are swarming with the displaced. It didn't take me long to fall into company with a group that called themselves the Memra. Their leader, Chanoch, fed me in exchange for any treasures I could find through thieving. I was a frightened seven-year-old boy scraping out a living on the streets—thieving—no better than my father."

As I listened, I hardly dared to breathe. He was describing things I could barely imagine. Even though we lived but two miles from Jerusalem, I was a village girl through and through, more comfortable in the fields than city streets. The savagery Uri had witnessed, and the desperation of his life thereafter, was hard for me to grasp.

"As I grew older, more was required from me to earn my keep. Chanoch was king of the city's underbelly. His reach extended from street rats such as me all the way to the elite. I did not understand the extent of his power until I was well-nigh crushed beneath it." He swallowed hard, the uneven rise and fall of his chest evidence of deep emotion.

"When I was twelve, I learned why they called themselves the Memra, what the word meant. They saw themselves as executors of God's word and will. While I and a thousand other urchins ran rampant among the streets, stealing whatever we could find, others carried out far more dangerous errands. When I turned thirteen, they required the same of me."

I was so captured by his story that I startled as he rose brusquely to his feet and strode a few paces away.

"Remember what I said earlier?" He turned back to me, one hand on his hip, the other raking through his hair in agitation.

I wobbled to my feet, light-headed from all the heaviness between us. Whatever our relationship had been, we were now entering something new, and both of us could sense it. "I remember," I whispered, meeting his desperate eyes. "These things are not who you are now."

At my words, his shoulders eased downward. Never breaking my gaze, he continued. "I was given orders to break into different nobles' homes. At first, I was to simply nab a treasure or two, and then it became vandalism. The targets were always those whom the Memra dubbed Roman sympathizers."

"They were Zealots," I breathed, the word throbbing with anger and death. I'd heard of such people who were so consumed by hatred for our foreign oppressors that they lashed out in violence.

Uri didn't contradict me, letting the word settle between us. "When I turned fifteen, they gave me a dagger—a jewel-studded beauty that I had nabbed myself the previous year. My errands were slowly taking me into more dangerous territory. The Memra were strategic with how they trained their members. They made you beholden to them, gave you a small task, and then a larger one. Pretty soon, you found yourself doing things you never thought you would do for a group that had somehow become your only family."

Uri shook his head, and I could tell that shame covered him like a cloak. "With the gift of that dagger, they initiated me into the inner circle, the Sicarii."

I didn't mean to, but I took a step back, staring at Uri with wide, disbelieving eyes. The Sicarrii were the most ruthless of the Zealots, famous for concealing daggers in public places and meting out justice on Jews who dared acquiesce to Rome. "Daggermen." I mumbled the word past numb lips, staring at Uri's hands, the strong hands whose steady pressure I had come to crave. Beautiful, scarred hands that had once wielded a dagger.

Uri immediately registered the shift in my mood and took a step toward me, then two, stretching out his hands. "Remember," he pleaded. "Remember, Martha."

With effort, I peeled my eyes from his hands to find his face. The anguish etched there broke through the horror nipping at my mind. "I remember," I gasped.

"My first mission was with five others at the theater. With no explanation, I was assigned a man to dispose of on the signal." Uri stood before me, nearly within reach, his arms loose by his sides, shoulders slumped, as if telling me this emptied him of all he had.

"In that moment, all I could see was my father's face as he stood up to the commissioner. Like him, I was being given a choice. When the signal came, I made no move. Five men fell dead around me, stabbed in the back by my companions. But my man lived, and because he lived, my life was forfeit. I dropped the dagger and fled during the commotion."

He was staring at the ground as if he couldn't bring himself to gauge my reaction. A slow burning filled my chest as I saw the tears wetting his cheeks. "The irony is, I hated Rome and all it represented." He looked at me then, with tired eyes rimmed in red. "After seeing my parents butchered in our own home, I loathed anything connected to Rome. And yet, I couldn't do it. I couldn't take a life, even though my parents' lives were taken from me, and the life I might have led was snuffed out before my eyes. Even so, I couldn't do it."

He was alone. My heart thudded painfully in my throat. He was alone in his pain. Alone with a past he wanted to forget.

"So now you know," he stated in an emptied voice. "Now that you know, are you still able to remember?" His question lifted with a touch of hope.

I closed my eyes with a deep breath, my lonely heart recognizing the ache in his. When I opened my eyes, I had my answer. With hurried steps, I closed the gap between us, standing on the tips of my toes to twine my arms about his neck. He exhaled sharply, stooping to wrap me in his embrace, straightening once more so that my feet dangled.

With a sob, I burrowed my face into his neck, and as his heart pressed against mine, whispered, "I remember."

Eleven

29 Sivan
18 AD

Only a few days remained before Uri left with the flock for many months. I spent those days in agony, already mourning his departure. During that time, Savta's health took an abrupt turn for the worse. For hours each day I stayed by her side, spoon-feeding her broth and holding her twisted fingers in my hands as her slim frame shook like a reed in a storm.

Her body had betrayed her, but I was thankful that her mind was as sharp as ever, unlike Saba, who had barely recognized the faces of his own family members toward the end of his life.

The eve of Uri's departure found me sick with worry over him and Savta. I sat by her side, unwilling to leave her but longing to be with Uri.

"Breathe, child." Savta stirred by my side and opened sightless eyes. "You sound like you've run a long distance."

"I don't know what's wrong with me," I gasped, hand tightening around her twisted fingers.

"Oh, you're filled with love. Anyone can see that."

"What?" I lurched back. I had yet to name my own feelings for the shepherd who had crept so steadily into my heart. Love?

"Don't act so surprised. I may be old, but I'm not dead . . . yet. And I can't see your dear face anymore, but I don't need sight to know certain things." She rested a curled hand over her heart. "To know them here."

Her voice was cracked, weak, and oh so dear. At her words, I curled over her thin form and wept.

"Oh, come now." Savta rested a hand on my head. "What's this about?"

"I'm worried for you. I'm fretful over Lazarus. He's so broken and sad. Mary is as wild as ever. Abba is . . ." I had no words to describe the darkness I sensed in him lately. "And I'm feeling . . . I'm feeling . . ." I couldn't bring myself to put words to the way I felt for Uri.

The fading sunlight streamed in through the high window, its beams dancing over the packed earthen floor. The last light of the last day before Uri would leave. I put my hands over my head and wailed.

Savta didn't speak for a while. She simply stroked my hair and let me spend my tears. I had always brought my emotions to Ima as a child. She was the one whom I could count on to welcome them. Savta had a blunt nature that she'd passed on to Abba. I was unaccustomed to confiding in her and was surprised that she welcomed my tears this night. Finally, I roused myself, simultaneously sniffling and hiccupping as I tried to rein in my emotions.

"Ah, Martha, you are carrying a heavy load on your young shoulders." Savta moved her hand to my cheek, tracing the paths of my tears with her thumb. "You are troubled and worried about so many things. Worry is like a ravenous beast, child. The more you feed him, the more he wants and the harder he'll go after it. Take it from an old woman who knows . . . do not give your worry one more scrap of food."

I exhaled a long, shaky breath. "It's hard to control something as wild as thoughts."

"It helps to focus those thoughts onto one thing." Savta let a hand drop over the side of her bedroll, spreading her twisted fingers as far as they would go into the dirt and raising her other hand to the sky. "We are but dust, and our heart and flesh will fail us, but Yahweh is our strength and portion forever. We do well to tether our thoughts to the One who is our strength."

Savta grew quiet, and we sat in companionable silence as I tried to focus my thoughts like she'd said. But for all my effort, my thoughts kept flying down the hill to Uri. How could I last a whole summer without seeing him? The tears flowed again, this time quietly, but not so silent that Savta couldn't detect them.

"It's pent-up love that makes you weep, is it not?"

Now that Savta had named it, I saw that it was true. My heart was filled with an unbearable love. "Yes," I gasped.

"I recognize your tears. They come from a place of longing. The way I long for my Ezra even now after all these years."

"I haven't heard you speak of Saba in a long time."

Savta sighed and turned her face away. "Not a day passes that I don't miss him." Her jaw moved as she chewed on her next words before releasing them. "I met Ezra for the first time on our wedding day. I was terrified that he'd be ugly or cruel or, even worse, ugly *and* cruel." She laughed, but it turned into a cough that violently racked her frame.

I offered her water, but she shook her head, so instead I held her hand as we waited for her breath to return. "But you ended up loving him," I prompted when she was resting easy again.

"Yes, praise be to God, he was the kindest man I'd ever met." Savta closed her eyes, as if imagining her groom on their wedding day. "And such a delight to the eyes."

I blushed at her words.

"Sometimes love engulfs us suddenly, like a consuming fire.

Other times it comes over us slowly, like a sunrise. That's how it was with my Ezra. Like the dawning of a new day."

She grasped my hand tightly—no easy feat for her gnarled hands—and raised herself slightly off the bed. "Love is a great gift from Yahweh. Don't forget it, Martha." She sank back down, her energy clearly spent.

"Thank you, Savta, but I'm afraid my love is impossible."

"Bah, and why? Because he spends his days with sheep?"

My mouth gaped open.

"I'm no fool, Martha. That Uri's name is on everyone's lips since Lazarus' accident, and every time he's mentioned you act as cheerful as birdsong."

"Oh, Savta," I moaned and dropped my face in my hands.

"Don't 'Oh, Savta' me." There it was—her natural pragmatism emerging. "Stop blubbering, child. There is no shame in loving a shepherd."

"But Abba!"

"He's grieving and broken, yes." Savta sniffed, tears coursing down her weathered cheeks. "He loved your mother more than life. He stopped living in many ways when Devorah died."

I resisted the temptation to wipe away her tears, afraid it would embarrass her.

"All we can do, child, is give ourselves up to our Creator. He knows our frame. He remembers that we are dust. It is He who gives and takes away. It is our part to bless the name of Yahweh."

Savta seemed to be tiring rapidly, her voice growing fainter as she spoke. The truth of her words burrowed deep in my bones. I tucked a blanket around her frame and smoothed her thin white hair back from her forehead. "Shh, rest now. Save your strength." I leaned over to plant a kiss and, as I did so, she grasped at my tunic.

"Love your shepherd, Martha, and may Yahweh bless you both."

I stayed with her long into the night, lying by her side and watching the rise and fall of her chest, one hand on hers.

I woke before dawn, startled by the pounding of my own heart. Savta lay next to me, and I hastened to check her breath. It was calm and even, so I stood and shook the folds from my tunic.

I hadn't meant to fall asleep. Was I too late to bid Uri farewell? As I entered the courtyard and donned my mantle, I glanced upward. The first light of dawn wasn't far off, and Uri would want to leave early to beat the midday heat. The thought that I'd missed him, that he'd been waiting for me beneath the tree, only to be left disappointed, caused my insides to quiver.

Sneaking out of our home unobserved had become a familiar routine for me. Never had I done so, however, in the early morning hours. As I unbarred our front entrance, I recognized that my errand would have to be brief so I could return before the household stirred.

Uri was leaving this time on his own. Having proved himself trustworthy to my father, he'd been given the position of head shepherd, meaning Tzvi would remain home for the season. I was both pleased and distressed. Pleased that my father clearly esteemed Uri. Distressed that he would be alone for so long.

The morning dew soaked my feet as I ran swiftly toward the hillside, a path I knew well. As I crested the hill, no eager form rose to greet me from beneath the tree. With a dismayed cry, I flew down the slope, checking under Azariah's canopy to be sure, stifling the gasp of despair that rose to my lips upon finding it empty.

The hillside was calm and quiet. The birds weren't even out yet to sing. Surely he had not left already. I ran to the sheepfold, restraining the urge to shout out to him. As I raised my hand to knock, the door opened, and there he was, murmuring my name, pulling me into his arms.

With relief, I choked down a sob and clung to his neck. *"Love your shepherd, Martha."* Had Yahweh seen my lonely heart, and was He giving me this love? Dare I accept it?

I pulled back to find resignation etched on Uri's face. "What is it?"

"Our meetings . . . our conversations . . . are the brightest things in my life."

His words, although beautiful, echoed with a finality that shook me. I rocked back onto my heels, head spinning. "But?"

"I cannot ask you to wait for me, Martha."

"What are you saying?" My eyes fluttered in surprise. "You don't . . . want me to wait for you?" Panic clawed its way into my voice.

"No!" Uri's brows drew together sharply. "Of course I want you to. I meant I shouldn't ask you to." He stumbled over his words, cheeks growing ruddy in his struggle. "If you only knew how much I want you to. But it's not a matter of what I want. It's a matter of what you deserve."

He leaned a shoulder against the side of the sheepfold. "I cannot ask you to wait all these long months without looking at another man. It's too much to ask."

Quietly, I observed his defeated form. He was so sure of my response, and it hurt. "How can you say that? Am I so flighty as to run to another man when you leave?" My voice was growing shrill as I squeezed back tears and tried to push out my confused words. "It's not as if I go sneaking out to meet strange men all the time, Uri bar Gavriel!" These last words left in a strangled hiccup, despite how intently I tried to maintain control. Thoroughly embarrassed, I hugged myself tightly and bit my lip.

Pushing himself off the wall, Uri approached me with a new light in his eye. "You would wait for me? Truly?"

"Yes, truly," I muttered, still miffed with him. "Look at another man?" I snorted. "Why would I do such a thing?"

"You're not . . . ashamed of me?" He swallowed hard. "My past, the thieving, all of it?"

My roiling emotions began to settle as I noticed the insecurity in his face, the raw hope that edged his voice. How could he be so unsure of his own worth? He was standing in front of me now, arms loose by his sides, expression suspended as he achingly awaited my reply.

Slowly I placed a hand on his chest, feeling his racing heartbeat beneath my palm. "You don't see what I see," I whispered.

Drawing a ragged breath, he rested his hand over mine.

"You asked me to remember, but, Uri, it is you who needs to remember. Those things are not who you are now."

With a groan, Uri ducked his head. "I don't deserve this. I don't deserve you."

I gazed into his eyes with their gold-ringed pupils. "None of us deserve Yahweh's good gifts. I'll wait for you," I breathed. "Of course I'll wait for you."

The word *love* was a hot coal on my tongue that I ached to release. But I held it back, frightened by its strength, unsure what would happen if I let it go.

"Then you'll wait with a reminder. A reminder that I'm devoted to you." Pulling back, he tugged a necklace out from under his tunic, slipped it over his head, and held it between us in his palm. "A dear friend gave this to me several years ago."

From the simple leather cord dangled a wooden pendant. I traced the delicate design—a long feather, the length of my finger. "It's beautiful," I murmured.

Gently, he eased the necklace over my head. "My friend made it for me when I was at my lowest point. I haven't removed it until this moment."

"Oh, I can't accept it. I can't accept something so valuable to you." Flustered, I moved to take it off.

"No, please." Uri stilled my hands. "Up until now, this was

the greatest reminder of Yahweh's love in my life." He raised a hand to catch a stray wisp of hair by my temple. Slowly, he rubbed the strands between his fingers, eyes dancing over my features, as if memorizing them for the long days ahead. "Now that reminder is you."

With a small cry, I burrowed deep into his arms, nestling my head against his chest. "I will treasure it." I choked the words out. "Always. I won't remove it. Ever."

The first sunbeams of the day tugged on the horizon, and a smattering of birdcall filled the cool morning air.

"I must leave before the sun rises." His voice rumbled against my cheek.

Like an obstinate child, I shook my head, which elicited a deep laugh from Uri. Gently, he pried my arms from him. "Prepare yourself, Martha." He quirked an eyebrow at me. "In six months, I'll be back for the winter with nothing better to do than pester you for attention." He chuckled, but there was yearning deep in his eyes.

Wordlessly, I watched him go, hugging myself tightly to keep my aching heart from flying right out of my chest, already missing his warmth. Uri was ahead of the flock and disappeared before the sheep did.

With hope in my heart and a feather in my hand, I stood still and watchful until every last sheep rounded the hill and was out of sight.

Twelve

20 Elul
18 AD

Savta's health declined rapidly that summer. Abigail, Mary, and I stayed close to her side, ensuring she lacked for nothing. It hurt to see how little Abba visited her. She called out for him deliriously, as if a dream gripped her and she couldn't awaken.

For his part, Abba kept his distance from us all. He had turned into someone I hardly recognized. Never once, though, did I harbor shame over him . . . until the night he returned home stupid with drink, crashing against the wall and stumbling to the ground.

It was already dark out, and Mary was abed. At the sound of Abba's carousing, however, she entered the courtyard to find Lazarus and me each gripping one of Abba's arms, supporting his bulk, painfully guiding him one staggering step at a time to his chamber.

At Mary's small squeak of terror, I jerked my head in her direction. "Back to bed, Mary. He's fine." I didn't linger to see if she obeyed. We stumbled over the doorstep into his chamber.

"I should've married her," Abba moaned. "So young and pretty.

I should've married anyone, someone." His head lolled back as we eased him to his mat.

"What are you saying, Abba?" Lazarus questioned, his face pale, the long scar on his forehead standing out starkly in the lamplight.

"Hush. Don't try to engage him," I snapped. "He doesn't know what he's saying."

Abba grunted and burrowed into his mat. "Devorah, why? I should've remarried. Should've sired more sons. What was I thinking? The firstfruit of my strength is weak. He is weak! Why did I not seek to sire more sons?"

With a cry like a wounded animal, Lazarus stepped back. I bowed my head with grief. The fear that had begun to grow of late ripened in that one moment. Lazarus would forever be a disappointment to our father. There was no way to undo the damage.

My intelligent and kind brother, the dearest of young men, was breathing hard at our father's words. I lifted a hand to him. "Don't listen to these words. They're spoken from drunkenness. They are not truth! You are loved and valued."

"Obviously not by him." Lazarus shook my hand from his arm and fled from the room. I was about to follow when Abba's next words rooted me to the spot.

"Your *friend*," he spat out the word. "I'm sure she wishes now that she had not turned me away. The gall to turn me away! Now she is due with that hypocrite's child."

I gasped. "Gilah?" What could he mean? Gilah turned him away?

He grunted, letting out a prolonged belch that smelled of barley beer.

Disgusted, I left the room in search of my brother.

My hunt led me to the roof, where the wind whipped across the fields and caught at my head covering. I shivered and tugged my mantle tighter around my frame. He was standing at the edge of the roof, facing east, where, many miles away, lay the Dead Sea. Since his near-drowning, Lazarus' thin frame had been racked with coughs that made me wince with worry. His body wouldn't release the memory of water. I approached him softly. "Do not let his words distress you."

"I show one lapse in judgment and this is what I receive." His words were biting, like the wind, ending in a harsh, barking cough.

"Are you speaking of . . . that night? Surely, Abba isn't still upset. . . ."

"I almost died that night, and he cannot forgive me." Lazarus turned, looking much older than his thirteen years. The scar, and our father's harsh words, had aged him. "But let's be honest. His disappointment runs deeper and farther than this most recent incident. I'm never enough for him, or at least not enough of what he wants."

His words, however painful, were also true, as much as I wanted to deny it. Nothing I could say would relieve the pain, so I lifted a hand to him. He took it and pressed a kiss into my palm. Sometimes there was no need for words.

Death and life occurred on the same day. As Gilah and Simon's baby drew its first breath, Savta drew her last. The village vacillated between mourning and rejoicing. But seeing as a girl was born to Gilah and not the preferred boy, they tipped the scales toward mourning.

Mercifully, Abba was sober for the burial. Since his drunken ramblings a week earlier, the household was strained and uncomfortable. No one had breathed a word about it in deference to him. Now, with the passing of his mother, he remained surprisingly stoic.

Benjamin's family came from Jerusalem for the burial. I stood with Aviva on one side and Lazarus on the other, staring, once again, at the family tomb. How many times had we come here? Each time a piece of me broke off and settled inside with the loved one who had gone on before.

"She lived a long and full life," Aviva whispered in my ear.

I gave her a tight smile, recognizing her words of comfort but missing Savta with an ache that wouldn't be soothed.

"She was pained over Abba," I dared to confide, casting my eyes to the man who stood silent and dry-eyed by the edge of the tomb.

Lazarus grunted in agreement. "She tried to speak to him over the years, to lessen his grief over Ima, but he wouldn't listen to her."

Hunching my shoulders, I bowed my head, recalling Savta's tears over Abba and shedding some of my own. Kind, dear Savta. Between her and Gilah, I'd been blessed indeed, even without a mother to guide me. With Gilah married and Savta gone, a new loneliness widened inside. I'd been to this place of grief before, had traveled the worn path of sorrow that left one weak of heart. How many times must I return here to this empty, tender place?

A warm hand on my back startled my head upright, and I turned to find Cleopas behind me. He regarded me quietly with kind eyes, saying nothing, simply pressing his hand to my back. Somehow, his wordless presence afforded me more comfort than all the earlier tears, wailing, and consolations combined. I dropped my face into my hands and cried silent, hot tears. Cleopas increased the pressure on my back, and I let him draw me into his arms, where I pressed my flushed cheek to his shoulder. Silently, he rubbed my back until the tears dried up.

I sniffed noisily as he hooked a finger beneath my chin and tilted my face to his. "Don't despair, Martha. Yahweh comforts the hearts of those who return to Him in death. Any pain your grandmother experienced in this life is being repaid tenfold."

I slid my eyes closed as the truth of his words settled like a weighty balm covering the hurt inside. If Yahweh was faithful to comfort His children in death, He would surely do so in life. He would surely do so for me.

The first rains of summer's end began, and farmers took to the fields with their oxen and plows to till the loosened soil. The arrival of the rains meant only a few more months until Uri's return.

Mary pestered me daily about visiting Lemuel's baby sister. Already, Gilah's fourteen-day period of purification had passed, and the sixty-six-day period until she would travel to the Temple to make her childbirth offerings had begun. Normally my eagerness to see the babe would match Mary's, but Abba's cryptic words resounded in my ears, constraining me. Finally, I could delay no longer without appearing rude. On a bright yet chilly morning, Mary and I traveled across the village to Simon's fine home.

A servant met us at the door and ushered us into the tiled courtyard, where we warmed ourselves by a coal fire before being summoned to the upper room. Gilah looked resplendent as she reclined on a couch, holding a tightly swaddled bundle. She made to rise, but I bid her stay seated, kneeling over her to kiss each cheek.

"I was beginning to wonder if you'd ever come." She beamed happily at me.

Confusion had kept me away, but now a burst of anger flared in my breast. Had Gilah not wanted me as a daughter? Granted, she was only eight years my senior, but if she'd been our mother, how might our circumstances have changed?

I stood before her, mulling it over like a piece of gristle. Gilah must have noted the contrary emotions crossing my face, for she motioned the servant to leave. "What is bothering you, friend? I was sorry to hear of your grandmother's passing."

Let her think it was grief that contorted my face. I nodded and motioned to the babe. "May I hold her?" As Gilah transferred the bundle into my arms, I tried to settle the uneasiness in my stomach by focusing on the small miracle before me.

Zissa had recently announced her own pregnancy, and jealousy, surprising and fierce, had leapt to life. Thoughts of forming a family of my own flooded my mind. As always when these longings rose to the surface, I thought of Uri. His necklace pressed against the skin beneath my tunic—a precious secret.

"What have you named her?" I watched as the little one's mouth puckered, seeking nourishment even in sleep.

Gilah leaned back and patted the seat, indicating for Mary to join her. As my sister nestled against her side, I swallowed a lump in my throat. She could have been Mary's mother too. What a difference that might have made!

"Simon named her Tehilah."

I rocked the babe gently. Tehilah—majestic, noble. Such a big name for such a tiny girl.

"Where is Lemuel?" Mary gazed up at Gilah and kicked her legs back and forth.

"He started school. Simon wanted him to start sooner, but I'm glad we waited until he turned six."

Mary stuck out her lower lip in a pout.

"I'm sure Rhoda will give you a sweet in the kitchen. Why don't you go and see?" Gilah kissed Mary on the head before patting her bottom and urging her on her way. When she'd left the room, Gilah turned toward me with a shrewd look. "All right, what's troubling you?"

I sat at Gilah's side and weighed the value of voicing Abba's drunken ramblings to her. We'd grown apart since her marriage, which was natural, as she was now the lady of an impressive household. But she was still Gilah. Still the one who knew me so well.

Sitting by my dear friend, I realized there was a chance Abba's words were incorrect. If the frustration building in my chest could be dispelled with one word from her, wouldn't I want to know? There was no sense in wrestling with an untruth.

"There *is* something on my mind." The words came slowly, pulled out of me one by one.

"Ah, I figured so." Gilah bumped my shoulder playfully with hers.

I didn't return her bright expression, choosing instead to stare hard at the sweet babe in my arms as I tried to keep my tone light. "I'm sure it is nothing. My father had too much to drink the other night. People say all sorts of things in such a state."

Gilah's body stilled next to mine. "What did he say?"

Her voice was tight, and the unease returned to my stomach. It was too late now, though. I had to follow through.

"That he sought to wed you . . . but you refused." My light tone seemed grossly inappropriate, but I was powerless to change it. I was locked into a mirthful sound that belied my inner turmoil. I risked a glance at Gilah, who had averted her face.

"But that can't be true, can it?" I prompted. "How strange to even think of it. You as a mother to us?" Even as I said it, longing tinged my voice.

Still no response. Gilah had covered her face with a hand and now let out a sharp gasp. I leaned forward to assess her expression. "It's not true, is it?"

The babe chose that moment to awaken. She'd been stirring for several moments, her lips moving as if suckling, frustration mounting. Finally, she'd had enough. Her eyes scrunched tight, and she let out a sharp wail of protest.

Gilah turned to take her daughter from my arms. Our eyes met over the wailing babe, and in them I saw the truth.

As Gilah soothed the babe with her breast, I turned my face away with a strangled "Why?"

"Martha, try to understand."

"When did he approach you?"

"He approached my father a little over a year after your mother's death. I was seventeen and ready for a family."

"Not our family, apparently."

"That is not true!" Gilah protested, voice distressed, causing the babe to lurch back with a startled yelp. Gilah soothed her daughter, rocking her back and forth, speaking gently to her, urging her to eat. Finally, she spoke again, this time in a whisper. "That is not true, my friend."

"Then help me understand." I tried to mimic her soft tones for the babe's sake.

Gilah hesitated, casting her eyes about the room as if searching for the right words. "Like I said, it'd been a full year. You and I had already developed a dear friendship. You were confiding in me and I in you. I saw you as a sister and friend. I was afraid all of that would change if I became your mother."

Something in her tone didn't ring true. "You're saying that you didn't want to become a part of our family because you loved me too much?"

"No, Martha . . ."

"Or was it because you'd be responsible for three children who weren't your own?" I hated how cutting my words were becoming.

"I love you all! Please believe me."

"The irony is, I would have resisted you as mother early on. But after a year? You were already mother in my heart. I would have rejoiced to call you mother in truth."

Gilah bent a stricken face over the nursing Tehilah.

"And Mary . . ." My voice caught as I fought back tears. "We are so dissimilar. I do not know how to guide her. I fear I am failing her." I choked back a sob. I would not cry. Not in front of her. "But it's up to me!" My voice rose, shrill even to my own ears. "Now Savta is gone, and I am the only mother Mary knows! But I cannot do it, Gilah. I am so tired and alone and do not know how to do it!" I shrouded my tears with anger.

"Martha, I never wanted to cause you pain." Gilah's voice was beseeching. "At the time, our friendship seemed like a valuable thing that would be threatened if I married your father. I wasn't willing to risk what we had worked so hard to build."

"What I don't understand is that you willingly married Simon, even though he was a widower like my father. You entered this union knowing you'd become mother to Lemuel, and now you adore the boy. Yet you were unwilling to do the same for us, for my family. Is our estate so mean compared to Simon's? Was that it?"

At the mention of Simon, Gilah's lips formed a thin line and hardness entered her face. "Please don't speak of my marriage."

I stared silently at her for a long moment, surprised by her tone, trying and failing to read her face. "I don't believe it," I finally muttered. "I don't believe it was simply you wanting to preserve our friendship. There's something you're not telling me."

A flicker of guilt and confusion swept Gilah's features. I pounced on that look with an accusing finger. "Ah, there is! There is something you aren't saying. I deserve to know, Gilah."

"Stop pushing me, Martha. You can be unbearable when you decide you have the right to something."

I ground my teeth at her words, shoving aside the hurt. "But I *do* have the right to know this. You made a decision that forever altered our family, and I deserve to know why."

"I don't want to speak ill of anyone. What is the use in dragging up the past? Let it go, Martha. Accept the way things are and let go of what could have been."

"No!" Perhaps I was pushing past my right to do so, but I could only see one thing: Mary could have had a mother. *We* could have had a mother. My heart was raw and obstinate from the loss of Savta. I'd already lost Gilah to Simon, but to learn that she could have been in my family was too much for me to bear. "I will not let this go. Why didn't you want to be my mother?"

"Fine!" Gilah snapped. Her harsh tone woke Tehilah, who began to whimper. Gilah rose and paced the room with agitated steps as she rocked the babe.

"If you insist on knowing everything, then so be it. I *did* want to be your mother, Martha. Was I concerned what that might do to our friendship? Certainly. But I would have risked it to call you my own. I almost said yes to your father, but remember, by this time I was well acquainted with your family. I'd been in your home daily for over a year. Your father neglects Mary and is a brute to Lazarus. He drinks too much, and when he does, he's unbearably mean. Maybe I should have been selfless enough to still enter the union, but I couldn't do it, Martha. I've seen what happens when a woman marries a harsh man. It eats away at happiness, and I didn't want that for myself! So I refused. I was selfish and I refused! There—are you satisfied?"

Gilah finished her speech with fiery eyes, arms bouncing Tehilah roughly.

Mortification filled my bones. Certainly, Abba had become withdrawn soon after Ima's death. Was his volatile nature obvious to others? Was I so accustomed to his mixture of aloofness and harshness that I'd failed to recognize how undesirable it was? "And yet you married Simon." The words were out before I had time to untangle their meaning.

Gilah stilled. "What did you say?"

My mind raced back to Gilah's worried ramblings shortly after her wedding, her staunch silence over Simon. "How that must have pained you. You denied one marriage because of a harsh father only to end up in a different marriage with a harsh father." I barked a mirthless laugh. "What cruel irony that is."

"Martha! You're being spiteful." Gilah looked horrified.

"And you, Gilah, do not have the right to chastise me." I rose shakily to my feet, not recognizing the cruel bite to my words, unable to stop their flow. "You are not, after all, my mother."

I left quickly, despising myself. As I fled the room to find Mary, I sensed I left behind more than Gilah. A whole part of my life was detaching, pinched off like a lump of dough for the oven.

Thirteen

11 Heshvan
18 AD

During the month when our family would typically harvest the olives from our grove, a sullen mood fell over the household. With no crop to harvest and the flocks not due back for over a month, Abba stayed closer to home than usual. His increased presence did nothing to lift our spirits. Lazarus still nursed his hurts, and I thought of Gilah every time Abba walked into the room.

A strange defensiveness rose within me. Was Gilah's assessment of our family correct? Abba could be neglectful and mean, but it wasn't always so. For all her allegations, Gilah didn't see the way his eyes could soften over a late evening fire, how sometimes I caught him looking at me and knew he was thinking of Ima. He wasn't all harsh words and hurt. There was a tender core to him still.

With a mixture of panic and shame, I recalled my biting words. I was angry with Gilah but also so filled with remorse that some days I could barely breathe. I should not have touched upon her marriage. I should not have tried to cause pain with my words, but I couldn't see how to undo the damage. So I turned my focus, as I usually did, to the work of my hands.

Our summer figs had been plentiful that year, with the autumn figs also promising bounty. What we didn't consume or sell fresh, we dried on our rooftop and stored in earthen jars. Abba decided to sell the excess harvest in the Jerusalem marketplace, choosing to make the journey himself rather than send Samu. Lazarus traveled with him, and I prayed for Yahweh to restore their relationship during their time away.

While the men in the family were absent, Mary pestered me with questions. She'd grown sour and peevish upon hearing that Lemuel was attending school. It was incomprehensible to her that she, who was a full year older than Lemuel, had to stay at home while he got to go and sit under important teachers and learn the Torah. My explanations of the way things were for girls compared with boys did nothing to assuage her frustrations.

Mary had begun to follow Lazarus around and would often accompany him home from synagogue each day. Now that Lazarus was away, however, Mary's attentions had nowhere to land except upon me. Time, I discovered, passes slowly when a seven-year-old girl trails your every step, talking nonstop.

Abba and Lazarus were gone less than a week, but when they returned, I noticed a marked difference in them both. A smile played around Lazarus' lips that hadn't been there before. Abba, too, seemed lighter in spirit. What could have transpired to cause such a change? The next night, as I was serving the evening meal, Abba reached out a hand and snagged my wrist. I nearly dropped the dishes from surprise.

"Daughter, I've neglected you of late." His words were cordial, warm even, but still I looked at him with suspicion. "I carry news of great interest for you." He turned and flicked a hand in Tzvi and Samu's direction. Both men rose to leave, and my head grew light with trepidation, although I could not say why. I looked to my brother for reassurance but found none. He simply scooped another morsel of stew into his mouth.

Perhaps noting my hesitation, Abba nodded to Mary, who stood in the doorway. "Take the dishes from your sister. Martha, sit down."

Sit at the table with the men? I tried to keep my hands steady as Mary took the dishes, her expression as confused as my own. I sat and looked pointedly at Lazarus. He gave me an unconcerned grin as a dribble of stew streaked down his chin.

"While we were in Jerusalem, we lodged with Benjamin. Cleopas, as you recall, thrives in his father's trade. Benjamin could not stop praising him." Abba looked to Lazarus, who nodded his affirmation.

"I remember." Why was Abba telling me this? Why did he look so delighted with himself?

"The boy—excuse me—the man is twenty and ready for his own home and family. Usually, deputies would be involved for such negotiations, prolonging the process, but seeing as we are family, Benjamin acted on his own. Cleopas wants you as his bride." Abba stopped and beamed broadly at me, no doubt expecting a jubilant response.

My mouth dried up, my tongue unable to form speech. I looked swiftly at Lazarus. He'd stopped chewing to give me an expectant expression, clearly as excited as Abba was at the prospect of my marriage.

"I . . . I don't know what to say." My mind whirled with this new information. Cleopas? The boy I'd known all my life? The one I teased and laughed with? He wanted me . . . as a wife?

"They're coming in a week to finalize the agreement." Abba returned to his food, convinced of my acquiescence. "They'll bring the *ketubah* at that time." He paused his eating to reach beneath the table. "Already they send gifts." He withdrew several items—an exquisitely carved oil lamp and a set of beautifully painted bowls.

I recognized the bowls immediately. They were the style and pattern I had so openly admired in their home last year. "He . . . made these?" I squeaked. "And gave them to you . . . for *me*?"

"Yes. Skilled, isn't he?" Abba resumed eating, sopping up the last of his stew with a piece of bread. "Benjamin said they've received wealthy clients over the last few years due to Cleopas' skill with the paintbrush. Some of his handiwork even adorns Herod's table. Can you imagine if he became an official royal potter? One of our own frequenting the palace!"

I stared at the bowls. They were indeed beautiful and fit for a king. Cleopas would have spent countless hours working on them, face lined in deep concentration as his large hands patiently formed and painted these bowls . . . for me.

The new image of Cleopas as a husband loomed large in my mind. I had never viewed him this way and could barely begin to make sense of it. I admired him greatly and appreciated his company, but my heart was not tied to him the way it was to Uri.

When I'd spoken with Cleopas at our family's sheepshearing, I'd been harsh with him, a blunder I'd tried to smooth over when we'd traveled to Jerusalem for the Feast of Weeks. I closed my eyes with a groan, remembering how I'd sought Cleopas out, laughed at his stories, smiled openly into his face, trying to undo any damage I'd inadvertently caused our relationship. Cleopas must have mistaken my friendliness as interest. My hands leapt to my burning cheeks as I recalled how tenderly he'd held me by Savta's grave, how willingly I'd gone into his arms.

"What say you, daughter? A week isn't long to prepare a feast, but let's spare no expense for when they arrive, eh?" He smacked his lips as he finished his meal, and out of habit, I offered him a small bowl of water to rinse his fingers. My body was operating as usual, while my spirit roiled within me.

"It is a fine match, sister." Lazarus finally spoke. "Cleopas is a man of excellence with a bright future."

I shot a withering look at him. Since when did he speak so authoritatively to me? Had he indeed bonded with Abba—over this? I gathered my courage in both hands and turned to Abba.

"I appreciate the match, but I . . . would rather not accept it."

Abba had stood after washing his hands, but at my words sat back down . . . hard. "What did you say?"

"I do not wish to wed Cleopas."

"And why is that?" Abba's voice was low and even, but I could sense the anger rising from him like steam from a hot oven.

I stood and gathered his dishes, bowing my head in a posture of humility as I uttered words that were anything but meek or compliant. "I do not wish to wed him. Can we return the gifts without hurting family relations?"

"I don't think you understand, daughter. We made a promise, Benjamin and I. In the presence of Cleopas, we promised you to each other."

"A promise is not a betrothal, though," I whispered. Where had I received such courage to speak out, to contradict him? I barely recognized myself as I uttered the soft words of defiance.

Abba's voice was lined with iron as he responded. "What did you say?"

With difficulty, I swallowed and bowed my head lower. "A promise is not a betrothal. We can break it without repercussions."

The blow came swiftly and with no warning. The sting of his palm across my face made me gasp aloud with pain and embarrassment. My hands released the dishes, and they crashed to the floor, shattering on impact.

"How dare you refuse this arrangement." His voice was calm and precise.

I stifled a sob and backed away from him, both palms over my cheek, hiding the shame.

"It is unthinkable to refuse. Cleopas' prospects are immense.

He could pick any bride but chooses you, an ungrateful girl who doesn't know what's best for her. If you refuse, you will not receive such a match again."

I stumbled toward the door, stuttering, "I-I'm sorry." Gaze averted, I could not see my brother's reaction.

"You are but a woman, and don't you forget it. You will do as I say. Now leave me. You disgust me with your disrespect."

My breaths came in deep, shuddering gulps as I complied. Turning, I fled from the room. Abigail and Mary hovered outside the door, most likely listening in. I dared not look them in the eye as I darted through the courtyard, out the door, and down the hill to my one place of refuge.

I heard him before I saw him. His voice was pained as he shouted my name. For a moment, I considered concealing myself further between Azariah's roots, shutting my eyes and ears to my brother's concerned calls. When he neared my location, however, I swiped at my eyes and lifted myself from my hiding spot.

"There you are." He approached and sat on a raised root. "Abba is still seething."

"I'm sure he is." I sniffed and sat back down in the little alcove, missing Uri's warmth.

"It's just . . . he didn't expect such a response from you. You should have seen him when Benjamin approached him. He was pleased and honored—happier than I'd seen him in a long time."

"And is his happiness more important than mine?" I hated my sulking tone.

"Of course not. I understand what it's like to receive his wrath." Lazarus bowed his head under the weight of harsh memories. "He should not have struck you," he murmured.

I placed a hand over my throbbing cheek. "I was insolent."

"You were honest. You were not speaking out of defiance."

There was a strained silence between us, and I could tell that my brother was aching to ask me something.

"Tell me why, Martha."

There it was.

"You've always liked Cleopas. When we last visited them, you were especially keen to talk to him. And I've seen the way he looks at you. He's taken a liking to you. Why not agree to the match?"

"Because . . . I cannot." It was unfathomable to promise myself to one man when my heart belonged to another. My own words came back to me. *"I'll wait for you. Of course I'll wait for you."* I'd spoken words that bound me to a man whom I couldn't share with anyone. The feather seemed to hum beneath my tunic, reminding me of a certain shepherd's devotion.

There'd been relief when I'd talked about Uri with Savta. The burden had eased when I'd offered it to another. I gazed at my brother and wondered. Should I bare my soul to him? Would he understand at thirteen years of age?

"But why not?" Lazarus persisted. "I will miss you, but Jerusalem is not so far away. Cleopas is an honorable man, and he speaks highly of you."

"He does?" I sniffled, thinking of those strange glances Cleopas was prone to giving me.

"Oh yes! I remember when we visited them last year, he couldn't stop talking about you. He said you'd grown into a lovely young woman. And earlier this year, he asked me if you had a suitor."

"Why didn't you share this with me before?"

"I don't know." Lazarus shrugged a shoulder. "I suppose I didn't think anything of it at the time." He laughed at his own obliviousness. "You have cause for joy. He is kind, and he admires you."

"I also admire him," I conceded, "and enjoy his company. Although I've never considered him as a husband." My voice caught on this last word. "It's not Cleopas himself that gives me pause." I drew the words out slowly, testing each one before releasing it.

My brother liked Uri. Indeed, he owed Uri his life. Surely, he would welcome the news that my heart belonged to his rescuer. "I cannot agree to the betrothal because my affections lie elsewhere."

Lazarus' brows shot upward, and his mouth gaped open in complete befuddlement. "Who? Who?" With the second *who* he rose to his feet with outstretched hands.

"It's someone unconventional."

"Does he share your feelings?"

I nodded and tried to stop the warmth creeping over my face.

"Does Abba know? Who is this man?"

I shook my head. "I haven't told anyone because I'm afraid." It was true. Afraid to lose a relationship I had come to rely upon. Afraid of what people would say about me.

"Martha, who is it?"

I had never seen Lazarus so adamant. For the second time that day, I gathered whatever courage I could muster and opened my mouth. "Uri. It's Uri. I love him and he loves me." The words rushed from me like a fountain.

Love? Did Uri love me? We hadn't used those words, but my heart knew them to be true. "He is good, Lazarus. He is a kind, wonderful man, and he's lived such a harsh life."

"Stop!" Lazarus held up a hand as if to stem the flow of words, his features clenched.

I bit my lip until I tasted blood.

"You mean to tell me that you love the hired shepherd? Uri. The man we pay to watch our sheep."

"When did you become judgmental?" Hearing the way Lazarus spoke of Uri ignited anger that surpassed any previous concerns I'd harbored. "That *hired shepherd* is the one who saved your life, remember?"

Lazarus began pacing. "Of course I remember."

Agitated, I rose to my feet as well, drawing my arms about myself for warmth.

"I'm not questioning his character. I'm pointing out his unsuitability."

"I've thought of that, but it doesn't matter to me."

"Doesn't matter? But it affects more than you."

He was right, for I was a woman. When I married, my family would no longer benefit from my work as I went to live in my husband's home and contributed to his household. The only compensation was the *mohar,* the bride price. And what could Uri possibly offer that Abba would find desirable? My head understood all of this, and yet my heart deemed it a weak argument.

"I realize this comes as a surprise," I said cautiously.

"A surprise? It's more than that, Martha. Abba will never agree to the match. You must know that."

"I'm hoping that since Uri saved your life . . ."

"Abba is not going to give you to his hired shepherd simply because he saved my life. He would never consider that a fair exchange. Never. You see how he views my life. I've lowered considerably in his eyes since the accident."

"But you are his only son—his heir."

"And his perpetual disappointment. Mary is a long way off from marriage, but you? You have a chance to increase our family's wealth by making a match with Cleopas. Their station in life is—"

"You sound like Abba!" I spat out my interruption.

Lazarus stopped pacing to scrub a hand over his face. "Is that such a bad thing?"

"Sometimes . . . yes." My voice grew quiet as I thought of Gilah's accusations. "Haven't you noticed how he's handled the losses in his life? He's grown bitter, Lazarus. He neglects Mary and is overly critical of you."

"He's still our father, and we owe him our respect." Lazarus clenched his jaw into a firm line and crossed his arms over his narrow chest. "Martha, I don't want to see you become destitute. I don't want to see you estranged from this family—an outcast because of a bad decision."

Something in his voice raised an alarm. "But you won't tell Abba . . . will you?"

"I must. Don't you see? To protect you, I must tell him."

My knees grew weak. If Abba had struck me for speaking out of turn, what would he do if he found out about Uri? He'd send him away. I would never see him again. "Brother, please keep this between us."

"How can you ask that of me? If Abba were ever to find out that I knew of this and didn't tell him, he'd disown me."

"There's no need for him to find out. No one else knows."

"But then you'd be free to continue in your relationship with Uri. And where could that lead apart from destitution and estrangement? I love you, sister. I don't want that for you."

"If you love me then you won't tell Abba!" I stumbled over a root on my way to his side and sank to the ground at his feet. I would humiliate myself if it meant I could keep Uri, keep him for a bit longer.

"Stand up." Lazarus backed away, casting my hands off his feet. "You are above this. Stop begging."

"You need to see how deeply this affects me," I sobbed. "I cannot bear it if Abba sends Uri away. Please, at least talk to Uri yourself before you act on this knowledge."

"I cannot speak with him about this. To do so would be to conspire with you against the family. I cannot do that."

I curled into a ball of misery. Why had I trusted my most valuable secret to my brother? If Lazarus would not accept Uri, then Abba most certainly would not. My wishful thinking of him happily granting Uri my hand out of gratitude was brutally unveiled as a ridiculous dream.

"I'm sorry." Lazarus' voice was farther away. He was leaving—perhaps going even now to tell our father.

"Are you doing this out of love for me, or for yourself?" Anger exploded through my pain, and I rose to my knees to shoot him an accusatory look.

"What do you mean?"

"You say you must tell Abba out of love for me, but I don't believe you. It is love for yourself that drives you. You think in doing this thing that you will gain esteem in his eyes. I beg you—think carefully over what you do." I channeled all my hurt and pain into fury, letting it seep from my eyes and onto the boy backing away from me.

He looked into my eyes one more time—a pleading, sad look—before turning and running toward home.

I let him go. I watched his fleeing form stumble once, twice on the uneven ground. I watched him until he was out of sight. And then I curled over again, forehead in the dust.

Abba returned the beautiful lamp and painted bowls. There were no special guests and no betrothal feast. He sat me down one more time, his voice dripping with anger, but my resolve was firm. I would not give my consent and so the conversation was short.

I eyed Lazarus like he was a pot ready to boil over. Surely at any moment he would tell Abba of Uri and the consequences would unfold, but day bled into day with no repercussions. As improbable as it seemed, Lazarus was keeping my secret, although what held his tongue I could not say.

As the weeks stretched on, Lazarus avoided me and I him, the rift between us throbbing like an open wound. Even with the harsh words spoken between us, there was also a close kinship, as we both lived under the weight of our father's disappointment.

Then the day arrived when Abba casually mentioned the imminent return of the flock. He spoke Uri's name in passing, and I watched, frozen, as Lazarus' eyes widened. If he'd been waiting for an opportune time, certainly this was it.

We both stood still and let Abba talk, neither of us moving or saying a word. I looked at my brother, tried to catch his eye, but he turned away from me without a word and left the room. I longed to reach out to him, to understand what restrained his hand, to thank him and beg him to give me even more time.

I began waiting under Azariah's branches each evening in anticipation of Uri's return. Night after night I stood silent and still with my mantle wrapped tightly against the cold, staring across the rocky hillside, fearful and anxious. Uri had a way of unfurling the hard bundle of worry that often clutched at my chest, tossing it as effortlessly as a winnowing fork, separating the grain from the chaff so that I could see clearer, breathe easier.

Refusing Cleopas' suit had solidified my love for Uri into something serious with real consequences. How could we be together? We had to be. I was holding out everything on the belief that we would be. Was Lazarus right? Was I being selfish and hurting our family? Was I resigning myself to a bleak future?

Three nights of waiting. Three nights of worry and doubt. And then the fourth night.

He crested the hill as the sun was lowering in the sky. I shaded my eyes to be sure. The clear sound of his flute came dancing across the slope, a harbinger of hope. At the sound of it, all doubt fled. I girded my tunic and ran with all my heart and strength in his direction.

Fourteen

27 Chislev
18 AD

Having left astounded that I might wait for him, Uri returned with a settled certainty. He swooped me up in his arms with a shout of joy, full of endearments. "At last, my Talitha!" he crowed.

I turned a blushing face into the crook of his neck and wept tears of delight.

With the days growing dark earlier and the night temperatures dipping lower, time together was often brief and always precious. I had been timid with him before, stepping carefully around his past, not pushing too much with my curiosity, but now we entered each other's stories boldly, with a confidence bred from a deepening intimacy. So it was without hesitation that one night I traced the familiar trail of his scar with gentle fingers. "You still haven't told me how you got this." I moved my hand to the pendant resting against my heart. "Or this."

We sat side by side in a hollow between Azariah's roots. At my inquiry, Uri drew me closer. "The necklace and the scar . . . they are both parts of the same story. Hope and pain all bundled together." He was quiet for a moment, and patiently I waited with my hand resting over the thump of his heart. "The scar came first," he finally shared, voice tight. "When I refused to take part in the Sicarii's attack, I marked myself as a traitor."

"Because you refused to kill a man?"

"Chanoch required absolute obedience, no questions asked. In refusing to follow orders, I was seen as a deserter, an enemy. So, when I dropped my dagger, I fled, both the theater and Sepphoris itself."

I shivered, and Uri drew his mantle over my shoulders before continuing.

"They chased me relentlessly. No matter how hard I tried, I couldn't shake their pursuit. Finally, I felt confident I'd lost them. By that time, I was near the city gate. Chanoch's network was so vast, however, that soon others were aware of my rebellion—others who were waiting for me on the road outside the city."

My body clenched with foreboding.

"They let me travel halfway to Nazareth before acting. They let me think I was safe, toying with me before striking."

I curled against Uri's side as I imagined his terror. He had escaped with his life, obviously, but still fear and panic clutched my chest.

"I shouldn't have taken the main road, but I foolishly thought I'd evaded Chanoch's men. They were waiting for me at a turn in the road—standing there, blocking my way." He let his voice trail off. I wrapped an arm across his chest and nestled my head into his shoulder, trying to infuse what strength I could into him.

"That's when I received this." He gestured to his scar. "They beat me nearly to death. They were armed and could have killed me instantly, but again, they toyed with me. God help them, they were enjoying themselves. But then, as abruptly as the attack began, it stopped. I was barely conscious, but I heard a voice across the street call out to me. It was a priest. He'd interrupted my assailants. I was filled with relief, but he just stood there, across the street, inquiring if I was all right."

"Clearly you were not all right!" Silent tears wet my cheeks as I imagined Uri half-dead on the side of the road.

"I suppose inquiring made him feel better about himself. Seeing that I was still alive, he pronounced a blessing over me even while he shuffled past me and down the road."

"No!" I trembled with outrage.

"When he left, I was sure that Chanoch's men would be back to finish the job, but I must have lost consciousness. The next thing I remember, I was on the back of a cart, and a boy some years older than me was holding my head in his lap. I was confused and terrified. I thought I was being taken to a gruesome death and struggled to free myself, but the boy held me tightly and told me I was safe. He and his father had found me on the side of the road and, upon seeing that I was still alive, loaded me into their cart. The boy had begun treating my wounds and had bound my head with strips of cloth torn from his own garment."

Uri's voice filled with deep emotion as he talked about the boy. I swallowed past the lump in my throat, grateful beyond words for the people who had saved him.

"They took me to their home in Nazareth. They didn't ask for my history but simply gave me food and shelter. The father owned a carpentry shop, with their home adjacent to it. They took me in as one of the family—and what a family it was!" Uri's tone grew wistful. "It was the kind of family I wish I'd grown up in. One I would like to build myself someday."

He cleared his throat as if embarrassed. "A mother as gracious as you can imagine, and a whole slew of children, who were loud and boisterous and full of life. The boy I'd met on the road was the oldest and spent most of his time by the father's side in the shop."

"They sound like a kind family. Is that where you received

this? Did the boy give it to you?" I held the feather pendant in my hand, imagining the warm home it'd come from.

"Yes. Every night the boy would whittle whatever scraps of wood were left over in the shop. He made all sorts of small toys and trinkets for his siblings. Those are some of my fondest memories." Uri stared off into the distance. "Evenings spent by the fire while the father quoted the Torah and the boy whittled and the mother spun thread and the little ones lay in small heaps on the floor, playing and listening."

"How long were you there?"

"Several months. They would have let me stay longer, I'm sure, but I couldn't impose on their hospitality anymore. They wouldn't let me repay them, even when I offered them my services in exchange for room and board. They gave without any thought of recompense."

"How generous," I murmured, beginning to grow sleepy, lulled into a quiet calm at the depiction of familial harmony.

"He made this for me especially." Uri rested his fingers on the pendant. "I'd commented on how much I enjoyed his small carvings, and so, unknown to me, he began working on one as a gift."

"And why a feather?"

"I asked him that when he gave it to me. He said it was a reminder that Yahweh would cover me with his pinions, and under his wings I would find refuge."

I recognized the ancient song. "This carpenter boy knew his Scriptures."

"Indeed. But what was truly astounding was that . . . he seemed to know *me*, even though I shared next to nothing about myself."

"What do you mean?" I twisted in Uri's arms so I could see his face. He was frowning, as if years of mulling over the situation had yet to bring clarity.

"He couldn't have known from whom I was fleeing, and yet he encouraged me not to be fearful of those who lie in wait for blood. He couldn't have known the choice I'd made that caused my flight, and yet he commended me for not walking in the way of the wicked. He couldn't have known my family history, the things I'd seen and experienced, and yet he extended comfort by reminding me that Yahweh binds up the brokenhearted. He was only a couple of years older than me, and yet he exuded wisdom that surpassed anything I'd ever experienced. It was his words that set me on the path to healing, that made me realize I was more than where I'd come from."

By this time, the night was growing colder, and I could not keep my shivering at bay. Uri wrapped me deeply in his arms, and I could sense that he was loath to let me go. Reluctantly, he drew me to my feet. "I need to see you home. Is your curiosity satisfied, my Talitha?"

I rejoiced in his tenderness toward me. "I suppose . . . for now."

He walked with me until home was in view. My nose and fingers were numb, but I didn't want to leave him. He wrapped me in his arms again, and I whispered against his chest, "I'm sorry you had to endure such horrible things, but I'm thankful—so thankful—that you're safe, that someone found you, took care of you." I paused, thinking of Uri's tone as he'd talked about the carpenter and his family. "It sounds like this boy meant a lot to you."

"He did. He does. He saved my life in more ways than one."

I climbed the hill toward home but stopped as a thought occurred to me. "What was his name, Uri?" I tucked the pendant back beneath my tunic and pressed a hand over it. Knowing its origin, I was even more touched by the gift. "What was the name of the boy who gave this to you?"

"Jesus." Uri offered up the name softly. "Jesus bar Joseph."

Fifteen

As the winter months stretched on, I was cautious with Uri in a way I hadn't been before. Early on, I'd let myself grow careless, running every chance I could find to the sheepfold, hardly caring if I was seen as I held my love tightly in both hands like a treasure. Now I realized the real-life repercussions of our relationship, saw clearly that one or both of us could end up wounded and bereft, so I was more mindful with our meetings. Although few and far between, our encounters were filled with a sweetness that sustained me.

I continued to learn more of Uri's past—how he traveled south from Nazareth, finally ending up as an undershepherd to a man named Meir. Next to Jesus of Nazareth, Meir seemed to have had the greatest influence on Uri.

"I came to him with nothing, no skills except what I'd learned on the streets. I was fast and sure on my feet. I could handle a weapon and pick a purse off a man without him knowing a thing. But I lacked skills that would help me make an honest living. Meir showed me that I could harness what strengths I did possess and use them in shepherding. He owned land in Bethel and had two sons and a sprawling estate. I spent many nights out in the plains south of Shiloh, listening to Meir's stories, learning all I could from him. His sons, however, were not as kind and generous. They resented my relationship with their father, so when he died, they immediately released me from their employ."

Hand in hand, we walked the long, terraced pathway that led to our fig grove. "I am sorry for his death." I squeezed Uri's hand. "But I cannot pretend I'm sorry it sent you straight into my arms."

Uri's story unfolded like a rich tapestry in my mind, with the thread of Yahweh's faithfulness connected throughout. "Beacons of light," I mused. "Yahweh keeps providing beacons of light in your life to guide you when you need it most. First Jesus, then Meir."

"And then you," he murmured, turning to gaze at me with a world of love in his eyes. "It's been a winding path." He dropped my hand and spread his own wide, taking one step, then two, backward. "I confess that I've often not understood it. I've not understood the winding path Yahweh placed me on. All I do know is that it led me here . . . to you."

He stepped close and grasped my hand in his own, drawing it to his lips. Shooting me a sideways look, he slowly kissed my knuckles. It was the first time he'd dared to kiss me, and my breath caught in my throat as I watched his lips move from knuckle to knuckle.

"It's led me to you, and I'm grateful," he murmured against my skin, voice husky. His eyes pooled with a question as they traveled to my lips, and even though my heart burst with desire, the trembling in my limbs and the blankness flooding my mind caused me to duck my head instead. Breath uneven, I rested my forehead against his chest, registered the wild beating of his heart, and waited for my own to calm.

We shared our histories in bits and pieces over the winter months. Rather than hardening in bitterness under life's burdens, Uri had grown a strength and determination that emanated from him like rays of light. When I examined my own life, however, the broken pieces didn't seem to fit together. There were tender spots that had no purpose, aching gaps that yearned to be filled. Uri had endured so much in life, traveled so far, and experienced so much. Where had I been and what had I done? How could I rise in strength like he had?

"I have scarcely been beyond Jerusalem," I admitted one night. "I've seen next to nothing compared to you!" I felt like Mary, petulantly pouting while Lemuel ran off to school. Embarrassed by my tone, I turned my face away, but he wouldn't let me hide. With a gentle hand, he cupped my chin and turned my face toward him.

"Ah, don't wish others' lives upon yourself." Then he softened his words by drawing me into his arms. "A quiet life is, in itself, a blessing, and who knows what is yet in store for you, Talitha."

"Ah yes, they will talk of my deeds for years to come," I jested.

Knowing Uri as I now did, my love for him deepened, although I had yet to be brave enough to use the word itself with him. As we entered a new year and spring loomed on the horizon, I could not shake the fear that had begun plaguing me, keeping me awake at night. It was only a matter of time before Abba would approach me with another marriage proposal.

Like a coward, however, I basked in my relationship with Uri without acting on my fears. I spoke with neither Abba nor Lazarus on the subject. Indeed, I hadn't even told Uri of my near-betrothal for fear of the conversation that would ensue. Would he start talking again about how I could do better than him? Would he draw away from me, wanting me to set my affections elsewhere? I couldn't bear the thought of hearing him, once again, belittle himself, and so I kept silent. We had time, I believed, to simply enjoy each other.

The time we thought we'd have, however, was cut unexpectedly short. There had been less rain than usual over the winter, which meant the spring harvest was not as bountiful. Typically, shepherds would allow their flocks to graze on the freshly harvested fields, but with so little harvest and the summer heat moving in sooner this year, Abba decided to send Uri away early to find cooler, more abundant pastureland. Instead of six months, I would be away from Uri closer to seven. I was left reeling with the news and with only a few days to mentally prepare before he left.

The morning of his departure found me shaking with a swell of emotion but firm with resolve. I had too many burning things inside that had been left unsaid. When I was within sight of Azariah, I picked up my pace until I was fairly flying down the hillside. Uri's dear form rose at my approach, and wordlessly I crashed into his arms. How familiar and necessary these meetings had become to me.

"You are trembling, Talitha." He drew me closer and murmured against my hair, "I'm especially pained to leave you this time."

"Why this time in particular?"

He took hold of my arms and pressed his lips to my forehead. "Because each passing day I come to love you more and more, making it increasingly hard for me to leave you." He pulled back, and there it was . . . the door wide open for me to walk through.

Huge, silent tears coursed down my cheeks. "And I . . . I love you too. From the very beginning, I think." Like a river bursting its dam, I dissolved into a rush of words, heart swelling painfully in my breast. "Oh, Uri, if you only knew how much I love you!" I raised my face to the sky, blinking rapidly, trying and failing to rein in my emotions. "You're dearer to me than my own soul," I sputtered, dropping my face into my hands.

His declaration had been calm and sweet. Mine was a mess of words, tears, and wailing.

Gently, he took me into his arms. Slowly, he tilted my face to his. Patiently, he waited until I dared look at him again. And when I did, I found his eyes filled with tears and light. This time, when his gaze dropped to my lips, I did not shy away.

Trailing his thumb across my cheek and down my neck, he rested a strong hand behind my head, threaded his fingers into my hair, and drew my face up for his kiss. I stilled, breathless as his lips found mine. His kiss was gentle and slow. I scarcely knew what to do and stood mute and alert like a young gazelle. But when he pulled back, I felt the absence so keenly that I tugged him right back down, crushing his lips to mine.

Uri returned my hungry kiss, grunting in surprise, as if he'd bitten into something decadent. I shivered at the sound, and he pulled back slightly. "Martha?" His voice was ragged and filled with wonder. "I—" He seemed unable to speak and instead pulled me tighter against him and dipped his head to kiss me again.

I was shaking and thankful he was supporting me, or I would surely have fallen at his feet. When he pulled back again, he looked so dumbfounded and happy, I laughed out loud. A crooked smile spread across his face in response, and soon we were both laughing and he was burying his face in my hair and rocking me back and forth in a relieved and dizzying dance.

When we'd calmed, he captured my face in his hands, suddenly growing solemn. "I need to ask you something important." His hands trembled where they rested on my face. "Will you . . . be my Rachel?"

"What do you mean?" I questioned, although a moment later understanding dawned on me.

The narrative was a favorite among the young women of Israel. How Father Jacob years ago fell irrepressibly in love with his cousin Rachel, working not seven but fourteen years for her hand in marriage. Such earnest desire was every girl's dream.

"I have nothing to offer you." He released my face and stepped back with arms outstretched, as if displaying his lack. "I am not a choice husband for you. Your father will certainly not deem me worthy of your hand."

My heart caught on the word *husband,* and I moved toward him, desiring his arms around me, his lips on mine, but he restrained me with a hand on my shoulder.

"I need to say this." His voice was quavering.

I obeyed and took a step back, although every piece of me yearned to leap at him, tell him "Yes, yes, and yes!"

"Jacob came to Rachel with nothing but the ability to work with his own two hands. He did, however, have his lineage behind him and, eventually, his father's inheritance. I come not even with this to offer. You know from whom I come. You know my past, every shameful part of it." He cleared his throat and scrubbed a hand behind his neck. "But you also know . . . you remember that this is not who I am now."

I shuffled from foot to foot, trying to keep still and silent for his sake, which was hard to do with my heart pounding so hard in my chest.

"And who I am now is a man who dares to ask . . . who needs to ask . . . for your hand in marriage. You are dearer to me than my own life. I cannot imagine any other woman but you by my side for the rest of my life. Which is why . . ." He swallowed with difficulty, his eyes joining mine then leaving again, as if overcome by the emotion he found there.

For my part, I was fairly dancing in place, trying to wait for him to finish, not caring that I was antsy with delight while he so solemnly shared his soul.

He cleared his throat. "Which is why I intend to ask your father for your hand in exchange for my services, for however long he deems necessary. I will work Jacob's fourteen years for you if need be. Anything to call you my own." He released a deep sigh. "If . . . if you deem this a good plan, that is. If you . . ." He finally looked up at me and kept his gaze locked on mine.

"If you would agree to become my wife. If that's your desire as it is mine."

The question in his eyes finally gave me permission to respond. With a happy laugh, I threw myself at him, nearly knocking him off his feet. Relieved giggles escaped me, a heady joy filled me, and a renewed hope leapt to life.

Uri steadied himself, adjusting his feet to support me. "Does this mean yes?" He looked at me with wide eyes, clearly unsure how to respond to or interpret my wild emotions. His, it seemed, were still in suspense. I quickly sought to put him definitively at ease.

"Yes! Over and over again, my answer is yes! You are like light and air to me. I would consider it the greatest honor and joy to be your wife. There is nothing I desire more."

With a shout of triumph, Uri lifted me off my feet. He spun me around with a loud whoop before planting me once more on the ground. I watched astounded as his face abruptly crumpled and he let out a sob.

Grasping his face in my hands, I pleaded, "What's wrong?"

"I didn't dare to hope. I didn't . . . I'm not worthy."

A fiery boldness filled my bones, and I longed to lift his countenance, for him to see what I saw. "There will be no more talk of unworthiness. We are promised to each other. I will have you for my husband, so there will be no such talk about the man I love with all my heart."

He turned his face into my palm and pressed a kiss into its center, absorbing my pronouncement before raising his eyes to mine once more. "All right, then. No more." He nodded firmly. "We are promised, one to another."

"Equal in every way before God."

"Equal in every way before God," he agreed.

In studying his eyes, I saw the resolve in them. "And we will approach my father together."

His eyes leapt eagerly across the hills in the direction of home. "Should we go now?"

Uri held so much hope in his face, but my sinking heart knew we had to wait. Abba had been drinking heavily the last few days, and his mood was darker than a stormy night. "We will need to time it just right," I murmured, chewing on my lower lip in thought. Abba might see my marriage to Uri as an out, a way to relieve himself of his unruly daughter while also garnering gain through Uri's free services. Uri's plan might find favor in Abba's eyes . . . but only if we caught him in an affable mood.

"When you return, we will choose the right moment to approach him," I said.

He groaned and buried his face in my neck.

"Can you bear it now, my love?" I whispered. "Can you bear the separation now that we share this promise?"

He shook his head, keeping his face pressed to my neck, where he murmured, "On the contrary, it makes me even more desperate to return to you." He kissed the skin beneath my ear, then moved to my jaw and finally my lips.

I clung to him, trembling with joy as he supported me with a strong arm, keeping me close against his chest as he kissed me lingeringly—with both restraint and promise.

We had already pressed past the time Uri needed to leave. He went to the sheepfold and I, like one of his lambs, followed behind, suddenly so filled with loss I could barely breathe. He unlatched the gate, and I let out his name on the ends of a sob. "Uri."

He turned, and I was back in his arms. "Ah, I'll have none of that. Do not weep, my Talitha, my beloved." He cupped my face in his hands and kissed the tears away. I placed my hands over his, closed my eyes, and wished myself a sparrow that I might fly away and keep him company throughout the long stretches of the night.

But I let him go. With a final kiss, I let him go.

He led the sheep from the pen, touching each on the back with his rod as they ambled to the pasture beyond. I held all our shared moments like jewels in my hands as Uri cast me a long, loving look before turning to lead the flock up the slope that led to the Judean wilderness. I lost sight of him then but could hear his high call as he communicated to the flock.

Running past the sheepfold, I strained my eyes to the horizon, keeping watch until every sheep crested the hill and was lost from sight.

"Love is a great gift from Yahweh. Don't forget it, Martha."

I pressed the feather to my lips with steadfast determination. I would wait for this man for seven months. I would wait for him for years and years if that was what it took for him to be mine.

Sixteen

22 Sivan
19 AD

For weeks I went through the motions of life, present but not present. Memories of my parting with Uri flooded my mind day and night and left me restless. I would gaze unseeing into the corner of the courtyard as I ground grain, a smile playing on my lips, then turn to run and hide when tears threatened out of nowhere. I was heavy and light, so full of an aching happiness that I hardly knew what to do with myself.

It was the beginning of the dry season, and Uri had been gone over a month when Bethany was shocked with an onslaught of rain. In denying us the moisture over the winter, the world was making up for it in force.

Dawn had arrived with a hint of rain moistening the air, and by midmorning, the dark tenor of the sky promised its imminent arrival. By late morning, I had finished preparing the day's food when a hand on my shoulder jolted me upright. Abigail stood nearby with a sour look on her face.

"Where is that little scrap of a girl? I need her help spinning wool."

"Mary? But I sent her to you hours ago!"

"I haven't seen her all morning."

A mixture of alarm and guilt filled me. I'd been so preoccupied lately that Mary had gone unnoticed and untended. How had I lost track of her for a whole morning? "I'll find her."

"You best start outdoors. I've already searched throughout the house."

I cleaned my hands, mind racing. Mary's cat, Chana, was due to birth her kittens any day now. Perhaps that's where she was. Taking Abigail's advice, I left our home and headed for the field just as the rain began in earnest. It ran in rivulets down the back of my neck, soaking my tunic.

Abba and Lazarus had left early that morning to help a neighbor harvest his wheat. My stomach sank with foreboding at the thought of rain during the wheat harvest. Rain almost never occurred this late in the season, and when it did, people saw it as judgment, for the pounding of the rain meant the destruction of the wheat, which would mat together, making it nearly impossible to harvest.

A deep rumble of thunder spread across the plains. I hurried my steps as guilt warred with anger. Yes, I should have been keeping closer watch over Mary, but at seven years old, Mary shouldn't need such close tending.

In the distance was a straggling group of men—the harvesters on their way back from the field, Abba at the front. I ran to meet them.

"What are you doing outdoors?" Abba approached with a scythe over his shoulder, his face shrouded by the pounding rain. Lazarus and the other harvesters were all gazing at the sky, tension thick. "This is quickly becoming a torrent too strong for harvest." Abba gestured to me. "Get yourself inside."

"It's Mary!" I grimaced, anticipating the reprimand that

would undoubtedly follow. "I cannot find her. Have you seen her?"

Abba's face flushed, his gaze turning more thunderous than the sky. "Martha, how many times must this happen before you learn to take responsibility for that child? Why is Mary not with you?"

"She was . . . early on," I stammered. "I sent her to help Abigail, and she apparently ran off."

Abba swung the scythe from his shoulder down onto the sodden grass, where it stuck at my feet. "Martha! Do not try to shift the blame." His tone bit through my tunic more than the rain, chilling me to the bone.

"You will find her." Abba stabbed a finger in my face. "And bring her back." Roughly, he turned to grab Lazarus by the shoulder and shoved him in my direction. "Both of you! Find that girl before this storm sweeps her away."

Lazarus stumbled against me, and together we hung our heads as Abba plucked the scythe from the ground and brushed past us. "And you will not let this happen again!" he shouted over his shoulder, his form already receding from view behind a sheet of rain.

Our steps were laced with urgency, and I did not try to hide my fear. We ran through the garden, shouting Mary's name, my mind reeling with the memory of a similar hungry search nearly eight years ago when I had misplaced my brother.

"The hillside," I shouted. "It's rocky. Perhaps Chana hid her kittens there."

We ran through the barley field, screaming Mary's name all the while, only pausing when we crested the hill. "There!" I pointed to a large outcropping of rocks. There were enough nooks and crannies to hide five litters of kittens. I nearly slid down the hill on my backside, so slippery was the ground. Finally, we arrived at the rocks, both of us breathing hard and drenched to the bone.

I gulped in air and spluttered as rain entered my mouth. With foreboding, I circled the rocks.

Huddled in a cleft of the largest rock, Mary sat, lap overflowing with bawling kittens. My chest loosened with relief as I sank to my knees before her. I turned to shout for Lazarus, but he was already scrambling to my side, half falling through the mud as he threw himself at Mary.

"Sister, we were so worried!" His words stopped short, however, at the grief on Mary's face.

She pointed a shaking finger to a spot not far from me. Both of us turned to look, and I let out a surprised yelp, leaping back and bumping my head against the rock.

Chana lay motionless in the rain, her eyes wide and still, mouth open in a wordless scream, her insides spilling out across the rain-slick ground.

"An animal got her." Mary sniffed, her young voice cracking with emotion.

"Oh, Mary." Lazarus was the first to respond, snuggling in close to her side with an arm around her shoulder.

There wasn't room for all three of us beneath the ledge, so I sat miserably in the rain and watched my siblings. Any words of reproof died on my lips as I witnessed my sister's grief, her eyes flooding with tears, round face framed by matted hair, and cheeks streaked with dirt.

Abba's harsh words had landed hard on me. They needed someplace to go, or I would internalize them, swallow them into my very being like poison. In such instances, I usually lashed out at Mary, all my anger and frustration finding a home as I chastised her errant behavior. But now, in the face of her grief, I swallowed back the anger and refused to unleash his wrath upon my sister.

"She was protecting her babies," Mary moaned, lifting one of the kittens to her cheek.

I looked back at Chana, who was, in truth, not the original Chana. About a year ago, I'd found Mary's beloved cat half-eaten by a wild animal. I'd wasted no time in burying the remains and seeking out another cat who resembled Mary's pet. I'd spent numerous fretful days searching our village for a close-enough counterpart to fool a six-year-old. The ruse had worked, and Mary had been none the wiser. I could not, however, guard her from grief forever.

"Then she died nobly," I spoke softly. The rain had eased up a bit, the thunder more distant. "It's a noble thing to die in the place of another. Chana sacrificed herself for those she loved. And look." I gestured toward Mary's arms. "Yahweh led you to her babies. It's a blessing you found the kittens." I gazed at her lap, counting five squirming bodies. "Now you can step in and nurture them. They will not come to harm because you are here."

Mary turned grateful eyes to me. "Do you think Chana knows? Do you think she knows I'll take care of her babies?"

I swallowed hard at the plaintive question. Was death so final that those who passed couldn't experience peace beyond the grave? With an aching heart, I recalled words of comfort spoken over me at Savta's grave, of Cleopas' warm tone, eyes filled with compassion. How I missed his friendship! *"Don't despair, Martha. Yahweh comforts the hearts of those who return to Him in death."*

"Yes." I smiled widely, bravely at Mary. "Yes, I'm sure she knows."

Lazarus leaned his head against Mary's. The rock ledge provided enough coverage so that they remained dry. Their two heads full of bountiful black curls melded perfectly.

The rain continued to pour down its judgment, and I sat beneath its weight with my stick-straight hair plastered to my skull, filled with aching joy as I watched my siblings. The harvest was uncertain, the weather volatile, and our father's favor was a capricious beast. But despite all of this, I was not alone and adrift in the world. My dear brother had stepped in where Abba had not. Together, we would always seek out our sister, bring her back, raise her up. In all the wild uncertainty of this world, I had these two.

Seventeen

28 Elul
19 AD

Endless months of waiting with still three more to endure and yet my heart remained steady and hopeful. Abba had not broached the topic of a suitable husband, and I wondered if he'd given up looking. Daily I prayed that Uri's request would find favor in Abba's eyes.

As late summer loomed, Abba sent Mary and me out to the sycamore fig trees, awls in hand, to pierce their unripe fruit for fertilization. It was a favored task of mine, but a first for Mary. I helped her into Hananiah's branches and showed her how to use the small wooden tool with the iron tip.

"Be careful as you climb," I instructed, "lest you prick your hand or worse."

We straddled the thick tree limbs, gathering the figs into our hands, careful to keep the fruit attached to the branch, gently piercing it, then releasing it once more. Oh, the irony that future growth and health depended on this small violence. The fruit must undergo what seemed a rough and senseless process so it might reach its full potential. As Savta had said, *"Pain before blessing. Dark before light. Sadness before joy. All good things come in time."*

Mary started singing a childish rhyme, and I good-naturedly joined in. Soon, Hananiah's boughs were filled with song. As I neared the top of the tree, I gazed across the field to where Azariah stood proudly over the sheepfold, diligently awaiting a certain shepherd's return. My heart swelled at the sight and sang, *Three more months. Only three more months.*

Mary was still prone to wander off, so I began rising extra early, before she or any of the household stirred. With bare feet, I began each day by stoking the courtyard fires and grinding the grain for the day's bread. By the time Mary appeared, the dough was already cooking on the sides of the oven, the sharp scent of leaven piercing the air and nipping at the tongue.

Mary would look at me and groan, perceiving that it would now be impossible to sneak away. I was thankful for the reprieve. Her wildness had caused no amount of unrest, especially since Savta's death. I kept a close rein on her, attempting to do for her what Gilah had done for me.

After Gilah's outburst concerning Abba and the harsh words we'd exchanged, our relationship had remained strained, neither of us making the first move toward the other. The longer we'd gone without repairing the friendship, the more my heart ached for her. Time had allowed me to reflect, and in doing so, I imagined the events from Gilah's perspective: young and longing for marriage, receiving a proposal from a much older man, desiring to be close to me but also desiring to love and respect the man she married. If there was one thing I did know about Gilah, it was that she did nothing rashly. She would not have turned down Abba lightly.

Could I resent her for wanting to marry a kind man and experience love with him? Could I resent her for declining a proposal from a man she did not love when I had done the same thing? My stubborn heart wanted to stay wounded, but after tasting Uri's love, I was also filled with a new compassion and understanding for my friend. Therefore, it was with great joy on a bright summer day that I accepted an invitation from Gilah to visit.

The steward let me in and instructed me to wait on a bench in the tiled courtyard while he fetched his mistress. I eased myself onto the seat, clutching a package of nut cakes in my lap—a feeble peace offering. It'd been Gilah herself who'd helped me perfect the sweet dish.

A moment later, Gilah herself entered, standing primly before me, thin arms crossed at her waist, a slight frown creasing her brow.

"It was good of you to come, cousin."

Cousin? We were indeed third cousins, but our relationship had never found its grounding in that vein. I swiftly rose to my feet, nearly dropping my gift in the process.

"I was happy to receive the invitation. We haven't truly spoken since . . ." My voice trailed off as I observed Gilah's tight expression. Nervously, I wet my lips. "Here, friend, some nut cakes for you. I remembered how much you like them." I extended the package, but instead of taking it as I'd expected, Gilah nodded to Rhoda, her cook, who stood in an open doorway.

Quietly, Rhoda crossed the courtyard and took the package from my hands. I swallowed past the lump in my throat, confused and not a little hurt.

"That was unnecessary, but thank you," Gilah said.

Instead of inviting me to the upstairs chamber, she simply gestured that I sit back down. Thoroughly confused now, I complied.

"I'm afraid this isn't a social call. I must discuss a delicate matter with you." Gilah stood calmly in front of me, her demeanor so unlike herself that I grew concerned.

"It's come to my attention that Mary keeps sneaking into our home to lure Lemuel away from his studies."

My jaw dropped.

"She's been caught numerous times climbing the acacia tree behind our home to scale the wall. And she's taught Lemuel to escape by climbing down the same tree. We've had numerous scares—unable to find him anywhere. And when we do find him, he is in such a state . . ." Gilah broke off as if overcome with emotion.

"He is in such a state of disrepair that it is shameful—filthy with torn clothes!" She shook her head sorrowfully. "But perhaps even worse than this is his attitude. The boy talks back to Simon most egregiously, earning him repeated beatings. He's even begun mouthing off to *me*!" She paused and placed a hand to her heart, chin quivering.

"The boy *is* at the age to test parents' authority," I interjected, managing to loosen my tongue. I was mortified over Mary's actions but strangely even more so over Gilah's manner and tone. It was one thing for me to exhibit frustration over my sister. It was another matter entirely to hear her put down so vigorously by others—blamed, even, for another's choices.

"Mary didn't force Lemuel to do anything," I reasoned. "The boy has a will of his own. I'm not condoning her actions by any means. Heaven knows she can be aggravating at times, but she is, after all, only a girl. It's hardly fair to place all the blame on Mary for Lemuel's actions."

Gilah's jaw tightened. Her manner, which had been constrained before, turned brusque. "Of course Lemuel is responsible for his own actions, but there is such a thing as a poor choice of friends. Simon . . . *we* believe Mary is a poor influence on Lemuel."

My heart dropped. This conversation wasn't from one concerned friend to another. It was delivered dispassionately, as if she hadn't known Mary and me from birth. As if she hadn't spent years pouring into our lives, assisting me with Mary as she could.

"It grieves me to hear you talk so," I said. "I understand your love of Lemuel and your concern over his well-being, but—"

"Then you will understand that Mary cannot associate with him anymore. She is not welcome here, and we forbid them to interact with each other."

"She will be devastated," I protested. "She considers Lemuel her dearest friend. Please, Gilah, consider that it is children we are talking about. Children who can be molded and corrected, guided and trained."

"Clearly Mary is not receiving such instruction."

Her words hit me like a slap in the face. She of all people knew how I struggled with Mary and how alone I was in my struggle. Gilah had a mother and mother-in-law. She had capable, caring servants as well as a tutor. I had no such support, none. Yet I tried. Every day I tried to be for Mary what she needed. I bit my lip to keep from crying aloud from the pain searing my heart.

"I suppose, then, that there is nothing left to say." My words were clipped, delivered in short bursts past hot tears clogging my throat.

For a moment, Gilah's stern expression wavered, and I caught a glimpse of the merciful woman beneath. How had she changed so drastically? Had our previous conversation soured her this much to me and our family? Could the old Gilah be coaxed out again?

"This is unlike you." I tried to deliver the words kindly, but they left my lips on the ends of a hiss. "Is this you expressing concern, or is this Simon speaking through you?"

At my harsh tone, the veil lowered once more, Gilah's jaw tightening so hard it looked like she was grinding her teeth. "I am not my husband's mouthpiece." Each word was a dagger.

"I'm not so sure of that." I could see the damage my words were doing but was powerless to stop. "Simon didn't want the embarrassment of targeting a small girl, so he sent you to do it for him, is that it? When did a girl become such a threat, anyway? And when did you become so hard-hearted?"

"Get out!" Gilah's command came softly, her hand trembling as she pointed to the door. "How dare you speak to me in such a way in my own home! After all I've done for you."

"After all you've done for me?" I snorted. "You would hold that over my head now? All you've done is be a false friend." My voice broke. Were these even my words coming from my mouth? I had come ready to reconcile. How had things turned out so badly? I only knew that if Gilah was forcing me to choose between her and my stubborn, infuriating little sister, I would choose my sister time and time again.

My mind was full of sadness and rage as I staggered to my feet. "You deny my family a mother and then cast a stone at me for not being more of a mother to Mary. How can you do that?"

"Get out!" This time Gilah's voice was a scream, her face so red I feared it might burst like an overripe fruit.

With a ragged breath, I lifted my tunic in both hands and violently shook its folds along with my feet.

Gilah reared back, recognizing the gesture. Her face transitioned from red to white as I turned on my heel and stormed from her home, having shaken the dust off my feet, ridding myself of her and her family.

Eighteen

14 Tishri
19 AD

Just when I thought my tired heart could not bear anything more, it stretched to accommodate this newest loss: Gilah, her sweet friendship, her comforting smile and knowing presence. I spent many nights in agony, remembering how things used to be and mourning where things now stood. I instructed my heart to move on, but like a stubborn mule, it kept crying out for her.

The bigger surprise was how I also continued to ache for Cleopas. The last time we were together, I'd tried to talk to him, to feel my way back toward friendship. But he'd given me short answers laced with hurt, refused to look at me, and quickly made an excuse to leave. Afterward, I'd wept privately, sick with the realization that I'd caused him such pain and had no way to alleviate it.

Deeper than the longing for Gilah and Cleopas was my longing for Uri. I craved the steadfastness of his love in a new way. Each passing day tugged my heart closer to his, threading them inseparably together. If we could just get to the point of his return, my burdened heart would lighten, and his presence would soothe the deep ache in my breast.

Enough time had passed that I more confidently rested in Lazarus' silence. I stopped anxiously watching him and instead observed our father and his moods to assess when Uri and I should approach him. There was a pattern to his temperament. In the summer months leading up to Mary's birthday, he became increasingly sullen and withdrawn. These were the months that we'd happily anticipated Mary's arrival. These were the joy-filled final months of Ima's life as she delighted in the babe growing in her womb. Abba's mood was blackest the whole month of Tishri, only lightening once the winter rains whipped in, as if he received satisfaction from the elements mimicking his dark thoughts.

Despite the heaviness Tishri brought into our family, it was also the month of our nation's most important festivals, including the Festival of Booths. This year, despite the weight of separation from Gilah and the brooding presence of Abba's dark looks, I focused on the meaning behind the festival as my family journeyed along the southern route to Jerusalem to construct temporary shelters. These shelters reminded us of Yahweh's hand of provision during the forty years of wilderness wandering. Despite our people's sin, Yahweh had never once deserted us but continued to come and dwell with His covenant people. Even in His discipline, He was gracious to provide.

We would construct our booth in the Kidron Valley, in sight of the pinnacle of the Temple. The surrounding countryside would be filled with similar booths. Come nightfall, the landscape would be dotted by campfires, like the stars had fallen from the sky.

Abba had been irritable all morning. When we arrived in the valley, he barked out orders. "Look for branches! Be quick about it." We'd brought wood from home for the booth's walls. We would need to forage, however, for the branches and brush that would compose the roof.

We spread out, Mary tagging along behind Lazarus. I ambled

along the slopes of the mount, arms full of fallen branches. As I grasped another dead branch, a splinter entered deep into the fat of my palm, causing me to yelp with surprise and discomfort.

"Did a snake bite you?" Abba's voice sounded behind me.

I whirled around in surprise, hand to my lips. "No, only a pesky bit of wood."

"Let me take a look." He reached out.

Dumbfounded at his show of concern, I set down my bundle and gave him my hand.

"It certainly drove deep," he murmured, twisting my palm for a better view. "I can dig it out." He produced a small knife, and I quickly withdrew my hand with a nervous squeak.

He raised an eyebrow at me. "If you don't let me pry it out, you'll need to wait until it works its own way out."

"That's okay. I'll leave it."

"Eh, you're too soft." He said the words on the end of a grumble, but his eyes were looking at me with surprising affection.

I wasn't used to his full attention. Since my refusal of Cleopas' proposal, we'd avoided prolonged conversation with each other. Now, beneath his strong gaze, I squirmed uncomfortably, finally turning to regather my bundle.

"I hear you love a young man."

Abba's blunt statement hit me like a blow, and I stood trembling, back turned to him.

"Is this true?"

I was quaking so hard, I thought I'd fall to my knees. Somehow, I found the strength to turn and face him. How much did he know? We were so close to Uri's return, so what was the use of denying it?

"Who told you this?" I finally responded.

"Your brother."

My eyes closed in silent panic.

"He didn't come right out and tell me. He was mumbling

to himself one day. You were being especially moody, apparently, and he was complaining that if this was what love did to someone, then he wanted nothing to do with it." Abba's lips quirked in humor. "I asked him what he meant."

Here it was. There was no way my brother refused a direct question from our father.

"He refused to give me any details." Abba's eyes bore into mine in disbelief. "I questioned that boy until I thought he'd cry, but still he would only admit that you loved a young man. Nothing more." He raised both eyebrows, waiting for my response.

Uri and I had decided to approach Abba together. If I did this thing alone, I risked his releasing Uri from our employment as soon as he returned home. I wouldn't even be able to say goodbye. It was the worst possible timing to trust Abba with this request, nearly on the eve of Ima's death. But could I withhold this information from him? I risked his wrath either way.

"It's true that my heart belongs to a young man." My voice cracked as tears flooded my eyes. How I hated to appear weak! Abba despised such emotion. In response to my tears, however, he sighed deeply and sank to a nearby boulder, his strong forearms resting on his thighs.

"I'm sure this is why you turned down Cleopas?"

It was a question, but I gave no answer, simply standing still with my arms full of dead branches and a lump in my throat as I waited with suspended heart.

He ran a weathered hand through his whitening hair. "I know a thing or two about love. Your mother was the love of my life. We were the rare couple who formed an attachment before our betrothal."

Never had he spoken so openly of Ima. I stood as still as I could, afraid any movement would spook him.

"Devorah was . . . unique. But I don't need to tell you this, do I?" He turned to me but kept his eyes from meeting mine.

It wasn't the harsh and demanding father sitting before me but the father of my childhood, the one who had laughed at Ima's stories, kissed her while sweaty from the fields, and held her crying form as they lost one baby and then another. I swallowed hard as tears gathered again. This . . . this was the man Gilah didn't see.

"She was unique, and I simply could not replace her." Abba stared at the ground. "My decision put an additional weight on you." He cleared his throat. "But perhaps you have come to understand the nature of love. It always takes more than it gives."

He looked me full in the face then, and seeing my tears a second time, grunted and brusquely rose to his feet. "I'll take those." He grabbed the bundle from my arms and strode away, leaving me with mouth gaping in confusion.

He had not pressed me for the identity of the young man. Was that a good sign? I longed for another glimpse of the father I once knew, but I feared such glimpses would remain few and far between. I held his pain-filled words in confused hands.

Savta had said love was a gift, but Abba claimed it was a thief. Which, I now wondered, was the more accurate depiction?

Nineteen

25 Heshvan
19 AD

Only a month away from Uri's return, and my nights were sleepless and filled with daydreams. Was he sleepless too? I gazed at the stars, imagining him doing the same, shivering at the memory of his lips against mine, barely able to believe he would soon be in my arms once again.

It was nearing the end of the olive harvest, the sky spitting out intermittent rainfall, the air beginning to hint at the cold to come. A request arrived early in the day to help my cousin Zissa brine a portion of her husband's olive harvest. With a small babe to tend and another on the way, she often sought out my help, and gladly I gave it.

We layered the olives in a stone box, with generous portions of salt to drive out the bitterness. My hands were scraped raw from the salt when an urgent banging on the front door disrupted us. We both looked over our shoulders in confusion as another volley of thumps rained down on the door. Before anyone could respond, the person outside threw open the door. I shot to my feet in surprise as Abigail stumbled forward, disheveled and panting with exertion.

"Ah, Martha!" Abigail hunched over, hands on her knees, words coming through wheezing puffs. "Come quickly! Lazarus sends for you. There's an urgent family matter, and he needs you home right away."

"Go." Zissa nodded.

Such was Abigail's state that I didn't even pause to wash up. With a frightened glance at Zissa, I lifted my tunic with fragrant hands and ran.

I expected wailing to greet me as I rounded the corner toward home, but there was no such display. The street was still, and there were no sounds of grief. What could be so urgent that Lazarus would send for me so dramatically?

As I neared our front door, it groaned open, and Lazarus himself exited, sprinting to intercept me.

"Sister, wait." He placed a hand on each of my shoulders, grasping me firmly, stilling my frantic steps. "Come. Not here. Come with me."

"Lazarus, what is happening? Is Mary okay?" My hands trembled as Lazarus led me away from the door, through the garden and the barley field, down the slope to Azariah's canopy. It was a well-known and welcome path, but I traversed it now in a state of dread.

When we reached the tree, Lazarus released my arm and bid me sit on a gnarled root. I shook my head, then changed my mind and sat, then stood again and paced—my body buzzing with nervous energy.

"A man arrived with news, and I . . . I need to be the one to tell you."

My brother's face clouded over with pain, and I sank to my knees on the ground. "What can this news be? Who is this man?"

"His name is Dan bar Simeon, a shepherd from Sychar."

"Sychar? What can a Samaritan shepherd want with us? What would bring him this far south?"

"He found . . ." Lazarus broke off, unable to look me in the eye. "He saw our mark on some sheep and, in making inquiries, discovered to whom the mark belonged."

"You aren't making any sense. How would he see our sheep? Where did he see them? They are with Uri."

Lazarus paced before me, his face taut. Since his accident and its accompanying scar, he'd appeared older than his years, but now he looked like a frightened boy. His wide eyes and nervous twitching reminded me of another dark night when we'd gained our sister and lost our mother.

"Lazarus . . . where did he see our sheep?" I repeated the question, fear breaking my voice.

"He found them barricaded in a cave along the Jordan Valley, north of Phasaelis," Lazarus finally answered. He wasn't meeting my eyes, and his lips had begun to quiver.

"Barricaded? As in trapped? Who . . . how?" I stopped talking then as the fear in my chest clutched so close that I ran out of breath. I sat gulping for air at Lazarus' feet.

"He found the sheep—all unharmed but nearly half-mad with terror, thirst, and hunger." Lazarus stilled, placed his hands on his hips, then abruptly threaded them behind his head. He was all agitated motion and halting words, and my patience was running out. "He says they—the sheep—must have been trapped inside for many days." He dropped his hands by his sides, as if giving up.

I closed my eyes and hunched over my knees, breathing heavily.

"Dan is an undershepherd for a wealthy man near Mount Gerizim. Help from a Samaritan—who would have thought it possible?" Lazarus shrugged at the implausibility. "This man is generously caring for our flock, helping to nurture them back to health until Tzvi can fetch them. In fact, he's already left."

I dug my fingers into the ground, the soil lodging beneath my nails as I let out a low moan. *Uri.* I thought I'd said his name out loud but found that I hadn't—couldn't. *Uri. What happened to Uri?* My mind screamed with questions while my body clenched in agony. Lazarus knelt by my side and laid a hand on my back.

"Sister, you need some water. Let me fetch some."

"No," I gasped.

Lazarus' breath hitched and for a moment I didn't think he'd continue. Finally, he said, "It was clear to Dan that Uri had barricaded the entrance to the cave to keep out wild animals. That part of the Jordan Valley is notoriously deep."

The Jordan Valley was webbed with rifts, some crevices running so deep that no man ventured near. A thousand plants thrived along the banks of the Jordan as it wound its way through this deep and hidden land that teemed with wildlife. Good pastureland must have been scarce for Uri to have traveled so far north and so near the rifts.

Lazarus' hand was heavy on my back. "Uri must have heard the wolves coming and barricaded the entrance—in time, thankfully, to keep them all out."

I raised my head then and searched my brother's face, praying.

"He kept them out, but at a cost." My brother bit a trembling lip and quickly looked away. "I-I don't know how to say this. Yahweh help me!"

"Say it," I whispered.

Tears wet Lazarus' cheeks as he hung his head.

"Say it!" I screamed, throat raw, mind and heart hollowed out like a gutted deer.

"Dan . . . saw bodies outside the cave, which made him investigate. Oh, Martha, I'm so sorry!" Lazarus broke off and covered his face with his hands, as if he couldn't bear to look at me. "Dan found the bodies of three wolves outside the cave . . . with Uri." He choked on the words. "My heart aches for you, sister.

I knew no one else would understand your grief. I'm so sorry . . . so sorry."

The words hung in the air, but I didn't comprehend them. I rose slightly, still crouched on my knees. "That doesn't make any sense. Uri will be home soon. We've waited so long, and he'll be home soon."

"He's not coming home, sister." Lazarus uncovered his face to gaze at me with stricken eyes. "He died protecting the flock."

"No, that doesn't make sense." My eyes were wide and dry as I stood. "He wouldn't be careless with his life. We are promised to each other. We were going to approach Abba. He wouldn't lose his life for *sheep*. I do not care about our sheep!" My voice rose in a shrill yelp.

"He was doing what any good shepherd would do—more so, since the sheep were not even his own. His actions are honorable."

"It doesn't make sense." My mind grappled with my brother's words—disbelieving them, trying to make them untrue with my own logic. "Why wouldn't he be inside with the sheep?"

"There would have been no way to barricade the cave from the inside—at least this is how Dan describes it. Uri needed to draw from the brush and the stones surrounding the cave to ensure the flock's safety."

"No, no, no." I shook my head vigorously and let out a laugh that horrified me. What was happening? My body was separated from my mind. I managed to gain control over the laughter that shook my body, swallowing it into submission, hiccupping from my efforts.

Lazarus had backed away at my outburst, unsure how to respond. "They buried him that same day. It's a comfort, at least, that he's beneath ground."

At the words *beneath ground*, the full import of what Lazarus was saying hit me. The blood drained from my head, and I collapsed against Azariah.

"No." The word was a whisper, a prayer.

"No!" I turned to stare at the empty sheepfold.

"No! No! No!" I arced my body toward Azariah and screamed the word over and over, pounding my palms violently against the trunk with each word, shredding the air with my howling denial.

"It's not true! It's not true!" I drove my words into the tree, deeper, louder, harder. I was shaking hard yet achingly light, a storm of confusion finding release along the length of Azariah's deep, rough, and ragged grooves.

"Sister, stop! You're bleeding!"

Only when Lazarus placed a restraining hand on my shoulder did I notice the ribbons of blood coursing down my arms. I paused, gulping air, and turned my hands to see the mess I'd made of my palms. I didn't feel a thing.

"Those are deep." Lazarus' voice wobbled. I turned to face him, still feeling nothing. His face was streaked with tears, and he sniffed noisily. "We need to get help. You've hurt yourself."

My wounds were nothing compared to Uri's. And my life was nothing now that he was gone. Sinking onto my knees, I threw my head back with a prolonged, guttural scream.

"Sister!" Lazarus knelt, took me in his arms, and held me as my body began convulsing with thunderous sobs. They tore through my frame with ferocious strength. I was sick with them and lay powerless and shuddering in my brother's arms as wave after wave of grief clutched me.

I had never experienced such pain—not when Ima died, nor the poor babes before Mary. Not when Savta had breathed her last or Saba before her. My face was flushed, and my tears ran hot, burning trails down my face.

Earlier this year, Uri and I had stood right here and promised ourselves to each other. How could it be that one moment a man was alive and strong, holding you in his arms, breathing promises into your ear, trailing kisses down your neck, and the next moment he was lifeless and alone beneath the ground? It was cruel and senseless. After all he had endured in his hard life, to go down in this way—it was unthinkable. And the deep happiness we had shared . . . was he not worthy of that? Was not I?

Lazarus stroked my hair and held me close. I was so numb that I could derive no comfort from his presence. Instead, I cradled my bleeding hands in my lap and gazed up at him with empty eyes. "Leave, please," I mumbled past numb lips. "Please leave me alone."

Pain crossed his face at my words. "Are you sure?"

I hunched back over my knees and moaned, unable to answer.

"I-I'll go and get help. Your hands—they will need to be treated." He hovered above me, briefly resting a hand on my head before turning and scrambling back up the hillside.

Alone now, I sat beneath Azariah's canopy. My nose was stuffy, my head clogged as well. The sobs had drained me of all energy, so I sat silently and stared past the empty sheepfold and over the terraced hills in the direction of my beloved's body.

Eventually, I rose to my feet, using Azariah's thick trunk for support, wincing as I finally registered the throbbing pain in my palms. On unsteady legs, I stumbled toward the sheepfold and clutched the doorframe with one bloodied hand, the feather pendant in the other, my eyes trained on the horizon.

I gazed in the direction I'd last seen him go. Surely, at any moment, he would return, coming to me with long, powerful, eager strides, arms and heart open to me. *"I'm home, Talitha,"* he would say. *"I've come home to you, beloved."* He'd lift me in delight, press me close to his heart, and we would never be parted again. Never.

I closed my eyes and imagined that moment, wished for it with all my soul—his arms sheltering me, his warm lips exploring mine, his very life bound to mine.

"Love is a great gift from Yahweh. Don't forget it, Martha." I let out a harsh rush of air. How could love be a gift if it was stripped

from you? Uri was my one treasure, the dearest thing in this life. How could Yahweh have taken this away from me?

I opened my eyes and took in the empty hillside. There would be no homecoming now. The future I'd lovingly cultivated in my mind would never come to pass.

Abba was right. Love was no gift. It was a thief.

Returning to Azariah, I laid a hand on the trunk, ignoring the pain in my hands. Here, this canopy that had held our dearest moments would now hold my desperate hurt. I would be unable to publicly mourn my sweet Uri. There would be no tomb to visit, no allotted days of mourning, no sackcloth and ashes.

I would have to make my own way for grief.

With a slow gesture, I pulled the veil from my head, letting its folds fall silently behind me. My torn hands felt ice cold as I knelt to scoop a mound of dirt from the ground. Tucking my chin to my chest, I released the dirt over my head, letting it slide through my fingers and into my tresses. Some of it fell out and past my ears, dirtying my collar and trickling down my back. I took another handful and another, repeating the gesture until my bloodied hands were caked with dirt and my head was full of earth.

Yahweh had formed man from dust, and to dust Uri had returned.

And me?

I was now a woman of dust.

He raises the poor from the dust and lifts the needy from the ash heap.

Psalm 113:7 NIV

PART TWO

Twenty

12 Ab
29 AD
Ten Years Later

Birdsong accompanied by morning's first light greeted me as I lay trembling on my bed. A sheen of sweat trickled down my brow, and I wiped it away wearily, blinking my eyes to rid myself of the vivid dream. I'd had many dreams over the years, but this one was new. In this dream I was surrounded by curly-headed children, and my heart was full of laughter and joy. It wasn't until a man entered the room, his eyes meeting mine, that I realized these children were ours. I gazed back down at them in shocked delight before jolting awake.

With a groan, I turned on my bed and willed the faces of my dream children away. *Yahweh, why must You give me a picture of things that will never be?* The light grew longer across the floor. The day's work was about to begin. With Lazarus away on business, I had plans to visit our family's workshops in his absence, a task I usually enjoyed.

Swinging my feet to the ground, I turned my mind away from dreams and said out loud the daily blessings I normally recited silently, trying to ground myself in my reality.

"Blessed is He who gives sight to the blind." I would turn my eyes away from long-dormant desires that would never come true. I stood, pushing back the longing that threatened to consume me.

"Blessed is He who sets the captives free." Yahweh would free me from the lingering effects of this dream. He must, for there was much to do today, and my mind needed to focus. Throwing my mantle around my shoulders, I stooped to tie my sandals.

"Blessed is He who clothes the naked. Blessed is He who provides for all my needs." I would not resent Yahweh today. I would not. I would choose to turn my eyes from what I lacked and look instead to what Yahweh in His wisdom had chosen to give me. I would not waste this day weeping.

By midday, Samu and I had finished visiting the family's various workshops and were crossing the field toward home. Both the work and his company had proven effective remedies for driving the morning's dream away.

Samu continued to be a trusted and valued member of the household. He'd recently walked through his own share of grief, for during the previous year, Abigail had passed suddenly. I recognized the quietness that flooded his face, the intensity with which he turned toward his work, as if he could outpace the emptiness.

Our workshops were all located in the field east of Bethany. The years following our flock's rescue from near destruction had been filled with bounty. Like Jacob's portion of Laban's flocks, God's particular blessing seemed to rest upon our small flock until it was no longer small but a massive business that had substantially raised our fortunes.

We'd expanded our holdings and begun processing our flock's raw goods for market. Wool, leather, and rich dairy dishes, such as creamy leben, found their way from our field to the Jerusalem marketplace and beyond. My brother was meeting with a merchant, freshly arrived from the port city of Joppa, who was interested in selling our leather to foreign markets.

About five years earlier, around the time we'd established our workshops, Abba had undertaken building a large estate for his fine household. As Samu and I traversed the field, my eyes lifted to that home—the two-story stone dwelling that loomed large over its surrounding neighbors and looked proudly across the field and the wealth it represented.

The home that had killed my father.

On a blustery day in the middle of construction, Abba had flown into a rage over building materials that arrived damaged. He'd been alone with Lazarus on the roof, throwing tiles over the side, ignoring our brother's pleas for calm. They'd argued, Lazarus uncharacteristically standing up to Abba's brashness. In the heat of the argument and fueled by his fury, our father had fallen off the roof to his death, snapping his neck and leaving a distraught Lazarus as head of our home.

Cleopas had stepped in and helped Lazarus shoulder his new responsibility. Ever Lazarus' friend, he had willingly become a mentor, spending copious hours in our home and away from his own business to help my brother succeed. With our home half-finished, Cleopas had personally overseen its completion, and under his stable and encouraging presence, Lazarus had grown into a mature capability.

My heart caught, as it always did, when thinking of Cleopas. He'd put his own interests on hold for us, and it had cost him. He should have been an official royal potter by now, but the years spent helping us had taken him from that path. Never once, however, did he begrudge the time invested in our family.

Over the years, some of the former ease between Cleopas and I had returned as we were thrown so often into each other's company. Regularly, I communicated my gratitude to him for the way he'd guided Lazarus, and he always accepted my gestures with warmth. Even so, there was still an unspoken tension between us that I regretted.

I rejoiced to see Lazarus steady, capable, and flourishing, and only wished the same could be said of Mary, whose young life had become more volatile the older she'd become. Now I cast a wary eye over the field and turned to Samu. "Have you seen Mary?"

Samu's lips tightened as he shook his head.

As if conjured from my mind, a figure arose in the distance, and I nearly shouted my sister's name aloud before realizing that it wasn't Mary but Gilah's son, Lemuel. I left Samu to meet him as he returned from the fields.

At seventeen, he was young but trustworthy, eager to learn and hardworking. He'd grown into a handsome young man, with dimpled cheeks and thick, black hair that curled pleasingly around his neck. Unlike his father in every way, Lemuel had retained his sweet nature, which had since matured into a compassionate heart. Hiring him to assist in attending our fig grove had been one of my better decisions.

"Are you headed home for the day?" I asked, drawing near. When he nodded his assent, I indicated for him to follow me. His dark eyes lit up with anticipation as he complied.

I was accustomed to sending food home with Lemuel whenever I could. I'd do so every day if Gilah's pride would allow it. When I first started the practice, she'd outright refused my gifts, sending them back untouched. But as her need had deepened, her pride had given way to acceptance.

Thoughts of my old friend flooded me. The beginning of our friendship had been forged in the fires of loss and need, fertile ground that had given our relationship deep roots. *Gilah.* My heart cried her name as my mind tried tracing, once again, the tangled path of our friendship's demise. *No.* I would refuse to think of the friendship as dead. It was not so, at least not on my end.

"How is your mother?" I questioned gently, eager for news.

"She's managing," Lemuel replied quietly, his averted gaze telling me more than his words. "Her work as a fuller keeps her busy."

I'd seen Gilah on several occasions at the creek, sleeves rolled up, head bowed over soiled garments as she scrubbed away at other peoples' stains.

"And Tehilah?"

"Bright as a little bird." Lemuel's voice softened at the mention of his half-sister, and he flicked a happy look in my direction. "Cheerful and full of questions."

"Ah, I remember Mary at that age." I broke off at the mention of my sister, and both Lemuel and I fell into a somber silence. Mary and Lemuel's childhood friendship had disintegrated after Gilah had confronted me so bluntly, but it was apparent that he still remembered her with fondness. I had caught him more than once looking at Mary longingly but had never seen him approach her.

We entered the reception courtyard, and I motioned for him to rest on a bench beneath a decorative myrtle while I continued into the inner courtyard. The kitchen, my favorite room in the house, was a bustling hub of activity.

"Make haste, Tovah, and gather a basket of food for Lemuel to take home."

I joined with our cook in readying the food, tucking rounds of bread, dried fruit, olives, nuts, and salted fish into the basket. Tovah clucked her tongue when she saw the fish, muttering, "So generous, mistress."

"What good does it do to hoard God's blessings?" I waved a hand, dismissing her praise.

"Gilah must be grateful with how much you add to their table."

I bit my lip at Tovah's words. Grateful? Yes, perhaps. But it still wasn't enough to repair a friendship that had become wrecked beyond recognition. No number of gestures breached the wall between us.

And when Simon had contracted leprosy . . .

It'd been a dark day for Bethany when Simon the Pharisee was declared unclean and driven miles from the village to live out the remainder of his days in a leper community. Considered good as dead, Simon's estate had passed to his son, who had barely been fifteen. Gilah had stepped into the role of trustee until Lemuel came of age. But Simon had accrued debt, and it wasn't long until the creditors came collecting. I'd watched in horror as the estate was bled dry, until all that was left were the bones of the home.

Gilah continued to live in Simon's fine home, but with no means to maintain it. Her station in life had plummeted, and my heart along with it. She drew inward, pushing away all who would offer comfort. The bright light that once lived in her was all but snuffed out. The disease had robbed her of a husband, the creditors of her money, misfortune sweeping through the household, taking and taking. As she fell, my family continued to rise, but I never forgot that sometimes what you love the most is snatched away like dry grass in a fire.

When the basket was ready, I rejoined Lemuel and found him weaving in and out of the pillars surrounding the courtyard. The sight caused my lips to quirk in amusement. Such a small, juvenile action, revealing the little child still inside the young man. Intercepting him in one of the long, covered galleries, I handed him the basket.

"You are too kind, mistress." Lemuel lifted the basket to his nose and took a deep whiff, his face alight with appreciation.

At that one gesture, my mind raced back to twelve years earlier, when I'd handed a different young man a basket full of food. Hands trembling, I stumbled backward a step and blinked rapidly. It was no longer Lemuel standing in front of me, but a scruffy young man with a long, jagged scar and a smile as piercing as the sunrise. This morning's dream resurfaced with a vengeance, mixing with memory and leaving me gasping, clinging to a pillar for support.

After all these years, a memory could still spring up and surprise me. After all these years, I still remembered what his skin smelled like and the exact tenor of his voice when he was delighted. After all these years.

"Are you all right?" Lemuel regarded me with worried eyes.

I blinked and swallowed with difficulty, refocusing to the present. "Y-yes, I'm fine. Only a bit light-headed."

"Should I call for assistance?"

"No, but thank you." I straightened and smoothed my hands down my mantle to steady myself. "Tell Tehilah hello from me." I knew better than to pass along words of friendship to Gilah. I had tried before, and she'd returned the basket untouched, as if punishing me for the effort.

"I will, and thank you."

I stood still and watched Lemuel leave, quickly ascending the stairs to my bedchamber as soon as he was gone.

Once alone, I sat on my bed and covered my face with scarred hands. The marks of my pain had grown faint over the years, but they were still present, serving as jagged reminders of my loss.

It had been years since I'd shed tears over this broken part of me, and I would shed none now, but I still needed a moment alone. Rising, I crossed the room to a table, where I poured cool water into a basin and moistened a linen cloth. I lay on my bed and placed the cloth over my eyes, allowing the sensation to focus me.

The simplicity of my room was calming—unlike Mary's room, which contained lavish curtains over her latticed window, a fine fur rug, and elaborately dyed bed linens. I could not bring myself to spend money in such an indulgent way and instead had chosen plain but functional furnishings.

Lazarus certainly would not complain if I chose to spend more, for our brother was caring and affectionate with us. There wasn't much we could ask for that he wouldn't try to grant. In fact, he'd often urged me to spend more time and money on myself.

"Sister, you work harder than anyone in this household. Why not add to your wardrobe as Mary does?"

"I possess everything I need."

"But you dress no differently from when we were young. At least let me purchase some dyed cloth. Surely a colorful mantle would be pleasing to you."

"I have no need of it."

"I simply want to show you the honor befitting the lady of the house. How about jewelry? May I not gift you with pins for your hair?"

I had steadfastly refused. I had all the ornamentation I needed beneath my tunic—the wooden feather pendant that pressed close to my heart.

Sighing, I shifted on my bed. How could I make my dear brother understand that it was more than modesty that restrained me? I could not spend the family's fortunes on myself, not when they had come with a cost that I bore daily. Our family had risen on the back of Uri's death. We had grown prosperous off the flock that he'd saved. How could I then take the money from such a sacrifice and use it to give myself frills? It was unthinkable.

I thought often of the carpenter's home and the compassion that family had shown Uri. One act of kindness had saved his life and set him on a new course. If they hadn't opened their doors to Uri, I never would have met him. Couldn't I do the same for others? I liked to think I was doing it for Lemuel and for the many who came to our door seeking help. By living generously, I could honor Uri's sacrifice.

The years had been hungry as I'd yearned after Uri with no hope of satisfaction. For a long while, I'd pushed Lazarus away. I didn't want my younger brother to view me as weak. But he was the only one who knew of my loss, so eventually I'd gone to him. Lazarus had taken my weeping frame into his arms and shaken me from my grief with searing, pointed words.

"You can stay in this place, Martha, defeated with grief, or you can do something. You can remain lost in anger, or you can choose not to be. But you must decide for yourself."

And so I had decided, and every day since, I decided.

Bitterness crouched at my door, gnashing its teeth for my soul, but through focusing on faithful stewardship, I could keep the beast at bay. I could keep my soul from becoming something unrecognizable—the way it had our father.

Twenty-One

The evening meal passed without any sign of Mary. My earlier curiosity now morphed into worry as my steps hastened in search of our handmaid, Nenet. I found her tidying Mary's room and laying out her bedclothes.

It was no secret that Nenet favored Mary. The young Egyptian girl was close in age to my sister and enjoyed enhancing Mary's already-beautiful features with powders and creams or trying new hairstyles to show off her thick curls. I didn't mind the unequal split of Nenet's time, but I did worry that she added to Mary's vanity.

"Do you know where Mary is tonight? I haven't seen her since this morning."

Nenet jerked like a startled rabbit in a snare. "Oh, mistress! Excuse me, I did not see you there. No, I haven't seen her."

"Surely you have some idea where she is?"

Nenet fidgeted, worrying her hands. "She did mention, perhaps, that she had a . . . meeting tonight."

"A meeting? With whom?"

"I couldn't say, mistress."

Something about Nenet's tone caused me to look at her sharply.

Suspicion clawed at my thoughts. "She isn't meeting a man, is she, Nenet?"

"I couldn't say, mistress."

Biting my tongue before I let out a stream of harsh words, I silently backed from the room and retraced my steps downstairs, leaving the tight-lipped Nenet behind me.

On the heels of the suggestion of an illicit meeting came the image of Aharon, one of our recently employed fieldworkers. He was handsome and somehow always managed to be near my sister. I'd caught them conversing more times than seemed natural.

My steps turned purposeful as I exited our home and strode across the field in the direction of our workshops, the fading sunlight forming long shadows around me. I'd start with the buildings. If my search was fruitless, I'd send Samu into the fields.

As expected, the workshops were locked up tight for the night. My frenzied steps drew the attention of several watchdogs, who growled and skulked in the shadows before recognizing my voice and slinking back with whines of shame.

I was about to return home and call for Samu when soft noises from behind a storage shed arrested me in my tracks. With trepidation, I approached the small building, realizing the sounds belonged to a man and a woman.

Yahweh, please let this not be what I fear it is.

For a moment, I considered walking away, retaining my ignorance of whatever was transpiring. But I couldn't. Fear compelled me as I slowly rounded the small building.

In the dim light, I could barely make out the two forms. As my eyes adjusted, I recognized Aharon's broad back. He was leaning over a smaller form, his hand pressed against the shed, blocking my view. My throat tightened as he ducked his head and whispered something to his companion.

A feminine giggle greeted my ears. I recognized that soft laugh even before my eyes confirmed it as Aharon shifted and twisted her face upward for a kiss. Fear ignited into anger as my sister pressed in close, snaking her arms around his neck.

Hours later, we were still at it. Me pacing frantically, Mary huddled in a corner, alternately weeping and spitting out words.

"Did it ever occur to you that *he* approached *me*?" Mary hugged her knees to her chest and shot me a defensive look.

"It didn't look like you were an unwilling participant, Mary." I'd torn her arms from Aharon's neck, startling them both, dragging her back home and smuggling her inside. But not before releasing Aharon from our employment.

Mary sat on her bed, a defeated look on her face. "He'd been approaching me for months. He wouldn't let up."

"So your only choice was to give yourself to him?"

"You're overreacting. You always do!" My sister wept, but it appeared to be tears of rage rather than sorrow.

She'd grown into a stunningly beautiful woman. The whole village said it was like having Devorah back again. Her big eyes were trimmed with lush lashes, and her cheeks were rosy and round. I'd caught many a young man passing comments one to another as she walked past. Her long mantle couldn't hide the beauty of her figure, nor her veil the perfect symmetry of her face.

Mary attracted male attention wherever she went, so it was no surprise that she'd caught Aharon's eye. Still, I couldn't help but think that if she conducted herself with more modesty, she wouldn't draw half the attention she received. Aharon was one in a long line of admirers. I'd caught Mary in our fig grove, and once even near the synagogue, each time with a different young man. She was like a bee in a field of flowers, never stopping long enough for me to truly assess the damage.

Lazarus had brought up the subject of finding a husband

for Mary many times over the years, but our sister stubbornly refused all mention of marriage. Her determination seemed so mixed with desperation that I always ended up interceding for her. I was loath to force her into a betrothal and said as much to Lazarus. At times like these, however, I wondered at the wisdom of my advice. If Mary were safely married off, then I wouldn't be dealing with such instances.

"Well, you no longer need to worry about Aharon being such a nuisance. When will you learn that your actions don't affect only you? Now, as before, I am left with the problem of concealment. Did you . . . ?" I averted my gaze and tried to keep my voice steady. "Was this the first time you've met? Have you . . . given him your virtue?"

"No," Mary snapped. "I wouldn't do such a thing." She turned her face to the wall.

I longed to believe her, but a part of me would always doubt my sister.

"You won't mention this to Lazarus?" Her tone was dull.

"Of course not." I pinched the bridge of my nose with furrowed brow. "I won't mention this to *anyone*."

Mary's purity weighed heavy upon my mind, and I had worked tirelessly to keep her questionable behavior hidden. Not only her reputation but also the family's was at stake, so I kept my eyes wide and ears alert for any whisper of my sister's indiscretion.

"Praise God it was *me* who found you." I shuddered. "I'm tempted to throw Nenet out of this house."

Mary lurched onto her knees. "No, please! She had nothing to do with this. I swear it! I only told her I was meeting with a friend."

Groaning, I scrubbed a hand over my face and gazed upward, seeking divine wisdom. I was tired, so tired, of Mary's obtuse nature and of the way I constantly doubted myself when dealing with her.

Although I wouldn't admit it to her, Mary's displeasure with me stung, leaving me alone with my resolve. Would I forever be looking after her, seeking her out, bringing her back, trying so hard to give her what she lacked? How could I be her sister when what she'd always needed was a mother?

"Fine. Let's speak no more on the subject tonight."

I left her curled in a ball of misery on her bed and retired to my own room, where I proceeded to stare dry-eyed at the ceiling, wishing for sleep that wouldn't come. When it finally did come, it was dreamless.

There were no more curly-headed children with eyes full of promise.

Twenty-Two

13 Ab
29 AD

Whenever harsh words passed between Mary and me, uneasiness entered my spirit. Like a tangled knot in my hair, our discord would irritate me until I brushed it out. After our late night filled with tears, Mary expectedly avoided me and, uncharacteristically, I let her.

Our stoic silence bled into the rest of the household. Everyone sensed something was amiss and responded appropriately with subdued expressions. Although externally quiet, my insides were churning like the waters of the Jordan after rainfall. With pain I remembered the small girl with the wide eyes who alternately clung to my skirts and ran off into the hills. I had failed her.

Lazarus returned from his business trip late that morning with an abounding cheerfulness that shattered the tension covering our home. Only the bright presence of our brother could draw Mary and me together, both of us rushing to the courtyard to greet him.

"Sisters, how I've missed you!" Eyes gleaming and arms stretched wide, Lazarus attempted to embrace both of us at once.

He crushed my face against his collarbone, his full beard tickling my brow.

"Why are you so cheerful? You've been away less than a week—hardly enough time to miss anyone." My tone was huffy, but I turned a pleased expression into his collar.

"I come with good news to share." Lazarus led us to his study, a spacious and beautiful room off the inner courtyard. Whereas other men might exclude women from the study, our brother was open and free with us. Indeed, he'd taught both Mary and me to read and encouraged us to browse his extensive personal library.

"Your meeting with the merchant was successful?" I prompted.

"Yes. He's originally from Arimathea, with holdings in Joppa, from whose port he conducts a massive amount of business. He's agreed to purchase a large quantity of leather from us."

"That's wonderful news."

"But more interesting still is the man I heard speaking in the Temple courts while I was there. Cleopas heard him speak before and says there has never been a rabbi like him—not since the days of Elijah. Do you remember the rabbi who overturned tables in the Temple last year?" Lazarus asked.

"Yes, there's been a lot of talk surrounding him."

When I'd first heard of the unusual teacher named Jesus from the small town of Nazareth, I'd been unable to draw breath. For days I'd clutched the feather pendant, experiencing once again the well-worn story of the carpenter boy and his whittling knife, hearing the warmth in Uri's voice as he'd told the tale. Could it be that the boy who'd rescued Uri on the road was the teacher now drawing a following and befuddling the Scribes and Pharisees?

Impossible. Jesus was a common name, and what carpenter's son could possibly arise to such a high-profile position? So I'd placed my suspicions in a box and put it away alongside the stubborn rumblings of grief.

"They say he's performed miracles. He turned water into

wine at a wedding in Cana and even healed those who were lame." Lazarus was pacing before us, eyes alight with excitement. "People from all over are beginning to adhere to his teachings. Why, even the Samaritans believe in him!"

I raised a brow at the mention of miracles. Jesus wasn't the first to perform a sign in order to amass a following, and he wouldn't be the last. Esteemed rabbis came and went. Leaders rose to power every day and fell just as quickly. What use was it, then, fixating on any one of them? Lazarus, however, studied the latest teachings with zeal, investigating every claim from every would-be Messiah.

"You think he's someone to pay attention to?" Mary spoke for the first time.

Lazarus stopped pacing to plant two firm fists on the table. "I do. I heard him speak myself. It's hard to explain. There is fire behind his words, as if he possesses divinely appointed authority."

I raised the other brow, skeptical. "Is he political when he talks? Do you think there could be another uprising?"

"Not political, but unsettling to the religious rulers. He sees right through people to the heart of things, and it makes them uncomfortable."

My brother's joyful words unsettled another memory inside me, where it rattled, demanding attention. Uri's Jesus had made him feel seen and known. The box I'd so neatly set my suspicions in shook. Stubbornly, I clamped down the lid. It couldn't be.

"He also cast out a demon . . . on *Shabbat* no less!" Lazarus spoke the shocking words gleefully. "How I wish I'd been there! What's more, Cleopas' friend Nicodemus spoke privately with Jesus and is inclined to believe he is a prophet sent from God."

I narrowed my eyes. "You're predisposed to think kindly of anyone Cleopas admires, brother."

"But I heard him speak myself! What's more, we'll soon be able to make up our own minds. He's coming to Bethany."

"Why here?" Mary questioned.

Lazarus thumped a hand on the table for emphasis. "Because Gilah pleaded for him to come."

"What?" Mary and I spoke simultaneously, giving our brother dumbfounded looks.

"That's right." Lazarus eased back with a smug expression on his face. There was nothing he liked more than being the sole owner of interesting information. "I was there when the request was made. She sent a messenger to her cousin Thomas, who is one of Jesus' disciples, begging him to approach Jesus about healing Simon."

"What?" For the second time, Mary and I stared at our brother in astonishment.

"I can't believe that she would be that forward," I stammered.

"Or deluded," Mary added. "No one can heal leprosy!"

"Like no one can turn water into wine?" Lazarus was enjoying our obvious perplexity with too much relish.

"And he agreed to come?" I shook my head in disbelief.

"He did, and I told him that he and his disciples could stay here. He agreed to come the next day. But this was yesterday, so that means today. They'll be arriving today."

"Why didn't you lead with this information?" I scrambled to my feet and wrung my hands in frustration. What were we doing sitting here chatting when guests would arrive this very day? Oh, this was so like my brother! All talk, talk, talk.

"There's so much to make ready," I exclaimed. "Mary, come."

Gone, for the moment, was the tension between us as we united over the imminent arrival of guests. I shoved aside the astounding fact that Gilah had reached out to this rabbi and that he had responded.

A man who could cure leprosy? What did Gilah expect him to

do? What did *he* expect to do? Would he disgrace and undermine himself with the attempt?

I sighed. Deluded or not, we would welcome this Jesus and his disciples. We would open our home to the strange rabbi with fire behind his words.

⸻ ✦ ⸻

We kept a well-stocked storeroom, which meant we could host a decent meal on short notice. Even though every servant we could spare was on kitchen duty, I joined in the task myself, relishing the pull of sticky dough against my hands as I prepared bread. The time I spent with such tasks had diminished greatly, and I missed it.

Lazarus had already left to await our guests on the western outskirts of town so he could escort them to our home. Even though I kept busy, I experienced the familiar prick of anxiety every time someone new entered our home—the desire to please and satisfy.

We were putting the finishing touches on the platters of food when a commotion at the front gate announced the guests' arrival. I shoved errant strands of hair back under my headdress with nervous fingers before entering the reception courtyard, which was filled with loud, sweaty men. I hadn't expected so many and prayed that we'd prepared enough food for them all.

Most of Jesus' disciples were from Galilee, and many were fishermen by trade. I wondered which of the bunch was the rabbi, my eyes roaming quickly over the tanned and dusty faces, finally lighting upon a large and impressive man who let out a booming greeting to my brother and clapped a hand on his shoulder. His was the most commanding presence. Here, then, must be the mysterious Jesus.

I approached the men quietly, and when the large man turned around, I offered him a deep bow. "Peace be on you. You honor us with your presence, Rabbi."

A stunned silence fell upon the courtyard. I risked a glance upward to find that the man's face had blanched of all color. Quickly, my own cheeks flooded, and I worked hard to keep from groaning with embarrassment and confusion.

As suddenly as the silence had descended, so did the laughter commence. First the large man and then the others. There was no mockery in the laughter, only enjoyment.

"I do not deserve the honor, mistress. I'm but a poor fisherman."

"And a loudmouth," someone chimed in.

"This is Peter," Lazarus said, coming quickly to my rescue. "One of the first to follow Jesus."

I dipped my head, acknowledging my error and wishing myself anywhere but here. Peter stepped aside, revealing an average-looking man who was grinning widely at me. He stood but a handbreadth taller than I, with nothing imposing about him. Over half of the other men were taller and broader than he and commanded more attention, and yet something about *this* man had compelled them all to drop everything and follow him. I bowed low and tried to find words to rectify the situation.

"And on you, peace, Martha," he offered on the end of a chuckle, smoothing over the embarrassment, eradicating any need for an apology.

Lazarus gestured for the men to sit as a servant entered bearing a copper basin to wash their feet. I took the opportunity to slip away and check on the food. Already I was inclined to like the man who had so readily forgiven my blunder.

The evening meal was filled with laughter and conversation. I took the opportunity to observe each man as I served, noting how the one named John leaned intimately against Jesus' breast and how Peter was prone to dominate the conversation unless reined in by the others. In their own way, however, each man's attentions and affections were centered on Jesus, and it was clear how they deferred to him—even Peter, who fell deeply silent and observant whenever Jesus spoke, as if he couldn't bear the thought of missing even one word.

For his part, Jesus was nothing like I expected. Many rabbis lorded their esteemed position over those beneath them; this rabbi seemed content to exist with a warm comradery that neither elevated nor diminished him.

As I served him a dish of carrots seasoned with honey and cumin, he glanced at me with a warm expression and murmured his thanks. Not once, but every time he was served, he paused to offer gratitude. What rabbi noticed the hand that served him, elevating the lowest through special notice and appreciation?

In the back of the room, I watched with fascination as Jesus laughed at a story, his hand coming to rest on John's shoulder, his eyes bright with fun as he turned to gesticulate animatedly, adding to the story with fresh details. Had this voice cast out a demon? Would these hands soon heal a leper?

I wanted to see what my brother saw in this new rabbi, what Cleopas had also witnessed and affirmed. But my heart? My heart said there was risk in opening itself up to new things. It trembled now, scared to believe.

Twenty-Three

14 Ab
29 AD

Word spread like fire that a rabbi was in town who could heal the sick and lame. That morning, our home was swarmed with people waiting for a glimpse of Jesus, many bringing their sick loved ones with hope that he would heal them. I watched with fascination as the disciples formed a barrier of sorts that allowed Jesus to pass through the crowd.

"I cannot believe we are doing this." Mary shivered and stepped closer to my side as a crush of people moved around us. "It's unsafe."

"But don't you want to see? Aren't you curious?" I glanced behind me to ensure that Nenet was nearby. She was shouldering our day's provisions and keeping close on our heels.

"Certainly, but I'm not sure that I'm curious enough to actually seek out a leper community."

It was true, such a journey was unheard of. Before I could reply, a piercing wail silenced the jostling crowd. I recognized the voice instantly.

Up ahead, Gilah had managed to shoulder her way through

the crowd. She'd brought Tehilah with her, and with another shrill cry, she threw her daughter and then herself at Jesus' feet. "Rabbi, Master," she moaned, "our lives are in your hands. Heal my husband, I beg you."

Murmurs spread through the crowd. Could this be my Gilah? The proud woman who took my food basket one day and refused it the next? My gut twisted with compassion at Gilah's desperate plea. The flesh of her flesh was living out his decaying days without hope in the wilderness.

Thomas knelt and raised her gently from the ground as Jesus himself bent to speak into her ear. Who was this rabbi who stopped to listen so compassionately to the heart-cry of a woman?

"What is he saying to her? And where is Lemuel?" My sister fairly danced by my side.

"Do I look like I have answers?" I sighed. "I know nothing you don't know yourself."

Gilah disappeared into the crowd as more neighbors dropped their work to join us on the road leaving town. The leper community was miles away in the Judean wilderness, which meant we all had a long day ahead of us. We traveled north out of town, two miles down the road to Jericho, before cutting east. We were now off-road, and many turned back at this point, unwilling to journey farther.

"Shouldn't we return as well?" Mary's voice cracked with concern. "Or at least wait on the road for word?"

"We won't draw too close, Mary. But how else can we verify what happens unless we see it for ourselves?"

The air was dry, the heat excessive. I raised a leather pouch to my lips and let a stream of cool water glide into my mouth before handing the skin to Mary.

Lazarus appeared at our side and laid a protective hand on my arm. "We're close now. When we reach the crest of that hill, we'll stop and proceed no farther."

I nodded my approval as others stopped at the ridge as well. Mary, Lazarus, and I pushed our way to the front, watching with a mixture of horror and admiration as Jesus continued.

"Will you accompany him?" Lazarus turned to Thomas, who somberly shook his head.

"We have yet to witness this kind of healing. He's filled a boat with fish until it nearly sank, and with a single word healed a boy who wasn't even present, but this? It's something we've never seen before."

I swallowed anxiously. Even his disciples had yet to see this kind of miracle? What were we doing here? What had we come out into the wilderness to see?

With bated breath, we all watched as Jesus picked his way carefully down the rocky incline toward the valley below. Caves pocked the surrounding hillsides, and out of one such opening, a white figure appeared. Even from this distance, we could hear the wrenching cries of "Unclean! Unclean!" I heard the catch in Mary's breath as she snagged my hand.

Another figure appeared and then another, their whiteness marking them as the walking dead.

"Oh, I cannot stand it." Mary moaned and buried her face in my shoulder.

"They make me think of Ima—all wrapped in white." Lazarus spoke softly by my side, his voice rote and emotionless.

I glanced between my siblings, both frightened and moving closer to me, although neither would acknowledge it. Was I the only one left with her wits about her? As I often did when nervous, I laid a hand over my chest, capturing the feather pendant beneath my palm, drawing strength from this small gesture.

As Jesus continued to descend, the cries of "Unclean!" heightened in volume and pitch. No one had ever seen a person voluntarily walk into the camp of death. He stopped at the bottom and stood quietly, surveying the surrounding figures. The anxious mutterings of the watching crowd silenced as we all stood transfixed, waiting to see what Jesus would do next.

"Simon!" His voice was thunder. I drew a quick breath and held it. How had I ever thought him any less than commanding? This was a voice you obeyed unquestioningly.

"Simon bar Ezriel!"

At the second cry, one of the white figures detached from a group and slowly, painstakingly descended to meet Jesus in the valley. My whole body tensed as the figure approached Jesus, stopping short and falling to the ground.

Someone in the crowd let out a sharp cry and began sobbing. I glanced wildly around until my eyes found Gilah. She was kneeling, eyes trained on her husband below, tears streaming, body shuddering. Lemuel was by her side now, one arm around her and the other around Tehilah.

In the valley, it was apparent that Simon couldn't or wouldn't go any farther. We watched in disbelief as Jesus crossed the remaining distance. Horrified cries erupted from the crowd.

"He's already too close!"

"Surely he won't touch the man!"

Heart pounding, I watched as Jesus knelt in front of Simon, extended a hand, and touched him.

Startled screams rippled through the crowd, and even some of the disciples looked like they were going to be sick. Were we witnessing the grisly end of this kind man? A sob caught in my throat as I thought of this man dying a devastatingly slow death, turning white and deformed as his body decayed.

A moment later, however, our cries of despair turned into calls of astonishment as both Simon and Jesus stood. As quickly as he rose, Simon was soon back on his knees, his face pressed to Jesus' feet.

"What is he doing?"

"Is he healed?"

"They're coming! They're coming!"

Sure enough, both Simon and Jesus were now walking in our direction, back up the slope to the astonished crowd on the ridgeline. Jesus had a hand on Simon's shoulder, and Simon no longer appeared ghostly white. Behind them, a swarm of the diseased descended the slopes, crying out for mercy. My breathing quickened as two strong men walked upward toward life while death screamed at their heels.

"They'll contaminate us all! Run!"

"No, he's healed! Look!"

"But the others! Flee while you can!"

As the pair approached, many screamed with terror, convinced Simon was still unclean. Some scrambled back down the path toward the main road, yelling warnings all the way. Instinctively, I shied away, but I could not leave without seeing the truth with my own eyes.

When they were fewer than twenty cubits away, it was clear that Simon was indeed clean. Strips of bandages hung loosely on his arms, no longer needed. His face was vibrant, healthy. His hair was no longer white but its former dark brown. When he extended his arms to Gilah, they were strong, unwavering, and whole.

"Woman, I give to you your husband." Jesus' words were ripe with compassion and joy as he held out a hand to Gilah, inviting her forward. His voice, firm and confident, coupled with the sight of Simon, infused the crowd with belief and awe.

Gilah stumbled forward, one hesitant step at a time, gulping in air as she repeated "Thank you" over and over. When she was close enough, Simon grasped her arms. For a moment, they stared at each other in disbelief before Simon crushed her to his chest in an embrace.

Tears wet my cracked lips. I moistened them, tasting the sharp tang of salt, and watched as Jesus left the couple to return to those of us who remained. We parted silently to allow him through. Many reached out to touch him as he passed—desperate, hungry hands, longing for one touch, one taste of this man's power.

My body tensed as he drew near. This man . . . he'd been in my home. I'd fed him at my table and watched him interact like any other man with his friends. How could such power reside in him? A noise at my side momentarily drew my attention away from Jesus.

"Why not the others?" Mary sobbed, staring at the dozens who had stopped short on the hillside, unable to come closer—a forest of despairing white. From here we could see their twisted features and hear their pleas for help and calls to family members. "Why? When there are so many hurting souls? So many in need?"

The crowd was slowly, silently following Jesus back to the main road. Thomas, who was nearby, heard Mary's cry and stopped to look searchingly into her eyes, his own mirrors of wonder and pain.

"The true question," he said quietly, "is why the one?"

I gripped Mary's hand tightly and pondered those words in my heart. Why the one? God help us, why mercy at all?

Twenty-Four

15 Ab
29 AD

As abruptly as Jesus had arrived, he left, taking his disciples with him, leaving behind a wake of confusion, hope, and belief. Bethany would never be the same again, and neither would our family.

Simon was examined by the priest and officially declared clean. Joy fell over the village like the blessing of a long-anticipated rain, moistening dry and weary hearts, bringing life, promising harvest. Daily, the elders met in the synagogue, hearing eyewitness testimonies of Simon's miraculous healing and speculating on this Jesus and his claims.

I was shocked to hear that Lazarus had asked to accompany Jesus when he'd left. "You'd leave our home? You'd leave us?" I yelped in disbelief and hurt.

"To be this man's disciple . . . yes, I would!" Lazarus' eyes were bright.

"But he wouldn't accept you?" I asked slowly, watching as my brother's face crumpled.

"He said he had need of me here."

"As do we, your family. We need you here, not off wandering from place to place with this man."

"*This man* possesses the power to give life, to restore what is broken and beyond repair. I believe . . . sister, this must be the long-awaited Messiah!"

My breath caught at his bold words. "Does he claim to be?"

"He hasn't directly referred to himself as such, but many are claiming that he is, and he isn't denying it. He has, however, said he's the Bread of Life. Think of it—as Moses fed our ancestors the bread from heaven, this man comes claiming to be that bread."

"A gift from heaven? He claims to be sent from God?"

"A second exodus. We could be living in the time of our second exodus. Finally, free from our oppressors, led by the Messiah, who can snatch a man from the jaws of death."

My brother's words fed the fuel of my confusion. There could be no doubt that this man had power, but a man sent directly from God?

Silence—we'd lived with four hundred years of silence from God. What were the chances that this silence would be broken now, in my lifetime? Hadn't every Jew before me wished for the same? That, finally, in their generation, the silence would be broken? It was arrogance at the worst, or wishful thinking at the best, to throw one's hope behind any one man as the Messiah.

We attended a public meeting at the synagogue, and I listened as person after person affirmed what my brother was saying.

"This must be the Messiah!"

"How else do you explain his miracles?"

"He claimed as much to a Samaritan woman."

"Would the Messiah reveal himself first to the Samaritans?"

On and on the conversation swirled, and my mind along with it. Over half of Bethany agreed with Lazarus. Gilah, especially, was a transformed woman, and this alone gave me cause to seriously consider my brother's words.

I longed to extend the hand of friendship to her, but years of her refusal stayed the gesture. Instead, I watched her with eager, hopeful eyes, my heart thrilling when one day she returned the look and I saw, once again, a glimpse of my old friend.

The change in both Gilah and Simon was immediate. Once a proud and aloof man, Simon cried unashamed tears of gratitude before the elders, recounting how his whole body was flooded with strength at Jesus' touch.

We listened raptly to his words, hungry to experience in our own flesh what he had—the moment of complete healing and well-being.

There was one, however, who remained untouched by Simon's story and all the whirling speculation. My sister regarded Simon warily, shrinking back whenever he looked our way.

One evening, as I ascended the stairs to my bedchamber for the night, I found Mary standing in her room with her back to the door, staring wordlessly out her latticed window into the night sky. Compassion stirred in my breast as I entered quietly, observing her for a moment before crossing the room and laying a warm hand on her back.

She jumped as if I'd struck her, turning around and staring at me with wide, fearful eyes.

"What worries you, sister? Won't you tell me? You've been quiet and withdrawn ever since the healing."

Mary's face battled with emotion as she decided whether to remain silent or speak. Finally, she crossed the room and closed the door, turning to me with desperation. "I cannot stand the sight of him," she groaned.

"Simon?" I prompted gently.

"I cannot bear to be near the man. He loathes me. He is a snake, a wolf in sheep's clothing."

"Mary!" I gaped, astonished at her harsh words. "Watch what you say."

"He's never liked me, never approved of my friendship with his son."

The truth in Mary's words gave me pause. "Be that as it may, I still don't understand why you're so agitated." I tried to smooth over Mary's ruffled feelings.

"Because it was me." She let out the words in a rush of air, as if she'd been holding on to them for a long time. "Because it was me," she said more calmly, sinking to her bed in defeat. "I was the one who discovered and reported his leprosy, and he will never forget it."

The air grew still in the room as her words sank in. Mary dropped her face into her hands and moaned, "Yahweh forgive me, I was thankful the day he was driven from Bethany."

My stomach churned at her words, my mind hardly grasping what she was saying. "I don't understand. How were *you* the one to discover his leprosy?"

"He'd pulled me aside privately to speak to me about . . . my relationship with Lemuel."

"What relationship? You haven't interacted since childhood."

Mary was silent, and it took me a moment to deduce her meaning. As I did and realization dawned slowly across my face, Mary sighed, shoulders drooping.

"You kept seeing him," I murmured. "Secretly?"

Mary nodded. "Not so much as children, but . . . later we met."

"Why would Simon be angry?"

Again, the unnerving stillness, the hooded looks, the heavy silence full of hidden meaning. I scrambled to fill in the gaps on my own.

"Unless you were meeting as . . . more than friends?"

Mary groaned and turned her face to the wall.

"Is there no man in Bethany that you haven't fornicated with!" I shocked myself by my own outburst but couldn't stop the stream of words. "God help us, Mary. When did you become a loose woman? It pains me, sister! I cannot abide it." Tears pricked my eyes. Sweet, impressionable Lemuel. No wonder he looked at Mary with longing.

"How dare you jump to the conclusion that anything immoral passed between us." Mary stood with hands defiantly on her hips.

"Like nothing immoral happened with Aharon?"

For a moment, Mary's hard gaze faltered. "I cannot deny that there are things I'm ashamed of."

It was the first time I'd heard her admit guilt.

"But that's not what this was," she continued. "Lemuel . . . he was my first love . . . we always . . . we are . . ."

"You are *children*." I gritted my teeth. "Perhaps Simon was right after all. Perhaps you *were* a bad influence on Lemuel."

"Don't say that!" Mary shrieked. "It's not true."

"Are you still seeing him?"

Mary was sobbing now, tears of anger and desperation. "I never see him anymore, thanks to Simon. He found me with Lemuel and threw me out. And then he followed and threatened me. He said if he ever found me near his son again, he'd make my life miserable. He was cruel and belittling, and it was horrible. I can never forget it. He called me names I still hear in my dreams and gripped me so hard I bruised. . . ."

"He should not have put his hands upon you," I conceded. "Or called you names. But I can understand his desperation if you were blatantly disregarding his wishes." I tried to restrain my anger, but it wriggled from my grasp and leapt into my tone.

"You haven't listened to a thing I've said," Mary lamented. "If you had, you wouldn't be taking his side in this."

"I'm not taking sides."

"But you are! You're making excuses for Simon's poor behavior while extending no understanding to me." Mary had stopped crying and was now looking at me with a dazed expression, her voice dull, lifeless. "Somehow, I didn't expect that. I should have known better than to confide in you. You only see what you want to see in me. Somehow, I am always wrong. Always wrong." Her voice trailed off, and she turned her hollow gaze away from me.

Her tone more than her words unsettled me. Only later, when I'd poured out my tears to Yahweh in the privacy of my own room, did I begin to think a bit clearer.

It appeared that Mary was nursing a broken heart over Lemuel. Was that why she'd so ardently rejected all mention of marriage over the years? Had Simon indeed been inexcusably cruel to her? In discovering his leprosy, did Mary somehow blame herself for the downfall of Lemuel's family?

And the most probing question of all: Was she right? Did I blindly assume the worst when it came to my sister?

Twenty-Five

10 Elul
29 AD

Worry buzzed in my mind, threatening damage like locusts before the harvest. After my conversation with Mary, I couldn't sleep, could barely eat. I had been shouldering Mary's care for so long, and I was weary of heart. *What would Ima do?* It was the question I constantly asked myself. It was the question that had no answer.

Rarely did I come to Lazarus about Mary. With the care of the estate on his young shoulders, my brother had plenty to occupy his mind and hands. At least this is what I told myself. A closer truth was that I didn't quite trust him with our sister. Lazarus was full of vision and ideals, his heart always yearning for the best in himself and others. His loving nature endeared him to everyone, but it also meant he was less useful when it came to hard matters.

With Mary's revelation about her past with Simon and Lemuel, however, an urgency entered my body and would not leave. Which is why, on a dry day toward the end of summer, I sought my brother's counsel concerning Mary for the first time in years.

He was in his study, shuffling rolls of parchment in a distracted manner as if preparing to leave.

"Do you have a moment?" I rested a hand on the doorframe and tried to relax my face and keep the harsh bite of worry out of my tone.

"Not really." Lazarus shot me a glance and then paused. Apparently, I had not successfully adjusted my features, for his brow furrowed. "But I can tell something bothers you." He shoved aside the parchment and waved a hand of admission.

Swallowing hard, I closed the door and shuffled nervously to his desk.

"What troubles you, sister?"

With that soft question, the floodwaters of worry overflowed, my tongue loosening in a stream of words. "It's Mary. Oh, brother, I'm so concerned for her. Surely you have noticed how quiet and withdrawn she has been. We exchanged harsh words that unsettle me. She . . . she is scared . . . scared of Simon, and I don't know how to advise her."

Lazarus leaned back in his seat, raising his eyebrows along with a hand, trying to slow the torrent of words coming from my mouth. "Wait. Mary fears Simon?"

How far should I go? I didn't want to taint my sister in the eyes of our dear brother. They adored each other, and I couldn't bear to interfere, to see the look of disappointment on Lazarus' face. Mary would never forgive me if she discovered I'd spoken to him, but I needed his help.

"She is . . . missing her friendship with Lemuel."

Lazarus shook his head, confused. "They were friends as children."

"Yes, and it's a friendship that Simon has long discouraged."

"I didn't realize that." Lazarus worried his lower lip, then suddenly narrowed his eyes. "Are Mary and Lemuel involved in a romantic way?"

"No!" The untruthful answer burst from my lips before I could make a conscious decision as to how to reply. "I mean . . . I don't believe so," I tempered my answer, praying for forgiveness as I let the half-truth hang awkwardly between us.

"I'm not sure what you're trying to communicate, sister." A tinge of impatience laced my brother's words. "Mary missing a childhood friendship is hardly a concern that needs my attention. This will pass."

Heat leapt to my face as I pushed back my irritation. I'd bumbled this conversation. "I will make myself clearer, then. Mary mourns her childhood friendship, yes, but it's her fear of Simon that is the most worrisome."

Now I had his attention.

"Simon has long discouraged Mary's friendship with Lemuel, which in turn has caused Mary to become fearful of the man."

"Why should she be fearful?" Lazarus snorted. "Why would Simon's opinion of her as a young child hold any weight now?"

"Because he holds ill regard for her still!" I blurted out, eager for my brother to understand enough . . . but not too much.

For the first time, true concern laced Lazarus' features. "I don't like the thought that someone thinks poorly of our sweet Mary."

I inwardly cast my eyes to heaven. *Sweet* Mary.

"You know Simon," I continued. "He likes control. Once he has decided a matter, he rarely changes his mind. Not too long ago, he . . . discouraged Mary's friendship with Lemuel directly to her face."

"Mary needs to let it go." The concern drained away as Lazarus stood and began shuffling the rolls of parchment once more. "If she respects Simon's wishes and stops pursuing the friendship, then I'm sure his good opinion of her will return. Besides, she isn't a child anymore. She shouldn't be seeking out the friendship of a man anyway."

I was losing the conversation, and with it any hope of help. "She discovered his leprosy," I whispered.

Lazarus paused and looked at me closely. "What?"

"In their confrontation over Lemuel, Mary noticed the leprosy and reported it. You can see now why she might be so fearful of the man."

Lazarus kneaded his brow with a groan. "Oh dear," he sighed and sat down again . . . hard. "She had no choice but to report him. Any of us would have done the same before the sickness spread and even more lives were ruined. She shouldn't blame herself for what followed. If she had not discovered it, then someone else would have. It was only a matter of time."

"Yes, of course *we* know that, but put yourself in her place." I grimaced, imagining the emotional toll on Mary as she reported Lemuel's father.

"What I don't understand is why she kept it from us." Lazarus gazed up at me with a mixture of confusion and irritation.

I didn't have the heart to tell him that Mary kept much more from him than he could imagine.

"You should reassure her. Tell her that there is no lingering bitterness on Simon's part." Lazarus shoved some rolls of parchment into a leather satchel. "If he had any true concerns, Simon would speak to me directly as the head of the household. I've spent many hours in his company since the healing, and I sense only gratitude from the man. I doubt that he holds a grudge against Mary. It's unfortunate that she found herself in the position she did, but there's no reason for her to fear Simon now." Lazarus rose to his feet, the conversation clearly over.

The abrupt outcome was partially my fault. In trying to protect Mary's image with our brother, I had failed to solicit his help. But it was also true that Lazarus clearly did not want to be involved and was leaving the pesky details to me. I moved to the door, heart beating hard, then spun to face this dear, infuriating man. "You don't need to try so hard. You try too hard not to be like Abba."

Lazarus froze. "What did you say?" His gaze refused to meet mine.

"You don't want to find fault in others the way he always did." I tried to soften the blow of my words. "And that's admirable, to a point. But you can't let fear of him control you still!"

"Who says it controls me?" Lazarus slammed the satchel down onto the table, his demeanor thunderous. "I am my own man, Martha. My own man!"

"Yes, I know you are," I stammered, surprised at the uncharacteristic outburst. "You have always been your own man, but I suspect at times that you overcorrect. I'm afraid that in trying to not find fault, you are blinded."

"You cross a line." Lazarus' voice had transitioned from thunderous to defeated.

"But can't you see what I'm saying?" Frustration over my brother had compelled me at first, but now, seeing the haunted look in his eye, love begged me to continue. "Oh, dear brother, he has been gone these past five years, and you barely even mention Abba's name."

"I don't hear his name cross your lips either." Lazarus' eyes shone with unshed tears. I longed to hold him as if he were a small boy and not a strapping man heads taller than I, but I kept my distance to preserve his dignity.

"Abba found faults where there were none. You experienced that more than most." Love for my brother poured from my eyes, and I hoped he could see it and receive my words in the spirit they were intended. "Finding endless fault and dealing with true conflict are two separate things. Don't let fear over his tendencies direct your life."

Lazarus covered his face with a hand.

Tears pooled in my eyes. "You want to simply be Mary's brother." I spoke the words softly, squeezing them out past the lump in my throat. "But sometimes she needs more. Fair or not, like it or not, sometimes she needs more from us."

Twenty-Six

15 Elul
29 AD

Lazarus and I rarely exchanged heated words, so after our argument over Mary, we were skittish around each other. Then, one day, he snuck up from behind and snaked his arms around me, anchoring me to his chest. I leaned back, letting my eyes close with a deep sigh. Ever a man of words, Lazarus now had none. I could tell after his embrace, however, that he had taken my words to heart, for he watched Mary with new thoughtfulness.

After such an event as Simon's healing, Cleopas should have been a constant visitor, since there was nothing he loved more than discussion with Lazarus. But it wasn't until weeks later that he finally arrived.

Cleopas was kind toward me but still without the ease we'd enjoyed growing up. Neither of us had broached the topic of our near-betrothal, which somehow made the relationship harder to untangle. He'd remained unmarried, a fact that made me jittery around him, an enigma I couldn't puzzle out.

Aviva had married a wealthy landowner from the southern town of Ein Gedi, a prosperous and bustling city along the coast of the Dead Sea. I rarely saw her, as she usually came to Jerusalem only for the major festivals, but on one such occasion, I'd summoned the courage to ask her why Cleopas had never married. She'd shrugged and claimed he was married to his work. The answer, however, didn't rest easy with me.

Should I be open and friendly with Cleopas or more reserved? Would he misinterpret my friendliness? Would he be hurt by my avoidance? Undecided, I alternated between the two, and, after each encounter with this inscrutable man, put myself through exhausting questioning. For his part, Cleopas remained unruffled by our interactions, which only flustered me more.

So it was that I anticipated seeing Cleopas with nervous energy. When he arrived, however, Lazarus sequestered them in his study, and I saw no more of them, catching instead the occasional burst of animated conversation from behind closed doors.

I hovered like a mother bird near her young, fiddling with tasks that didn't need doing, eventually ending up in my prized kitchen garden, hands in the earth. When the men finally left the study, they stood opposite my sunny garden. I lurched abruptly to my feet and called out a greeting. "Peace to you, Cleopas."

"And to you, Martha."

"What weighty things are you and my brother discussing this time?"

"More news about Jesus," Lazarus interjected.

Cleopas placed a large hand on my brother's shoulder, as if harnessing his enthusiasm. "Your Jesus is quite notorious. Caiaphas speaks poorly of him in the Sanhedrin."

The high priest's skepticism bode ill for Jesus. With such ominous news, my earlier nervousness flew from my mind. "Why take a stance against him?" I wondered aloud as I brushed the dirt from my hands and joined the men.

"Because his claims exceed what I originally thought." Lazarus was beaming with boyish excitement.

"He claims God as Father," Cleopas confirmed. "I heard as

much directly from his lips. To justify his work on the Sabbath, he said that his Father is always working and therefore he must do so as well."

My eyes widened at the implication behind the words. "He would make himself equal to God? And to work on the Sabbath . . . Would he place himself above the Law?"

"Not above," Cleopas mused. "But the fulfillment of the Law, yes."

"What's more," Lazarus crowed, "he claims that those who listen to his message and believe will come into eternal life. After witnessing his power, I believe it! Simon was as good as dead, and he returned him to life. Is there nothing he cannot do?"

The trembling I experienced out in the wilderness as we witnessed Simon's restoration returned as a flicker of belief. "Where is he now? If he's ignited the attention and anger of the Sanhedrin, Judea is not a safe place for him."

"He's returning to Galilee," Cleopas confirmed.

An argument arose that hadn't occurred to me before. "He's from Nazareth, correct? The Messiah won't come from Galilee."

"That's what others argue as well, but he wasn't born in Nazareth." Cleopas, who was generally a more reserved man than my brother, began beaming, his expression matching Lazarus'. "He was born in Bethlehem." He drew out his answer, enjoying its effect.

My mind and breath caught with the new information. Bethlehem—the House of Bread, the House of David. The man who claimed to be the Bread of Life coming from the House of Bread, as prophesied by Micah. Could it be that a man had arisen from the line of David to claim the throne? Dare I hope that such things could happen during my lifetime?

"I'm returning with Cleopas tomorrow to hear for myself what they say about him." Lazarus' joyful demeanor sobered. "I want to know what our religious leaders think of the Messiah."

"Be careful, brother." Lazarus' exuberance could land him in trouble. "If he is returning to Galilee, perhaps he could stop by our home one more time."

Lazarus' face lit up at the suggestion as my mind busied itself, pondering and wondering.

Had I invited the true Messiah back into our home?

The time spent in the charged atmosphere of Jerusalem had taken a toll on some of Jesus' disciples. I noticed it in the creases around their eyes. They had seen wonders, and with that sight had come public scrutiny they were not expecting.

I served a simple but hearty fare: a steaming pot of lentil stew, warm rounds of bread, juicy figs, and boiled pears for dessert. Remembering how Jesus had liked the spice, I added extra cumin to the lentils and watched with satisfaction as he dipped his bread heartily into the stew and closed his eyes briefly with appreciation upon taking a bite.

From all accounts, members of the Sanhedrin were conflicted. It was curious to me how a man who did so much good could stir up so much trouble.

"He doesn't speak like other teachers," Lazarus had confided. "Instead of quoting other rabbis, Jesus references God Himself, as if there's no other authority between him and God. This, among other things, troubles our leaders."

I understood how emotional tension could create physical weariness and was glad I'd opened our home again, affording these men a comfortable night before the long road ahead to Galilee. Providing food and lodging was the least I could do, after all, for the man who had transformed Gilah's life.

Having heard Jesus was in town one more night before departing the region, Gilah and Simon had joined us at the table, Gilah quietly helping as I served the men. We exchanged few words.

I could sense her eyes turning to me often, but each time I tried to meet her gaze, she looked away quickly. That she would come under our roof was enough cause for hope. Had Jesus healed more than Simon's physical body? Had his touch also mended a hurting family?

Later in the evening, long after appetites were sated and the dishes were cleared, Jesus and his disciples reposed in the inner courtyard around a fire before retiring to the upper room we had prepared for them. Half of Bethany had shown up at our door as news of Jesus' presence spread. We let in as many as could fit into the courtyard, with more spilling out into the street.

Even with the press of people surrounding him, Jesus' eyes flicked to the covered colonnade surrounding the courtyard, and I followed his gaze to where small shadows scurried back behind a pillar. Jesus' expression lit up as he turned toward the scampering shadows and opened his arms in welcome. He gestured for the shadows to come, and to my surprise they did—two small, curious children emerged from their hiding place.

"Mordecai's children," Lazarus explained. "Our porter."

"And what are your names?" I heard Jesus ask as he welcomed the children close to the fire.

"Daniel, and this is Levi," the eldest replied.

"Strong names for two strong boys." Jesus smiled and withdrew a small piece of wood from the scrip attached to his girdle. "Do you have a favorite animal, Levi?" He turned to the youngest, who had yet to speak and was currently sucking on two fingers, observing Jesus with hooded eyes.

Upon being directly addressed, Levi froze before finally shrugging his shoulders.

Jesus narrowed his eyes at him as if deep in thought and then turned to the piece of wood, dancing it between his fingers as he withdrew a small knife and began shaving off slices of wood with short, firm strokes. As he worked, both boys leaned in closely, and I found myself doing the same, easing myself from the outskirts, drawn forward with a lump in my throat and a dawning realization that clawed at my chest.

"He's a former carpenter by trade," Philip, one of Jesus' disciples, interjected, noticing my deep concentration.

A carpenter. I'd stuffed my suspicions over this Jesus of Nazareth securely out of sight, but now they sprang outward, shattering the box where I'd hidden them. It couldn't be . . . but it *was*.

All around him, our visitors talked, largely ignoring the two young boys and the quick, harsh scrapes of the blade as Jesus turned the wood over and over in his calloused hands. Finally, he sat upright with a pleased expression and held the piece of wood to the light, angling it in his inspection, the firelight throwing shadows over carved fins and a wide, gaping mouth.

"A fish for the boy who longs for the sea." Jesus admired his work for a moment before turning, tousling Levi's hair, and nestling the figure into the center of his palm. "Share with your brother, young man."

"Yes, Rabbi, I will. Thank you."

As the boys ran off, Jesus turned his attention once again to the fire and the surrounding conversation, but I couldn't tear my eyes away from what I'd witnessed.

It was improbable, impossible even, but my heart throbbed with a new understanding that would not be denied.

As the flames continued to flicker, throwing light and shadows onto our visitors' faces, I—who was too far away to feel the heat—sensed it nonetheless. Burning like a branding iron against my skin, the feather pendant raged hot. I wanted to tear it from my flesh and throw it at Jesus' feet. I wanted to scream away the hot tears burning behind my eyes and demand that this man answer me.

I knew him.

More truthfully, I knew *of* him. How had he come to be here in my home? How had a lowly carpenter risen to such prominence? What did it all mean?

I stood, clutched by fear and desire, not knowing whether I wanted to cast myself at Jesus' feet or bid him never to come near me again. My seething emotions pushed me backward until I stood silently by a pillar, one hand on the cool stone, the other over my racing heart. Abruptly, I sensed his attention, even though he hadn't looked my way once. Could he detect my new understanding? Did he know me the way I knew him? Or *did* I know him?

The carpenter Joseph and his son Jesus had become a fable to me, a story by which I had come to understand my life. But what did I know of anything? I inhaled sharply, closing my eyes, transported to that moment when Uri had told me his story, sharing what Jesus had done for him. So many years had passed, and what did I really know?

I knew this man was kind and compassionate, filled with warmth and light, and yet he was unsettling. Sitting silently, he was an ember softly burning. But when he talked, he was a slowly building fire, until you realized he was pulling you closer, warming you with his very words.

Could one be burned, I wondered, by drawing too close?

Twenty-Seven

29 Elul
29 AD

Mary continued to keep her own counsel. Even though it was the heat of summer, she spent long hours outdoors, returning slick with sweat, eyes hooded beneath her veil, an animal or plant in her hands. She was finding solace in her typical way, out in God's creation.

I did not begrudge Mary's methods, but the longer her silence stretched, the more worry gnawed at me. I needed to break the tension between us, but a mixture of fear and pride restrained me. Fear that I would learn new things about Mary that I didn't want to know. Pride over the surety that I was in the right. And hovering over it all, a thick layer of guilt that weighed my every step.

To distract myself, I mulled over Jesus of Nazareth with a fervency that matched Lazarus', latching on to every story that passed through our gates. Even though we were far removed from Jesus' current ministry in Galilee, news of him swept over the whole nation as he performed such miraculous wonders that they could not be contained by geography. With each new report, my excitement grew, as did the undercurrent of hurt and confusion.

My hand sought my necklace so often in those days that Lazarus took note of it. "Do you wear something beneath your tunic, sister?" I brushed his question aside and for a moment considered taking the necklace off. I hadn't removed it for eleven years. Day and night for eleven years, it had graced my neck in secret. No, I would not remove it now. But I schooled myself to stop seeking it out, no matter how much my hands itched to hold it.

Mary excluded herself from our conversations, but one day I overheard her confiding in Lazarus. "I don't understand why Jesus would choose to heal someone like Simon and yet overlook so many others. It makes no sense."

I stood silently in the shadows, brow furrowing at the pain evident in her voice.

"If he's the Messiah—the Son of God, even, as he now claims—then surely he knows what kind of man Simon is."

Lazarus took a deep breath, his large hand cupping her shoulder as he replied. "Everything about him is unexpected, Mary. He's changing how people think."

Mary's agitated form stilled beneath our brother's touch. "Why would he choose the unworthy out of all those in need?" Her voice was small now, her eyes pleading with Lazarus to help make sense of it all.

"I don't know why he chooses to do what he does." Lazarus' arm had come to rest across Mary's shoulders as he drew her close to his side. "There's truth in his words, though, that it's the sick who most need a physician. He comes to the sinners, and I find it interesting that the righteous do not like it."

Mary's face grew conflicted as Lazarus turned her to face him. A lump formed in my throat as he engaged with Mary's distress rather than turning away.

"Sweet sister, I know some of what burdens you, the deep fear of Simon you harbor."

"How . . . ?"

"Martha confided in me."

"Of course!" Mary spat the words out, and I cringed at the hardness in her tone. "I should never have told her."

"No!" Lazarus grasped both her shoulders tightly. "If you could see how much our sister loves you! How much she has sacrificed for you. It was love that compelled her to share with me."

Mary was weeping silent tears.

"I've been reminded that sometimes in an effort not to find fault, I can overlook hard truths." Lazarus sighed and bowed his head. "You're right, Mary. Simon has a hard streak that I've noticed throughout the years."

Mary whipped her head up at his words. I covered my mouth to smother the sound of my own disbelief.

"I do not like to see the worst in people," Lazarus continued.

"That's not a bad trait," Mary assured him.

"But sometimes it is an excuse." Lazarus dropped a hand from Mary's shoulder and ran it over his face wearily. "Loss can lead to bitterness. Knowledge can lead to pride. Both the hard and good things in our lives can take root in ways that produce death."

He paused thoughtfully. "This is why the greatest commandment in Scripture is to love Adonai with all our heart, with all our soul, with all our might. In loving Him with our whole being, our hearts will be fertile ground, ready to receive all that Yahweh ordains for us. So that when the hard and the good come into our lives, they land in soil that will produce fruit."

Mary leaned her head on our brother's chest as she soaked in his words. The image struck me sharply of Uri holding a newborn lamb.

"When bitterness chokes the life out of a man, he comes to love his hurt more than Adonai. And when knowledge becomes its own reward, a man comes to love his mind more than Adonai. I have seen both things happen, and the death they produce." Lazarus rested a hand on the back of Mary's head, pressing her close.

"We turn our love to Adonai, and we leave our love fixed there. We have no need to fear the man who refuses to do the same. Instead, we entrust him to Adonai."

I closed my eyes and breathed deeply through the ache in my chest. Was I holding on to my hurt the way Lazarus described? I might be, but I feared the introspection that would uncover the truth.

"Jesus is coming to plow hard hearts, Mary. He is coming to shake people from their slumber. We cannot begrudge his hand of mercy to those who need it most."

It would certainly be like Uri's Jesus to reach out to the lowest, those outcast by society. Uri had wrestled with the deep shame of his heritage, but I had loved him despite it all. Jesus, too, seemed to love those who needed it the most.

Months passed, and in many ways our lives returned to normal, but our hearts, like Lazarus had said, had been plowed, and there was no going back. Slowly, and with few words, Mary and I made amends, although there was still a tender spot between us that needed tending.

Gilah and I were speaking, but not with our former closeness. Soon after the Festival of Weeks, she announced her pregnancy, and the whole town responded with excitement. The baby was called a miracle child, sired by a father who was brought back from the edge of death. Gilah was showered with attention, but my heart was conflicted. There was a time when Gilah would have shared such news with me first and privately, but I had found out from Tikvah, who by now was married with three children of her own.

"Can you believe it?" Tikvah exclaimed. "Gilah isn't exactly young anymore." She let out a barking laugh. "This child is a miracle in many ways!"

I barely managed a pinched smile in response as my mind traveled back over the years. Every time Gilah had become a mother, she'd moved a bit further away from me. Would this new child sever the burgeoning relationship between us?

As the summer heat blazed its trail across the Judean plains, I tried and failed to resist the searing thoughts that forged a path across my mind. I was a bundle of nerves and sorrow, pain and hope. There was something keeping me from joy, but I could not yet name it. I could, however, trace the beginnings of my rumbling discomfort.

Jesus had arrived on the scene and pried open a part of me that had long been hidden. No matter how I squirmed, I could not remain as I had always been. Jesus' presence demanded change, but my harried heart did not know how to respond.

Twenty-Eight

26 Tammuz
30 AD

Jerusalem was swollen with discontent. Almost a year had passed since we'd seen Jesus. As his ministry continued to expand in and around Galilee, those of us near the Holy City experienced the aftershock like the sharp joy and pain of childbirth. Even as the ripple effect of wonder and excitement reached us, so too did the deep displeasure of the religious leaders, who met daily to debate every word, action, and claim of the carpenter rabbi.

"They seek his life," Cleopas told us. "I don't think they'll dare do anything in public, though, as his popularity with the people is growing."

"Will we see him again?" I wondered aloud. "If his life is in danger, then he will need to stay far away from Jerusalem."

What if I *never* saw him again? The thought was unbearable. I hungered for Jesus' presence and yet also dreaded it, for in his presence I felt uncannily seen. If I had learned anything over the past year, it was that my heart was a twisted cavern in which I became easily disoriented. Did I want this man seeing into that darkness?

As the first grapes were ripening, with the heat of summer not far behind, Lazarus told us that despite the growing animosity among the religious rulers, Jesus was on his way back to Jerusalem. At the mention of Jesus' imminent arrival, my conflicted heart leapt with a decisiveness that surprised me. "Invite him here, brother." I could not bear the thought of not seeing this man who had figured so prominently in Uri's past, the man with the power of God behind his every move.

As Lazarus traveled to Jerusalem, I made the house ready for Jesus' arrival. The last time I'd seen him, my preparations had been rushed, but now, with proper notice, I would make sure that Jesus and his disciples benefited from my best hospitality and lacked for nothing. The nomad life of traveling from town to town with never a place to call one's own was taxing. As he had once sheltered Uri, I would now shelter him. The thought filled me with more joy and aching pain than I could manage.

A barrier kept me from my brother's certainty and settled joy. Mary had wondered, *Why Simon?* I wondered, *Why not Uri?* Why had I been left arms empty, bereft of the future I thought I'd enjoy?

The words of the psalmist rang loudly, words Jesus had repeated to Uri: "He will cover you with His feathers, and under His wings you will find refuge. His faithfulness is body armor and shield."

If Jesus was the Messiah, why had he given false promises to Uri? He'd given Uri a feather, promising protection, and yet the one he called Father had not protected Uri when it mattered most. How could I trust a Messiah whose actions seemed capricious?

And yet I longed to trust him. The desire to care for his needs as he'd done for Uri was overwhelming. I hated to think of him pouring out for others with no one to pour into him. It reminded me of Uri, alone in the wilderness, guarding and guiding day and night.

Lazarus sent word to expect Jesus the following day, which gave us plenty of time to prepare. The whole house was busy, and yet I could not find Mary. She remained elusive all throughout the evening, and while I would typically stop my work to track her down, I couldn't spare the time and was frustrated that she was pulling this stunt on such a special occasion.

The following morning, I instructed the servants to slaughter and roast a choice lamb and sent Nenet to find Mary while I started on the other dishes. When Nenet returned an hour later saying she had not located my sister, I threw up my hands and put Nenet to work. Mary and her problems would have to wait.

Jesus arrived earlier than expected, beating the heat of the day. He brought with him not only his twelve disciples but also a handful of followers from Jerusalem, including Elchanan, a Sadducee who was a member of the Sanhedrin and whom I recognized as someone Lazarus had spoken with on numerous occasions.

Our courtyard filled quickly with dusty, hot travelers. They were weary, both physically and in spirit. The toll of their journey was evident on their faces, but behind the exhaustion throbbed an intensity of purpose. I listened to snippets of their conversation, shocked to hear that not only Jesus but also his disciples had driven out demons. Both brash Peter and demure John had performed miracles in the name of Jesus. Even this man's *name* was enough to perform the impossible?

I shook as I stood before him, this man who looked entirely normal but who was slowly turning the world upside down. The necklace against my heart insisted I demand answers from this man, but the small flame of faith in my breast whispered to wait.

"Your hospitality is most welcome, Martha." He gazed at me kindly and pronounced a blessing over me and my home.

The men rested in an upstairs room, sheltered from the heat

before the evening meal. I served drinks and finger foods while they reclined, staying close to attend to their needs while also keeping an eye on the kitchen activities.

"Tell again how you answered that lawyer who tried to test you, Rabbi," Elchanan spoke. "Not everyone here heard it. You should have seen the Master." He turned to elbow Lazarus. "The lawyer wanted to know how to inherit eternal life but wasn't satisfied with the Law of Moses. He wanted clarification on who his neighbor was."

I didn't appreciate the goading tone of Elchanan's voice, as if he was also attempting to test Jesus through having him repeat himself.

"A man was going down from Jerusalem to Jericho, and he fell among robbers, who stripped him and beat him and departed, leaving him half-dead."

My body stilled and grew attentive, for I was well acquainted with the road to Jericho.

"Now by chance a priest was going down that road, and when he saw him, he passed by on the other side. So likewise, a Levite, when he came to the place and saw him, passed by on the other side."

I was holding a nearly empty platter of walnuts, which I now fumbled. No one appeared to notice as I clawed at the nuts. Several escaped me and tumbled to the ground. Embarrassed, I knelt to retrieve them, my face flaming with heat. This story—I knew this story!

"But a Samaritan, as he journeyed, came to where he was, and when he saw him, he had compassion. He went to him and bound up his wounds, pouring on oil and wine. Then he set him on his own animal and brought him to an inn and took care of him."

Help from a Samaritan? This was an unusual turn of the plot.

"Which of these three proved to be the man's neighbor? The

Samaritan!" Elchanan interjected the question and provided the answer all in one breath, stealing the climax of the story.

There were appreciative and surprised murmurs throughout the group as some, hearing it for the first time, tried to process the meaning.

My face flushed hot and then cold. Having rescued all the walnuts, I was still crouched near the door, unable to move.

And then I sensed his eyes on me.

Slowly, I looked to Jesus, meeting and holding his piercing gaze. As the others chatted among themselves, picking apart their interpretations of the story, Jesus sat silently, with his eyes resting upon me. Even as some began asking him questions, he did not break his gaze. So pronounced was his focus that others began looking to me as well. I hardly noticed the handful of curious faces that swiveled in my direction, so captured was I by Jesus' eyes.

Apart from my own brother, I had not looked a man full in the face this intimately and for this long since I had last gazed into Uri's dear face. Could Jesus see that I had made the connection between his story and the real-life events he had lived as a youth on a road leading from Sepphoris? Did he know why I'd been withholding my belief from him, and did he judge me for it?

Behind his gaze, I sensed an invitation.

I was the first to break eye contact, nearly casting all the walnuts back onto the floor as I scrambled to my feet and out the door. Heart racing, I retreated down the stairs, only breathing easily once I entered the kitchen. An enticing array of smells and sounds greeted me, a familiar and welcome distraction from my storming emotions.

When it was time to call the men to supper, I sent Nenet, choosing to remain among my spices, jars, and simmering sauces. I couldn't bear to re-enter Jesus' presence and so hovered outside the dining hall door instead. I spent most of the meal this way until embarrassment over my avoidance consumed me.

It was shameful to hide my face from our guests, especially when we had one of such distinction beneath our roof. No matter that his gaze pierced through to the inner spirit. Especially after his story of the Samaritan, in which he'd so clearly extolled the value of loving service, would I then deny him my own personal care out of fear and pride that he would see and discern too much in me?

Intercepting a servant in the hall, I took the basin and pitcher of water from her. The washing of the hands after the meal was usually performed by a servant, not the lady of the house. What better way to show my desire to serve Jesus than to personally attend to him in this way?

I entered the room quietly and stood still for a moment, allowing my vision to adjust to the dim interior. My eyes sought out Jesus so I might serve him first. He was seated, as expected, at the right side of Lazarus, in the place of honor. Sitting upright, he towered over the others, who were still reclining at the table. They listened with rapt attention as he taught. As I rounded the table, I tried to pick up on the threads of his teaching but stopped abruptly as I saw who sat at his feet.

Mary.

She was here. All day yesterday and today I could not find her and now to see her *here*? Yes, she was brazen, but to sit at Jesus' feet in the position of disciple, a role reserved for men, extended beyond anything I thought her capable of.

Mary's expression was transfixed as she stared into Jesus' face, hanging on his every word. Rage boiled in me at not only the impropriety of her position but also the desire expressed in her actions. She who had largely avoided conversations about this man over the past year was now acting like one of his disciples.

I had spent countless hours contemplating Jesus, going over and over his claims, trying desperately to reconcile the Jesus from the past with the Jesus before me. I had also singlehandedly served him today. And what had she done? Avoided me, avoided service, avoided talk of Jesus, only to now swoop in and assume the position of worshipful supplicant?

Perhaps what stung the most was the fact that to reach Jesus, she must have snuck past the kitchen, knowing I was there and that she should be there as well, and yet ignoring it all out of her own selfish desire.

My earlier resolve to humbly serve Jesus no matter the personal cost shattered at the sight of my sister. I stood suspended over a void, the only sign of my turmoil the slight tremor on the surface of the water in my hands. Willing my body forward, I quietly approached Jesus and stooped to offer the pitcher. He kept talking as he lifted his hands over the bowl, and I dutifully poured water over them and into the basin. Out of the corner of my eye, I saw his face turn to me as he dried his hands on the cloth flung over my shoulder, but I steadfastly looked at the grain of the table, willing the whole process to end.

When he was finished, I moved to Lazarus, and then to Thomas, slowly making my way around the table. As I reached the opposite end, I dared a glance back in Mary's direction, surveying the others as I did so.

Why had no one spoken up at the impropriety of Mary's actions? They were all joined in mutual learning, unconcerned that my sister was making a mockery of my service in favor of elevating herself to the position of disciple.

"Which of you who has a friend will go to him at midnight and say to him, 'Friend, lend me three loaves, for a friend of mine has arrived on a journey, and I have nothing to set before him.'" Jesus' voice resonated throughout the room.

"And that friend answers from within, 'Do not bother me; the door is now shut, and my children are with me in bed. I cannot get up and give you anything.'"

I poured water over Judas' hands, the stream faltering as my body tensed. It was clear that this friend Jesus spoke of was in the wrong for withholding the means of hospitality, no matter the inconvenient hour.

"I tell you, though he will not get up and give him anything because he is his friend, yet because of his impudence he will rise and give him whatever he needs."

My eyes widened with surprise. Perhaps this was a veiled rebuke to Mary, who was certainly showing a persistent impudence by inserting herself where she shouldn't be. Satisfaction welled up in me at the thought that Jesus might openly rebuke my sister.

"And I tell you, ask, and it will be given to you; seek, and you will find; knock, and it will be opened to you. For everyone who asks receives, and the one who seeks finds, and to the one who knocks it will be opened."

I sloshed water over Matthew's hands too roughly. He blinked up at me in brief surprise as water soaked his lap. Quickly adjusting my grip, I waited patiently as he dried his hands. The last of them.

There, I had finished my task and had been witness to a confusing story where Jesus encouraged not hospitality but shameless persistence. He was still talking, but I was no longer listening as I made a hasty retreat to the door.

Hurt and confusion warred within. By letting Mary stay at his feet, Jesus was endorsing her position as his disciple. Such validation stung like a slap in the face. Wasn't I the one who was embodying the qualities from his earlier story? If Jesus valued hospitality and service, why was he letting Mary so flagrantly avoid it?

Nearing the door, I realized I couldn't leave, not with my sister still in a position of unchecked defiance. I turned and stared straight at Jesus, clearing my throat to gain his attention. When that didn't work, I slammed the pitcher and basin onto a side table, louder than I'd intended. At the sound, several heads turned in my direction, including Jesus'.

I pushed past the ache in my heart to give voice to my concern. "Lord, do you not care that my sister has left me to serve alone?"

Silence descended upon the room as all eyes turned to me. Why had I spoken so publicly? I wished I could take the words back, stuff them down my throat.

Seeing as I could not unsay what had been said, however, I had no choice but to plow forward. "Tell her . . . tell her to help me." I forced myself to meet Jesus' gaze. If he could indeed see inside me, then surely he knew that my words rang true. Seeing as no one else would set the situation right, I must do it myself. Mary wasn't only humiliating me but also embarrassing herself.

Jesus rose slowly and crossed the room. For a moment, he stood before me silently, his eyes unflinchingly meeting and holding mine. Then he dropped his gaze to my hands.

I was agitatedly twisting my fingers, a rushed, habitual gesture. He cupped my hands in his own, stilling their frantic movement, and slowly, intentionally turned them over so my palms were exposed to him.

My hands throbbed with the memory of pain. The scars were faint now, most of them hidden in the twining swirls and grooves of my palms' natural lines. Jesus gently rubbed his thumbs along the scars, finding and tracing each one, a twist of sorrow entering his face. When he looked back up at me, tears shone in his eyes.

"Martha, dearest Martha." He released my hands to grasp my face, framing me between his rough carpenter's hands. "You are anxious and troubled about so many things."

Tears slid silently down my cheeks and seeped into his hands.

"There is only one thing worth being concerned about, only one thing that is truly necessary."

More tears. I couldn't stop or conceal them. Like that old winnowing fork I used to imagine, he was unfurling all that bound me up inside, tossing my worry to the wind. Up swept the winnowing fork, away blew the chaff. What remained was what was needed.

Tenderly, Jesus wiped a tear away. "This one necessary thing—Mary has discovered it. She has chosen the good portion, and it will not be taken away from her."

His words, rather than a rebuke, were an invitation. I sensed it clearer this time, and my heart leapt with a desire to respond. Whatever Mary had discovered, I wanted it too, and here was Jesus, offering it to me. The room was achingly still but for a strangled gasp in the corner. I tore my eyes from Jesus to see my sister, standing silent and wide-eyed in the corner with a hand over her mouth.

It wasn't the look on her face that drove me from the room. It was the love in his.

And so I fled.

We walked with him an hour on his way out of town as befitting the departure of an esteemed guest. Those who had arrived with him from Jerusalem returned that way while we continued with Jesus and his disciples along the northern road, which traveled past Bethphage and in the direction of Shiloh.

Mary was still avoiding me, but this time it seemed more out of embarrassment than laziness. Neither she nor I was used to her being singled out in such an exemplary way.

I had spent the evening with Jesus' words pounding in my head. "*Martha, dearest Martha.*" The phantom pain I sometimes experienced in my hands had been subsumed with the memory of his gentle, firm strokes as he not only uncovered my hurt but also seemed to understand it.

Lazarus often said that Jesus was doing a new thing in people's minds and hearts—changing their thinking, unearthing the fuller meaning of the Law, and ushering people into an intimate relationship with Yahweh that extended far beyond rule-keeping.

Could it be that what I thought I understood of myself, my past, and my current place in the world was being transformed before my eyes? Was Jesus welcoming my impudence, inviting me to come to him shamelessly and persistently with all my hurt? Perhaps he was larger than my history, more powerful than my pain. Perhaps I did not have to understand him completely to trust him.

Now, as we traveled the dusty road with the sun to our backs, I moved toward my brother and whispered, "Let's make a contribution to his ministry."

"Already done," Lazarus assured, nodding his head toward Judas. "I gave their treasurer some coin before we left."

Satisfied, I fell back a few paces to walk with Mary, who turned her head aside at my approach.

When we had traveled a mile beyond the Mount of Olives, Jesus turned to my brother with a warm expression. "There is no need for you to travel farther, my friend."

He and Lazarus embraced before he turned to Mary, bent over her head, and murmured into her ear. My breath hitched as he finally turned to me with a gentle expression and took my face, once again, in both hands, drawing me close and pressing a kiss of blessing on my forehead. When he released me, I instinctively clutched the feather pendant that lay nestled beneath my tunic. Jesus' eyes rested on me thoughtfully for a moment before he spoke.

"You are weary, are you not, Martha?"

I gulped convulsively, throat suddenly dry. "W-what do you mean?"

He sighed deeply and placed a hand over mine so that both of our hands cupped the hidden feather. "You are weary and burdened." He increased the pressure on my hand, eyes never leaving mine. "Like an ox straining too long alone, you are overwhelmed and heavy-laden."

How could this man elicit even more tears from me? My eyes flooded so I could barely see him.

"Ah, Martha, come to me. My yoke is easy, my burden is light, and it is for you. Come to me and find rest."

"I don't know how," I choked, turning grief-stricken eyes to him, letting him see the depth of my pain.

Jesus nodded slightly, acknowledging my words. "Old patterns are indeed hard to break. New wineskins are needed for new wine."

I blinked rapidly, scrambling for his meaning. "Yes, for an old skin would burst, and the wine would be wasted."

"Likewise, no one patches what is old with something new, for the new will pull away from the old, making the tear worse than before. I have come into the world to fulfill the Law and the Prophets and to make all things new."

Belief, small and flickering, burst to life in my chest. I had seen the new life this man brought. I had witnessed his power, tasted his compassion, and my soul discerned his words to be true.

"My words will be folly to those who are perishing." His eyes were alight with recognition, as if he saw the belief that had blossomed in me. "But to those who are being saved, my words are life."

Joy broke through the pain and confusion, and I trembled in its wake.

"Every sheep of mine will recognize my voice." Jesus' tone softened as he squeezed my hand before releasing it. "You have seen that a good shepherd lays down his life for the sheep and that the sheep will follow closely after that good shepherd."

My tongue cleaved to the roof of my mouth as Jesus laid bare the most hidden, hurting part of me. There was no doubt left in my mind that he had picked up the threads of our connected history and that he had the power of God to weigh the thoughts and intentions of the heart.

The feather thrummed beneath my tunic, sending waves of assurance into my being. *He sees. He understands. He knows it all.* The intimacy of his knowledge, which had frightened me the day before, now covered me with peace. I did not have to understand all his ways to give this man my allegiance. I could surrender my understanding as I came to trust his above my own.

I stood silently next to my siblings as we watched the Messiah leave with his disciples.

The nation was desperate. I had known this from childhood. Israel yearned with groaning for her Messiah. Until this moment, I hadn't known that I'd been yearning too. I was also desperate for personal deliverance, as burning and urgent as the nation's need. I had been groaning in spirit for years, for this moment, for this man.

And here he was.

Twenty-Nine

15 Adar
30 AD
Shushan Purim

Summer passed in a languid haze. As the winter rains descended and our flocks returned from pasture to be wintered close to home, I was surprised to find that my spirits remained uplifted. So often my thoughts darkened this time of year, my eyes lifting irrepressibly to the hills as if Uri might manifest himself on the horizon. The vise that normally gripped me had loosened its relentless hold.

Breaking my joy, however, was the news that Gilah had lost her miracle baby. As the cold rains of winter lashed the countryside, the news broke over Bethany like a harsh blow.

"It's no wonder," Tikvah clucked, "at her age."

I grimaced at the harsh pronouncement, and on a soggy, misty morning I swallowed my pride and knocked on Simon's door, hoping to see my old friend and offer comfort.

"She is refusing all visitors," the reply came.

There was a time when she would have made an exception for me, but I dared not ask for that exception now. So I retreated and resorted to praying for her from afar.

As the weather continued to grow colder, we traced Jesus' movements and ministry as well as the blackening cloud of disapproval that hovered over Jerusalem. When we received an invitation to visit Elchanan for the Feast of Purim, my heart did a hesitant flip.

According to my brother, Elchanan had not voiced dissension over Jesus' ministry. He had, however, often made a point to be present whenever Jesus was near Jerusalem. His lack of commitment, one way or the other, worried my brother, coupled with the fact that he was a close companion of the high priest Caiaphas, who decidedly opposed Jesus.

Still, we would not refuse such an invitation, and so we joined the throng of pilgrims on their way to the Holy City, bearing baskets of food as gifts for our relatives and carrying extra coin to give to the poor. Having fasted the day before, our stomachs were ready for the upcoming feast and our spirits for the reading of the *megillah*, the Scroll of Esther. Elchanan lived near Caiaphas' home in the Essene Quarter, so we traveled to the nearest synagogue for the reading.

Many months had passed since Jesus had last been in our home, during which time Mary and I began cautiously moving toward each other.

"I didn't mean to slight you, sister." Mary had sought me out not long after Jesus had left. *"I . . . I realize you might expect such behavior from me, but please believe me . . . I did not mean to humiliate you. I sensed an invitation that compelled me to respond. I needed to be near him, to listen to him."*

"He is like fire." I recalled my original observation of Jesus. *"He is like a fire on a cold and dark night. To be near him is to receive life."*

"Yes." Mary's eyes glowed with agreement. *"He was the first man in a long time who looked at me and saw a person. There was no contempt in his gaze."*

I thought of Simon's disapproval, of Aharon's attention, and of the many men beforehand who had sought my sister. Did Mary often experience contempt from others? Did men only see her beauty and interpret it as either a threat or something to possess? My heart softened in a new way toward my sister.

As we listened to the reading from the Scroll of Esther, a deep joy shone from Mary. I settled beneath the familiar story of God's deliverance and cast glances at my sister, who sat still and observant, hands clasped and pressed tightly to her lips as if she was hearing the story for the first time.

Later that evening, we saw many well-known faces among Elchanan's guests. Cleopas was in attendance, along with his friend Nicodemus, a Pharisee who was a part of the Sanhedrin. Also present was Joseph of Arimathea, the wealthy merchant with whom Lazarus had done business.

Elchanan's impressive banquet hall was bustling with festivity. We made ourselves comfortable among the women of the household, the youngest of whom was Elchanan's daughter, Adina. Many in the company were dancing, and Adina outshone them all, with voice and hands lifted in praise, elaborate collar necklace gleaming in the lamplight, and a hint of her glossy black curls peeking from beneath a beaded veil.

"For all his travels here and interactions with our host, our brother never mentioned Elchanan's beautiful daughter." I leaned close to Mary, whispering my observation.

Mary smirked as she picked at a cluster of grapes. "I'm sure he's never mentioned it because he doesn't want to admit that he's besotted." She inclined her head to where our brother sat like a statue, eyes never straying from Adina as she swayed with others in the middle of the room. The dancers made a sudden turn, and Adina swept past Lazarus in a whirl of fine linen. Our brother sat back in his seat like a felled tree, eyes widening.

Mary and I giggled behind our hands, relishing the sight of our characteristically chatty brother struck dumb. My giddy enjoyment, however, was checked by a soft voice near my shoulder. "Martha, a word if I may?"

Cleopas' serious brown eyes regarded me. Flustered, I stood and brushed the crumbs from my hands before joining him at the side of the room. It had been a while since Cleopas had singled me out like this, and despite my best efforts, my cheeks flushed as he stood much closer than usual. A sharp jolt of awareness shot through me as his hand hovered at the small of my back. I shivered and moved slightly away, but he moved with me, and to my continued surprise, bent his head until our faces nearly touched.

"Lazarus is on the verge of making irrevocable enemies," he murmured in my ear. "The kind of enemies no man wants to make."

My response to his closeness evaporated at his somber words as I turned to him. We were now nearly nose to nose. His face softened for a moment, hand pressing tighter into my back.

"What do you mean?" I whispered a little too loudly. Cleopas placed a finger over my lips and indicated I should keep my gaze trained on the celebration in the center of the room. Trembling, I did so, murmuring from the corner of my mouth, "What kind of enemies and why?"

"Lazarus has been one of the most outspoken supporters of Jesus' ministry." Cleopas' voice was low and strained, contrasting sharply with the unchecked merriment in the room. "You know your brother . . . once he is passionate about something and believes in it, there is nothing that can restrain his enthusiasm or his tongue."

I closed my eyes briefly as I let the truth of his words sink in. "Yes, he lacks the cautiousness present in most other men."

"Exactly," Cleopas hissed. "I share his belief, but there is a time and a place for everything. Didn't our own King Solomon advise that a word fitly spoken is like apples of gold in a setting of silver? I fear that Lazarus doesn't understand the potential consequences of his words."

A cord of fear threaded its way through me, binding up my heart and catching at my breath. I stared at my brother's young, handsome face as he delighted in Adina's dance. It had taken him years of working through our father's rejection to regain his open nature. And the fruit of his labor was evident. His inner person, which felt so deeply, was the result of a passionate and intentional cultivation through years of hurt. I would not see him return to the withdrawn and tentative spirit that had held him captive for years.

"Who could ever wish that dear man harm?" My voice cracked at the mere thought. Cleopas shifted at my side, and my mind flew back to another night, during the merriment of our family's first sheepshearing, when Cleopas' intuition had proven tragically correct. I had spoken to him then with a rash tongue that I had later regretted. If he now suspected our brother was in danger, then I believed him.

"Lazarus' name is being linked to Jesus in every conversation, good or ill. He continues to associate himself so closely with Jesus that I fear the fate of one will be the fate of the other."

I surveyed the crowd with worried eyes, now wondering who could be trusted. "Thank you for bringing this to my attention." I turned to find Cleopas watching me intently. My eyes met his briefly before he jerked away.

"Yes, of course. I've tried to counsel him myself, but he doesn't heed my words. He values and respects you, Martha. I'm confident he'll listen to you."

I glowed under his compliment even as skepticism rose within me. If my brother would not listen to Cleopas, I doubted he would heed the words of his sister. As abruptly as he'd drawn me aside, Cleopas left, and my body instantly missed the warm pressure of his hand while my heart chided me for the thought.

Later that night, guests from Jerusalem retired back to their homes, while pilgrims stayed either in one of Elchanan's upper rooms or in another relative's home. We were preparing to leave for Cleopas' home when my brother looked up sharply at a cluster of men. My gaze followed his to where Elchanan and two others stood talking.

"He claims to carry the authority to lay down and pick up his own life. Can you imagine? No man can do that," one of the men said urgently to the others.

"No one can deny his power," Elchanan interjected. "His works speak for themselves. The question remains: From where does that power come?"

"That is the central issue," the third man acknowledged. "Some of his teachings sound like the ramblings of a madman. And some of his claims reek of blasphemy. What conclusion can there be, then, but that his power comes from Satan?"

"Can Satan drive out Satan?" Lazarus' voice boomed loudly through the courtyard. I jumped at the sound, heart fluttering to my throat.

"Can a demon open the eyes of the blind or give a leper back his life?" Lazarus looked like a madman himself as he crossed the courtyard, gesticulating wildly into the night.

My eyes flitted about fearfully until they found Cleopas, who was watching the exchange with clenched jaw. I longed to run to his side for comfort and to urge him to intervene.

"I have seen it for myself. How can his power come from Satan, the father of lies, when he speaks truth? How can his power come from Satan, the destroyer of life, when he brings life?"

Elchanan separated himself from the group with a strained expression, arms outstretched. "Friend, you make good points. It is only friendly debate."

"Jesus' words don't allow for lukewarm debate. Either you

agree with him, or you don't. Either you are for him, or you are against him. One cannot be neutral in this matter, Elchanan, and you know it."

I'd never heard my brother so insistent. His voice was filled with fire and challenge. I sent Cleopas another poignant look. As if sensing my gaze and hearing my silent plea, Cleopas crossed the room as Elchanan clapped a large hand on Lazarus' shoulder.

"Your zeal is admirable, although some would disagree with your reasoning. Surely a man claiming equality with God invites inquiry and healthy debate. That is all we are doing here."

"And the hour is late for such debate." Cleopas finally reached Lazarus and placed a restraining hand on his arm, subtly pulling him out from underneath Elchanan's grip. "All debate is merely rambling when wine flows freely. Why not revisit the discussion in the light of day?"

"If this is friendly debate, as you say, I'd much prefer to stay." Lazarus shrugged off Cleopas' hold.

Elchanan inclined his head and spread his hands in acquiescence. "That is your prerogative, friend. My home is your home. You are certainly welcome to stay."

"I'll stay with you," Cleopas interjected quickly.

Lazarus shook his head. "No, I would much rather you accompany my sisters to your home. I don't want them out on the streets at night alone."

Cleopas hovered between us. Neither he nor I could argue with Lazarus' words. There was no clear reason for Cleopas to stay with Lazarus when there were two women who needed an escort.

Reluctantly, Cleopas joined Mary and me at the door, and we exited the home with the sound of Lazarus' voice ringing in our ears. The chill in my bones mimicked the sharp nip of the night air. I turned silently to Cleopas and saw my concern mirrored in his eyes.

More people clogged the narrow Jerusalem streets than usual as late-night revelers made their way home with staggering steps. Cleopas stayed close as he led us from the Essene Quarter to his home in the business district.

A modest dwelling, the home included his potter's shop facing the street with his private rooms in the back. We entered the shop, and Cleopas fastened the door behind us. "Your usual room is prepared. Let me know if you're in need of anything. I'll stay in the front and wait for Lazarus."

As Mary and I made ourselves comfortable in the guest room, we laid out a mat for Lazarus, although I remained skeptical that he'd make it back in time for sleep. Mary quickly settled on her own mat, and soon her deep, even breathing filled the small room. I, however, sat upright and worried at my lip, finally succumbing to curiosity and padding softly down the hall.

Cleopas sat silently in a corner of the shop, chin on his chest, eyes closed. I paused in the doorway, unsure why I'd come. As I turned to head back, Cleopas straightened and spoke my name, voice thick with tiredness.

"I didn't mean to disturb you." I stood perched in the doorway like a bird on its branch, ready for flight at a moment's notice. "How long do you suppose he'll be?"

"I couldn't say." Cleopas yawned and scrubbed a hand over his face.

Something about seeing him so sleepy and unguarded put a twist in my stomach. I looked away quickly and turned to head back. There was no need for me to stay alert when Cleopas was keeping watch.

His hesitant voice stopped me in my tracks. "Won't you stay . . . for a moment?"

I turned to find him looking at me with softly pleading eyes. "I suppose I can keep you company for a bit." I took the seat he offered, with rigid hands clasped tightly in my lap.

"There's something I've been meaning to ask you."

"How is Aviva doing?"

We spoke almost at the same time. When I realized what he'd said, my face blanched, and I mulishly pressed forward with a stream of chatter to stop whatever he was going to say.

"She's due soon with her third. Have you heard any word from her? I so rarely see her these days and miss her so. The last we'd spoken she seemed better after her husband's accident."

"Y-yes. . . . I'm thankful Yahweh preserved his life." Cleopas seemed disoriented after my outburst and turned away slightly to stare at the door, as if willing my brother to walk through it.

"And the rest of your siblings. How are they? Who would have thought that out of all eight of you, only you and Lieba would remain in Jerusalem?"

"Martha, I need to tell you something." Cleopas turned to me abruptly. His voice was pained, cutting through my anxious chatter like a knife. "Please. I haven't known how to say it for so long, but now is as good a time as any."

I sat dutifully silent and watched as his mouth moved for a moment, as if trying to form his words as he formed clay.

"You refused me once, a long time ago, and our relationship lost something after that." My eyes flicked to his in surprise. He was leaning forward, his strong forearms coming to rest on his thighs, large hands dangling between his knees.

"What I want to say is . . . I miss you." He glanced up at me. Something in my face must have embarrassed him, for he looked back down at his hands quickly.

"I don't hold your refusal against you. I never did. Many times I wanted to tell you this, but at first hurt and disappointment restrained me, and then so much time had passed that I simply let it lie."

Mind whirling, I tried and failed to summon words to contribute to the conversation.

"I suppose I wanted to say that I miss the way things used to be between us." His words were soft, simple, humble . . . irresistible.

Hadn't I thought of Cleopas over the years? Hadn't I wondered how my life might have changed if I had said yes then? Would I have been spared the hurt I had endured? I closed my eyes as the pain swept over me in strong currents, battering me with relentless fury. *No,* my heart whispered. I could have made no other decision at the time.

"Martha . . ."

His voice brought me back to the present. I opened shimmering eyes to find him gazing at me in earnest.

"Ah, Martha."

He sat upright, broad chest expanding as his breath quickened. "I might possibly be making a muddled mess with this. I merely intended to tell you how much I missed you, but my heart is not letting me stop there."

Cleopas. I knew what he would say before he opened his mouth. But I let him say it anyway and tried to listen through the fresh pain filling me.

"My regard for you is still bright after all these years." Our eyes were locked, the tension between us so great that it rooted me to the spot. I couldn't have moved even if Lazarus had come bursting into the room that very moment.

"If anything, I've come to hold you in even higher esteem as I've seen how you manage your family's home with such wisdom, hospitality, and grace."

He rose from his seat as if launched from a sling and sat by my side with such fervency that I almost lurched off the bench in surprise.

"I've observed how dedicated you are, Martha. Others may not see it, but I do." He grabbed my hand and threaded his fingers effortlessly through mine. "So many rely on you, and you give of yourself without holding back and without asking for anything in return. You are a mother to Mary and a confidant to Lazarus. It makes me think of Ruth. You are a woman of noble character. I've already spoken with your brother to receive his blessing, which he was happy to give. I must ask you again, dear Martha, if you would consider becoming my wife."

He spoke in one long stream of words, his eyes finding and holding mine. I could not look away, even as heat flooded my cheeks and a lump formed in my throat. I could not look away. Cleopas noted my hesitation and raised our clasped hands to his lips, where he pressed a kiss into the back of my hand.

"Say something, Martha. What are you thinking?"

All the small pieces of suspicion scattered over the years converged into a startling whole. I'd underestimated Cleopas' continued regard and was struck dumb beneath the import of his words as he, slightly out of breath, waited for my reply with my hand still grasped in his.

It had taken many years to accept my life as it stood, and here was Cleopas offering me something I had long thought outside my reach. I could not deny that his regard, now so bluntly spoken, was deeply attractive.

Saying yes, however, terrified me. How could I leave my siblings? They needed me, and my heart was frightened to open itself up again.

But was it unwise to simply disregard everything Cleopas was offering? A possible family of my own. Little ones to raise in the fear of the Lord.

I'd been staring at a shelf of pottery as I let my thoughts tumble through me. Turning to Cleopas, I saw how his face had fallen with my prolonged hesitation.

"I don't know what to say," I began hesitantly. "I'm honored, and I . . . I miss you too." My admission caused a flame of hope to leap into his face.

"You've been so kind to us throughout the years. Even when I turned you down." I gulped hard, unable to believe we were finally talking about this hard part of our history. "You never let bitterness turn you away." I squeezed his hand. "And you've sacrificed so much for us." I turned to gaze at our humble surroundings. "The wealthy clients you turned down so that you could help Lazarus." My throat caught with tears. "You should be serving Herod himself by now."

Cleopas grunted and waved his other hand. "There is no need for continued thanks. I willingly made the sacrifice. Lazarus is like a brother to me." His words were earnest but laced with dismay. He wanted my love and here I was giving him gratitude instead.

The many years of our connected past stretched between us, serving in their own way as an inseparable bond. I turned to him, looking into his familiar face, longing to make his expression light up the way I used to in childhood. Could I give him what he wanted? He deserved a wholehearted response. He deserved a woman who was whole. And I could give him neither of those things.

A stab of guilt entered my breast and leaked through to my voice as my hand went slack in his. "I've always regretted the distance that crept between us. I admired you greatly then, and I still do."

He had spoken to me as a lover, but I was responding as a friend, and we both immediately sensed the shift. The flame of hope in his face died as he slowly untangled our fingers and returned his hand to his lap.

I was bungling this badly. Part of me wanted to grab his hand, entwine our fingers once again, and tell him yes. But the other part of me hesitated, remembering the promise I'd given Uri and all the long years of sorrow afterward.

Cleopas hung his head and turned slightly away. How could

I explain to him what held me back when I couldn't articulate it to myself?

"I don't know what's restraining me," I blurted out. Honesty. I owed him that. "There is restraint in my spirit, and I cannot give you the answer you desire."

Cleopas looked down at his hands and shook his head, as if dismissing his own disappointment. "No matter. It's okay, Martha. We do not need to discuss it further. Look at me—this is an ill time to even be mentioning this. Here, while we wait for your brother, who may even now be throwing fuel on an already-hot flame."

"No, don't be hard on yourself." I extended a hand unthinkingly and placed it over his own, where it rested in his lap. He jerked at my touch and made no move to reciprocate it.

"You should rest." His voice was soft, but I could detect pain. "I'll keep watch."

I removed my hand and sat observing him somberly for a moment before finally rising and returning to the door. Casting one more look behind me, I left slowly with heavy feet.

What had I done? Did I carry a perverse nature that was keeping me from happiness? Was I clinging so closely to hurt that I could not welcome anything else? Or was I showing wisdom in my restraint?

I settled myself on a mat next to Mary and gradually drifted off to a fitful sleep on the turbulent waves of doubt.

THIRTY

16 Adar
30 AD

Something was pulling me slowly and steadily from sleep. I fought to return to my dream even as my mind tried to remember the details, but a voice was calling my name persistently, dissolving the edges of my dream as my body began to shift in response.

"Martha." The voice was close and urgent. "It's your brother."

My eyes shot open at this information, half expecting to see Lazarus. Instead, it was Cleopas' worried face that greeted me.

"Still nothing. It's nearly dawn, and there's been no word from him."

With a gasp, I sat up, my foggy mind finally latching on to his words.

"I'm returning to Elchanan's home to see if he decided to stay the night there. In truth, I should have gone back to check on him sooner, but I fell asleep." He shook his head angrily, and I could tell he was thoroughly upset with himself.

Struggling to my feet, I barely had time to respond before Cleopas was out the door. I roused Mary, and we entered the shop to wait anxiously among the pottery for Cleopas' return.

Hours passed, and as the sun rose in the sky, our spirits continued to drop. Finally, unwilling to wait any longer, Mary and I traveled back to Elchanan's home ourselves, only to find that Cleopas had come and gone.

"I'll tell you what I told your cousin. Lazarus left here a few hours after you did last night," Elchanan's steward informed us. "My master knows nothing of your brother's whereabouts." His tone was peevish, his temperament unhelpful, and we left more frustrated than we'd been before.

We returned to Cleopas' home slowly this time, peering down each alley.

"This is unlike him," Mary voiced the concern that clawed at me. "He would never intentionally cause us such worry, would he?"

I squeezed her hand tightly, unable to say a word for the fear that clutched my chest.

As we neared our destination, I stopped abruptly and pointed to Cleopas' door. It gaped open, a streak of blood on the doorpost, its dark hue begging death to pass over.

Mary gasped, and then we were both running, stumbling over each other in our haste. I reached the door first, pushing through into the dark interior, where I stood blinking in confusion.

Lazarus lay bloodied and battered, Cleopas hovering over him.

Mary shoved past me with a shriek, sinking to the ground and grasping at our brother's torn tunic.

Cleopas turned desperate eyes to me. "I found him near the theater. I've already sent for a physician."

I fell to my knees in the doorway, watching the scene from a distance.

Mary was rocking as she screamed our brother's name over and over. Her voice was muffled, for a roaring was spreading through my head, drowning out all else as a sickening familiarity descended upon me.

Violent trembling seized me, and my vision narrowed. Cleopas was calling my name, grasping my arm.

My body met the ground with a thud, but my mind barely registered it, so strong were the grief and fear filling me. My thoughts beat a weary refrain, over and over. *How could this happen again? I've already lost so much. Yahweh, please . . . not my brother too. Oh, my brother. Not again. Not my Lazarus.*

Each rattling breath was a gift. In the dimly lit room that had become our constant place of vigil, Mary and I sat, waiting on that next breath from our brother, only drawing breath ourselves in response to his. Waiting, praying, pleading, day after endless day.

"He's never quite recuperated from that accident," Mary rasped, her voice clogged with tears. "I was so scared that night. I thought he would die."

"Me too." The memory was sharp with both painful and joyful moments, for it'd been that accident that had ignited my relationship with Uri.

"That's when I stopped resenting you so much." Mary sniffed and wiped her eyes.

"What do you mean?"

She let out a shaky sigh. "I've carried the weight of Ima's death for so long that it became part of me. Lazarus never made me feel responsible for her death." She paused to stare lovingly at his face. "But I interpreted your harshness with me as anger over what I'd cost the family. And in a way, you were right. If it hadn't been for me, Ima would still be alive."

"Oh, sister, no! You cannot think that way." I grasped her hand tightly.

"For years I resented you because I thought you resented me. I tried to shelter myself from your anger by convincing myself that I didn't care about you."

Tears fell silently down my cheeks as I stared at my sister's pained face.

"But that night, when we were both so scared and you comforted me, I realized that maybe you were simply trying to mother me, and that maybe you didn't know how. I had never experienced your love in such a deep way."

I was weeping now, noisily, my head bowed over our clasped hands.

Mary gently stroked the back of my head, fingers fluttering over my hair. "Do you think we will ever learn to get along?"

I let out a sharp, humorless laugh before crying all the harder. Mary joined me, and together we wept tears of regret, tears of hope.

We'd spent several days with Cleopas, as Lazarus had been unable to withstand transport. Attended to by the best of physicians, his health still hadn't improved enough for our comfort. Seeing as there was nothing left to do but watch and pray, the physician had released us to travel, urging us to make our brother as comfortable as possible, surrounded by the familiarity of home.

Our household had seen its share of grief with the death of our father, but now, with the illness of his son, the worry and dismay were boundless. Samu, who had known Lazarus from infancy, could barely keep his composure. Other more recent hires were similarly affected, for our brother was a kind and fair employer. Mary and I rarely left his side, Nenet quietly ministering to our needs.

More than the beating he'd endured, the time spent shattered and bruised in the chill of the night had taken the heaviest toll on our brother. An invisible fist gripped his chest and wouldn't ease up. Each breath was fought for and won through painful labor.

In one of Lazarus' rare lucid moments, we were able to piece together the narrative of that night. He'd left Elchanan's home after several hours of heated debate, barely making it down the street before being jumped from behind. A bag had been thrust over his head, denying him a full view of his assailant, but from his account it was clear there'd been more than one. He'd fought back, but the element of surprise and numbers were against him. Having relieved him of his purse and outer garment, the assailants fled, leaving him half-naked and vulnerable. Hours passed, during which time Lazarus painstakingly dragged himself in the direction of Cleopas' home. The grueling effort had cost him almost more than the beating.

I didn't believe for a moment that the attack was a mere robbery. "They were trying to silence you, brother. You've been so outspoken in your support of Jesus. Did you expect no repercussions?" I hated to chastise him when his life was still uncertain, but fear for him loosened my tongue. "You repeatedly walk willingly and blindly into the nest of vipers that is the Sanhedrin, and you expect to come away unscathed?"

Lazarus' battered face was resolute. "Jesus said he had need of me here. Perhaps this is what I'm intended to do. Bear witness to him in the fiery smelt of the Sanhedrin."

"Beware of ending up like his cousin John," I warned. "Don't fancy yourself a herald. John was beheaded for his quick tongue."

And yet part of me admired my brother for his unflagging belief. Did I possess the faith to stand defiant and vulnerable if it meant championing the Messiah?

As Lazarus' lucid moments dwindled, he spent most of his time tossing feverishly on his bed, calling out for Adina.

"Should we fetch her?" Mary whispered. "Is his connection to her so great that he calls for her on his deathbed?"

I shushed her immediately. "This is not his deathbed. We are not there yet." But I sent for Adina. It was the least I could do for my brother, who unconsciously and fervently longed for her. My message was returned with a brusque decline from her father.

"I'd hate to think that Elchanan had anything to do with this," I spat out, angrily pacing the hall with his reply in my hand. "Why would he deny our brother this? What harm can there be to let Adina say good-bye?"

I stopped and choked on my own words, realizing that we were indeed nearing the time when we'd need to say good-bye. Crumpling to the floor, I buried my face in my knees and let Mary wrap me in her arms until there were no tears left.

The idea came as I lingered in my herb garden, taking a much-needed break from my brother's bedside.

Of course—why hadn't I thought of it earlier? The man for whom Lazarus was willing to risk everything was also the one man in all the world who could help us.

"Mary!" I streaked through the garden and back up the stairs, breathlessly entering the bedroom, where she was scrambling to her feet. "We must send for Jesus."

I composed a strongly worded message, and that same day, we sent two servants on horseback for Bethany beyond the Jordan, a location many miles to the east of us, where we had last received reports of Jesus.

"He will come," Mary said fervently. "He will. After all, he came for Simon when Gilah called, and he didn't even know them at the time!"

My mind settled at her words. Yes, Jesus would come for his friends. "We should have sent for him sooner," I muttered, twisting my hands, but Mary shook her head.

"No, he will receive notice in time. The message will reach him quickly, and if he leaves right away, he will be here in time."

That very evening, however, Lazarus took a turn for the worse. His fever increased, leaving him limp and motionless. Mary and I sat through the long watches of the night, unwilling to leave his side.

I must have fallen asleep, for I startled upright, disoriented, to find Mary yawning next to me and rubbing her neck. "You should have woken me," I scolded.

"One of us should rest, don't you think?"

"How is he?"

"About the same. No change."

"You should rest, then."

Mary yawned again and curled up on a mat next to Lazarus' bed. Instead of closing her eyes, however, she observed me, her head resting in the crook of her arm as she looked at me with large, languid eyes.

"What is it?"

"I've been thinking. All that time we spent with Cleopas . . . I couldn't help but notice how tense things were between you. We're all worried for Lazarus, but the two of you clearly avoided each other."

I looked away at my sister's words. It was true. I feared things would never be the same between Cleopas and me after this second refusal. And yet surely the recent events had proved my decision right. How could I consider marriage when my siblings needed me so?

"It made me wonder at the nature of your relationship," Mary continued, yawning and curling up tighter, eyes peeking up at me sleepily. "Perhaps he still loves you after all these years."

I tried to laugh off her words through the jumble of my emotions but merely succeeded at a twisted grimace that did nothing to hide my inner conflict.

Mary was silent for a moment before propping herself on an elbow and piercing me with a now more-alert gaze. "He does, doesn't he? He loves you." At my continued silence and pinched expression, Mary leaned toward me and placed a hand firmly on my knee. "Could it be that you refuse to consider him as a suitor because of your love for Uri?"

The shock of her words tore through me like lightning, leaving me terrified and fiercely, uncomfortably alive. "How did you? What? How?"

"I've known," Mary said softly. "I've always known . . . from the very beginning."

I stared at my sister—this woman who had caused me so many sleepless nights over the years—and realized that I barely knew her. "How did you find out?" I managed to squeak.

"Well, I *was* a pesky little girl when you two met, and I *was* prone to wander off into places I shouldn't be." She smirked. "I followed you the day you brought him a basket of food. Even at barely six years old, I could tell the two of you were completely besotted."

"But you never said anything."

"He was away for so long after that, and it left my mind completely. It wasn't until much later when I caught the two of you under a fig tree"—she looked slyly at me—"in each other's arms." She drew out the words, and my cheeks reddened at the thought of her observing such a private moment. "Then I understood how serious your connection was."

"I don't know what to say," I spluttered. "I can't believe you kept this to yourself all these years. Why would you do that?"

"At first, I was terrified over what might happen to you if Abba found out. And then . . ." She met my eyes, and I saw pain and love there. "And then I came to love you, truly. And Uri as well. I didn't want to see either of you unhappy."

Tears fell down my cheeks. While I'd viewed her as a problem

I couldn't solve, she'd viewed me with love and a desire to protect my happiness.

"You could have thrown this in my face, Mary. All these years that I've rebuked you for your male admirers . . . you could have brought this up in your defense, and yet you didn't."

"I love you, sister." Mary looked at me, her eyes swimming with tears. "Why would I twist a knife into your wound? Love bears all things for the beloved."

With a groan I clasped my sister's face in my hands and looked at her—truly looked at her—for the first time in years. Her striking resemblance to Ima that had often caused me pain now deepened my love for her. This girl, this wily child turned woman . . . she was like our mother in ways I had not seen before. She saw people, flaws and all, and loved them anyway.

"I love you too, more than you can know. And I am sorry, so sorry." I pulled her close and murmured the apology over and over into her hair. My throat was so tight, I couldn't bring myself to say more. I was sorry for not seeing her, for blaming her, for never working past my own grief to fully embrace her. In some ways, I had come to love my hurt more than Adonai, more than the people right in front of me.

I'd rebuked Lazarus once for not helping me with Mary in the way I wanted. And while there might have been truth to my complaint, I had also missed the ways Lazarus had cared for Mary all these years. He had given Mary exactly what her parched heart had needed: unequivocal love.

"How is it that Lazarus loved us so well when we have been so stubborn?" Mary voiced what my heart was crying. Gently, she brushed aside the unruly curls that had flopped into his face, her slender fingers exposing the old scar on Lazarus' pale forehead. "He loved me so much." Her voice was elevated and squeaked with emotion. "And I've been so undeserving of his love, so undeserving." She buried her face in Lazarus' side as fresh sobs overtook her.

I wrapped her in my arms. She turned into me, and I held her as I'd done on that other fearful night so long ago.

We clung to each other in the silent presence of our brother, who had always seen and loved us both so well.

Thirty-One

20 Adar
30 AD

For a whole day we lived with breathless expectancy. Even as Lazarus worsened, Mary and I passed each other in the corridors with tight expressions that declared, *"But he will come!"* Jesus had performed powerful miracles for strangers. He would come to aid his friends. For a whole day we lived with this hope aching in our chests, but when the second day dawned and there was still no word from Jesus, the ache turned to a stab of pain.

"Surely he would have at least returned our message by now," Mary fretted. "Perhaps he didn't receive it."

The burden of our sorrow, the waiting, and the uncertainty were beginning to show on us both. In Mary's haggard and haunted eyes, I saw a mirror of my own despair.

Many of our neighbors had come and gone, bringing us words of comfort. Gilah had visited frequently over the last few days. She still wouldn't speak of losing her babe, and I didn't press her. Having experienced such loss, Gilah seemed especially tender to the sorrow we were now facing.

As she arrived this day, however, her expression was changed. Features pinched, she gripped my hands with surprising ferociousness. Her red-rimmed eyes sought mine as she spoke in a hushed and urgent voice. "Simon is grumbling against Mary."

"Why? What cause does he have?"

Gilah bit her lip and shook her head. "I cannot say. But even now he's stirring up dissent in the synagogue." Her eyes welled with tears. "I chose his side once, and it cost me your friendship. And although he is my husband and a changed man, I will not make the same mistake twice. You deserve to know what is said of your family."

I didn't wait for her to say more. With purposeful steps, I left for the synagogue.

Betzalel, the village scribe and Lazarus' old tutor, sat in the Moses Seat, with clusters of elders nearby. A smattering of other villagers were present, men on the left and women on the right.

"What you are suggesting, then, is that you attempt to drive out the demon?" Betzalel, advanced in age, sat hunched in his seat as he addressed Simon.

I stepped back silently in the shadows as Simon answered. "It's the logical course of action."

One of the elders shook his head. "It is unclear who sinned—Lazarus, or his father, or some other member of the family."

"Oh, but it *is* clear." Simon stepped forward, arms outstretched, looking beseechingly at the men around him. "The youngest sibling, Mary, has a history of exhibiting shameful behavior, and it would seem that a demon has been sent to torment her brother as punishment."

Gasps rippled throughout those gathered, the loudest of which was my own. In horror I watched Simon stroll casually around the room as he dissected the morality of my family.

"It can be no secret that Mary is a loose woman, a perpetuator of sexual sin. What other explanation can there be, brethren, than that this sickness comes as a direct result?"

"That is untrue!"

All eyes turned to me as I stood slumped against a pillar, close to fainting.

"Someone remove her." Simon pointed to me. "She should not be here."

"I have every right to be here." The trembling in my limbs increased as my anger nearly overcame me.

"But not to speak," Simon retorted.

Betzalel looked at me with kind, rheumy eyes. "I understand your grief, Martha, but Simon is correct. You must remain silent or leave."

"I cannot remain silent when you slander my sister." I nearly whispered the words, my head growing light as I swayed where I stood. Was this how Mary had felt at the feet of Jesus as she disrupted convention? Or Lazarus, when he confronted Elchanan in his own home? Was this what it meant, then, to take a stand?

Instead of responding to me, Betzalel turned again to Simon. "The Torah demands that a woman be caught in the act of sexual sin for punishment to be executed. Have you such proof?"

My light-headedness increased as I thought of the many times I'd rebuked Mary. She had always assured me that she was pure, but I had allowed doubt to flourish. Even as doubt crept up again, I called to mind the adoration in Mary's eyes as she'd declared her love for me. *"Love bears all things for the beloved,"* she'd said.

If I was truthful with myself, I'd been embarrassed by her beauty, embarrassed by the way she drew attention, embarrassed that I could not control her in the ways I wanted to. My embarrassment had become a burden I grew tired of bearing, so I had chosen to grasp at control and fear. I forced several deep breaths into my lungs and bent my head, trying to steady my resolve.

"I ask you again, Simon, have you such proof of this sin?" Betzalel's voice crackled with age and impatience.

Simon was surprisingly silent as the murmurs in the crowd increased with speculation. Finally, he broke his silence with a halting voice. "She brought shame upon herself and her family by seducing my son."

The crowd erupted like bees from a hive, some outraged and some disbelieving. There was a time when I would have believed the worst of Mary and accepted any gossip as true, but that time had passed. I had finally beheld my sister's soul, and I would not believe the worst of her now.

Betzalel raised his hands, and the room slowly quieted. "But is there proof of fornication?"

Simon fidgeted where he stood, eyes shifting before finally landing on the ground. "No."

"Then I am afraid it is hearsay. However—" he raised his hands again as the crowd reacted to his pronouncement—"However, I can see no harm in you visiting the family and praying over our brother Lazarus. It could indeed be that some evil spirit holds him captive."

"I will not let this man enter our home!" All light-headedness had blessedly left me, and I stood rigid and certain, pointing a finger at Simon.

Betzalel turned and nodded to two of the elders, who began making their way toward me.

"Know this, Simon bar Ezriel, you will never enter our home again."

By this time, I could see that they intended to throw me from the synagogue. Hastily I retreated before they could reach me. They would never let me back in, but the thought didn't concern me.

Back through the marketplace and toward home I fled, tears of outrage and hurt nearly blinding me. I had ruined my own reputation, but I hardly cared. I only wanted to reach home and clasp my dear sister in my arms once more.

Chest heaving, I neared our door to find Mordecai anxiously pacing in the street.

"*There* you are, mistress. Come quickly. These may be Master Lazarus' final moments."

New distress clutched me as I tore through our home, scrambling up the steps, slipping and tripping in my haste. I ignored the sharp pain in my shin, limping down the hallway and thrusting open the door.

Mary rose at my entrance, her face anguished.

"Is he . . . ?" I gasped.

She shook her head. "Not yet, but soon."

With a sob, I threw myself down by our brother's side, both thankful I wasn't too late and horrified that Jesus, in fact, was. "If only he'd come," I moaned.

"We tried," Mary whispered. "We did all we could."

A handful of breaths later, our brother died with both of his sisters clasping his hands.

There had never been a man more dearly loved in both life and death. With great care, Mary and I prepared him for burial. We kissed his face, washed his bruised body, and anointed him with the choicest of perfumes.

When it was time to wrap his body in a shroud, Mary broke down and had to leave the room. Silently, I performed the duty alone, tucking more spices among the folds, wrapping tighter and tighter until all that was left was his familiar face peeking from the cocoon. Mary returned in time to help me adjust the sudarium over his face, and we finished by binding his hands and feet with strips of cloth.

We'd last performed these rites for Abba, Lazarus being present to help support us in our grief. Now it was just us two. I clung to Mary fervently. My love for her blossomed as we experienced a deep and mutual dependence. We had leaned on Lazarus for support all these years. Now we would find that support in each other.

Soon after we finished our preparations, we received an influx of friends and family. Cleopas came, as did Lieba. Lazarus was a respected and well-known businessman and scholar, and the love and honor he'd elicited in others was evident as people arrived in droves to say good-bye and offer us comfort.

Mary and I welcomed our visitors and accepted their sorrow and kind words until Elchanan arrived. His presence was a stinging blow.

"There's no proof that he harmed Lazarus," Mary whispered to me.

"Maybe not directly, but I cannot shake the notion that he was involved."

Adina also came, and her grief was so pronounced that Mary and I were convinced that whatever Lazarus had harbored for her had been mutual. I was further incensed with Elchanan, who had refused Adina a chance to see Lazarus alive one last time.

As the day ended, we transported our brother on a litter to the family tomb, the line of mourners snaking all the way through the village. The ground itself shuddered with the weight of our grief.

We stood facing the large stone painted a blinding white. Three men grunted and strained as they rolled it aside.

"I don't want to go."

I gasped and closed my eyes tight, but the image of Lazarus as a scared little boy wouldn't leave me.

"I don't want to go in there."

I shook my head, trying to release my mind of the memory.

"I don't ever *want to go inside."*

A sharp sob tore through my throat as I remembered the small boy who was afraid of death, afraid of the dark, afraid of being alone. Tears leaked from my closed eyes.

"I'm here," I whispered. Did he know? I was here, right here.

Opening my eyes, I turned and placed a shaking hand on his bound body. "I'm here, beloved." I rested my forehead against his side, the musky scent of nard enveloping me. "There is no need to fear."

We laid him on a stone shelf in the presence of so many who had gone before. As Mary wept at his feet, I planted my hands on the ledge beside him.

"Do not fear, brother. I will watch over her." I gazed down the length of his body to Mary's bent head. "Until we join you, I will love her well as you did. It is only for a little bit; I promise," I whispered shakily. "I will join you one day, and until then there is Abba and Ima, Saba and dear Savta." I leaned over and kissed his bound head, my tears staining the cloth. "You are not alone."

Please, Yahweh, I pleaded, *comfort the heart of this loved one who has returned to You in death.*

I saw the life I would now lead without him, the unexpected road before me that would be devoid of his laugh, empty of his presence. With sharp clarity, a future without Lazarus spread before me, making my body go cold with shock, then flush hot with dread.

The servant we'd sent to fetch Jesus returned, verifying that the message had been delivered but bearing none in return. The silence was frightening, overwhelming, confusing.

Had Jesus simply been unable to arrive in time? Or had he stayed away? And, if so, why would Jesus deny us in such a horrible way? Why would he allow a man who had championed him in life to then suffer and die? And on his own account? For there was no doubt in my mind that my brother had been driven to his death out of loyalty to the Messiah.

Thirty-Two

24 Adar
30 AD

The first night after Lazarus' burial, I woke up screaming, sweat drenching my body, the nightmare still clinging to me with persistent claws. Mary, who had chosen to sleep by my side, was awake in an instant, but even with her soothing presence, I could not shake the dream. I sobbed like a child, refusing to share the dark images with my sister. Lazarus, alive and trapped in the tomb, scratching the stone walls in desperation, pacing and crying among our family's bones, pleading with me to come and retrieve him.

It was the beginning of many nightmares to come. Even though my mind recognized that I wasn't responsible for my brother's death, my heart said I'd failed him. I was his big sister and should have anticipated how volatile Lazarus' words had become in the current religious climate. I should have urged him to caution, compelled him to discretion.

And yet . . . I was also deeply proud of my brother's unwavering faith, his passionate nature that refused to let him stay silent concerning his belief. He had put himself in danger for someone he loved. He had deemed Jesus worthy of the sacrifice, and I couldn't blame him.

On the third night, it was Mary who woke up in a sweat. I held her as she shuddered against my shoulder.

"I saw his spirit depart," she moaned. "He was roaming the gravesite one moment and the next he was exhaled into the air—gone, like a vapor."

I cringed at the image, knowing the source of Mary's dream. Some said the soul of the deceased remained near the body for three days, hoping to return. We were now facing the dawn of the fourth day, when the spirit was believed to be fully departed.

Our home was especially somber this fourth day as our guests contemplated the full removal of Lazarus' soul. It was nearing the first day of a new year, a time typically ripe with joy and possibility. Instead, we, along with our neighbors and friends, were cast in a shadow of grief and left musing over our own mortality.

We congregated in Lazarus' study, drawing comfort from his favorite room. Occasionally, Mary would rise and circle the room, trailing her hand along our brother's beloved scrolls, lingering over each one.

Surely at any moment Lazarus would come barging in, bright-eyed with news and knowledge, eager to share with us the light burning inside him. It was hard to accept that such vibrancy was snuffed from our lives forever.

Of those gathered, Simon was noticeably absent, apparently respecting my wishes, or perhaps avoiding us out of cowardice. Gilah, however, had stayed close to our side the last three days, neither of us mentioning my outburst in the synagogue. Mary remained blessedly ignorant of the accusations that had been hurled against her. Bethany was being gracious in our grief, the usual gossiping tongues surprisingly silent in the light of our deep sorrow.

Close to midday, I left the study for my herbal garden, my stomach roiling within me. I was plucking mint, remembering a different day when I'd settled my little brother's belly with the same herb, when Lemuel crashed into the courtyard, wild-eyed and panting.

"He's here!" Lemuel's frantic presence was jarring in our somber home.

"Who?"

"Jesus! I was coming in from the grove and saw him and his disciples headed this way."

My heart tumbled to my toes as I dropped the herbs, grasped my mantle in both hands, and hurried past Lemuel without a word.

I ran east, in the direction of our fig grove, in the direction of the Messiah. Movement barred deep thought, so I focused on the next step and then the next, my breathing jagged, my heart pounding in time with each step.

When I crested the hill that sloped down to our grove, I saw him. He was following the terraced path that snaked upward, his disciples trailing behind him, like sheep behind their shepherd. Without stopping, I plunged toward him, nearly falling down the hill in my haste.

Barely meeting his compassionate gaze, I crashed at Jesus' feet, where I greedily gulped in air, filling my lungs, trying to speak. Up until that moment, I hadn't realized how desperate I was to see him. The longer he'd tarried, the more I'd wondered if perhaps his absence was judgment. Had we displeased him in some way?

Then again, we were so close to Jerusalem. Perhaps concern for his own safety outweighed his love for us. But no, he was here, and my heart was a tangle of emotions.

"Lord," I gasped, bowing my head over his dusty sandals. With a trembling hand, I snagged the hem of his robe, grasping tightly as if tethering him to myself.

He was here. He had come after all. He had not forgotten us.

I raised my eyes to his face, barely able to see past my veil of tears. "Lord, if you had been here, my brother would not have died." My words were ripped out of my chest, ragged and raw, all my pain and fear pooling into this moment. I lowered my eyes, fearing that my rushed words had come across as a reprimand. What would Lazarus say to the Messiah if the roles were reversed, and I was the one in the grave? How I wished I had the strong faith of my brother!

Past Jesus, along the gently rounding curve of the hill, stood Azariah, its wide-sweeping canopy speaking of love and loss. My gaze dimmed. Everywhere I looked, the earth was full of graves. It was too much. The burden of death was too much to bear.

First Ima, then the father I once knew. Savta and then sweet Gilah's friendship. The precious gift of Uri. All taken from me. And now this last crushing blow. The losses stacked one on top of the other until I was buried beneath them. I could see nothing else, feel nothing else but the relentless weight of grief.

Everyone who mattered most to me had been snatched away. I cradled my empty, scarred hands in my lap, aching with a loss that refused to be filled, my mind roaring with pain that refused to be silenced. I had been left hollowed out and alone.

You are not alone.

The thought arose unbidden.

You have not lost everyone. You have gained more than you have lost. You are not alone.

My head bowed under the truth flooding my mind. I'd been given the gift of a lifetime, a privilege my ancestors could only dream of.

I'd been given the chance to love and befriend the Christ.

He was looking at me with tenderness as I raised my eyes to his again. Even though I didn't understand how one so good as

Lazarus could be taken from this earth, even though my heart was burdened with crippling disappointment in Jesus' delay, I wanted him to know that my belief was still his. I did not need to fully understand his ways to give him my allegiance, and so I tempered my previous rushed words with words of faith. "But *even now* I know that God will give you whatever you ask."

Jesus knelt and extended his hand to me. I grasped it tightly, blinking back tears as I let him draw me to my feet. His voice, warm and sure, greeted me like a kiss. "Your brother will rise again."

We were standing face-to-face now, his disciples observing us with strained expressions. I recognized the risk they were all taking by even being here.

"Yes, I know that he will rise when everyone else rises, at the last day." I acknowledged Jesus' words, recognizing them as a balm meant to comfort me, like the words others had spoken during the last few days. But Jesus was shaking his head as if I misunderstood him. My brow furrowed in confusion as a sheen of tears glimmered in his eyes. He seemed to be having difficulty speaking, and my chest constricted in response.

"Martha," he managed to say, "*I am* the resurrection and the life." He dropped my hand to thump his chest adamantly, eyes igniting with fervency, voice quavering with emotion but growing stronger and more urgent as he continued. "Anyone who believes in me will live, even after dying, and everyone who lives and believes in me will never die."

The words coming from this man's mouth were ones only God Himself could say. The weight of his meaning fell upon me like a comforting embrace, and in the direct and unwavering hold of his gaze I saw that he was inviting me into deeper truth, deeper intimacy.

Jesus searched my eyes. "Do you believe this?"

His blunt question hung in the air between us. Jesus had

denied me his presence and power, and now he asked me to confirm my belief in him. I could take great offense at such a request.

In the corner of my eye, Azariah's branches billowed, beckoning my heart to remember its loss, suggesting that I hold back my belief from this man as he had held back his power from me. And yet, stronger than the loss and hurt was a calm certainty. I had seen things I could not deny, heard words of life that pierced the soul, and there was no going back. I would not close myself to truth or cling to my hurt more than to Adonai. And so, I looked Jesus straight in the eye and accepted his question with an open heart.

Did I believe that the man standing in front of me didn't simply have access to life, access to God, but was, in fact, these very things himself? Was I ready to publicly confess with my mouth that Jesus was who he said he was?

The image of Uri, young, hopeful, and deeply in love, filled my mind. I closed my eyes at the memory—Uri's strong arms outstretched as we walked this very path. *"I confess that I've often not understood it. I've not understood the winding path Yahweh placed me on."*

I opened my eyes and stared at the Christ. I didn't understand this path. In truth, I did not want this path. But it was the path that Yahweh had given me, and perhaps that was enough.

Jesus was waiting, patiently gazing into my eyes. "Martha," he repeated, "do you believe this?"

The path—winding, mysterious, and painful—had led me here to this moment with this man.

And I was grateful.

"Yes," I gasped. "Yes," I repeated, louder, raising scarred hands in surrender. "Yes!" I released a surprised laugh, body shuddering with the magnitude of the truth before me.

Jesus grasped my trembling hands, steadying me, and I clung

to him. "Yes, Lord." The conviction was a gift, blossoming in my heart and flowing from my lips. "I believe that you are the Christ, the Son of God, who is coming into the world."

Gladness, bright and glorious, spread slowly over Jesus' face. He closed his eyes briefly, then drew me close and pressed his forehead to mine. "Go and fetch your sister," he murmured.

I returned home with no less urgency than I'd departed. Mary was where I'd left her, sitting in the study, fingering the single open scroll on Lazarus' table. Rather than make a public announcement, I drew Mary aside with great anticipation, for the one at whose feet she'd found refuge was now calling for her by name.

"Jesus is here and wants to see you," I whispered in her ear. "He's near the grove."

Mary's eyes jumped to mine for a moment before she turned and crashed headlong into the table. Yelping in pain, she rubbed her leg, stepping to the side and knocking over a tall jar of scrolls before finally stumbling from the room.

Numerous pairs of startled eyes watched her, and soon their feet followed. Surprised murmurs rippled through the crowd when Mary turned in the opposite direction of the graveyard. She sprinted toward the grove and beat us all there. Jesus was still on the terraced pathway, and Mary had nearly reached him by the time we came into view.

Down the crowd streamed, and me along with it. Mary crumpled, sobbing, at Jesus' feet. I was too far away to hear what she said, but at the sight of her grief, many in the crowd began to wail and pound their chests. And then, much to everyone's surprise, Jesus knelt next to Mary. Instead of lifting her to her feet as he'd done with me, he stayed on his knees in the dirt and wrapped Mary in his arms.

As the crowd joined them and mingled with the disciples, sorrow increased, and many of the disciples began to weep. My heart swelled at the great show of love for my beloved brother.

Jesus looked up at me from his position in the dirt, still clutching a sobbing Mary, his face ravaged with grief as he asked, "Where have you laid him?"

"Lord," I sniffed, barely able to utter the words, "come and see."

As Jesus stood, supporting Mary against his side, a deep sob shook him. He lifted his face, eyes furiously piercing the blue of the sky. Tears streamed unchecked down his cheeks as he opened his mouth in a silent wail. He stood transfixed like this for a long moment, as if in the grip of something unbearable, before finally drawing breath once more in a deep, prolonged gasp. The crowd watched in astonishment as he dropped his face into his palm with a groan.

"See how he loved him!" Gilah spoke from behind me, and I heard others echo her words as we all traveled up the slope and to the tomb.

As we approached the graveyard, Elchanan began to frown and mutter, "They are all touched by his show of sympathy, but couldn't someone who opened the eyes of a blind man also have kept this man from dying?"

His pointed words illuminated the root of my disappointment. On the heels of the hurt, however, came the remembrance of Jesus' bold declaration: "I am *the resurrection and the life*." In remembering his words, the lesser words of a spiteful man had no power over me.

The path to our family tomb was narrow. Many of those who accompanied us stationed themselves off the path, on high outcroppings overlooking the tomb, their wails amplified as they resounded off the craggy cliffs.

Jesus strode purposefully, almost angrily, to the tomb and smacked an outstretched palm hard against its surface. He left it there for a moment, head bowed, then slid his hand down and raised his head to gaze at his surroundings. Jaw clenched, he took in the mourners high above us as well as the cliffs pockmarked with white stones.

A rush of air left him, sounding sharp and indignant. He strode several paces away from the tomb, then abruptly whipped back around, as if confronting an enemy. With a long and steady arm, he pointed to my brother's resting place and in a loud voice commanded, "Take away the stone."

I glanced worriedly at Mary, who was standing still in shock. "He must not realize how long Lazarus has been dead," I whispered, hoping that she'd say something. When she remained silent, I looked to Cleopas, who was several paces behind me, and to Gilah, who was on a ledge to my right. They were open-mouthed and confused. The wailing fell silent as Jesus' words reverberated throughout the crowd.

Swallowing hard, I stepped forward and gently relayed the hard news. "Lord, he has been dead for *four days*." When his determined stance did not change, I stated the obvious, my words halting with embarrassment. "By this time, the smell will be . . . terrible." Couldn't he mourn from out here? Why open the tomb and expose himself to the stench and ritual uncleanness?

Jesus' eyes bored into mine. Gone was the soft and tender side that had comforted my sister and me moments before. In its place I saw fire, purpose, power. "Didn't I tell you that if you believed you would see the glory of God?"

At his words, I fell silent.

Cleopas had come to stand quietly at my side, his hand resting protectively on my arm. I turned to him and nodded, eyes wide. Without questioning either me or Jesus, Cleopas threw his shoulder against the stone. Lemuel joined him, and then Samu. As they heaved the stone aside, I fell back against Mary, my mind whirling, breath short. She clutched at my arm, her labored breath loud in my ear as we watched the opening slowly widen.

Everyone stepped back as the tomb opened. Jesus, however, moved forward until he stood alone before the gaping entrance. Spreading his hands wide, he gazed again into the sky, his voice simultaneously commanding and intimate. "Father, thank You for hearing Me. I know that You always hear Me, but I said this out loud for the sake of all the people standing here, so that they will believe that You sent Me."

He spoke to God with a poignancy I'd never witnessed before—like he could see Yahweh, so tender and sure were his words.

We were all silent, holding our breath. Jesus' next words resounded like thunder, leaping over the cliffs, stretching into the depths of the tomb, penetrating our wondering minds.

"Lazarus! Come out!"

I could hardly comprehend his words. Mary's grip on me tightened compulsively. Immediately, in response to Jesus' words, shuffling sounded from the tomb. It was unlike any sound I'd heard before—a slow fumbling, thumping sound that filled me with both excitement and panic. Mary and I stood rigid as the strange shuffling, bumping noise drew closer.

And then, gleaming like a beacon in the darkest night, a white figure appeared. I recognized it immediately as Lazarus. He was still bound head to toe, which made movement nearly impossible, but he flung himself forward, compelled by Jesus' words. Without the use of either arms or legs, he leaned against the side of the tomb for support, then half hopped, half slid forward, dragging his body in a bumbling, determined effort.

A shrill scream sounded from behind us and then another as the crowd's reactions finally caught up to our sight. I gripped Mary's arm nearly hard enough to break bone.

"Unbind him and let him go!" Jesus commanded, and instantly several men obeyed, stooping to loosen the binds around Lazarus' ankles and wrists.

Once free, Lazarus stood upright. A strange lightness filled my body as I moved toward him, dragging Mary with me. The closer I came, the harder my body began to tremble. My bones were featherlight, brittle things that threatened to break apart from the spasms that now shook me.

The men were still unwrapping the shroud, releasing my brother fully from his binds. I raised an unsteady hand that I hardly recognized as my own and touched his face gently before jerking the sudarium away in one smooth motion to uncover the man beneath.

Two bright brown eyes greeted me. The eyes of my baby brother.

I dropped the cloth and stared deeply into the face I thought I'd never see again. "Brother?" I murmured and cupped his cheek in my hand. It was supple, warm, alive, and at the touch, strength poured slowly back into my bones. "Oh, Lazarus."

He gave me a lopsided grin, and something within me released. I fell hard against his chest, which was now clear of graveclothes, and gripped him with the strength of ten men. He embraced me with a loud cry of joy, snagging Mary and nestling her beneath his right arm while he continued to clutch me with his left. Mary and I wept and spluttered, befuddled and overcome, while Lazarus laughed and praised God with abandon.

Behind us, disbelief and joy broke over the crowd like a thunderstorm, the exuberant sound of rejoicing outdoing even the previous display of grief. We were wild with it, swept up in it, delirious with the overwhelming certainty that the Messiah was among us, and he had the power to undo death with mere words.

All three of us turned to him. How was it that a man whom we could see and touch had plundered the grave? It could only be because Yahweh had come. He had seen and heard us, even as he had for our ancestors in Egypt so long ago. He had seen, heard, and acted. He was here with us as the prophet Isaiah had foretold. Immanuel—God in the form of flesh and blood. Immanuel—God in the form of an ordinary carpenter who was, even now, opening his arms to my brother with the widest of smiles on his face.

Lazarus' unhindered laughter now turned to sobs in the arms of the man who had delivered him. Never had a sight been so sweet as a man undead in the loving clasp of his deliverer.

Thirty-Three

1 Nisan
31 AD

A new year, and the world erupted around us. The intense and immediate aftershocks of Lazarus' resurrection spread far beyond our small village. As he'd done after Simon's healing, Jesus left almost immediately, even though we clamored for him to stay. We received word that he'd traveled north to Ephraim, a town near Samaria.

"It's safer for him there," Cleopas observed. "He was in disfavor with some before, but now he's caught the attention of those who possess the power to do something about it."

Nearly a week had passed since the miraculous event, and in that time our home received constant visitors as people came from far and wide to catch a glimpse of the man who had come back to life.

Lazarus could barely walk down the street without people grasping at his mantle as if some of Jesus' power remained on him. During such encounters, he would grow pale. "They look at me like I'm divine," he confided to me once, his voice shaking, eyes haunted.

"Only some," I reassured. "But think how many believe in the Christ because of his work displayed in you."

"I am unworthy," Lazarus cried.

He would not speak of the four days in the tomb, answering us briefly that some things were not meant to share. Privately, Mary and I speculated and wondered at what our brother had experienced, while outwardly we tried our best to acclimatize him to life once more. But life post-resurrection was proving more complicated than we could have imagined.

"The chief priests gave orders for anyone with information on Jesus' whereabouts to come forward," Joseph of Arimathea informed us one evening, having traveled from Jerusalem with Nicodemus.

Lazarus' expression was grim. "They mean to arrest him, then?"

Joseph nodded. "Jesus' actions spark belief in many but anger in others."

"How can they be angry with a man who restores life?" Mary questioned.

"They fear Rome will regard him as a significant threat. The root of the problem, though, is that he is interfering with their agenda and power, and they will not rest until he is silenced." Joseph stopped and seemed to consider his next words carefully. "That is not all, however." He turned to Lazarus. "They seek *your* life."

Mary gasped, and Lazarus shook his head. "But why?"

I closed my eyes briefly, knowing the answer. "Because you are a living testimony."

Joseph nodded, affirming my words. "Indeed—a walking verification of Jesus' power and claims. Your life points to him as Messiah, and the only way to undo what Jesus has done is to return you to the grave."

I shook my head. How could anyone hate the Christ and wish to undo his mighty works?

"Elchanan is the most outspoken of the bunch. In fact, it was he who left straight to the Sanhedrin and told them what Jesus had done."

At the mention of Elchanan, Lazarus sat up straighter.

"And to think, we've hosted him at our table numerous times!" I seethed.

"He's heard Jesus' teachings and seen his work firsthand," Mary added in disbelief.

"Some need no excuse for their hatred other than self-interest." At Lazarus' tone, we all turned to him. His face was pained. "He's a difficult man, certainly, but not until recently did I understand the full extent of his cruelty."

As we awaited further explanation, Lazarus kneaded his weary brow. "He's always strategically placed himself in the middle—not only in the matter of Jesus, but in all matters. He seeks no firm position that he might better curry favor. Such a man cannot be trusted."

"Having sat with him in the Sanhedrin for many years, I concur with your assessment," Nicodemus said somberly.

Mary placed a soft hand on Lazarus' arm. "You spoke of him as cruel?"

"Adina suffers horribly at his hand," Lazarus murmured. "When we were at their home for Purim, she confided in me how harshly he treats her since she refused to marry the man he has chosen." Lazarus rubbed a hand on the back of his neck and looked at his toes sheepishly. "I'm afraid Elchanan deduced our . . . um . . . connection that night."

"Which would further ignite his anger toward you," I interjected.

Lazarus nodded, his expression melancholy. "Adina has gone to live with relatives in Tiberias for the time being rather than sit under his wrath. She fears that staying at home will ignite her father's anger toward me. It is our hope that, given enough time, her father's wrath will dwindle. If we can simply wait things out . . ." Lazarus' voice trailed off, and I recognized the ache for a love that seemed impossible.

Joseph placed a hand on Lazarus' arm. "Bigger miracles have happened." He raised an eyebrow at my brother with a soft laugh. "In the meantime, you must avoid Jerusalem at all costs."

"We will keep our ears open on your account," Nicodemus added. "And relay news through Cleopas."

At the mention of Cleopas, my heart picked up pace. The unbridled joy of recent events had removed all former strain. Caught up in the miracle before us, there was no room for awkwardness. We'd celebrated together, eyes bright with belief. Normally a reserved man, Cleopas had clasped me in his arms numerous times as we experienced emotions that left us breathless and reeling. We were mutual witnesses to the glory of God unfolding in the world, and I discovered that I rejoiced in him as my companion.

On the heels of this realization, however, had come throbbing guilt. I had sought to honor Uri's sacrifice all these long and lonely years. The feather against my heart was a binding cord of love that tied me to him still.

What would happen to me if I chose this new path?

Thirty-Four

5 Nisan
31 AD

The summons arrived late at night when the time for social calls was over. "My mistress requests your presence."

I gaped in surprise at one of Simon's servants, then quickly donned my mantle, leaving a brief message for my siblings before hurrying out into the night.

We reached our destination quickly. Since Simon's physical restoration over a year and a half ago, the family's former station in life had been restored. Now as the doors groaned open, I was shocked to come face-to-face with the master himself.

"Martha, you are good to come." Simon stood before me, devoid of his typical Pharisaic dress, wearing instead a simple tunic in preparation for bed. He ran a hand through his whitening beard.

"Gilah asks for you. She will talk to no other." He gazed at me with weary eyes. "Would you please go to her? She's in the upstairs room."

With a lump in my throat, I moved past him as if skirting a

viper in my path. My gait quickened as I reached the steps, but Simon's voice from behind gave me pause.

"This means a lot to me, Martha."

I half turned toward him but kept my gaze fixed elsewhere.

"Especially . . . after all I've said . . . I wouldn't blame you for never coming near us again." He cleared his throat. "I wanted to tell you that . . . I appreciate you coming."

It was the clearest apology I would receive. I was here for Gilah, not for him, and yet I nodded my head in recognition of his words before scurrying upstairs.

Gilah paced her bedroom like a caged animal, one hand on her stomach, and the other at her mouth, where she gnawed at her fingernails. As soon as she saw me, she let out a groan in a long rush of air and sank to her knees, arms outstretched.

Without thinking, I entered her arms and held her as she sobbed against my shoulder. Terrifying thoughts flooded my mind as I crooned and stroked her black hair. Finally, as her tears subsided, I dared to ask the burning question, "Oh, Gilah, what is wrong?"

There was a pause before she replied in a shaky breath, "I am with child again."

"But this is wonderful news!" I leaned back in confusion. "Why the tears? I am so happy for you."

Gilah's long fingers splayed against her flat stomach. "Good news, yes, but I fear I will lose this one too." She closed her eyes and bowed her head. "I haven't told a soul yet, save Simon."

I gazed at this woman who'd kept me at arm's length for years. When life's hard moments had come, she'd closed the door to me and all others, as if through boxing in her wounds, she could deny them their power.

My hand fluttered to the hidden pendant. Not unlike what I'd done as well. I stretched a hand to Gilah, and she clasped it until my fingers went numb.

"You are afraid to hope."

Gilah's face crumpled as she nodded jerkily.

"It can be a fearful thing to open our hearts again to hope when we've been hurt so badly." I could barely squeeze the words past the tightness in my throat. "It requires bravery to live with an open and tender heart."

"I do not think I am strong enough," Gilah wailed, her tears wetting our clasped hands.

Who was I to counsel my friend in her hour of need? I, who had lived for years in the tight grasp of my own pain?

"Yahweh promises us strength. It is our part to trust Him." I placed a hand on her stomach. "New life is always a gift. No matter how long we enjoy that life, it is always a gift."

"I am still grieving the last babe. How do I grieve the one and hope for the other at the same time?"

Grief and hope, how often the two mingled in my own breast. "If there is one thing I am learning, it is that Yahweh is still working. He has not forgotten Israel, and He has not forgotten *us*." I gestured to us both with tears in my eyes. "The Christ has come and shown us a better way to live."

The words trembled as they left my mouth. The certainty that had filled me on the hillside upon Jesus' arrival flooded me again. "The Christ is calling each of us to come, and I don't think he begrudges the fear and hurt we bring with us."

Gilah sighed deeply, eyes sliding closed. "He is tender toward our pain. I felt it when he healed Simon."

"But he doesn't want us to live bound by that pain." How I needed to believe my own words! *Yahweh, help my unbelief.*

Gilah was silent for a moment, then lifted her eyes to mine. There was a new determination in her look. "Yahweh has given me a gift . . . again. A chance to love . . . again. I will pray for the courage to hope."

Bowing over our hands, I pleaded, *Yahweh, I also need the courage to hope!*

Gilah placed her free hand on my head, and together we wept. We both had been irrevocably touched by the healing power of the Christ and knew there was nothing impossible for him.

When our sobs had turned to sniffles, Gilah threaded her fingers through mine, giving me the crinkled-nose smile from our younger days. "My spirit rests easier having you here. I've missed you desperately, but I never allowed myself to admit it. You've been so kind to me over the years, and I wouldn't receive it."

"We don't need to revisit it."

"I let Simon's persuasions guide me for so long, and it influenced me more than I realized. Before the sickness took him, he was a hard man to love, and in trying to love him I became a hard woman myself. I spent many years sick with regret." Gilah bit her lip and looked quickly away. "I mourned you as the daughter I could have had. I was angry with Yahweh. . . ." She broke off, her confession requiring all her strength. "I was angry that I had refused one marriage only to end up in another like it." Gilah turned tormented eyes to me. "I love my husband now; I truly do. But for many years, I was filled with so much fear, anger, and regret that I couldn't love him, you, or anyone."

"Oh, Gilah." Our shared history spread before us like a tangled pathway with the blame never arriving at any one doorstep. "I'm not guiltless," I managed to choke out. "I've spoken my share of harsh words out of hurt and anger. I let my desire for a mother blind me to my friend." I smiled at her through the tears. Finally, in our mutual confession, I glimpsed the road to our friendship's true repair.

She walked with me to the courtyard. Simon was no longer in sight as a servant unbarred the gate.

"Simon and I . . . we want to host a banquet in honor of Lazarus and Jesus." She looked nervously into my eyes.

I was pleased to pursue a restored relationship with Gilah,

but her husband was another matter. Could we comfortably celebrate under his roof after the malicious words he'd uttered in the synagogue?

"I understand your hesitation, but there is no ill intent here. Simon wishes to celebrate the great goodness done to your family. He believes in Jesus now, as you and I do."

"*Now* he believes? Despite his own miraculous healing?" Instantly I regretted my harsh intonation, but Gilah seemed unaffected.

"Simon is a bullheaded man, set in his ways. It took multiple acts of God to pierce his thick skull." She smirked. "He was changed after his own healing, yes, but now that change has turned into true belief. There is something about seeing a dead man walking again that undeniably changes the world."

I couldn't disagree. Nearly all in Bethany now celebrated Jesus as the Christ. Was it so hard to believe that Simon also had changed? I was recognizing more and more the malleable nature of man. I saw it in my brother's faith and my sister's devotion. I saw it in the softening of my own hurt and calloused heart. Humankind was destined to change under the touch of an unchanging God. The times we were living in—who could traverse them and remain the same? Not I, and certainly not even Simon.

Keeping people at arm's length had not served me well in the past. The years of strain between Mary and me were a constant reminder of my own willfully stubborn heart. And so, as we parted with a kiss to the cheek, I promised to relay the message to my brother.

Lazarus was gratified to accept the invitation the following day, although we all wondered whether Jesus would dare to show his face again so close to Jerusalem, especially during Passover, when the city and surrounding villages were teeming with pilgrims.

But accept he did. With intense excitement, I helped Gilah

prepare the feast, setting aside my qualms at entering Simon's home as we all anticipated seeing and serving the Christ once again. My mind traveled back to all the times I'd served before. With clarity I remembered which were Jesus' favorite dishes and relayed this information to Gilah. We prepared roasted quail with a citrus honey glaze; dates stuffed with minced meat, fresh mint, and parsley; and my signature nut cake dessert, among numerous other dishes.

My heart softened toward Simon as I saw him spare no expense. Whatever Gilah and I deemed necessary, he granted. I worried, however, for Mary, who joined in our preparations only when doing so allowed her to remain in our home. She stoutly refused to enter Simon's home and avoided answering me when I asked what she would do the day of the feast.

Part of her reservation was due to Lemuel. I'd overheard the two engaged in a heated debate in the middle of our courtyard. Ducking low in my herb garden, I'd hidden behind a raised bed of sage as Mary angrily wept. "You never once stood up for me, fought for me!" Risking a peek, I saw Mary with her hands clenched at her sides, facing Lemuel, whose face was racked with emotion.

"I wanted to, but why would I when I'd been discarded? How else could I interpret your actions when you leapt so quickly into the arms of another man?"

"So quickly? I hardly—"

"And then another after him and another? How was I to trust your words of commitment to me when you acted this way?"

"I will not be defined by my past anymore. Even then you must have seen that it was I who felt abandoned by you. I was alone and facing threats from your father and you did *nothing*."

The pain in Mary's voice was evident. She'd been nursing her woundedness for so long, and now I saw her past as cries for help, attempts to soothe a relentless ache. My heart throbbed with compassion as I risked another glance to find Lemuel storming off, leaving Mary collapsed on a bench.

Oh, Yahweh, I prayed, *guide and guard these young ones.* They had such a long road ahead of them, these childhood friends turned sweethearts.

Apparent in Mary's outburst was her continued fear of Simon, and I sensed that between her terror of the man and her hopeless love of his son, it would be nearly impossible for Mary to attend the banquet.

My predictions proved true when the day of the banquet arrived and Mary remained home while Lazarus and I, dressed in our finest clothes, left for Simon's home. No amount of cajoling from Lazarus could persuade her, although she hedged by saying she had a headache and would come later.

Simon's large home was alive with activity. With the Passover so close, there were many in attendance from all over the nation, northern accents mingling with southern, relatives reuniting with loud exclamations and kisses. When Jesus arrived, dusty and weary with travel, the celebration became even more boisterous. Many of the guests had been present at my brother's graveside miracle, but some had only heard of this Jesus of Nazareth, believing in him from afar and rejoicing now that they saw him in the flesh.

In all the commotion, he took the time to personally greet Lazarus and me, his tired face creasing warmly in welcome. "My friends," he murmured, releasing me from his arms to place calloused hands on my shoulders. "How I've missed you." He turned and drew Lazarus into an embrace, looking at us with eyes flickering with emotion.

I served along with Gilah and other women from the village. With each fragrant dish that I brought to Jesus' side, I prayed that the mental distress I detected in him would ease. When I brought him the nut cakes, he immediately popped one onto his tongue, lolling it to the side of his mouth, where it appeared to lodge in his teeth and bulge from his cheek. He looked up at me with a lopsided grin. "Now *these,*" he mumbled around the sweet, "I have been looking forward to."

My heart swelled at the simple pleasure I was able to afford him. I stood silent and happy as he took another and then another, grazing my hand in a thank-you before allowing me to pass the plate to Lazarus.

As the evening progressed, I kept alert for Mary, praying that her earlier promise to come later was truth and not bluff, but as the demands of serving grew, my mind slipped from my sister. It was a surprise, then, when I rounded a corner and bumped into her in the courtyard.

She jumped and clutched at the object in her hands, pressing it tightly against her chest. "You startled me, sister," I yelped, relieved to see her. "Praise God you've come. I would hate for you to miss seeing Jesus. Here." I stretched out the full pitcher of wine in my hands. "Serve this while I fetch the bowl for the men to wash their hands."

Mary stood silently, staring at the proffered pitcher, finally lifting tearful eyes to mine. Only then did I notice what she was carrying. She held an alabaster flask, its pleasing curves narrowing into a slender neck sealed with wax. The whiteness of the flask nearly glowed in the dimming light. I glanced from it to Mary, confusion lacing my voice. "What is this?"

"Something . . . of great value," Mary breathed.

"Why bring it here tonight, and where did you receive it? I don't recognize it."

Mary closed her eyes as if in pain and bowed her head slightly. "It was a gift . . . from a man. Something I've held on to as a dowry but which I no longer need. Please, sister." She opened her eyes, and I could see the deep resolve in them gleaming like diamonds. "I must go in now."

For several long moments, I studied her with uncertainty. Clarity eluded me, but I sensed a holy resolve that I dared not interfere with. Once I would have reprimanded Mary for not helping, might have even demanded to know exactly what she was going to do. The need to control her actions had consumed me for far too long. I was recognizing more and more the need to relinquish my hold, so I nodded and stepped to the side, allowing Mary to pass.

I followed her silently into the room and stood by the doorway, pitcher in hand, while Mary padded quietly, unswervingly to where Jesus reclined at the table next to Simon, who was laughing at something Lazarus was saying.

Mary stood still for a moment behind Jesus, and as she did so, the room grew quiet. Jesus shifted in his seat, glancing up at Mary. As his gaze rested upon her, Mary fell to her knees, bringing the alabaster flask down with her in a calculated swing, aiming the slim neck at the side of the table, where it shattered upon impact, her eyes never leaving his.

A collective gasp filled the room as the head of the flask rolled across the table and the deep, earthy smell of spikenard flooded the house. The smell was of royalty. In one swift movement, Mary had transformed the dining room into a throne room.

The guests were utterly silent as Mary rose and gently poured some of the costly amber liquid over Jesus' head. I stood with a trembling hand over my mouth as Jesus' eyes closed in deep pleasure, the thick perfume flowing into his hair, bathing his scalp, trickling down his neck. Kneeling behind him, Mary then poured the rest of the perfume over Jesus' bare feet.

When she unveiled her head and let down her thick hair, scandalized whispers traveled like fire throughout the room, for no decent Jewish woman uncovered her hair in public. Slowly, Mary worked the expensive oil into Jesus' feet, rubbing it over and under and between his toes, her hair falling in waves around her face. Even though the room was full of people, it felt like a private, holy moment. No one dared say a word as Mary pulled her thick hair over one shoulder, allowing the black tresses to pool over Jesus' feet, hiding them from view. Mary began wiping his feet with her hair, gently patting them dry.

People began finding their tongues at the conclusion of Mary's display. First one voice, then another, rose with objections. "What a waste," one man mumbled.

"Why would she do such a thing? That was at least a pound."

I glanced with gritted teeth at Simon. As host, he had the authority to silence the voices, but he sat rigidly with a shocked look on his face.

Finally, one of Jesus' own disciples, Judas Iscariot, rose to his feet and gestured angrily. "Why wasn't this ointment sold for three hundred denarii and given to the poor?"

At his pronounced outburst, others became vocal, some even directing their comments to Mary, who sat quiet and unmoving under their heated criticism. Simon broke through his stupor by placing a restraining hand on Judas, urging him to keep calm, asking him to sit. Lazarus extended a comforting hand to Mary as more and more hurtful words flew about the room.

"Enough!" Jesus' voice pierced through the complaints. He thumped a fist on the table and sat up. Instantly, the quarreling voices quieted. "Leave her alone!" Anger leapt into his eyes as he came to my sister's defense. "Why do you trouble her so?" His voice was disbelieving, frustrated. "She has done such a beautiful thing to me." He turned and gestured to Mary, who had raised her head to look at him with soft eyes.

"You always have the poor with you, but you will not always have me." His voice cracked. "This woman . . . she has done what she could. In anointing me, she has done so to prepare me for burial."

An eloquent defense, for no one would begrudge love outpoured for the dead. So why do so when the extravagant gift was for the living, who could receive it with gratitude?

I recognized in Mary's gift a great exchange. Knowing my sister's woundedness and broken past, I could sense the statement she was making. She was "wasting" her dowry on this man, declaring him worthy of it all. She was trading her past for his declaration of her worth.

My sister had become a devoted woman—whole, restored, pure. Such was the great love and gratitude coursing through me that Jesus' next words aroused no envy. Rather, I marveled at the weighty import of them.

"Truly, I say to you, wherever the gospel is proclaimed in the whole world, what she has done will also be told in memory of her."

Thirty-Five

10 Nisan
31 AD

Jesus and his disciples stayed the night at our home, rising before dawn. "He has turned his face toward Jerusalem," Philip told us somberly. "We tried to talk him out of it, but he is determined. He walks toward danger, but God forbid he do so alone. We will go with him."

Not only his disciples, but all of Bethany flooded the streets to escort Jesus from the village. Rather than the southern route we were used to taking, Jesus headed north, toward the small village of Bethphage at the northernmost point of the Mount of Olives. A sharp breeze carried the earthy scent of imminent rain as my siblings and I joined the crowd on the winding road. I recalled Joseph of Arimathea's solemn warning that Lazarus' life was in danger and laid a protective hand on his arm.

Sensing my concern, Lazarus squeezed my shoulder. "Do not fear, sister. Look at the crowds." He gestured around us. "I'm hardly in any danger surrounded by so many."

Ahead and behind us, people young and old, highborn and

lowborn, packed the road. If Lazarus was safe in such a crowd, then surely Jesus would be safe too.

It was still early morning when we arrived in Bethphage. The crowd waited in the surrounding palm grove as Jesus tarried. The smell of a king still clung to him, evidence of Mary's gift from the previous night.

"What is he planning to do here?" I questioned Lazarus, but he had no more insight than I. Two disciples entered the village while Jesus remained behind. "You should ask him," I prodded my brother. "See what he intends to do."

As I spoke, a loud commotion broke out to the west from the direction of the Holy City. In bewilderment, we watched as a crowd, much larger than our own, wound their way up the slope, shouting and waving palm branches, a sign of national victory. I had harbored such anxiety for Jesus, fearful that he'd be met with clubs and swords, but this? I had not expected this. Shouts of "Hosanna!" drifted through the air, and my heart pounded in excitement.

"They're worshiping him," Mary murmured in awe.

Hope filled me at her words, swelling to the point of overflow as the shouts of praise grew clearer with the crowd's approach. "Blessed is the king who comes in the name of the Lord, the King of Israel!"

"They're recognizing him as king!" I turned joyously to Mary.

The crowd joined ours at the top of the mountain like two crashing waves on the Sea of Galilee, jubilation rising to the surface upon impact. We were caught up in it like a helpless boat.

Two burly men seized Lazarus and pulled his arms upward in exaltation. "He's here! This is the man who once was dead and now is alive again!"

Mary and I watched wide-eyed as Lazarus was jostled away, barely managing to give us a bewildered look before being fully consumed by the crowd. Jesus was surrounded as well, although his disciples managed to maintain a protective guard around him.

"Do they intend to make Jesus king?" My voice sounded shrill in my own ears.

"They're certainly declaring him so with their words." Cleopas drew close to my side, his hand coming to rest at the small of my back.

"Don't worry for your brother." Nicodemus joined us, nearly shouting to be heard. "This isn't the crowd we need to worry about. Most are from Galilee and only recently heard of Lazarus from those who witnessed his resurrection. He's somewhat of a national hero. Hearing of this miracle, they've come to escort Jesus into Jerusalem."

"They're doing all of this . . . because of Lazarus?" Mary questioned, disbelief in her voice.

"It would seem so." Cleopas laughed.

The air pulsed with exhilarating energy, like the moment when Lazarus left the tomb. My heart throbbed with longing for the crowd's cries to be realized, for Jesus to be recognized nationally as the Savior he was. Closing my eyes briefly, I let myself revel in the image of him high and lifted over our oppressors. Surely the Son of God, who had power over death, also had power over Rome. I opened my eyes to find Cleopas studying me.

"We should join them," I spoke eagerly, my breath leaving me in a rush of anticipation. Casting my eyes around the palm grove, I tugged at Cleopas' sleeve. "Come, let's gather branches and join them!"

I wasn't the only one with this idea. Others from Bethany had already begun dispersing into the grove. Small children shimmied up the shaggy trunks of date palms and began throwing down long fronds to people below. I giggled like a girl, not caring how I sounded or appeared as I darted into the grove with a loud cry of joy.

Being part of such a moment was the greatest of gifts and the truest of joys. While children continued to throw down branches, I scooped them up in my arms and began handing them to those around me. In all the excitement, I lost sight of Nicodemus and Mary. Cleopas, however, was sticking close to my side, and as I darted farther into the grove, he rushed to keep up with me.

He caught me behind a large tree, snagging my arm and whirling me around to face him. My arms were full of fronds, their long leaves spiking up into my face, obscuring him from my view. I laughed and twisted in his grip, trying to rid my mouth, nose, and ears of the leaves. My laugh turned to a gasp of surprise as he drew me sharply against him, causing me to drop the fronds.

"I cannot stand it, Martha. Each moment I'm with you, my heart confirms it. I love you—I always have." His face was close to mine, breath warm on my cheeks. "If you were simply indifferent to me, I might be able to stand that. I would begin the long, hard work of driving all love for you out of my heart. But you are not indifferent." He looked deeply into my eyes, piercing me beneath his gaze, laying my emotions bare with his scrutiny. "You are *not* indifferent." He said the words again, slowly. They poured over me like honey, sweet and thick, into my heart.

I shivered in his arms, which seemed to embolden him. He raised a hand to my face, tracing my cheekbone with his thumb. "I sense it when you look at me, and you *do* look at me—long and often, dear Martha. I see it in the preference you show me, serving me the choicest pieces of food. And don't think for a moment that I'm the only one who notices."

My mouth opened and closed silently, mind whirling and confused. Since when had Cleopas become so bold? There was a growing fire deep in my belly in response to his words, his touch, his look. He was a man who knew exactly what he wanted.

And what he wanted was me.

Cleopas rubbed his thumb along my jawline, his gaze dropping to my lips. "So this is what I'm telling you."

I swallowed hard and realized that my lips were parted and raised to him as if welcoming his kiss.

"I will continue to wait for you however long it takes. When you come to know your own mind, I will be here." He slid his hand from my face to my neck, where my pulse hammered hard beneath his palm. "Something restrains you. But I sense that it isn't a lack of fondness for me. If it is, then tell me now. Tell me directly and at once and let us be done with this." He stopped then, releasing me from his arms, and raised his brows, waiting for my word of release.

But I couldn't give it.

The warmth spreading through my body, the quivering in my knees, and the surprising, nearly overpowering desire for his lips to land on mine told me that I could not give him the definitive word that would drive him away. My face flushed with this new knowledge, and I blinked rapidly, looking away from his deep brown eyes and studying instead my dusty toes peeking from beneath the hem of my robe.

"As I thought," he murmured softly. There was no exultation in his tone, only a quiet statement of fact. He drew near again but didn't touch me, which only caused my body to ache for him. "You see, you dear and stubborn woman, you see how I cannot drop this conversation. I will wait for you to untangle whatever holds you back."

He left me then, and I stood rooted to the spot, letting his words settle within me, conflicting emotions leaving my head spinning.

"That looked intense." Mary's voice jolted me back to the present. She held a palm branch and looked at me with wide eyes. "It looked intense . . . and intimate. Of course you'll share with your beloved sister everything that happened."

Before I could reply, loud shouts pierced the air. Mary and I looked up to see Jesus' head bobbing through the trees. "What . . . ?" I frowned, thoughts of Cleopas set aside for now as I quickly grabbed a palm branch from the ground and rushed with Mary in Jesus' direction.

We neared the road as Jesus passed, riding on the back of a colt. People rushed to throw palm branches and the cloaks off their own backs to the ground, where they were trampled by the colt's hooves, a graphic display of their loyalty to Jesus as leader and ruler. The young animal, which should have been spooked, especially around such crowds, ambled calm and demure down the road with the bearing of an animal twice its age.

We tried to shoulder our way to Jesus, but the press of the crowd made it impossible. Instead, we raised high our palm branches and trailed behind our Lord and King as he traveled the road from Bethphage to Jerusalem.

As the road dipped down the western slope of the Mount of Olives, the cries of the crowd grew more focused. A woman behind us yelled, "Hosanna to the Son of David!" And soon her cry was repeated over and over by others. The Son of David—the long-anticipated king who would establish David's throne forever. "Blessed is the coming kingdom of our father David!"

The kingdom that I never thought to see in my lifetime . . . it was here! "Hosanna in the highest! Peace in heaven and glory in the highest!" Mary and I raised our voices along with the others, chanting these phrases over and over, singing them, rejoicing in them, calling them out for all to hear.

Not all in the crowd were pleased, however. A handful of Pharisees flanked Jesus with angry scowls, lips moving quickly, fingers jabbing at the crowd and at heaven. Jesus, however, wasn't stopping. He urged the colt forward, the Pharisees walking briskly to keep up, their extra-long *tzitziyot* on the hems of their robes flapping in the breeze. He responded calmly, gesturing to the side of the road as he did so, and then quickened his pace, leaving the Pharisees behind, where they quarreled and fumed to one another.

A little farther along, we reached a rocky outcropping overlooking the Holy City. Here, Jesus stopped, and the crowd hushed as the sound of his weeping filled the air.

"Why is he crying?" Mary's voice broke. "I hate to see him so." She pushed forward as if to comfort him, but I placed a restraining hand on her arm, sensing Jesus' need for privacy. Even his disciples stepped back a pace as he raised his face upward and wailed, "Jerusalem! O Jerusalem!"

"He's weeping over the city," I murmured to Mary, stating the obvious, my voice catching as I observed his distress. The question remained: Why?

From our vantage point, we could see the city stretched out below, its splendid walls and towers breathtaking against the skyline. "Look," Mary whispered to me. "The lambs."

Hundreds upon hundreds of pure and spotless lambs were being driven into the city through the Sheep Gate in preparation for sacrifice.

"If this gross display doesn't seal his fate, nothing will." The rush of angry words came from behind, and I turned quickly to see the same Pharisees from earlier now observing Jesus with livid expressions.

"None of this would have occurred if we'd simply seized Lazarus as I'd suggested days ago," one of them hissed. "This is exactly what I feared would happen."

"No one could foresee this level of public display," another countered.

The group moved off the road, and before I could think better of it, I followed them, dragging Mary behind me. She began protesting, but I silenced her with terrified and urgent words. "They speak of Lazarus!"

"We are gaining nothing," one of them moaned and pointed vehemently at the crowds. "Look, everyone is going after him!"

"Elchanan insists it's not too late."

Now Mary was listening as intently as I was. We stood silent and painfully still at the side of the road, eyes trained forward as the group of Pharisees continued to talk.

"Even now, he is raising witnesses who are willing to testify against Lazarus."

"Testify how?"

"Haven't you heard? It's common knowledge that Lazarus' proximity with this blasphemer Jesus has turned him into a blasphemer as well." The man's tone was deceptive and sly, indicating that the reports were planted. "In fact, there's a man willing to say he's heard Lazarus utter blasphemy against Moses and the Law."

"What's more," another added, "there are rumors that Lazarus himself is a sorcerer, conspiring with Jesus in an elaborate hoax. Two witnesses are willing to say as much."

They continued talking but moved farther from the road.

Mary turned to me with terrified eyes and spoke the words burdening my own heart. "We must find Lazarus."

Doing so, however, proved an impossible task. As Jesus continued down the Mount of Olives, Mary and I searched the crowds in vain. We didn't want to shout Lazarus' name and draw unwanted attention to him, so we silently scanned the crowds, asking those we trusted if they had seen our brother.

At the base of the western slope of the Mount of Olives nestled a peaceful garden called Gethsemane. Its well-tended pathways curved around gnarled olive trees interspersed with shrubbery. I had been in this garden many times before, and usually the tranquility of the silent, silver-leafed trees inspired calm, but today, they prompted worry.

We were now so close to Jerusalem.

Yahweh, please! We need to find Lazarus before he goes any farther.

As soon as the prayer left my heart to Yahweh's ears, my eyes snagged on an olive tree on the far side of the garden. It loomed large and towering over its brethren, keeping watch between the garden and the Kidron Valley.

Go there. The inward tug was like a physical prompt. Without hesitation, I pointed it out to Mary, and we ran to the tree, stopping short of the ridgeline overlooking the Kidron Brook.

Disappointment flooded me as my eyes scanned the crowd streaming from the garden, down the valley, and to the narrowest portion of the Kidron. I had been so certain we would find Lazarus here.

The crowd was beginning to cross the brook when I turned and came face-to-face with my brother.

He was out of breath and flushed, eyes bright and beaming at us. "There you are, sisters!" So casual, as if his very life didn't hang in the balance.

Thank You. I closed my eyes briefly before grasping my worrisome brother's arm. "We must leave."

"What are you talking about? We can't leave now!" Lazarus gestured to where Jesus was descending into the valley. "Not when we're so close to the city!"

"That's exactly *why* we must leave," Mary chimed in. "We've overheard a plot to frame you for blasphemy, sorcery, and God only knows what else!"

"I was jaded before." Lazarus spoke as if we hadn't relayed urgent information. He gazed thoughtfully over our surroundings. "I haven't spoken freely to you because I haven't been able to find the words. But it's been hard." He turned to us then, tears glistening in his eyes. "It's been hard to be . . . alive again."

Mary and I quieted at his admission, our frantic mission paused in the face of his vulnerability.

"As overwhelmingly glad as I am to be in the land of the living with those whom I love, it's also difficult being surrounded once again by the world's brokenness and man's sinfulness. And others' reactions to me . . ."

He broke off, swallowing convulsively. "I feared I was detracting from my Lord when people came for miles to touch my robe. I am but a man!" His eyes were fire, his face wrenched into an expression of anguish that I could not understand.

"I am not any different than they, and yet . . . and yet I *am*. In raising me from the dead, our Lord set me apart." His voice trailed off once again. "I can hardly explain it, but today . . . today, I see the purpose in it all and it gives me more joy than I can contain. These people—" he flailed his arms around in a wild expression of happiness—"they heard of what our Lord did for me, and it gives them the courage and the hope to claim him as king. Praise Yahweh that He saw fit to use my life for His glory!"

Mary and I stood woodenly in place, abashed and quiet, unwilling to break our brother's happy revelation and yet torn with the need to do so. Finally, I loosened my tongue enough to croak, "I am glad for you, Lazarus, and I share your joy. But, brother—there are those who even now are scheming to take your life from you once again. You need to do your part in exercising wisdom and discretion in preserving the life our Lord so graciously gave back to you."

"This is not hearsay." Mary grasped Lazarus' arm. "We overheard what Elchanan intends to do. Because of this very moment and your part in it, your life is forfeit."

"They have conspired to gather false witnesses against you." I took his other arm, trying to ground him in reality.

Lazarus finally appeared to hear us. His happy and distracted expression now sobered as he looked from one sister to the other. "You are certain of this information?"

"Very certain." I nodded. "We heard it with our own ears."

"Think of Adina," Mary added softly.

"Yes, please, brother. If you won't exercise caution for our sake, think of Adina, who suffers separation from her family, her home, and from *you* . . . all for your own sake."

Mary delivered the final blow. "Would you void her sacrifice by walking heedlessly into a snare?"

With the mention of Adina, we had won the argument. Lazarus' joy slowly morphed into frustration. He ground his teeth, wrenched his arms from our grasp, and strode away a few paces. For a long moment he stood with arms clenched, back turned before letting out a growl and whipping around to us once more.

"Fine." He spat out the word, although I could tell his frustration wasn't with us. "We will travel no farther."

Mary and I released deep sighs of relief. "We'll return by the Jericho Road," I decided. "It's not safe to return the way we've come in case some in the crowd still linger."

By this time, Jesus had crossed the brook, along with many others. Lazarus watched them with longing but allowed Mary and me to guide him to the safe obscurity of the garden grotto, a large cave containing several olive presses. There we remained until the last of the crowd had passed, their exuberant songs still lingering like a fragrant offering in the air.

Finally, we ventured out and began the trek toward home. Worry over Lazarus and the strange stirrings over Cleopas tore at my mind and drove me deeper into myself as we traveled the winding southern road back home.

Thirty-Six

It was midday when we reached home. Lazarus still had not spoken a word to us after we'd forced him from Gethsemane and now took immediately to the fields to select a one-year-old unblemished male lamb from our flock. Bringing it indoors, he housed it in a pen in the inner courtyard, where it would remain the prescribed four days until we sacrificed it at the Temple.

"Will we be able to make the journey this year?" Mary asked our brother tentatively, trailing a hand over the lamb's soft back.

Lazarus' reply was fierce. "We *will* be journeying to the Temple in four days' time, conspiracy or no conspiracy. If our Lord would risk it, then I can do no less."

"We must simply trust Yahweh in this," I said to Mary privately. "We've seen His power to restore our brother's life. Surely He can preserve Lazarus' life despite these new threats."

"Yes," Mary mused. "But we should also be prudent and not take unnecessary risks."

That evening, Mary and I supped alone, Lazarus choosing to hole himself up in his study.

"I hope he won't remain angry with us forever," Mary worried.

"I don't think he's angry with *us*."

"So." Mary's tone shifted as she shot me a sly look. "Cleopas?"

I flushed and stabbed at a chunk of carrot in my stew. "What about him?"

"Oh come, sister. We're past such hedging."

"He loves me, and I . . . admire him. He senses that something 'restrains' me, but I'm unsure how or if to tell him of Uri." There, I'd finally voiced the burden. It was a relief to talk about Uri with Mary. I was so used to bearing the weight alone, but I was learning to confide in this sister who was quickly becoming a friend.

"All those secret meetings between Uri and me, and yet word never leaked out. He's been a precious secret for so long. . . . I'm not used to talking about him, sharing anything about him with others. I honestly do not know how we managed to keep our love secret for so long."

Silence greeted me. I turned to watch Mary methodically picking apart a round of bread. "Back then . . . Lazarus and I spoke numerous times about you and Uri."

Mary's soft-spoken revelation nearly toppled me. "What?" I gagged, coughing up bits of carrot. "He never mentioned speaking with you. All these years and he never indicated that you knew a thing."

"Well, I don't think he wanted you to know how easily swayed he was by his little sister." Mary smirked. "When you threw Cleopas' offer of marriage back in Abba's face, I followed you." She shook her head at the memory. "I can understand some of your frustration with me back then. I was too sly and nosy for my own good. I heard your conversation with Lazarus. I saw his reaction and sensed your desperation. When he left you, I followed. When he ran to Abba, I stopped him."

"You convinced him to keep silent." My mind closed the gap between events, finally connecting the pieces of my history. Voice tense with unshed tears, I mused, "I always wondered what stayed his hand. He was so convinced that telling Abba was best."

"I was conniving, persuasive." Mary snorted. "I knew how to get what I wanted, especially from Lazarus."

I covered Mary's hand with my own and squeezed my thanks, throat too tight for words. To think my most precious secret had been kept by a stubborn little girl.

"Don't be afraid of this new thing with Cleopas." Mary returned the squeeze on my hand. "You will have peace when the time is right."

The evening meal had passed by the time Jesus and his disciples returned. Bethany was filled with pilgrims, and every family housed extra visitors. We'd extended an open invitation for Jesus and all in his company to stay with us, and Jesus had quickly accepted, eyes exuding his gratitude.

His return to our home was quiet and subdued, nothing like the fanfare that had accompanied him that morning. I checked the curiosity welling inside and chose to focus on ensuring his comfort and care.

"By the time he made it to the Temple, it was nearly time for us to return," John shared with us quietly.

"And what happened? When he entered the city?" Mary asked breathlessly.

John scrubbed a tired hand over his face. "Children, singing his praises in the public square. People pouring from their homes and businesses to follow him. The streets so congested it took us thrice as long to reach the Temple."

"And did no one object?" Lazarus questioned.

"None that I saw, although I doubt Rome is taking any of this seriously. It's our religious leaders who are the most put out by the display."

I swallowed hard, remembering the heated discussion Mary and I had overheard earlier that day. "Well, they will be forced to take it seriously when he comes to his throne," I mused aloud. "But when will that be?"

None of us knew. The exuberant crowd who had gathered, ready to pronounce him king, now followed his every step throughout the Holy City with dogged interest but little desire to enact a power change.

"Perhaps he's waiting until after Passover," Lazarus speculated.

As the days leading up to the festival passed, Jesus and his disciples continued to retire to our home each evening, where we heard a retelling of their day. Early in Jesus' ministry, he had driven out merchants in the Temple courts, a story that had amazed me at the time. The day after his grand entrance to the Holy City, we heard that he had done so again, with a whip and thundering authority. As he relaxed in our home, we heard snippets of how he had overturned tables and barred merchants from carrying anything through the Temple.

"He spends most of his time teaching in the Temple," Philip told us. "And it's not simply the Jews who are interested in his words. Today, some Greeks asked to see him."

"His teaching seems more somber of late," Andrew added. "He told the Greeks a confusing story about grain needing to die to produce fruit."

Philip nodded. "And he exhorted them to follow him but focused on their need to hate their own life to do so."

"It's not the first time we've heard this teaching," Andrew corroborated. "He's spoken before of hating father and mother and of losing one's life in order to gain it, but . . ." His voice trailed off as if he was unsure how to explain.

Philip placed a steadying hand on Andrew's shoulder. "But it's different this time. There's an urgency about him that puts all of us on edge."

"We heard a voice like thunder speak to him directly afterward, although we could not make out what it said." Nathaniel joined our conversation.

"It was only thunder," Judas interjected.

"Then why did our Lord say that the *voice* came for our benefit?"

The disciples continued to argue in troubled tones as I quietly exited the room. If there was one thing I had learned, it was that Jesus was worthy of my love and trust, even—and perhaps especially—when I didn't fully understand him. It was confusing and frightening to see this disunity of ideas among his own disciples.

If *they* didn't know his upcoming plans, then what hope did I have of understanding them? Could I hold onto belief in the face of such uncertainty?

---

14 Nisan
31 AD

The morning of Passover dawned uncharacteristically warm. Jesus rose early, and we walked with him for a stretch along the southern road to Jerusalem. I could tell Lazarus longed to accompany Jesus all the way, especially since he had declined our invitation to partake of the Passover meal with us that evening, choosing instead to celebrate within the city with his disciples.

Being apart from Jesus pained Lazarus, but he didn't push Mary and me, realizing we had compromised enough already by agreeing to travel to the Temple later that day for the sacrifice.

We walked with him halfway. At the lowest point in the road, before the path climbed the steep eastern side of the Judean mountain range, we stopped, and Jesus turned to us with shining eyes.

"Friends, I leave you now, but only for a short while. We'll see one another again." His words had the effect of a benediction as he approached Lazarus first, embracing him tightly as my brother clung to him.

When Jesus turned to me, his eyes softened, and he placed a comforting hand on each shoulder as he kissed my cheeks.

Mary let out a soft sob as Jesus turned from me to take her in his arms, gazing tenderly down at her.

This man was fire and kindness, strength and humility. I had witnessed the heat of his righteous anger, the tenderness of his compassion, and the bright light of his pleasure. Jesus left us now as if it was a solemn occasion. My heart constricted as the group continued along the path. He looked back at the bend in the road, casting us a long, loving look before turning to lead his disciples up the slope that wended its way toward Jerusalem. We stood rooted to the spot until every disciple rounded the bend and was lost from sight.

My heart thumped unevenly within me. We would see Jesus the very next day as the seven days of feasting began, wouldn't we? Why the somber departure?

That evening, as our household partook in the Passover meal, my mind kept wandering to Jesus and his disciples. We gathered around our table as Lazarus said the traditional blessing over the first cup of wine. "Blessed are You, Adonai our God, Sovereign of the Universe, Creator of the fruit of the vine."

Oh, to celebrate this most holy of days with Adonai's own Son in Jerusalem! My heart cried out for him as I closed my eyes and lifted the cup of dark red wine to my lips.

With each of the four cups of wine and the accompanying blessings, my mind settled into a deeper contentment. I was concerned for my brother's safety, but when had dwelling on my worries ever produced a thing? Tonight, we celebrated a God who was mighty to save, and I had witnessed His salvation firsthand as my dead brother walked out of his tomb. He had saved him once, and He could do it again.

It was deep into the night by the time we retired, and the moon was out, highlighting the planes of my sister's tired face as she bid me good night.

I was snug in bed when the wild shouting began. At first, I thought it a dream and snuggled deeper beneath my blanket, willing sleep to claim me once more. But the noise was persistent, and soon I could no longer deny that what I was hearing was real and nearby—as close as our own courtyard.

Hurriedly, I threw on my mantle and ran barefoot down the stairs. The noise was coming from our front door. Heart in my throat, I followed the sounds, stopping short as I found Mordecai closing the door behind a frantic young man.

He was bloody and naked, near to collapsing. Fear coursed through my body, and I wondered for a wild second why Mordecai would allow such a person entrance. I shouted for Lazarus over my shoulder, my voice hoarse and strained as I cautiously drew closer to the bewildering scene playing itself out in our own courtyard.

The man was close to fainting. He lay trembling on the floor, so stricken with terror that his own nakedness didn't seem to shame him.

"Grab a robe, Mordecai!" I barked the command and was about to question why he would open the door to the man, but a moment later I understood.

This young man was no stranger. This young man was Lemuel.

Thirty-Seven

By the time Mary and Lazarus reached the courtyard, I had a robe around Lemuel and was sitting next to him on the ground. Mary shrieked when she saw him and flew to his side, nearly shoving me out of the way in her haste.

"Lemuel, what happened?" All the bitterness of their previous encounter seemed to disappear as Lemuel turned to Mary with intense vulnerability, and she met him there with open arms.

"Let's move him inside, Mary." Lazarus knelt and gently pried Mary's arms from Lemuel. "Attend to his physical needs before questioning him."

"Yes, of course, of course," Mary mumbled, her tear-streaked face appearing scared and young in the moonlight.

Thankfully, Lemuel's injuries were superficial, with most of the blood coming from a long gash on his forehead that looked more alarming than it was. The terror in his eyes and trembling in his limbs, however, struck a chord of fear in all of us.

Long moments passed before we could coax him to talk. Lazarus plied him with sweet wine, and Mary stroked his hair, his cheek, his brow, and murmured words of comfort. Finally, the combined effort appeared to take effect as Lemuel gave a last deep shudder and blinked rapidly, eyes coming into focus.

"Mary," he breathed her name, eyes closing in relief.

She pressed his head to her breast. "I'm here, love. I'm here. Won't you tell us what happened?"

His trembling began again at her question, but his senses had returned enough for him to speak.

"They came for him. So many! A cohort at least. They came with lanterns and torches and weapons, like he was a ruthless insurgent. And not only them but the Temple police and chief priests."

His words sent chills down my back. A cohort of Roman soldiers numbered six hundred—a fierce sight indeed. "Who did they come for? Where?" I tried to keep my voice steady, even though I wanted to scream and shake the answers out of him.

"He could see them coming—we all could. From the garden you can see the whole valley. Why didn't he run away?"

"Gethsemane?" I whispered.

Instead of answering, Lemuel simply stared off into the distance, reliving the nightmare, his voice hollow and detached. "It was eerie . . . all those flickering lights extending over the valley and highlighting the bloody Kidron Brook. So red, so unnaturally red! Like the first plague in Egypt."

I could easily see what Lemuel described. There was a channel leading directly from the Temple altar down to the Kidron Brook, and during Passover, it streamed red with blood from all the sacrifices. For days on end, the brook was filled with blood.

"Why were you at Gethsemane, Lemuel?" Lazarus questioned.

"I followed him there," Lemuel moaned. "That traitor! How could he do such a thing?"

Now Mary herself seemed struck with irritation at the small snippets of knowledge we were gleaning. Taking Lemuel's face in both of her hands, she stared intently into his eyes. "You've clearly witnessed something terrible, so I don't blame you for being fearful. But it's important that you tell us everything. Don't leave anything out."

At Mary's measured and authoritative tone, Lemuel relaxed. "We stayed in Jerusalem to celebrate Passover with the family of Shabtai bar Absolom, one of Abba's friends. Late in the evening, I was disturbed from sleep by a large company in the courtyard. I overheard an elder saying they had an inside man to help them finally make Jesus' arrest."

My hand flew to my mouth. Mary grew pale, and Lazarus bowed his head, as if anticipating the rest of the story.

"They were leaving for Gethsemane at that very moment and had come to gather Shabtai, who is a member of the Sanhedrin as well as a chief priest. I didn't hesitate but threw on a robe and trailed behind, hoping to outpace them without being seen and warn Jesus. I was able to maneuver ahead of them once we were outside the city walls, but even then, I arrived barely before the whole company and not in enough time to warn anyone."

Lemuel hung his head, tears silently making trails down his cheeks. "The disciples were spread out in groups of two and three, resting or sleeping. I tried to shake them alert, ask them where Jesus was, but by that time there were torches. I found Jesus at the same time Judas did."

"Judas?" Mary questioned softly.

Lazarus' lips tightened, and his eyes grew hard and bright. "He was the inside man, wasn't he?" he stated. "Judas Iscariot."

My gut twisted as Lemuel nodded. Judas, a man who had been with Jesus from the beginning. He'd always appeared pragmatic, calculated in his thoughts and dealings, but I'd never thought him to be traitorous.

"He singled him out with a kiss." Lemuel's lips trembled. "Peter, James, and John were closest to Jesus. When the soldiers drew near, Peter raised a sword and lashed out at one of the servants. There was blood everywhere, and the man's screams were horrible. But then Jesus knelt, and we could all see what had happened. Peter had chopped off the man's ear."

Mary looked sick, turning her head away as Lemuel continued his story, all of us listening in stunned and horrified silence.

"He reattached the ear. He picked it up and placed it back on the man's head like he'd simply dropped a garment. . . ." Lemuel looked dazedly into the distance. "And in doing so, he certainly saved Peter's life. Jesus reprimanded the chief priests, asking them why they came to him like he was a robber when every day he's been openly teaching in the Temple."

Lemuel's voice grew strained. "When they seized him, we all . . . we all ran. It was mass confusion. I didn't plan to run, but then everyone was running. Someone ran into me and knocked me flat on my back. I would have gotten away unscathed if not for being knocked over. One of the soldiers found me stretched out on the ground and butted me in the head with his sword to knock me out. I managed to stand, and he grabbed my robe. I . . . I left the robe behind and ran."

He said the last words on a sob. "I'm so ashamed, Mary." He turned hollowed eyes to my sister, who had tears streaming down her cheeks. "I went there to warn him. If only I'd run faster, been quicker. But then instead of helping, I didn't even stay by him. I left my dignity behind and ran away like a naked, scared child." He spat the words out through clenched teeth, angry tears dripping from his chin and staining his robe with shame.

Mary tried to respond but was crying so hard she couldn't. I placed a gentle hand on Lemuel's knee and asked the question brewing in my mind. "Where did they take him?"

"I don't know!" Lemuel turned red-rimmed eyes to me. "I imagine they took him to Caiaphas."

"Nicodemus will have more information," Lazarus murmured and immediately rose to enter his study, most likely to pen a message to his friend.

"Mary, my pride is destroyed!" Lemuel was sitting upright now, clasping both of Mary's hands in his own, gazing fervently into her face. "I let myself be closed off in my hurt, believing that there was truth and rightness behind it." He dipped his head to rest his face against the back of her hands. "I am undone. I finally understand tonight who I truly am, and it disgusts me."

Mary shushed him instantly, her eyes ablaze, her voice like the spark from flint and stone. "None of us is worthy. We are all naked and undone before the holiness of God."

"Then who can stand?" Lemuel moaned. "Who can stand before this holy God?"

The answer came to me softly. "Those who align themselves with His Son."

The one who was now in the enemy's hands.

---

15 NISAN
31 AD

Jesus was being passed back and forth like an unwanted burden. This was the message we received in the early hours of the morning—a rushed, scrawled missive from a frantic Nicodemus. The high priest Caiaphas; his pompous father-in-law, Annas; Herod Antipas; and finally, Pilate himself—there was no official left in Jerusalem who wasn't playing a part in the unfolding drama.

Nicodemus urged caution, stating that he and several others in the Sanhedrin were working as hard as they could to voice reason in the ongoing trials but that it was a tricky situation that had exploded into a political scandal. He urged Lazarus to stay put until he had more precise information.

Pilate seemed favorably inclined toward Jesus, affirming his innocence multiple times, which made Nicodemus hopeful. Wait and pray, he urged us, and he'd update us soon. Nowhere in

Nicodemus' letter, however, was there a sign that Jesus was doing anything other than silently complying with his captors.

"He holds the power to raise the dead," Mary cried into my shoulder. "Why is he masking his power? Surely now would be the opportune time for him to reveal who he is."

We sat quietly in my room, sleep elusive, fretting while Lazarus locked himself away in his study.

We didn't receive word again until midmorning. Lazarus took the message in his study, Mary and I hovering by him with eager faces. Our brother unrolled the small scrap of parchment, barely looking at it before he dropped it with a low cry that shook me to my core. Turning from us, he sank onto his knees with a deep shudder that seemed forcibly wrenched from his body.

I approached the parchment like it was a cobra, reluctant to see what it contained but needing to know. I held it up so both Mary and I could see. It contained three words.

He is crucified.

The blood instantly drained from my face, and my vision narrowed as the room began to spin. Leaning over, I took in deep gulps of air, but nothing could keep the room steady. With a cry, I stumbled forward a pace and retched. There was nothing in my stomach, so it came out as a strangled gurgle. Again and again my body heaved, but there was no relief.

Mary stood rigidly by the desk, observing our afflicted forms as we lay on the ground. Her eyes had a manic sheen to them as she looked wildly from sister to brother and back again.

"It is a mistake!" Her voice was shrill and unnatural. "This isn't true. It can't be."

I turned miserable eyes to her. "It's Nicodemus' handwriting." The bile rose in my throat, causing me to double over quickly as I retched again, moaning. "Why would he lie about such a thing?"

Mary stared intently at me, eyes narrowing as she weighed my words, lips pinched and nose flaring as her breaths came faster and faster, her chest rising and falling and finally hitching with an audible gasp that turned into a prolonged scream full of rage and pain, which filled the study and left little room for anything else.

In one quick motion, she grabbed the parchment and threw it on the floor, stomping her foot, face reddening. I wanted to extend comfort, but the image of Jesus on a Roman cross filled my vision, compelling me to buckle over once again, body heaving as if trying to rid itself of the horror.

It was the worst way to die. Full of physical and emotional torture as well as public humiliation. It was so horrific that I wouldn't wish it on even the vilest of men. Why had such an extreme death been sentenced? Usually, it was reserved for the worst of criminals.

Stripped naked and beaten nearly to death, victims of this cruel torture were nailed to a rough post, arms outstretched on a crossbeam. Death often took days to come as the victim slowly suffocated, each breath a fresh agony as one had to pull the body upward for air. I had seen the twisted forms before on the sides of major roads—a visible reminder that Rome was in full control. Eyes averted, I would hurry by and pray fervently for death to come quickly for the hurting soul.

I could not reconcile the horrific sentence with my friend and dearest Lord. He had never once performed any physical violence or broken the Law. He was all that was good, kind, and true. I could more understand the earth opening and swallowing me whole, or for light to become dark and dark light than for the Son of God to die on a Roman cross.

Mary had collapsed on the ground, her arms covering her head, silent beneath the weight of shock and grief. Lazarus had stayed hidden from view behind his desk but stood now, face anguished.

"He will still be alive. I will go and bring what comfort I can."

At his words, both Mary and I lurched violently to our feet. Cleopas' warning echoed in my mind: *"Lazarus' name is being linked to Jesus in every conversation, good or ill. He continues to associate himself so closely with Jesus that I fear the fate of one will be the fate of the other."*

The thought of Lazarus suffering the fate of Jesus was unbearable and drove desperation throughout my body like a living fire, lapping at my nerves and giving life to my limbs.

"No! You cannot go!" I ran to his side, Mary close behind.

"They will kill you!" Mary screamed, close to hysteria.

Lazarus gazed forlornly into both of our faces, appearing like a young boy. "But . . . I cannot leave him alone to die like this. Not after all he did for me. The man gave me back my very life."

Mary grabbed his arm and pressed herself against his side as if she could tether herself to him and thereby keep him at home. "Would you null his work by throwing away that life?"

"Trust me, brother, going now would be your death sentence. If they could kill the Messiah this way, then they will not hesitate to do the same to you."

The image of Lazarus suspended between earth and heaven on the cruel wings of a cross consumed me. "I cannot lose you again, and certainly not to a Roman cross."

Through many tears, Mary and I pleaded with our brother.

My impassioned words raised further questions in my mind. How could Jesus be the Messiah if he was dead? He had raised my brother from death, given him back his life—therefore, why could he not preserve his own? It was all a garbled mess in my terrified mind, which chose instead to latch on to one thing: keeping my brother home.

Lazarus crumpled beneath the weight of our cries and pleas, although I could tell by the whiteness of his face that he no more relished the idea of suffering for the Christ's sake than we did.

It was nearing noon by the time we exited the study, all three of our faces pale and stained with tears. The air was wet and smelled of looming storms. Lazarus turned to say something to me but then, without warning, the whole world darkened, as if a hand had cupped the sun in its palm and snuffed its flame right out.

Thirty-Eight

Mary screamed, a short and piercing sound that echoed throughout our courtyard. And then silence.

Tense and wide-eyed, I stood gripping my brother's arm and staring up into the heavens. There was no moon, only points of stars too small to pierce the surrounding dark.

"But . . . there's a full moon this time of year," I stammered. Passover was always held during a full moon. Had something happened to the sun? Where was the moon?

The impending storm I'd sensed earlier rolled in slowly, rumbling and grinding like someone scraping the stone cover over a well, sealing in and pressing down. Impulsively, I gulped for air.

Over our courtyard walls, sharp cries of terror rent the air as others responded to the sudden darkness. Lazarus pried his arm from my grip and stumbled his way back to the study. A moment later, he returned with a lit oil lamp, which illuminated his pinched features.

Over the course of the next hour, we lit more lamps and accounted for all those in our household. Even with the lamplight, the darkness pressed close.

"Do you suppose this is what it was like in Egypt when darkness covered the land?" Mary whispered. "Is this another judgment?"

I could not answer her pressing questions—no one could. As time stretched on, we waited for the darkness to lift, and when it didn't, the panic set in deeper. Eventually, Lazarus approached me with a determined expression on his face.

"I've made up my mind to go." His words were blunt and allowed for no dissent.

I understood what he meant but asked anyway, my voice weak, "Go where?"

"I'll be under the cover of darkness. It will be safer this way. I'll travel straight to Cleopas and see what more I can discover."

"We will accompany you." Mary's firm voice surprised me. I studied her eyes, silently asking, *Are you sure about this?*

"We can at least be nearer to our Lord," Mary continued. "And perhaps learn where his disciples are housed."

The thought of being with others who had also loved our Lord was a compelling enough reason for me, so with a nod I agreed to the new plan, even though I still experienced dread.

Leaving the dark confines of our home for the open road was akin to leaving the warm depths of a blanket to enter a chilly and uncertain world. Each of us held our own lamp, enough to illuminate a few steps at a time.

With each step along the darkened road, my heart quaked, and soon it wasn't only my heart that heaved. As we neared the halfway mark, the ground shuddered beneath our feet. I glanced at the dry ground beneath my dusty feet and saw pebbles begin to bounce as another tremor shook the earth.

The Jericho Road was wide and uneven, meaning our passage had been slow and perilous up to this point as we painstakingly made our way over the rough terrain with what little light we had. With this newest difficulty, however, we stopped altogether, and I could see the gleaming whites of Lazarus' eyes as he glanced wildly about us, trying to determine our next course of action.

Angry rumbling filled the dark sky, growing in intensity as another tremor shook the earth. We were hemmed in, above and below, by the grief and displeasure of God. As it began to rain, I closed my eyes and lifted my chin, letting heaven's tears mingle with my own.

"The lamps!" Lazarus hovered over his flame, protecting it from the rain. We were at the peak of the Judean ridgeline. We should have been able to clearly see the Holy City, but the darkness was so thick that we could only make out small flickers of light from torches lining the walls and the sporadic trail of lights from others along the road.

Swinging my lamp around, I saw a craggy outcropping of stones by the side of the road and motioned for my siblings to follow me as I dashed to the shelter. We huddled beneath the rock, but there wasn't enough room for all our bodies and our lamps, so Lazarus passed his lamp to me and stood outside, bearing the wet and the wind, while Mary and I sheltered our three flames.

We sat in sodden silence as the earth continued to roil beneath us, not enough to dislodge boulders but enough to make travel imprudent. As I gazed at my brother's dark form keeping watch over us and squeezed my sister's slim, cold hand, which was tightly grasping my own, a bright and furious love warmed me.

So much had been taken from me over the years and yet these two—bone of my bone and flesh of my flesh—remained. There was little I wouldn't do or endure for them.

The uncertain earth continued to shake, reminding me of my Lord hanging even now from a cross. Apart from him, it was my siblings who meant the most to me in all the world.

There is another.

The quiet voice was immediate and soft, seeping into and warming my bones like a long swallow of good wine.

Cleopas.

Closing my eyes, I relaxed into the truth I had pushed aside for so long, letting its weight sit comfortably in me.

Cleopas.

The man who had quietly waited on the side all these years.

Cleopas.

The man who had never once pressured me but had always given of his love, time, and resources for the benefit of me and my family.

"Sister?" Mary stroked my cheek with a tender hand, and I realized I was quietly weeping. I looked at her with shining eyes, knowing that my tears were ones of relief because, for the first time, I could acknowledge the love I held for Cleopas. Yes, the *love.* I could name it and embrace it without guilt or shame.

A memory, sweet and clear, rose in my mind.

"Ah, Martha," he'd said with a grin. *"Isn't it better to behold beauty for a moment than not at all? Simply because something is fragile, does that mean it shouldn't be enjoyed to the utmost? Valued even more for its fragility?"*

Uri and I were like painted pottery—too beautiful to break. And yet our future had been shattered at my feet. Did it follow, then, that Uri had not been a gift? *No.* It was better to behold beauty for a moment than not at all.

"Love is a great gift from Yahweh. Don't forget it, Martha." I hadn't forgotten Savta's words, but I'd failed to believe them. I'd spent years thinking of love as a thief and myself as its victim. Capricious and cruel, once love left, it took hope right along with it, never to be seen again. But is this what Yahweh intended? Could Savta be right? Perhaps love was still a gift from the Lord who gives and takes away.

As the darkness overhead pressed in on all sides, I wondered—dared to believe—that love was a gift that Yahweh kept on giving. Gilah's brave words became my own cry. *"Yahweh has given me a gift . . . again. A chance to love . . . again."*

All these long years, I'd sought to honor Uri's sacrifice. But I'd also grasped at his memory, afraid to let go, afraid to find out what would happen to me if I did. The deep, dear tenor of Uri's voice sounded in my ear. *"Who knows what is yet in store for you, Talitha."*

Yahweh, give me the courage to hope! I moved from the shelter of the rock and stood with arms wide open, welcoming the weight of the rain, my face tilted to the dark sky.

"Sister?" Mary's voice pierced my rumination. Her face was eerily highlighted by the lamps. Tears mingling with the rain, I could not trust my voice with words.

"The rain, it's easing enough for us to travel." Lazarus ducked and took his lamp from Mary's slackened grip. "The tremors are infrequent enough that we should be safe."

The closer we drew to the city, the more people we encountered. Each person held the same uneasy, haunted look in their eyes, isolated within their own small pools of light, which cast shadows into the hollows of their faces.

Never had the streets of Jerusalem been so silent. There were no children calling, no scampering underfoot. Likewise, business had halted, for who could barter and trade when the day had been turned to night?

Cleopas' street was narrow and winding. We approached his door, and Lazarus rapped once, twice, the swift sound reminding me of hammer against nail. The door opened a crack before being flung wide, and there was Cleopas, arms and home open to us.

"Sometimes love engulfs us suddenly, like a consuming fire." Savta's words, cracked and hopeful. *"Other times it comes over us slowly, like a sunrise."*

The halos of light from our lamps were enough for me to find and catch Cleopas' eyes. *"Like the dawning of a new day."*

Not caring what my siblings thought, I shouldered past Lazarus and burrowed into Cleopas' wide-open arms with a sharp release of air, as if I'd been holding my breath for this exact moment.

◆

The warm glow of lamplight filled the shop with shadows that illuminated the soft earth tones of the pottery. I snuggled closer against Cleopas' side and imagined myself in a warm cave where no ill news could reach me.

His arm draped across my back, hand coming to rest at my hip. His other hand cupped my own, where he hadn't ceased to knead the tension out of each knuckle with smooth, comforting gestures.

Mary and Lazarus sat opposite us, where it appeared they were trying hard not to stare at our intimate forms. Lazarus cleared his throat and shifted his eyes to the ceiling. Mary worried her lip and covertly glanced at Cleopas' hand on my hip. I exhaled deeply, not caring if they were scandalized, only finding myself grateful for the presence of those dearest to me.

Soon after we arrived, the light of day returned. We were blinded by it. Cleopas rose to his feet and quickly stumbled, blinking rapidly. I saw rosy spots when I closed my eyes, as if the sharp rays of the sun were branded on my eyelids. The darkness had been suffocating, but the light was overwhelming. We were stupid with it—stumbling about with cries of deliverance.

Mary fell to her knees and raised her hands in praise, while Lazarus joined Cleopas at the door to observe the bright street. Dropping my face into my hands, I offered praise for the return of the sun and for the presence of life, but even so, my heart was unbearably heavy.

It took days for the condemned to die. My Lord was still on a cross, and he was still in unspeakable agony. At my muffled sob, the others turned to me. Cleopas was immediately by my side, arm back around me, and I turned my face into his shoulder.

We all sensed it—the incongruity of light when darkness was still such a present force.

Because it was the Day of Preparation, Lazarus urged Mary and me to return home to make ready the household for the Sabbath while he remained with Cleopas. Mary and I were reluctant to leave without firm information on our Lord and were beginning our argument when a sharp rap at the door drew our attention.

Nicodemus entered, furtive and with new, deep creases in his face. The news he brought was both devasting and a relief. The Jews, out of a desire to clear the crosses of their victims for the Sabbath, had asked Rome to break the criminals' legs, expediting death. I covered my face with my hand, imagining the crunch of bone, the groaning sag of the body, the now complete inability to draw breath.

"But Jesus was already dead," Nicodemus informed us. "It is over."

Relief that his agony was no more mingled with despair that he was no longer a part of this world. I was sick with the emotion tearing through me.

"Joseph is determined to ask Pilate for his body. He owns a new tomb not far away, and we will lay him there this very night."

Praise Yahweh, he would receive a decent burial—a small but significant comfort.

"And Peter? John? What of the disciples?" Lazarus asked, face drawn.

"Some were present at the crucifixion, but now . . . no one knows where they are."

I was full of gratitude for Nicodemus and Joseph, these two brave men who had both the means and the great love to properly care for our Lord. Until now, their devotion to Jesus had been masked, since they walked a dangerous path close to the religious and political seats of power, but now? Now they were stepping forward to perform this most important of tasks at the risk of their own necks. Even though so many of us were scattered and mourning, Jesus would not go to the grave unloved and unattended. He would receive the honor due him in these final moments.

I took Nicodemus' hand in my own and wept openly over it. "Bless you for this kindness. Send our love and gratitude to Joseph."

"I wish . . . if only . . . I could do more." Nicodemus' voice cracked.

After Nicodemus left and the newfound light began to dim into night, Mary and I could no longer press our brother to stay. We needed to return home before Sabbath began and travel was prohibited. Cleopas drew me aside to take me into his arms. I clung to him, trembling, and when he finally pulled back, there was a new look in his eyes. "Go with God, Martha."

"I'll see you soon?" I asked, reluctant to leave him when my heart had just found him.

"Very soon," he promised in a husky voice. His deep brown eyes held steadfast love as they met mine. I carried that look with me back through the winding city streets and along the country road as Mary and I returned to prepare for the strangest and most solemn of Sabbaths.

Thirty-Nine

16 Nisan
31 AD

It was unsafe to leave our home. It was unsafe to stay. The only comfort I derived was in the eyes of my sister, where I saw my own fear perfectly mirrored and with whom I now discovered a deeper kinship as we asked ourselves, "What now?"

Jesus' own disciples could not be found, but it would take the religious leaders next to no time to locate us in our Bethany home. All through that long and lonely Sabbath, Mary and I pondered what to do next. How long before the chief priests came knocking? We had distant relations in Hebron. Should we send our brother away for a while? Even so, it could not be forever, for we had an estate to run, businesses to manage.

Gilah visited that afternoon to inform us that the chief priests and Pharisees had requested that Jesus' tomb be secured with an official Roman seal and guard.

"They had an audience with Pilate?" I asked incredulously. "On the Sabbath?" Those who had been so vocal about Jesus healing on the Sabbath now broke it themselves!

"What are they afraid of?" Mary asked mournfully. "They're

merely testifying to Jesus' power by doing this. They're still afraid of him, and he's not even alive!"

I pondered the truth of her words. It was indeed baffling, the lengths to which the religious leaders were going in order to crush Jesus and his legacy.

As the Sabbath ended and we faced the beginning of an uncertain future, Mary questioned, "When do you suppose Lazarus will return? What does he hope to gain by staying in the city?" She lit her lamp and led the way upstairs to our sleeping chambers.

"I don't think he hopes to gain anything." I paused, trying to find the right words. "He's experienced Jesus in a unique way. I can't imagine what he must be feeling right now."

"Do you suppose he feels guilty?" Mary wondered, voice tinged with weariness.

"Perhaps some guilt that he is alive while Jesus is not," I answered.

It was unthinkable that the man who had raised our brother from the dead was now in a tomb.

17 NISAN
31 AD

The first day of the week dawned with a bright nip in the air. Normally, this day would be filled with expectant joy for the barley harvest to come, but what joy could be gleaned when our hopes were lying in a grave? The wind whipped down from the Judean range and passed over our village with ferocious strength, tumbling and nagging at the trees on its passage to the Dead Sea.

As for me, I needed to think. Uri's necklace was heavy on my chest, weighing me down with memory and something else I had yet to define. I spent the morning halfheartedly reviewing

Lazarus' business ledgers. If we indeed sent him to Hebron, then I would need to brush up on the accounts to better step into his role. But my mind could not focus. I kept staring at the same figures over and over, my eyes glazing over as my thoughts tumbled.

Had Joseph and Nicodemus had enough time to properly prepare the body? All foreign objects should be removed from the body before burial, and I could scarcely imagine the grueling, emotional work of removing each splinter from our Lord's inflamed back.

With a frustrated groan, I shoved the parchments aside and rose to my feet. I would achieve nothing today, so I might as well do something to relieve my mental strain. Finding Mary in the garden, I told her where I would be—under Azariah's branches.

Since Uri's death, I had ceased coming here on a regular basis, the spot holding too many painful memories, but now those memories were intertwined with others. Jesus, winding his way up these slopes, coming to rescue my brother. Jesus, with eyes alight and the wind plucking at his full beard, asking me, *"I am the resurrection and the life. Do you believe this?"*

I reached Azariah, and the tears flowed. How could the resurrection and the life now be dead? Did I still believe? I wanted to. With all my heart, I wanted to believe.

I had never removed Uri's necklace before but was compelled to do so now. Slowly, I pulled the leather cord over my neck and let the pendant dangle before me.

The intricate feather carving reminded me of the night Jesus had carved a small fish for a curious little boy. It was common knowledge that Jesus loved little children and often let them clamber all over his lap.

"Does he whittle for them?" I'd asked Andrew.

"Oh yes," came the swift reply. *"He's never without scraps of wood and a knife."*

"He's always making small toys and usually carries two or three ready to hand out wherever we go," John had added.

I sat in the hollow where Uri and I used to meet. With slow fingers, I traced the lines of the feather, imagining the young hands of Jesus patiently working on it, turning it over and over until it was perfect for his new friend. Hands that had helped Uri in his time of need. Hands that had held my face and wiped my tears. Hands that would one day be nailed to a rough, wooden crossbeam. Turning my body into Azariah's trunk, I gave myself over to grief.

Sleep claimed me, and the next thing I perceived was Mary's distant shouts startling me upright. Disoriented, I stumbled from my hidden spot, blinking in the light and shivering at the sudden impact of the wind.

She was half running, half tripping down the slope, waving something wildly in the air. I shaded my eyes, watching with surprise as Mary's shouts turned to laughter. She began leaping down the hillside like a young gazelle, jumping and dancing with a hidden inner purpose that was both beautiful and confusing to behold.

The wind was whipping away her words, so it wasn't until she was nearly at hand that I finally heard, "Good news, sister! The best of news!" She spun into my presence with a whirling, dizzying joy that was infectious. "It could not end this way. I knew we were missing something."

She was holding a piece of parchment that had become torn in her great hurry.

"What could possibly be this good right now?" I asked.

With an impatient gesture, she shoved the parchment into my hand. "He has risen!" She giggled like a young girl and clapped her hands before raising them once again into the air and twirling.

Heart suspended, I read the missive. It was from Lazarus.

Beloved sisters,

Early this morning, some women in our company traveled to our Lord's tomb in hopes of anointing his body. However, when they arrived, they were astonished to find the stone rolled away. The tomb was empty! Angels appeared to them saying that Jesus was not there but had risen. Both Peter and John ran to the tomb and verified that it is indeed as the women say. The tomb is open and empty!

Cleopas and I scarcely know what to think. Our hearts are burning within us. We have not seen him, but it must be true. For if Jesus the Christ could raise me from the dead, then truly he can raise himself!

Joseph of Arimathea departed first thing this morning for the port of Joppa, intending to first stay the night with relations in Emmaus. To our knowledge, he has yet to learn of these significant events. Cleopas and I are leaving immediately to relay these events to him and perhaps to learn more of the state of the tomb when he left it.

I pray that this fledgling hope finds firmer ground and we can know soon where our hope stands.

Cleopas sends his warmest regards and to you, Martha, his deepest love.

Looking up from the missive, I found Mary alternately watching me with happy eyes and lifting her gaze to heaven in worshipful wonder.

The fledgling hope Lazarus spoke of leapt to life within my own breast as the import of his words took root. I clasped the parchment close, staring at it wide-eyed.

Mary laughed at my reaction and snagged me in a wild hug. "Martha, he *is* the Messiah. As surely as he called Lazarus out of the grave and we touched the living flesh of our brother, Jesus has walked out of his own grave! His own grave! Can you believe it?"

My own words returned to me. "*Yes, Lord. I believe that you are the Christ, the Son of God, who is coming into the world.*"

"Yes," I whispered my belief out loud. "Yes." A little louder now as I wrapped my arms around my sister, anchoring her wriggling form against my chest. "Yes! Yes!" My voice grew stronger, firmer, more confident until I was gasping in delight and joy. "Yes, Lord; I believe! I believe!"

We held each other and laughed, spinning in loopy circles, tripping and righting ourselves in a delighted dance like children learning to walk.

"I must leave." Mary finally pulled back, snatching the parchment from me. "I must tell Lemuel." She began scurrying back the way she'd come, shouting over her shoulder, "I must go and tell *everyone*!"

I watched her retreating form for a moment, hand to breast, registering the emptiness there. "My necklace!" Hurriedly, I returned to the hollow in Azariah's roots, sighing deeply when I found the pendant peeking from beneath some leaves.

The carving that had earlier caused me so much consternation now nestled comfortingly in the palm of my hand. I held it up, letting the dappled light filtering through the branches play across the intricate grooves. Looking past the pendant into the branches, I sensed the urge to climb, to reach higher and higher and give release to the ever-mounting joy inside me.

Looping the necklace back over my head, I hitched up my tunic and tied it to give my legs free access to climb. Azariah's sloping trunk beckoned me, and I began my ascent, laughing at myself. Not since I was a girl had I climbed these branches. I'd spent many a happy afternoon dangling my bare legs, awl in hand. Now I climbed with no other purpose than to be up high and gaze over the land I loved.

One of Azariah's thick branches ran nearly parallel to the ground. I reached it and, grasping the branch above me for support, walked slowly along it, suspended between earth and sky. Pausing partway, I studied the landscape stretching before me. There, in the distance, were Azariah's brothers, Hananiah and Mishael. At the thought of these three brave men, the meaning of Azariah's name fell over me like a benediction: Azariah—Yahweh has helped. I closed my eyes and breathed in deeply before turning and resuming my climb with renewed zeal.

"Yes, You have helped us." I spoke the prayer out loud, grasping another branch and pulling myself up to the next height and then the next. "Yahweh, You have helped us. You have sent us Your Messiah." I reached higher, straining upward. With each physical effort, I blessed His name until finally I had pulled myself as high as I could.

Straddling a branch, I rested, my breath coming quickly. Above me, Azariah's branches thinned out until all that was left was open sky.

I could go no farther, but I did not need to. Yahweh Himself had come down, had come to me, and I welcomed the disruption of His winnowing fork. *Yes, Lord! Remove the chaff. Leave the truth. I accept Your life and hope.*

There was no grave He could not plunder, no darkness He could not pierce, and there was no one so lost that He could not find her and lift her up.

"Martha, I am the resurrection and the life."

Jesus' words returned to me, leaping straight to my heart, which beat hard with new understanding.

"Anyone who believes in me will live, even after dying."

"Even after dying," I breathed, chest tight, mind alive, heart thrumming hard. I tilted my head and carefully removed the necklace, gazing again at the beauty of the carved feather.

Love was not a thief, and death was not the end.

Praise Yahweh, He has helped. He has provided the Way. And I know Him.

My fingers fumbled the pendant, and with a gasp, I watched it slip from my grasp and snag on a branch barely beyond my reach. The worn leather cord tangled in a limb, and the pendant swung a low arc beneath, caught on the outermost edge of Azariah's canopy.

If I scooted forward carefully, I would be able to snag it and was preparing to do so when a brisk breeze lifted the pendant, causing the necklace to stretch taut for a moment before releasing into a joyful dance with the wind. I breathed a sigh of relief when I realized that the necklace was held fast, the cord so enmeshed in the limbs that it could not be blown away. Instead, it flew about with happy abandon—free to partner with the wind without fear of being thrown loose.

For a moment, the wooden feather danced in and out between the fingers of the wind, mirroring the flight of its real-life counterpart. I sat and let it be. The clouds shifted in the sky, briefly covering the sun, and in the distance, sheep bleated out their need.

I watched the feather dance until the sun broke through the clouds, spreading its fire slowly over the hillside, the light bringing life and dazzling the cold and darkness away.

author's note

Martha, Lazarus, and Mary—arguably the most famous set of siblings in Scripture. But what do we really know about them?

We know they opened their home to Jesus and His disciples on many occasions and that Jesus deeply loved all three, considering them among His closest friends. And then there are the standout events recorded in Scripture: the infamous Martha/Mary moment, the resurrection of Lazarus, and Mary anointing Jesus before Passover.

In these depictions, we're led to believe that Jesus already had a long-established relationship with the siblings, which led me to ponder the "before" picture, to imagine what the siblings' home life and relationships to one another might have looked like as well as the timeline for when they came to befriend the Christ and believe in Him as the Messiah.

Part One is largely fictitious and contains the biggest fictional element regarding Jesus in the form of the backstory between Him and Uri. Nazareth was a small town in Galilee, located just south of the larger metropolis of Sepphoris. Herod Antipas spent years reconstructing Sepphoris, and it was his capital until the founding of Tiberias. It's highly probable that both Joseph and Jesus worked in Sepphoris while it was being rebuilt and traveled often between it and Nazareth. I speculated that perhaps Jesus drew from His own life for His parables, and I depicted Him doing just that in the telling of the Good Samaritan, in which He draws upon His imaginary encounter with Uri outside Sepphoris, transplanting the location to one His hearers would readily recognize—the road to Jericho.

In constructing Uri's background, I included a fictional group, the Memra, who considered themselves the "executors of God's word and will." Memra is Aramaic for *word*, especially in relation to God's creative word. The group may be fictional, but their zeal is not. There were many in Jesus' day who saw active protest and violence as a justifiable response to their Roman overlords. The Sicarrii, or "dagger men," were such zealots, known for carrying knives during public events and meting out justice against those who acquiesced to Rome.

The fictional group, the Memra, headquartered in Sepphoris, served as an entry point for Uri's later inclusion into the historical and much more ruthless Sicarrii. Whereas it's believed that the group may have been in existence as early as 6 AD, we don't hear much of the Sicarrii's guerrilla and terrorist activity until the 50s. Therefore, I took some creative license in depicting the Sicarrii as executing active attacks during Uri's time in the group, approximately 14 AD.

Part Two required many thoughtful choices, one being Mary's anointing of Jesus. Matthew, Mark, and John place the anointing in Simon the Leper's home in Bethany. But only John names Mary of Bethany as the woman with the flask. Even so, it's widely accepted that these three accounts depict the same event.

The Lukan account contains many similar aspects to the other three. However, there are enough differences to separate this account from the others. The woman in Luke is a "notorious sinner" and the host isn't Simon the Leper but Simon the Pharisee. With enough differences between the accounts, most scholars agree that the event in Luke is a separate incident from the one depicted in the other Gospels.

Therefore, we cannot definitively claim that Simon the Leper and Simon the Pharisee are one and the same person, nor that Mary of Bethany was a "known sinner" in need of forgiveness. However, in carefully pondering all four accounts, I decided to leave open the possibility that Simon the Leper, who most likely had been healed by Jesus earlier in His ministry, could once have been a Pharisee.

What an interesting arc to consider! An outwardly clean man, a Pharisee, contracts leprosy and becomes known as Simon the Leper. Then in his reactions to Mary, shows that he needs not only the external cleansing from leprosy but also an internal cleansing of the soul. The arc was too good to pass up.

Likewise, we do not know much of Mary's own history. There is nothing to suggest she was a "known sinner," but perhaps she had a past she was ashamed of. And perhaps her anointing of Jesus was also a personal proclamation of an inner transformation. I found these suggestions exciting and in keeping with—or at least not contradicting—what we do know of the biblical account.

Therefore, in writing Simon as both Pharisee and Leper and in giving Mary a complicated past from which she needs forgiveness, I am not attempting to conflate all four Gospel accounts or claim that they are one and the same event. I am merely letting all four accounts inform the formation of this novel's characters.

Another choice was in the identification of the young man who flees naked from the terrifying scene in the Garden of Gethsemane. We learn of this strange account in just one of the Gospels: Mark 14:51–52. There are numerous theories as to who this man was, ranging from the bizarre to the plausible. Many believe it was Mark himself, but most conclude that we just don't know. In writing this unidentified young man as Lemuel, I provided both a way for the siblings to hear a detailed account of that harrowing night and for Mary and Lemuel's relationship to experience a breakthrough. In Lemuel's lament and Mary's response, we see ourselves. We are all, in a way, that naked young man fleeing in fear, desperately in need of the forgiveness and righteousness of Christ to clothe us. This is a lesson for Mary, for Lemuel, and for us.

In researching biblical events, I spent a lot of time in the book of John, where we learn that Lazarus' resurrection was a catalyst for some of Jesus' final moments. In fact, John explicitly correlates the resurrection of Lazarus and Christ's triumphant entry into Jerusalem (John 12:17–18). In seeing that "the world has gone after Him" (verse 19 ESV), Jesus' death sentence was accelerated, and Lazarus' life was in danger, as the chief priests made plans to put both men to death (verses 10–11).

Jesus' illegal trials and grisly death, then, must have hit the siblings hard on numerous levels. They had skin in the game in a way no one else did, for Lazarus had become a poster child for the legitimacy of Jesus' ministry and power in those tumultuous final days. In constructing Passover week, I relied heavily on the information and timeline in John, keeping in sight the personal and high stakes the siblings faced.

A final note on dear Cleopas. He is mentioned once in the Bible in Luke 24 as one of two disciples to whom Jesus appears postresurrection on the road to Emmaus. Because Cleopas is a close Greek equivalent to the Hebrew Clopas, some suggest the Cleopas on the road to Emmaus is the same Clopas, husband of Mary (John 19:25), and that perhaps Mary is the other disciple on the Emmaus road. Others argue that the second disciple was Luke himself, one of the apostles, or simply an unknown disciple. In constructing Cleopas' character, I chose to separate him from Clopas, husband of Mary, and identify the second disciple as Lazarus.

Throughout the story, we see these two cousins connected

in their love of knowledge, which makes the road to Emmaus especially fitting for their characters. "And beginning with Moses and all the Prophets, He interpreted to them in all the Scriptures the things concerning Himself" (Luke 24:27 ESV). What fun to imagine a larger story for this dear disciple who was one of the first to encounter the resurrected Lord and who was privy to what must have been the best sermon of all time!

In all things, dear reader, Scripture is preeminent. My hope is that *Up from Dust* ignites your love of Jesus and drives you deeper into the Word, where there is endless wealth to be found. In weaving this fictional account, my desire was to remain true to what we do know of these flesh-and-blood people who actually lived and loved the one we call Savior and Lord.

acknowledgments

Writing a book is such a strange endeavor! It begins with a seed of an idea in the heart of one person and then expands, taking on more people, growing deeper and broader, throwing down roots, unfurling branches, until finally, blessedly, it bears fruit. This book came to fruition under the tender care of many people over the course of many years.

Thank you to my dear agent and mentor, Cynthia Ruchti. You took a chance on me when I held just the beginnings of this story in nervous hands. I'm thankful beyond words for your guidance, patience, and dedication. I couldn't ask for a better companion on this journey!

There were several long and lonely years searching for a publisher, and I'm convinced it's because God was lining up just the right editor. Rochelle Gloege, from the beginning, your enthusiasm for this book and the way you caught and carried its vision deeply blessed me. Thank you for championing this story! Jen Veilleux, I'm thankful we were able to meet in person. In every conversation since, I've valued your insight and rejoiced that we share the same spark of passion over Jesus' tremendous heart for women. To all of the incredibly talented individuals at Bethany House, thank you for packaging and marketing this story with such loving care, ensuring that it captivates and reaches its readers!

My gratitude to Pastor Gary Armstrong, whose Easter sermon in 2016 sparked the very beginnings of this story. I still have the bulletin where I scribbled out that initial seed of an idea. Thank you to those who faithfully lifted me up in prayer and walked alongside me during the many highs and lows. Jordan Petty, Alicia DeMoss, Betsy Adams, Martin and Amy Winslow, Tom and Eileen Goebel, and my entire Choosing Hope family—you are God's gifts to me!

Love and thanks to Grandpa Mai, who has a soft spot for Martha, and in loving memory of Grandma Mai, whose last gift to me was *Daily Life at the Time of Jesus* by Miriam Feinberg Vamosh. She never doubted that one day this book would exist! Thank you to my parents for recognizing and encouraging a love of words in me. A special thanks to my sister, Laura, who helped me flesh out the feather pendant, and to all my siblings and family who were such enthusiastic cheerleaders along this winding road. Andrew, for being so kind, patient, and supportive. You consistently tag-teamed with the kids, even while exhausted, to create margin for me to write, and I'm beyond thankful! And to the three kiddos God has so graciously given me, who might be too young to fully grasp what I do, but who think it's kinda cool that Mommy makes books.

And finally, to the Heartbeat of this whole project. Abba, You have used this experience to draw me close to Your heart. With this book I bless Your name and earnestly pray that You would be glorified. The path has indeed been winding, mysterious, and sometimes painful, but it has led me here to this moment with You.

And I'm grateful.

discussion questions

1. All three siblings carry burdens they learn to work through in order to embrace freedom and new life in Christ. Discuss the trajectory of each sibling. Which sibling's journey did you resonate with the most?
2. Did you find Martha's father to be a sympathetic character? Discuss the ways his choices affected his children. Compare and contrast his grief with Martha's.
3. What do you think of Cleopas' assertion that it's better to behold beauty for a moment than not at all? Is there something in your life that feels fragile and perhaps shattered like "broken pottery"? How might God be redeeming that part of your story?
4. Discuss the feather pendant and the role it plays in Martha's life. What does it come to represent for Martha, and what do you make of the ending where she removes it for the first time in eleven years?
5. When Martha connects Uri's Jesus with the Jesus before her, she struggles to reconcile the two and wonders why the Messiah would give Uri "false promises." When Jesus

quoted Psalm 91 to Uri, was that a false promise? Why or why not?

6. Is Martha's hesitation with Cleopas understandable, given her background? Compare and contrast her relationships with Uri and Cleopas.
7. In what ways does Gilah and Martha's friendship change throughout the story? Are there scenes in which they prove their friendship to each other? What do you see as the contributing factors to their reconciliation?
8. Martha doesn't know how to be a sister to Mary when what she needs is a mother. How does Martha struggle with this tension and grow in her understanding and love for Mary?
9. When Lazarus falls ill, the sisters realize how much he'd seen and loved each of them uniquely. In what ways did Lazarus show his love and care for each sister?
10. Trace the theme of darkness/light throughout the story. What do you make of Martha's observation of Jesus as a fire?
11. Compare and contrast Uri and Jesus. Discuss the impact each has on Martha's formation.
12. Significantly, Martha never receives concrete answers about Uri. Likewise, we can experience hard things without concrete answers. How are you tempted to react in such moments? How do Martha's reactions shift throughout the story?

Heather Kaufman is the author of multiple books, and her devotional writing has appeared in such publications as *Portals of Prayer, Open Windows,* and *Guideposts.* A former editor turned writer, Heather worked eight years in the publishing industry while earning her master's degree and spinning tales late into the night. When she fell in love with studying the Bible through a cultural lens, the words of Scripture came springing to life, and Jesus became even more astoundingly beautiful. Now she delights in crafting stories that highlight the goodness of God and compel readers deeper into the Bible. When not reading, writing, or accumulating mounds of books, Heather can be found exploring new parks with her husband and three children near their home in St. Louis, Missouri. Learn more and stay in touch at hmkstories.com.

Sign Up for Heather's Newsletter

Keep up to date with Heather's latest news on book releases and events by signing up for her email list at the link below.

HMKStories.com

FOLLOW HEATHER ON SOCIAL MEDIA

Heather Kaufman, Author

@HMKStories

@HMKStories